DEATH
SENTENCE

ALSO BY DAMIEN BOYD

DEATH
SENTENCE

DAMIEN BOYD

Text copyright © 2016 Damien Boyd
All rights reserved.

Published by Thomas & Mercer, Seattle

www.apub.com

Amazon, the Amazon logo, and Thomas & Mercer are trademarks of Amazon.com, Inc., or its affiliates.

ISBN-13: 9781503939691
ISBN-10: 1503939693

Cover design by Stuart Bache

Printed in the United States of America

For Alison, Florence and Will

Prologue

Absolute darkness.

She'd never experienced it before. There'd always been a gap under the door, a keyhole, light filtering in through the curtains. Moonlight. But now there was none.

She held her gloved hand in front of her face, no more than a few inches away, but couldn't see it, couldn't even make out the outline. She tried moving it, waggling her fingers. Nothing. At least there was the sound of running water somewhere below her in the darkness.

'Spooky, isn't it?'

Prick.

Why not come caving? You'll love it!

Yeah, right.

'Can I turn my lamp on now?'

They'd only been in the cave for twenty minutes, but she was already soaked to the skin. And cold, if the chattering of her teeth was anything to go by.

'C'mon, let's get moving. You'll soon warm up.'

'How much further is it?'

'It's a four hour round trip to Sump One.'

Four hours?

'I'm not sure I . . .'

'Don't be silly. You'll be fine.'

She followed his light down towards the water, if only to avoid being left alone in the darkness.

'You'll need to crawl through this bit and watch your head.'

Face down in the stream, her helmet banging on the rock above her. Cold water again, just when she had been starting to warm up.

'Where do we go now?' Trying not to sound nervous.

'Down there,' he replied, turning his head to shine the lamp on his helmet over the precipice. 'The Thirty Foot Pot.'

'How?'

'Down this ladder, but I'll have you on a rope, so you'll be quite safe,' he replied, pulling her towards him and clipping the karabiner on to her caving belt.

At least the waterfall would muffle her screams and wash away her tears.

She looked at him, grinning at her from under his caving helmet as he uncoiled the wire ladder and dropped it over the edge.

All right then. But if you think I'm going through that bloody sump you are very much mistaken.

Prat.

Two hours later she slumped down on to a boulder, breathing hard, and unzipped her oversuit. Then she took off her helmet, careful to keep her head torch shining on a white nylon rope that disappeared into the water under the far rock wall.

'We go through there?'

'That's Sump One. It's only seven feet, and I'll be waiting for you on the other side.'

She shook her head.

'You'll be all right I promise.'

'No.'

'Look, I'll go through and then come back to prove it to you.'

She watched him lie down on his belly in the water, take a deep breath and duck down. Then he began pulling on the rope and kicking with his feet before he disappeared under the rock.

She waited.

Then he reappeared, grinning like an idiot.

'You see, it's easy.'

Seven feet. Underwater. She could do a full width of the swimming pool, but that wasn't cold and dark. And didn't involve crawling on your belly through a confined space hundreds of feet underground.

'All right, all right. I'll do it. What the hell.'

He sat in the water and smiled at her.

Is that supposed to be reassuring?

'I'll pull on the rope three times; then it's your turn. Just shut your eyes and go for it!'

She watched him disappear again and then waited for the rope to move, fear rising in her chest. If she'd had any breakfast, she'd have thrown it up by now.

Please don't move. Please . . .

Then the rope jerked. One. Two. Three.

Oh shit.

She lay down in the water facing the blank rock wall, both hands on the rope. The water was cold, far colder than further up the cave.

Were those footsteps behind her? She spun round.

Was that a light?

She closed her eyes, took a deep breath and ducked down, the cold water clawing at the exposed skin of her face. Then she began pulling on the rope.

The air in her oversuit made her float, and she had to wriggle and kick to dive down under the cave wall. Her helmet clattered on the rock above

her head, and the sound of her oversuit scraping along the roof was ampli-
fied by the water all around her.

She reached forwards, took hold of the rope in her right hand and
pulled. Now for the left hand. Inching forward.

What the . . . ?

She opened her eyes. The rope was right in front of her. She had a firm
grip on it with both hands now and was pulling as hard as she could. But
she wasn't moving. She tried harder. Nothing.

She tried to lift her head to see the rope ahead, but her helmet hit the
rock directly above her. The walls on either side ruled out turning around.

Only one thing for it. Crawl back out. Odd that she was still capable
of rational thought despite the panic that was taking hold of her.

She let go of the rope and dug her hands into the gravel in front of her.
Then she began pushing and wriggling backwards.

Nothing.

She tried kicking her feet, but they were jammed. Wedged.

How much longer could she hold her breath?

It can't end like this.

She began jerking the rope in the hope that he would come.

First his light. Then hands searching for hers.

Lungs bursting.

He had hold of her wrists and she could feel him pulling. But she was
stuck fast.

The end was near. She knew that.

But I'm supposed to be going skiing . . .

Then she took the involuntary breath, the gasp that she had been fight-
ing. She felt the water in her mouth, her throat, her lungs.

Convulsing now, yet oddly calm.

The light fading . . . convulsions slowing . . .

It can't end like this.

It really can't.

Chapter One

Plastic bottles. Cans. Broken glass. Carrier bags. Dog bags. Syringes. And the smell. What the hell was that smell?

Nick Dixon stepped back into the light and exhaled, his breath suspended in front of him in the freezing dawn air.

'I did warn you, Sir.'

'Thank you, Cole,' replied Dixon, taking a deep breath and turning back to the pillbox.

He peered in, shining his torch along the concrete walls to the left and right of the inner blast wall directly in front of him. Narrow shafts of light penetrated the darkness, illuminating abandoned machine gun placements piled high with green plastic cider bottles, squashed juice cartons, cigarette butts, dead snails and more beer cans. All of it covered in cobwebs and dust, the spiders long gone.

Otherwise it was pitch dark, far colder than outside, despite the fresh snow, and damp. So damp he could taste it.

Dixon stepped over the rubbish piled up in the entrance and on to a small patch of bare earth floor to the left of the inner wall. Bags of household waste were piled up along the side wall to his left next to a set of old tyres and a shopping trolley. Several piles of human excrement explained the smell.

It was no place to die.

Dixon shone his torch at the ceiling and watched the snowflakes falling through a small hole just above his head, presumably where the flue of a wood burning stove had once been. A lifesaver in winter no doubt, but now the stove was long gone and the snow was settling on several empty beer cans on the floor.

He tucked his torch under his arm and rubbed his hands together. Then he saw the body.

The man was lying with his back against the far wall, slumped over to his right with his head resting on a bag of garden rubbish marked 'biodegradable'. He was blocking the passageway around the inner wall to the other side of the pillbox.

The man was bald, but his deathly grey skin reflected little of the light from Dixon's torch. He had been dead for hours.

What hair he had was grey, although there were flecks of black in his moustache, which gave away his original hair colour. A jacket and tie, brown corduroys, brogues and a green waxed coat, a Barbour probably. Respectable? Certainly not someone you would expect to find in a place like this.

A pair of spectacles lay broken on the ground in front of him, the frames buckled, the lenses shattered.

Dixon squatted down and shone his torch into the man's face. A faint trace of brown powder was visible around his nose and mouth, and there was some bruising on his face and the back of his head, each bruise small and clearly defined. But no blood and no obviously fatal injuries. Still, cause of death would be someone else's problem.

He stepped back and shone his torch on the wall, reading what little graffiti there was.

How can you possibly spell that wrong?

And that?

It was odd, given that plenty of local lads would regard the pillbox as a blank canvas.

Written in faded green spray paint just above the body were the words 'old but still it'. The message looked like it had been there some years, but Dixon took a photograph of it on his iPhone before retracing his steps back to the entrance, stepping over the rubbish and into the right hand side of the pillbox.

More beer cans, plastic bottles and carrier bags, with the added extra of silver foil, the remnants of several candles and blackened spoons on one of the machine gun placements, everything covered by a thick layer of dust and cobwebs. More tyres too. And the remains of a small fire in the corner, ages old by the looks of it. From the smell, this side was also the urinal.

Dixon checked the walls for graffiti, but found none at all, except for Tracey's mobile phone number. A good time was guaranteed apparently.

He shone his torch down at the bottom of the far wall, lighting up the dead man slumped on the bag of garden rubbish. From the position of his hands, they must have been tied behind him, but it was impossible to see how.

Dixon turned to leave – or rather, make his escape – and noticed a large red admiral butterfly on the wall just under the ceiling. He reached up and touched it with his torch, sending it spiralling to the floor, its wings crumbling at his slightest touch.

'Everything in this bloody place is dead,' he muttered as he stepped back out into the snow.

'Where's Jane?' asked PC Cole.

'If you mean where is Detective Sergeant Winter, she's still in bed.'

'Celebrating, was it?'

'Well, it's not every day you get promoted, is it?' replied Dixon, smiling.

'And what about Detective Constable Willmott?' Cole grinned, revealing a missing front tooth.

'Louise is on her way. What happened to you?'

'Rugby.'

'I didn't know you played rugby.'

'I don't, Sir. It was a piss up at Burnham Rugby Club, and it got a bit out of hand.'

Dixon shook his head as he walked around the side of the pillbox, peering at the brickwork, each and every brick carrying a message of some sort etched into it. Several different people 'woz ere', some of them even taking the trouble to give the date. 'Kyle loves Tracey' caught his eye, and he wondered whether it was the same Tracey whose phone number was scrawled on the wall inside. Perhaps not.

Scratching a message into the red brick appeared to be the pre-ferred method of graffiti outside, and there was very little spray paint, although the same person had daubed the same messages that appeared on the inside walls. His spelling had not improved.

'Don't fall in, Sir,' shouted Cole.

Dixon looked down at the shallow water, which was gin clear beneath a thin layer of ice. Not surprising when boat traffic on the Bridgwater and Taunton Canal had stopped decades before. Patches of weed were still visible on the bottom, despite the snow that was settling on the ice.

The pillbox had been built where the canal narrowed, and small concrete pyramids were just visible in the brambles on the far bank. Dixon had seen enough war films to recognise a tank trap when he saw one.

He walked back around the side of the pillbox, taking care to step over anything that resembled a pile of dog mess. Not easy when it was all covered in snow.

'SOCO on the way?'

'Yes, Sir.'

'And a pathologist?'

'Roger Poland is coming. We've sent a car for him. He didn't feel well enough to drive.'

Dixon smiled.

I bet he didn't.

'Is the towpath blocked?'

'We've got cars at Huntworth Bridge and Fordgate, Sir.'

'Who found him?'

'Mr Rushton, Sir. He's waiting in my car,' replied Cole, gesturing into the field behind the pillbox.

Dixon was walking through the gate when his phone rang.

'Where are you?'

'On my way, Sir,' replied Louise. 'My husband's dropping me off. There's no way I can drive.'

Dixon sighed. 'Get him to drop you at the Boat and Anchor,' he said. 'You can walk in from there. South, away from the M5. The fresh air will do you good.'

'I'll be as quick as I can.'

Dixon rang off and opened the rear passenger door of the patrol car. A black Labrador jumped out, followed by a man wearing waterproofs and a wide brimmed hat.

'Mr Rushton?'

'Yes.'

'I'm Detective Inspector Dixon. I gather you found him.'

'Polly did actually,' replied Rushton. 'I don't usually let her go any-where near the pillbox because of the broken glass, but there was no stopping her today. Then she wouldn't come out. Just sat there barking.'

'What did you do?'

'I had to go in and get her. I carried her out and put her on her lead. Then I dialled 999.'

'Do you walk along here often?'

'Most days. We park at the Boat and Anchor.'

'When did you last come along here?'

'Friday. We went to the beach yesterday for a change.'

'Have you seen the man before?'

'I didn't get a very good look at him I'm afraid. It's dark in there and I didn't have a torch.'

Dixon nodded.

'It's not a place you want to hang about,' continued Rushton, 'and when I saw the body lying there I just grabbed my dog and legged it.'

'Very wise,' replied Dixon. 'We have your details?'

'The officer over there took them.'

'Good. Someone will get in touch to take a formal statement from you, but that's it for now. You can go.'

'Thank you.'

'Would you like a lift back to your car?' asked Dixon.

'That'd be great, please. I'm running a bit late now.'

Dixon watched the patrol car drive slowly back along the towpath to Fordgate, leaving fresh tracks in the snow. The towpath north of the pillbox was a narrow footpath, but south to Fordgate it was wide enough for vehicles, which explained the fly tipping.

The pain in his toes was becoming unbearable, so Dixon climbed into his Land Rover and switched the engine on before adjusting the heater to blow on his feet. He had a few minutes to kill before Scientific Services arrived, so he took out his phone and opened a web browser. He typed 'bridgwater canal pillbox' into Google and hit 'Search'.

He ignored the first two results, news articles about an old World War Two pillbox being turned into a haven for bats, and looked at the third result, the Wikipedia page for the canal. The short description in the search results referred to a 'pillbox which formed part of the

Taunton Stop Line', so he clicked on the Wikipedia page for that, which was directly below it.

Dixon scrolled down, reading as he went. The Taunton Stop Line was a World War Two defensive line designed to stop an enemy's advance from the west. It ran from Seaton on the south coast to Highbridge on the north, taking in the River Axe, various railway lines and the Bridgwater and Taunton Canal. Under 'References' he clicked on 'Somerset Pillboxes', then 'Taunton Stop Line'. Now he was looking at a complete list of all the pillboxes on the Stop Line, running north to south by the looks of things. Someone had photographed them all.

Dixon clicked on 'Huntworth (b)', a standard Type 24 pillbox according to the narrative, but this was further north, nearer the pub, so he clicked 'Back' and selected 'Fordgate (a)', the next in line south. And there it was. A Type 24 right at the water's edge where the canal narrowed. The photographs must have been taken some years before, judging by the lack of vegetation and the five concrete 'dragon's teeth' that were clearly visible on the far bank.

Dixon read aloud: 'Tanks attempting to drive over these obstacles would expose their vulnerable undersides to the fire of the defenders.' He wondered what those defenders, the Home Guard probably, would think of it now.

Next he went back to Google and typed in 'Type 24 pillbox'. The first result came from the Pillbox Study Group, so he clicked on it and found a diagram of an 'irregular hexagonal' pillbox, with rifle slits either side of the entrance and light machine gun slits in the side and front walls. This one was the 'shellproof' version, the wider window ledges, now covered in rubbish, designed to accommodate the tripod of the much larger Boys anti-tank rifle. Dixon recognised the shape of the inner wall too, to protect the occupants from the blast of a shell landing behind the pillbox.

His impromptu history lesson was interrupted by Louise, tapping on the window of his car. She was breathing hard.

'Have you been running?' asked Dixon, climbing out of the Land Rover.

Louise nodded.

'There was no need for that.'

'I wanted to get here before SOCO,' she gasped.

'Well, you just made it,' replied Dixon, turning to see two vans driving towards them along the towpath from Fordgate. PC Cole was behind them, with Roger Poland sitting in the passenger seat of his patrol car.

The vans turned into the field and parked either side of Dixon's Land Rover. PC Cole dropped off Roger Poland, turned and drove back along the towpath.

'Where's he off to?' asked Dixon.

'He went off duty half an hour ago,' replied Poland, dropping his bag on to the bonnet of Dixon's Land Rover. 'Bloody good job he turned up. The other lot just dropped me at the Boat and Anchor.'

'The walk would've done you good,' said Dixon. 'Look at DC Willmott here, all bright eyed and bushy tailed.'

'You look like death warmed up,' said Poland, frowning at Louise.

'You don't look much better yourself,' she replied.

'Are you going to allow your newest CID officer to speak to a senior pathologist like that?'

'Yes.' Dixon grinned.

'Thought as much,' said Poland, smiling. 'What've we got then?'

'I didn't get too close,' replied Dixon, 'but it's a man aged sixty-fiveish, possibly younger, slumped against the wall in the pillbox over there. Looks like he's been dead for a day or so.'

'How d'you know he's been murdered?'

'His hands are tied behind his back,' replied Dixon. 'That's a bit of a giveaway.'

'You've been in there?'

The voice came from behind him. Dixon spun round to see Donald Watson, the senior scenes of crime officer, climbing into a set of white overalls. He was standing on one foot, leaning on the open door of an Avon and Somerset Police Scientific Services van.

'I just had a quick look,' replied Dixon. 'I stayed well back.'

Watson reached into the back of the van and threw a set of overalls to Dixon and another to Louise.

'I've got my own,' said Poland.

'Give us twenty minutes,' said Watson. 'There are overshoes and masks in here. All right?'

Dixon nodded.

'You been in there?' asked Watson, turning to Louise.

'No.'

'Only you look a bit . . .'

'She was out celebrating her transfer to CID last night,' said Dixon.

'Celebrating?' muttered Watson, shaking his head. 'You must be bloody mad.'

Poland reached into his leather bag and took out a large Thermos flask.

'Coffee anyone?'

'Her need is greater than mine,' said Dixon, nodding in Louise's direction.

They were sitting in Dixon's Land Rover watching two scenes of crime officers covering the pillbox with a large tent. Bright shafts of light were shining out of the machine gun slits from the arc lamps set up inside, and despite the glare, camera flashes were still visible from time to time through the snow that was, if anything, falling harder now.

'No Monty?' asked Poland, looking over his shoulder into the back of the Land Rover as he passed Louise a mug of coffee.

'I left him at home with Jane,' replied Dixon. 'It's too cold for a Staffie to be sitting around.'

'It's too cold for me to be sitting around.'

'It's a shithole in there, Roger,' said Dixon, shaking his head. 'What the hell was he doing?'

'That's your department.'

'There's a brown powder around his nose and mouth, but he's no druggie.'

'You never can tell these days.'

'I suppose not.'

'I often wondered what these pillboxes were for,' said Poland. 'Second World War?'

'Yes. Built to stop a German invasion from the west. There's a whole defensive line right down to the south coast.'

'Manned by the Home Guard, I suppose?' asked Poland.

Dixon nodded.

'Give me The Novelty Rock Emporium any day,' he muttered.

'What's the . . . ?'

'Surely you've seen *Dad's Army*, Louise?' asked Poland. 'Even I know that one.'

'Nope, sorry.'

Dixon looked at Poland and raised his eyebrows.

'Here we go,' said Poland, pointing over to the tent that was now covering the pillbox. Donald Watson was standing in the entrance, waving at them.

Dixon opened the door of the Land Rover.

'C'mon, let's get this over with.'

'What is wrong with people?'

'Eh?'

'They bag up their dog shit and then just dump it.'

'D'you mind?' asked Poland, rolling his eyes.

'I suppose we should be grateful they didn't leave it hanging in a tree,' muttered Dixon.

'OK, let's get him on a stretcher,' said Poland, standing up. 'Better strap him on too. You'll need to tip it to get it out of here.'

'Anything in his pockets?' asked Dixon.

Poland shook his head.

'Nothing?'

'Nope.'

'Cause of death?'

'D'you want me to guess?'

'If you have to.'

'Myocardial infarction,' replied Poland.

'What?'

'Heart attack to you.'

'I know what it is.'

'That is just a guess mind you. I won't know for sure till I open him up.'

'What's the brown powder?'

'No idea.'

'A sample's going off to the lab,' said Watson.

'How long's he been here?' asked Dixon.

'A day or two,' replied Poland. 'Friday night or perhaps Saturday morning. Early hours. It's colder than most fridges in here don't forget.'

'What about the rope?'

'Bog standard nylon,' said Watson. 'You can get it in any hardware store.' He was holding up a clear plastic evidence bag with a knotted blue rope inside. 'We had to cut it to get it off.'

'And the bruises?' asked Dixon, turning to Poland.

'A hand was held over his nose and mouth. Like this,' replied Poland, clamping his right hand over his face.

'Then his heart gave out?'

'Looks like it.'

Dixon looked down at the man's face just as one of the mortuary technicians zipped up the body bag. Sixty-five had been a reasonable guess. His face was gaunt, moustache well trimmed and the marks either side of the bridge of his nose confirmed that the spectacles were his.

'Is there enough left of the lenses to get a prescription?' asked Dixon.

'Possibly,' replied Watson. 'We'll check fingerprints and DNA first, but if we draw a blank, then it's on to dental records and the specs.'

'What about missing persons?'

'Nothing that matches,' replied Louise.

'We're going to need more . . .'

'Ah, there you are.'

Dixon turned to see Detective Chief Inspector Lewis peering into the pillbox, blinking furiously as his eyes adjusted to the light.

'Mind stepping outside?'

'No, Sir,' said Dixon, stifling a sigh.

'What d'you need?'

Dixon stepped out into the snow, managing to jump over the puddle of mud and slush at the entrance to the pillbox.

'Is it melting already?'

'That's just where people have been walking,' replied Lewis.

'Then we'll need the dogs to search the surrounding area.'

Lewis nodded.

'And divers in the canal.'

'I don't envy them that one,' said Lewis.

'House to house at Fordgate and over there,' continued Dixon, pointing to a line of new houses five hundred yards away on the other side of the canal. 'And we need to track down and speak to anyone in the Boat and Anchor on Friday night.'

'What about identification?'

Dixon shook his head.

'What, nothing?'

'No.'

'Well, let's hope we get something from DNA and fingerprints. Dental records'll take ages.'

'And it's a bloody Sunday,' muttered Dixon.

Chapter Two

It was late morning by the time the dive team broke the ice and began a search of the canal bed. Dixon watched two divers crawling side by side along the bottom in the freezing cold water, feeling in the mud with their fingers. Maybe his comfy desk was not so bad after all.

The canal was still sealed off at Huntworth and Fordgate, much to the annoyance of the local angling club and their match secretary, who had to cancel the fishing competition at the last minute. He had calmed down when Dixon had pointed out the canal was frozen over anyway.

DC Mark Pearce was supervising the house to house enquiries at Fordgate, and Louise was over at the new development on the far side of the canal. DC Dave Harding was in the Boat and Anchor going through the bookings for the previous Friday evening. And then there were the locals who had not booked a table. The landlord was doing his best to remember who had been in that night, and there was CCTV footage of the car park, but it was going to take time to catch up with them all.

It had at least stopped snowing.

'Anything?' asked Dixon.

'Not yet,' replied the dive team sergeant, following his divers along the canal bank. 'We'll go as far as we can either side of the pillbox though.'

'Thank you.'

Dixon did not expect them to find anything. Anyone taking the time and trouble to empty the victim's pockets was hardly going to drop the contents into the canal right by the murder scene. And there was unlikely to be a murder weapon either, given Roger Poland's to-be-confirmed cause of death. Dixon checked the time. Another couple of hours and he could head over to Musgrove Park Hospital to catch the end of the post mortem. He knew from bitter experience that it was best not to arrive too early.

'Perhaps it was two consenting adults,' had been Jane's suggestion when Dixon rang her an hour or so earlier. He put it down to the fact that he had woken her up. That and her hangover. He shook his head. No, whatever the brown powder was, the victim had been forced to inhale it; the bruises around his nose and mouth and on the back of his head were evidence of that.

Dixon was reading the graffiti etched into the brickwork on the outside of the pillbox when his phone rang.

'I hope this is good news.'

'No, Sir. Sorry,' replied Louise. 'Nothing from the fingerprints.'

'What about the DNA?'

'We should get a result one way or the other by tomorrow morning.'

Dixon rang off and watched the scenes of crime officers loading their equipment into the back of one of the vans. The other was full of the rubbish that had been strewn inside the pillbox, each item bagged up for examination back at the lab.

'Saves the council clearing it I suppose,' said Watson.

Dixon nodded.

'Nothing from Fordgate, Sir.'

Dixon spun round to see Mark Pearce walking towards him along the towpath.

'There's only twelve houses,' continued Pearce. 'No one at home in three of them, and none of the others saw or heard anything.'

'Are you on foot?' asked Dixon.

'Yes, Sir. Dave's got the car at the Boat and Anchor.'

'Keep walking then and you can give him a hand.'

'How far is it?'

'Half a mile or so.'

'Hop in,' said Watson, climbing into his van. 'I'll give you a lift round there now.'

'Thanks.'

'Keep in touch with Louise,' said Dixon, 'and don't go without her. I may go over to Musgrove Park for the PM.'

'Yes, Sir,' replied Pearce.

Watson waited in the field to allow two Dog Section vans through the gate and then drove slowly back along the towpath. The vans parked next to Dixon's Land Rover, and a uniformed police sergeant got out of the driver's seat of one of them. The other van was rocking from side to side.

'That's Ajax, Sir. He gets a bit excitable.'

'Just the two of you?' asked Dixon.

'There's another on the way.'

'Good.'

'Where d'you want us?'

'The towpath north to Huntworth Bridge and south to Fordgate, plus this area around the pillbox.'

'Any idea what we're looking for?'

'His pockets were empty, so a wallet, car keys, stuff like that.'

'What about a murder weapon?'

'He died of a heart attack while he was being assaulted, so that's unlikely.'

'Leave it with me then, Sir. I'll let you know if we find anything.'

'Thank you.'

Dixon stamped his feet to keep them warm while he watched the dogs start their search of the immediate vicinity, one heading north along the towpath and the other south.

He waited for the third dog to arrive, another liver and white Springer Spaniel, and watched it searching the canal bank around the pillbox, weaving in and out of the undergrowth. By now, though, the pain in his toes was too much to bear. Much longer and frostbite would set in, but either way, getting to the post mortem too early seemed a small price to pay for getting out of the cold.

'You're all right,' said Poland over the intercom. 'You've missed the internals. Come in.'

Dixon sighed. He had been quite happy sitting on the radiator in the anteroom, and the pathology lab would be stone cold. Still, at least he could feel his toes again.

'He was a heart attack waiting to happen,' said Poland as Dixon walked into the lab. 'He's had one before too.'

'Any idea when?'

'Within the last year or two.'

'Time of death?'

'Friday night or Saturday morning.'

'And he died in the pillbox?'

'Yes. There's no sign he'd been moved.'

Dixon looked down at the body on the slab, still with no name. An incision held together by a line of staples ran the full length of the torso, another around the top of the skull.

'Approximately sixty-five years of age,' said Poland, reading from his notes. 'Sixty-three point five kilos and one hundred and seventy-eight centim—'

'What's that in real money?' interrupted Dixon.

'Ten stone and just over five feet ten to you. A bit underweight for his height and age.'

'What's this?' asked Dixon, pointing at the forearms.

'Old burns. They're on both arms, the backs of his hands and the right side of his face.'

'Serious?'

'Not life threatening. Serious enough though. The burns on his face have been touched up at some point. Cosmetic surgery.'

'How old?'

'No idea. Years. Decades even.'

'What about toxicology?'

'Nothing,' replied Poland.

'Nothing? What's that brown powder then?'

'No idea. It's still sitting in his lungs, but he died before it could be absorbed.'

'How much is there?'

'Not a lot.'

Dixon leaned over and peered at the dead man's moustache. Faint traces of the brown powder were still visible in amongst the greying hair.

'Anything from the fingerprints?' asked Poland, dropping his notepad into the pocket of his white coat.

'No.'

'Well, I've lined up an odontologist for tomorrow in case you get nothing from the DNA.'

Dixon nodded.

'He's looked after his teeth, so if he used a local dentist he should be fairly easy to find,' said Poland. 'Assuming he's local of course.'

'Let's hope it doesn't come to that.'

'Quite.'

'Is there anything else I need to know?' asked Dixon.

'Not really,' replied Poland. 'There's a historic leg fracture, he drank a bit too much, non-smoker, ingrowing toenails. How much detail d'you want?'

'Not that much.'

Poland smiled. 'You look like you could do with a hot drink. Coffee?'

'I thought you'd never ask.'

Dixon followed Poland into his office and sat on the corner of the desk while Poland boiled the kettle.

'You might as well have this,' said Poland, handing Dixon a chicken sandwich. 'My secretary got it for me from the canteen, but I can't face it.'

'Thanks.'

Dixon reached into his pocket and took out his insulin pen. Then he dialled up twelve units and pushed the needle into the side of his leg through his trousers.

'You really shouldn't be doing that through your clothes,' said Poland. 'It could lead to all sorts of—'

'Yes, Mother.'

'Jane still in bed I suppose?'

Dixon nodded.

'Bet you're glad you were driving last night,' said Poland, placing a mug of coffee on the desk next to Dixon.

'That pillbox was bad enough, but with a hangover? I'd have—'

'I nearly did.' Poland smiled. 'So, what's this training course Jane's doing?'

'Child Protection and the Internet. Then she joins the PPU.'

'Remind me.'

'The Public Protection Unit. It's based at Portishead.'

'Odd choice.'

'You go where the vacancy is, and it splits us up at work now we're living together. Then she'll transfer to the Bridgwater SCU.'

'Are you taking the—?'

'Safeguarding Coordination Unit,' mumbled Dixon through a mouthful of sandwich.

'You lot enjoy a good acronym, don't you?'

'And what are all those letters after your name?'

Poland shrugged his shoulders. 'So, what happens now?'

'We waste valuable time trying to find out who he is,' replied Dixon, shaking his head, 'before we can start finding out who killed him and why.'

'Is that you or me?' asked Poland, rummaging in his pockets as a phone started ringing.

'Me,' said Dixon, reaching into his coat pocket. 'Dixon.'

'Duty sergeant, Sir. We've had a missing persons call. It fits with your victim. Male aged sixty-five, bald, moustache.'

'Who made the call?'

'A neighbour. Not seen him since Friday. She's worried about his elderly mother, and the dog's been barking non-stop since yesterday.'

'Have we got a name?'

'Alan Fletcher, Sir.'

'Where?'

'Easter Cottage, North Curry.'

Dixon drove over the large rock on the edge of the verge and parked on the grass opposite the war memorial in the centre of North Curry. Two uniformed officers were sitting in a patrol car further along Church Road, but he recognised neither of them.

He walked across the grass, leaving the first footprints in the fresh snow, and along the pavement in front of the cottages. Easter Cottage was the second one along. Built of red brick with old fashioned sash windows, two either side of a white painted front door and three upstairs, it was definitely the right house, judging by the barking. A small terrier of some sort.

Dixon peered in through the letterbox, turning when he heard the doors of the patrol car opening behind him.

'What are we waiting for?' he asked, holding up his warrant card.

'The RSPCA, Sir, for the dog.'

'Which neighbour made the call?'

'Next door but one, Sir.'

Dixon turned back to the letter box and looked in. There was a small porch with a tiled floor and a glazed inner door. Behind that a small Jack Russell was barking for all he was worth.

'It's just a bloody Russell,' said Dixon, straightening up. 'Get this door open.'

'The RSPCA will be here within the hour they said, Sir.'

'We can't wait for them. Now get it open.'

One of the officers fetched a handheld battering ram from the boot of the patrol car and hit the door just above the Yale lock. The door swung open.

Dixon stepped into the porch and closed the door behind him. He glanced along the coat hooks to his left. A dog's lead was hanging on a hook behind an old coat, so he unhooked it and looped it around his neck before trying the inner door, which was unlocked. He opened it just wide enough to squeeze in. The letterbox moved behind him, and he turned to see one of the uniformed officers watching his every move.

The dog hesitated and then started barking again, more agitated this time, so Dixon sat down on the floor with his back to it and waited.

It took no more than a few minutes for the barking to subside. Dixon reached slowly into his coat pocket and took out a dog biscuit, which he dropped on to the carpet behind him. Monty could spare a couple. He waited for the crunching sound and then dropped another on the floor. Then another. The fourth he held in the palm of his hand, scratching the dog behind the ears as he took it.

'Hungry, aren't you, old son?'

Dixon checked the dog's collar. 'Nimrod', and on the back 'Fletcher', then a phone number.

He stood up and walked along the passageway into the kitchen at the back of the cottage; it was 'in need of refreshment', as an estate agent would say, and there were several piles of dog mess by the back door. The dog's water bowl was empty, so he filled it from the tap and listened to the slurping as he walked back to the front door.

'Call off the RSPCA, then have a look around, will you?'

'Yes, Sir.'

Dixon was opening a tin of dog food when one of the uniformed officers appeared in the kitchen doorway.

'There's an elderly lady dead in bed upstairs, Sir. Back bedroom.'

'Call it in.'

'Yes, Sir.'

'The neighbour says there's a daughter. Lives over Ilminster way apparently.'

'Give her a ring and get her over here,' said Dixon. 'There's an address book by the phone in the hall. We'll need Family Liaison too.'

'Ground floor is clear, Sir,' said the other officer.

'You got a dog?' asked Dixon.

'Yes, Sir.'

'Good. Feed this one, then put him in the back of my Land Rover. It's not locked. Here's his lead.'

Dixon stopped at the bottom of the stairs and looked at a small red pennant mounted in a wood framed glass case on the wall. A leek set on a red background encircled by the words 'Cymru Am Byth' in white on a blue background with a crown on top. Underneath it, engraved on a small gold plaque, were the words 'Presented to Captain Alan Fletcher DSO by the Warrant Officers, 1st Battalion, Welsh Guards, Pirbright, June 1991.'

That explained Nimrod.

A colour photograph next to it showed two army officers in full ceremonial uniform – black trousers, red tunics and bearskins, swords at their waists – both Welsh Guardsmen judging by the golden leeks sewn on to their collars. Dixon recognised the officer on the right with the big smile. Younger, happy and yet destined to end his days in a freezing cold pillbox on the Bridgwater and Taunton Canal.

She looked asleep, were it not for blue lips and grey skin. Dixon thought she must be well over ninety and in poor health if the different boxes of pills on the bedside table were anything to go by. He picked up a small red and white box and looked at the label. '1 Nitrolingual 0.4 mg Pumpspray, spray twice under the tongue when required. Mrs Lillian May Fletcher.'

On the bedside table was a silver framed photograph of a young Alan Fletcher with his bride on their wedding day, both of them grinning at the camera. The photograph looked very much like it had been taken on the same day as the one at the bottom of the stairs. Perhaps the other officer in that photograph had been Fletcher's best man. A second wedding photograph on the bedside table was presumably the daughter and her husband.

Mrs Fletcher was propped up in the bed on three pillows, her head back, mouth open and eyes closed. 'Peacefully in her sleep' the obituary notice would say. Unlike her son's.

'The neighbour's here, Sir.'

Dixon stopped on the landing and looked back. Then he turned to the uniformed officer waiting at the top of the stairs.

'I want this treated as a crime scene until we know otherwise.'

'Yes, Sir.'

'We'll need Roger Poland and SOCO out here. All right?'

'Yes, Sir.'

Dixon was halfway down the stairs when the neighbour appeared in the doorway of the sitting room.

'Is she . . . ?'

Dixon nodded.

'This is Mrs Westlake, Sir. The neighbour from two doors down.'

'Detective Inspector Dixon, Mrs Westlake. Can we have a word back at your house perhaps?'

'Yes, of course.'

Dixon followed her along the pavement and through her front door, which was standing open.

'How old was Mrs Fletcher?'

'Ninety-six, Inspector,' replied Mrs Westlake, opening a door on the right. 'Let's sit in here. I've lit the stove.'

'Did you know her well?' asked Dixon, sitting down on a chair opposite the wood burner.

'Yes, reasonably well. We met when my husband and I moved in here. That was eight years ago.'

'And was her son living with her at the time?'

'Yes. Alan. He keeps himself to himself really. He's her carer. She's got . . . had . . . angina and renal failure, amongst other things. I helped out if Alan was away. Beta blockers, statins, diuretics. She was always taking pills of some sort.'

'And was her death expected, if that's not a stupid question to ask of a ninety-six year old?'

'Not as stupid as it sounds. Her kidneys had packed up and she'd refused dialysis. Palliative care they call it, don't they? She was determined to die in her own home. Stubborn old . . .'

Mrs Westlake took out a handkerchief and wiped her eyes.

'And Alan was looking after her?'

'Yes. They'd got some nurses coming in next week from the local hospice. I'd better ring them.'

'When did you last see him?'

'Friday morning. He'd walked down to the shop for his paper as usual,' replied Mrs Westlake. 'Why, what's happened to him? He'd have said if he was going away . . . asked me to help with Lillian.'

'Did you see him again after that?'

'No.' Mrs Westlake was watching the flames flickering in the door of the wood burner and shaking her head. 'No, I'm sure I didn't.'

'Did you see anyone else that day? Anyone unusual. Someone you'd not seen before perhaps.'

'No.'

'When did you notice the dog barking?'

'Late Saturday I think. Yesterday. I went into Taunton in the morning.'

'Does Mr Fletcher own a car?'

'Yes, it's over there,' replied Mrs Westlake, gesturing back towards the war memorial. 'Opposite the cottage. The blue one.'

'He won the Distinguished Service Order—'

'In the Falklands. That's all I know. He never spoke about it.'

'What about friends? Did he have any?'

'Not that I know of I'm afraid. He was a churchgoer, though, if that's any use to you.'

'Down the road here?'

'Yes.'

'Thank you,' said Dixon, standing up. 'You've been very helpful.'

'Has something happened to Alan?'

'That's what we're trying to find out, Mrs Westlake.'

Dixon was walking back along the pavement when Louise and Mark Pearce arrived and pulled up behind a Scientific Services van that was double parked, blocking the road.

'Where's Dave?' asked Dixon.

'We left him at the Boat and Anchor,' replied Louise.

'I see you've made an arrest, Sir,' said Pearce, pointing at Dixon's Land Rover.

Nimrod was standing with his paws up at the back window.

'Shut up, Mark.'

'Sorry, Sir.'

'It looks like our victim is Alan Fletcher. He lived here with his elderly mother, who just happens to be dead in bed upstairs. Roger's on his way to have a look at her, but we're probably wasting his time. She was ninety-six with heart trouble and kidney failure.'

'Did well to get to ninety-six,' said Pearce.

'There's a daughter on her way here now,' continued Dixon. 'Right then. Mrs Westlake, two doors down. She's the neighbour who rang us. Go and get a statement from her, will you?'

'Both of us?' asked Pearce.

'Just you.'

Back at Easter Cottage, Dixon leafed through the address book on the hall table. He turned to 'F' and rang the mobile number next to 'Alan'. The handwriting was faint and spidery; Mrs Fletcher's no doubt. 'This is the Vodafone voicemail service for 07—' He rang off.

'This is his mobile phone number,' said Dixon, handing the open phone book to Louise. 'See if we can get a trace on it. Even if it's off, it might show up on a base station.'

'Yes, Sir.'

'Then see what you can find in the living room. Have you got some gloves?'

Louise nodded without looking away from her phone.

Dixon glanced along the hall to the kitchen and watched a scenes of crime officer dusting the back door for fingerprints. Another was dusting the bannister, and a third the front door.

He was staring at the photograph of Alan Fletcher on the wall at the bottom of the stairs when his phone started ringing in his coat pocket.

'Yes, Sir.'

'What've you got?' asked DCI Lewis.

'A neighbour made the call. It looks like our victim is retired Captain Alan Fletcher, ex-army. Lives here with his elderly mother. Only we get here to find she's dead.'

'Not another murder?'

'Doesn't look like it, Sir. She was ninety-six and terminally ill so, and I'm guessing now, but I reckon he went out on Friday, never came back and sometime between then and now she died in her bed. He wasn't here to give her her medication of course. There's no sign of forced entry or a struggle. It's possible he suffocated her I suppose, or overdosed her before he left, but Roger's on the way, so he'll soon tell us.'

'What about his car?'

'Still here, so either he went on foot or was picked up by his killer. He may have caught the bus to somewhere, but we'll check that.'

'Any other relatives?'

'A daughter is on her way over from Ilminster. We'll get her to do the identification when I've spoken to her. Family Liaison is on the way too.'

'Good. Keep me posted.'

'Yes, Sir.'

Dixon rang off and peered into the living room. Louise was sitting in front of an open bureau, flicking through the bundles of papers in the various compartments.

'See if you can find his Christmas card list. And find out what bus routes come through North Curry, will you?'

'Yes, Sir.'

Dixon turned when he heard voices behind him in the hall.

'This is Mrs Fletcher's GP, Nick,' said Poland. He was wearing a set of white overalls and blue latex gloves. The doctor was dressed casually.

'Dr Saltmarsh.' She shook hands with Dixon.

'SOCO haven't found anything, but we need a cause of death.'

'Probably heart failure,' said Dr Saltmarsh. 'I'm surprised she's lasted this long to be honest.'

'Let me know,' said Dixon. 'I'm going to give the dog a run in those gardens over there.'

Dixon was leaning on the gate of Queen Square Garden, a small walled garden opposite the cottage, watching Nimrod cocking his leg on the base of the flagpole when Dr Saltmarsh appeared beside him.

'Looks like the heart. I've notified the coroner. There'll need to be a post mortem anyway because of the way she was found.'

Dixon nodded.

'I've left Dr Poland in there,' continued Dr Saltmarsh. 'We couldn't see any sign of anything untoward.'

'Thank you.'

'You do know the sign says no dogs?'

Chapter Three

'The daughter's here, Sir. Mrs Painter.'

'What about Family Liaison?'

'Karen Marsden is downstairs.'

'Has Roger finished?'

'Not yet.'

Dixon was sitting in what had once been a spare bedroom at the back of the house. The bed had gone, but the bedside table was still there, in amongst several stacks of boxes piled high against the wall. Each box was sealed with tape and the contents written in black marker pen on the outside. Military style. Ornaments, dining room; pictures, living room, small; plates, kitchen; books, fiction; books, non-fiction. None of them touched since the day Alan Fletcher had moved in with his mother, judging by the dust.

It was a store room but also Fletcher's office. An old laptop on a camping table 'designed for Windows 98' according to the sticker by the keyboard, and a printer of pensionable age. Dixon took his phone out of his pocket and opened 'Settings', then he selected 'Wi-Fi'. He waited several seconds, but there were no networks in range, and a laptop of this vintage would need a modem cable anyway. He checked under the desk. Nothing.

On the floor under the window was a black bin liner, full and tied at the top. Next to it was a small shredder. Scientific Services would have fun with that lot.

The built-in wardrobe behind the door contained nothing but old clothes, moths and empty suitcases. It smelt damp, but not as damp as the pillbox.

Dixon closed the door behind him and walked across the landing to Mrs Fletcher's bedroom. Roger Poland was standing in the window, talking into a handheld Dictaphone, his large frame blocking what little light there was left coming in from outside.

'The daughter's here,' said Dixon.

'Show her up. There's no sign of foul play, but the PM will confirm it one way or the other.'

'Where is she?' asked Dixon, arriving at the bottom of the stairs.

'In there, Sir,' replied Louise.

'Find anything?'

'No.'

Mrs Painter was sitting on the sofa with her back to the door. Sergeant Karen Marsden from the Family Liaison Team was sitting next to her. Steam was rising from mugs of tea.

'Mrs Painter?' asked Dixon.

She stood up and turned to face him. Late fifties, early sixties – definitely Fletcher's younger sister – she had short, dark hair, professionally dyed no doubt, and wore a long wool coat and brown leather boots.

'This is Detective Inspector Dixon, Eve,' said Karen.

'What's a detective inspector doing here? Where's my brother? Where's Alan?'

'Mrs Paint—'

'He hasn't done anything stupid, has he?'

'What d'you mean?'

'He always said he wouldn't let her suffer. That he'd . . . you know . . . when the time came.'

'As far as we can tell at this stage, your mother died of heart failure, Mrs Painter,' said Dixon.

'Oh thank God.' She closed her eyes and bowed her head. 'Sorry, that must sound awful.'

'We understand,' said Dixon.

'Thank you.'

'Would you like to see her now?'

'Yes, please.'

Mrs Painter followed Dixon up the stairs.

'This is Dr Roger Poland.'

'You're not my mother's GP.'

'I'm the senior pathologist at Musgrove Park, Mrs Painter,' said Poland.

'Where's her GP?'

'She's been and gone,' said Dixon.

'Look, will somebody please tell me what's going on?'

'We received a call from a neighbour this afternoon and arrived to find your mother had passed away.'

'It looks like she died in the early hours of Saturday,' continued Poland. 'Heart failure as far as I can tell, but the coroner's been notified, and there'll need to be a post mortem, probably tomorrow now.'

'Why a post mortem?'

'Because she was found alone in the house,' replied Dixon.

'Will there be an inquest?'

'That's unlikely.'

'You still haven't mentioned Alan yet,' snapped Mrs Painter.

'No. We'll come on to your brother in a moment, Mrs Painter,' said Dixon. 'Would you like to spend a moment with your mother first?'

Mrs Painter looked down at her mother. A tear appeared in the corner of her eye and then was gone.

'No.'

'You confirm this is your mother, Mrs Lillian May Fletcher?' asked Dixon.

'Yes.'

'Right. Well, let's continue this downstairs, shall we?'

'Tell me about Alan,' said Dixon. He was sitting in the living room perched on the edge of an armchair next to the open fire and wishing it had been lit. Mrs Painter and Karen Marsden were sitting side by side on the sofa, with Louise behind them, at the bureau.

'He lived here with my mother. What more is there to say? Where is he? And where's Nimrod?'

'Mrs Painter, I'm sorry to have to tell you that we found a body this morning on the Bridgwater and Taunton Canal. We believe it to be your brother, but will be asking you to identify him formally, if that's OK.'

Silence.

Dixon glanced at Karen Marsden and then back to Mrs Painter.

'We believe it was a heart attack,' he continued, 'although I have to tell you that he appears to have been assaulted and died during the assault. For that reason we have opened a murder investigation.'

'Murder?'

'Yes.'

'When?'

'Late on Friday night or possibly the early hours of Saturday.'

Mrs Painter sighed and shook her head.

'Where were you?'

'You can't possibly think that I did it.'

'Forgive me, we have questions we have to ask, boxes we have to tick.'

'I was at home with my husband.'

'Do you know of anyone who might wish to harm Alan? Did he have any enemies?'

'We weren't that close, Inspector. Or at least we hadn't been for some time.'

'Why?'

'Family reasons.'

Dixon waited. Mrs Painter looked up and then back down to her feet.

'We fell out after he moved in here with Mother. Not that we'd seen much of each other before that.'

She took a sip of tea.

'It all changed when my father died and Alan came back from the Falklands. He came back a different person. Scarred inside and out I suppose.'

Dixon looked at her and raised his eyebrows.

'He was there when the *Sir Galahad* was hit,' continued Mrs Painter. 'He was the adjutant, 1st Battalion of the Welsh Guards. Watched the whole thing from the shore. His best friend, best man, actually, was on the ship and died in the fire. Alan could do nothing except watch. None of them could. They lost a lot of men that day.'

'Go on.'

'Is there anything stronger?' asked Mrs Painter over her shoulder to Louise.

'Er . . .'

'The sideboard over there. There's usually a bottle of gin or something.'

Dixon watched Louise fetch an open bottle of gin from the sideboard and waited while Mrs Painter tipped at least a double measure into her tea.

'It's all right, Inspector. My husband will come and pick me up.'

'You said it all changed when Alan came back.'

'He came back on a hospital ship, badly burnt. It was after Port Stanley fell. There was a fire on an armoured personnel carrier from what we could gather. He went in to get the men out. It was like he was trying to make up for not be able to help on the *Sir Galahad*. Got them all out too. That's when he won the DSO. His commanding officer told us that. Alan never spoke about it. Ever.'

Dixon nodded.

'He was bitter,' continued Mrs Painter. 'Blaming everyone and . . . poor Jean, she bore the brunt of it.'

'Jean?'

'His wife. They went their separate ways in the end, which is when he moved in here. She lives in Shropshire now. We keep in touch.'

'Is she in a relationship?'

'Yes. She lives with a man called Ian Newby. He's divorced too.'

'What about Alan? Was he in a relationship?'

'Not that I know of.'

'So, what happened when he came back from the Falklands?'

'His army career stalled. He was the youngest adjutant in battalion history, but when they got back it all went wrong. He left in 1991, slinked away really, still a captain, and after that it was one failed business venture after another. He went bust twice I think. And then finally Jean had had enough. He even managed to lose her inheritance from her parents.'

'Did they have children?'

'No.'

'Do you?'

'Is that relevant?'

'I'm just trying to build a picture of the family, Mrs Painter.'

'Two. And three grandchildren.'

'What about his failed business ventures then? What were they?'

'They bought a guest house in Lyme Regis, but it was repossessed. Then it was a letting agency. After that he just gave up I think and started taking it out on Jean. Drinking too.'

'So when they divorced he came to live here?'

'That's right. Look, you'll find out about it eventually, so I may as well tell you. He got my mother to change her will, leaving everything to him. She said I was financially secure and he needed it more, so she left him everything. That's when we . . . well, when we fell out.'

'You felt you were due half?'

'Yes. Why not? I was being penalised for being careful. He pissed all his money up the wall and gets bailed out. And what about my children?'

'Where did your mother make this will?'

'He took her to a firm of solicitors in Taunton. I don't know which one.'

'Did your brother make a will?'

'I've no idea,' replied Mrs Painter, shaking her head.

'Who inherits your mother's estate if your brother dies first?' asked Dixon.

He watched the blood drain from Mrs Painter's face.

'I don't know,' she replied. 'Me probably. Look, I don't need the money, I really don't. It was the principle of the thing.'

Dixon stood up.

'Mrs Painter, I'm going to ask you to go with these two uniformed officers to identify your brother. Then they'll take you home.'

'Yes, fine.'

'The coroner's officer will be in touch about your mother's funeral arrangements, but they are likely to be delayed because of the post mortem.'

'What about my brother?'

'It'll be some time before his body can be released I'm afraid, but Karen will keep you informed. We would like to speak to his ex-wife, if you could tell us how to get in touch with her.'

'Yes, of course.'

'And then there's Nimrod,' said Dixon. 'He's in the back of my car at the moment.'

'He'll have to be put down,' replied Mrs Painter. 'I can't have him . . . He fights with my Border Terrier.'

'Would you like me to take care of him?'

'Yes, please, Inspector.'

It was pitch dark by the time Dixon and Louise left Easter Cottage. Mrs Fletcher had been taken to Musgrove Park for post mortem the following morning, and Scientific Services had left with a vanload of papers, the bin bag of shredded paper and the laptop to go to High Tech. A search of the garden had revealed a small brazier that had been used for burning rubbish at some point, so how much of value was left would remain to be seen.

Mrs Painter had formally identified her brother, Alan Robert Fletcher, and the search of the canal had been completed and turned up nothing. House to house had drawn a blank too.

Dixon ignored the turning for the staff car park at Express Park and drove around to the back of Bridgwater Police Centre.

'You missed the—' said Louise.

'Kennels,' interrupted Dixon. 'They're round the back.'

Louise looked over her shoulder at Nimrod, curled up asleep in Monty's bed.

'You're not taking him home then?'

'Better not. They can be little buggers can Russells. One had a go at Monty on the beach a few weeks ago.'

'What'd he do?'

'He sat on it,' replied Dixon, grinning.

'You're not going to have him put to sleep, are you?'

'You heard Mrs Painter. I can take care of him.'

'That's what she said.'

'Good. So, we'll see if the charity I got Monty from can take him. Until then he can stay here.'

Dixon glanced up at the police centre while he waited for the steel gates to open. Several officers were visible in the huge windows at the front of the building, sitting with their backs to the glass. Mark Pearce had collected Dave Harding from the Boat and Anchor, and both were now being quizzed by DCI Lewis, who was leaning on Mark's workstation.

'Give me ten minutes, then get everyone together in meeting room two, will you?'

'Yes, Sir,' replied Louise, jumping out of Dixon's Land Rover in the staff car park.

A cup of tea with a spoonful of sugar would be enough to tide him over until he got home. He checked the time while he stirred it: 6 p.m. Not too late, so he dialled the number and waited.

'What's up?'

'Who died first, Roger?' asked Dixon.

'That's easy. Alan did. His mother perhaps twelve hours later. It'll be in my report.'

'Thanks. Let me know if you find anything tomorrow morning.'

'Will do.'

Dixon rang off. Then he leaned back in his chair in the corner of the staff canteen and closed his eyes. He had been up since just after 5 a.m. that morning and hadn't got to bed much before 1 a.m. Thank God he had been driving last night.

He just had time to send Jane a text message.

how's your head Nx

The reply came as he was finishing his tea.

banging

He smiled. They had been first in and last out of the Zalshah Tandoori Restaurant in Burnham-on-Sea, and Jane had been doing all right until the liqueurs arrived.

He typed out a reply – *serves you right!* – but thought better of sending it.

Dave Harding, Mark Pearce and Louise Willmott were waiting for him in meeting room 2, although it was more of a glass cubicle on the landing, a victim of the move from a good old fashioned police station to a brand new police centre. His office had gone too, replaced by a workstation, and not even his own at that. 'Hot desking' it was called. Bollocks. It was going to take some getting used to.

Dixon sat down at the head of the table and glanced around the room. He was going to miss Jane on this one. Mark was young and keen, Louise was bright but new to CID, and Dave's old grey suit was just as crumpled as ever. Not that Dixon would criticise a man for that, but the brown suede shoes were a different matter altogether.

'What did you make of the daughter, Sir?' asked Louise.

'What did you think of her?'

Louise shook her head.

'Trust your gut.'

'I don't think she did it.'

'Neither do I,' said Dixon. 'But we check all the same. Find the mother's will and get the solicitor's will file too. See if Alan made a will as well.'

'What happens if he didn't?'

'Nothing. He died before his mother, so the gift to him fails. It's about the mother's will now, and it'll soon tell us who inherits in his place.'

'It could be the daughter.'

'Yes, it could, but that doesn't mean she killed him. Not everyone left out of a will kills the other beneficiaries.'

'If they did, we'd be bloody busy,' said Harding.

'We would, Dave,' replied Dixon. 'Get anything at the Boat and Anchor?'

'Lots of names and phone numbers from the bookings. Some regulars and several number plates from the CCTV. Some people arrived by taxi too.'

'Well, you know what to do.'

'Yes, Sir.'

'Let me know if you need any help.'

Harding nodded.

'Mark, we need everything on Alan Fletcher's failed businesses. He went bust twice apparently. Find out who he owed money to. Check with the Insolvency Service to begin with, and see what they've got on him.'

'What about the ex-wife?'

'Leave her to me. Louise, see if you can find the solicitor who acted for him on the divorce, and set up a meeting with the ex.'

'Yes, Sir.'

'What about the brown powder?' asked Pearce.

'We should get a result tomorrow,' replied Louise.

'And we'll need some house to house in North Curry tomorrow evening. Catch people in after work,' said Dixon. 'Anything else?'

'Isn't this a double murder?'

'Eh?' Harding was shaking his head.

'Seriously, Dave,' continued Louise, 'you kill a carer and the person being cared for dies. Aren't you responsible for both deaths?'

'That's one for the Crown Prosecution Service,' said Dixon. 'Let's just find the bugger first, shall we?'

Chapter Four

Jane was fast asleep on the sofa under the duvet she had dragged off the bed, and not even the diesel engine nor Monty's barking had woken her up. Odd that. Dixon would have checked for a pulse had it not been for the snoring.

'You been fed, old son?'

Monty ran into the kitchen and sat on the floor by the dog food cupboard, wagging his tail.

'That's a no then, is it?'

The noise of the kettle boiling soon drowned out the sound of a metal dog bowl being pushed along the tiled floor.

'What time is it?'

'Just after seven,' replied Dixon, turning to see Jane standing in the doorway, the duvet wrapped around her shoulders.

'You've been had.'

'What?'

'I'd already fed him.'

Dixon rolled his eyes. 'Cheeky little—.'

'Have you eaten?' asked Jane.

'I had a sandwich earlier.'

'There's a chilli in the freezer.'

'What about you?'

'I might have some toast later. How'd you get on?'

'We got lucky, if you can call it that. A neighbour was concerned about the victim's elderly mother, only she was dead when we got there.'

'A double murder?'

'Don't you start.'

'But you know who he is?'

'Alan Fletcher. Lived over at North Curry.'

'Cause of death?'

'Heart attack. He was being assaulted at the time.'

'In a pillbox on the canal?'

'I reckon he'd have been killed if he hadn't died first. His hands were tied behind his back. Either way, it's murder.'

'I'm going to go and have a shower,' said Jane. 'Tell me about it later.'

Dixon dragged his laptop out from under the TV stand while he waited for the microwave to go ping. He would have time to cook his supper and eat it before it booted up, but then it was almost as old as Alan Fletcher's. It was a miracle it had lasted this long and a great shame it had survived the shotgun blast a few months earlier. A new one, paid for by his house insurers, would have been just the job.

He balanced his empty plate on the arm of the sofa, picked up his laptop and typed 'Falklands War' into Google. The first result came from Wikipedia, so he clicked on it and scrolled down to 'Land Battles', then 'Bluff Cove' and 'Fitzroy'. Thirty-two Welsh Guardsmen had been lost from a total of forty-eight killed when the *Sir Galahad* had been hit by bombs and caught fire during an attack by Argentinian Skyhawks. Dixon had seen the footage of helicopters hovering next to a ship billowing black smoke before, but he found it on YouTube and watched it again, trying to imagine how Alan Fletcher must have felt watching the attack and its aftermath from the comparative safety of the shore, powerless to stop it.

It was old news footage from the BBC and ITV. Soldiers milling about, helping the wounded ashore from the lifeboats and landing craft that were being used to ferry the injured to safety, and administering first aid. All of it against a backdrop of black smoke, flames and explosions as the fire reached the ammunition on board the ship. Dixon looked for Fletcher amongst the faces, but it was impossible to identify him.

Nine days later, on 11 June 1982, the 1st Welsh Guards had taken part in the Battle of Mount Harriet, when 42 Commando, Royal Marines, with 40 Commando and the Welsh Guards in support had captured the high ground above Port Stanley. Mount Longdon and Two Sisters fell on the same night to other units, the first phase of the approach to Port Stanley complete. Two days later Mount Tumbledown and Wireless Ridge were taken, and a ceasefire was declared the following day.

And Alan Fletcher had survived all of that to die in a shithole on the banks of the Bridgwater and Taunton Canal.

'What's that you're watching?' asked Jane, dropping down on to the sofa next to Dixon.

'A documentary about the Falklands War. My victim was there.'

'Really?'

'He was in the Welsh Guards. The adjutant.'

'What's an adjutant?'

'Personal staff officer to the battalion commander. He deals with the admin, that sort of stuff.'

'Was he still in the army?'

'No, he left in 1991.'

'Got any witnesses?'

'No.'

Jane shook her head.

'What's on the telly?'

'You choose,' replied Dixon. 'Just not a war film, all right?'

Dixon woke early the following morning. He never slept well during an investigation; 'in the heat of battle' he called it, although that seemed a bit crass this time. Yes, he'd had his house broken into by armed men in the dead of night and yes, he'd been shot at too. And stabbed come to think of it. But it wasn't quite the same as fighting for Queen and country, watching your friends fighting and dying all round you. He closed his eyes and saw the smoke billowing out of the *Sir Galahad* again, this time in slow motion and against a backdrop of Elgar's 'Nimrod'. The music had been going round and round in his head all night.

In Dixon's book, war veterans were to be treated with respect, not murdered in pillboxes on the banks of the Bridgwater and Taunton Canal. Alan Fletcher had done his duty for Queen and country, and he could rely on Dixon to do his.

He reached over and prodded Jane.

'C'mon, you've got to get up to Portishead don't forget.'

'What are you doing today?'

'Oh, y'know, places to go, people to see.'

Dixon was filling up with diesel in the Shell station at the entrance to Express Park when his phone rang in his pocket.

'Louise? Where are you?'

'Outside Harringtons Solicitors in Burnham, Sir. They made Mrs Fletcher's will, but they won't let me have it. Client confidentiality apparently.'

'Who are the executors?'

'They wouldn't tell me.'

Dixon looked at his watch. It was just after 9 a.m. He ignored the cashier banging on the window of the petrol station and walked away from the pump, still with his phone to his ear.

'We don't have time to wait for an interim death certificate. Tell them they've got three choices. They can either believe a member of Her Majesty's constabulary that Mrs Fletcher is dead and release a copy of her will, or you can take them to the mortuary now and show them the body.'

'What's the third choice?'

'Arrest them for obstruction.'

'Just a copy?'

'Yes, a copy will do. And a copy of their will file. And don't forget to ask them if they acted for Alan on his divorce.'

'Leave it with me, Sir.'

Every run-in with a solicitor reminded Dixon of his narrow escape from the legal profession, leaving the day he qualified. Much longer and it would have been a mortgage, commitments, and he'd never have got out.

Louise rang back just as he was parking the Land Rover in the staff car park.

'I've got it.'

'What does it say?'

'I give all my estate whatsoever and . . . blah . . . blah . . . Here it is . . . For my said son Alan absolutely but if he dies before me then to be divided between such of my grandchildren as shall survive me and if more than one in equal shares on their attaining the age of twenty-five years.'

'Mrs Painter's going to love that,' said Dixon. 'Who are the executors?'

'Where's that?'

'Top of the first page.'

Paper rustling.

'Er, I appoint my son Alan Robert Fletcher and the partners at the date of my death in the firm of Harringtons Solicitors of—'

'That'll do,' interrupted Dixon. 'What about Alan's divorce?'

'No record.'

'Get back as quick as you can then.'

'Yes, Sir.'

A quick check on Nimrod in the kennels and Dixon arrived in the CID area on the first floor just before 9.30 a.m. Late for him perhaps, but Sunday had been a long day.

'Where's Dave?'

'He's gone to interview people who were in the Boat and Anchor on Friday night, Sir,' replied Pearce. 'Louise has gone to get the old dear's will.'

'What about Alan's businesses then?' asked Dixon.

'The guest house was repossessed. They couldn't keep up the mortgage payments.'

'Which bank was it?'

'Northern Rock. They both ended up doing individual voluntary arrangements.'

'How much did they owe?'

'Not a lot. It was mainly the bank and some local tradespeople in Lyme Regis.'

'And the letting agency?'

'That went pop big time,' replied Pearce. 'The company was wound up. He was done for trading while insolvent and disqualified as a company director. Owed thousands.'

'Who to?'

'I'm waiting for the file, Sir.'

'Copy it for me when it arrives.'

'Will do.'

'Anything from scientific?'

'Nothing amongst the papers except an old letter from Harringtons thanking Mrs Fletcher for paying their bill. It was in the bureau. They're making a start on the shredding.'

'Jigsaw puzzles are bad enough,' muttered Dixon as he walked over to the kettle.

'Here it is, Sir,' said Louise, dropping the copy of Mrs Fletcher's will on to Dixon's keyboard. He picked it up, glanced at it and then threw it to one side.

'Did you get the will file?'

'Yes, Sir.'

'Any mention of the son being there when she gave instructions?'

'No. Listen, I've been thinking about it,' said Louise. 'I really don't think Mrs Painter killed him.'

'Why not?' asked Dixon.

'Firstly, she's not the direct beneficiary. Her adult children are, and the youngest is twenty-nine.'

'Wouldn't you do that for your daughter?'

'No.'

'Your brother will be pleased,' said Dixon.

'I haven't got a brother,' replied Louise, frowning. 'And what if Alan had inherited? He doesn't have children of his own, so chances are he'd leave it all to her children anyway, his niece and nephew. And if he didn't make a will, then it would go to Mrs Painter or her children under the Intestacy Rules, wouldn't it? He'd already had one heart attack, so why kill him for it?'

'What if his will left it all to someone else? The Welsh Guards Benevolent Fund, for example.'

'Is there one?'

'I expect so. And he's hardly good with money, is he?' continued Dixon. 'She might have thought she had to kill him before their mother died to see to it that the money stayed in the family.'

'Are you saying you think she did it now?'

'No,' replied Dixon. 'But she could've done. There's a motive there, even if it is thin.'

'And she volunteered it don't forget.'

'She knew we'd have found it anyway. Have you found his will?'

'Not yet.'

'Well don't just stand there then. And see if you can track down the ex-wife too.'

Dixon smiled. He thought Louise was right about Mrs Painter, but for the wrong reasons. Although if pressed he could do no better than 'it didn't feel right'. The will gave her a tenuous motive, more so if Alan's will was found and really did leave the estate outside the family. No, Mrs Painter had some questions to answer, and they would have a close look at her finances, but Dixon's mind was already elsewhere.

He had spent the last twenty minutes scrolling through pages and pages of old posts on several web forums, reading the grievances of landlords and tenants who between them had lost thousands of pounds in rent and deposits when Fletcher Lettings (South West) Limited had gone bust. It looked like Alan Fletcher had had his fingers in the till too. There were a lot of very angry people.

Beacon End House was on the hill above Ilminster. It was a large Victorian property with four chimneys and a slate roof, not much else being visible from the road thanks to the high box hedge.

Dixon pulled in opposite the drive and wrenched the handbrake on.

'What time was she getting down here?'

'She was leaving Shrewsbury this morning and getting down for lunch, so she should be here by now,' replied Louise.

'Can't see a bloody thing,' mumbled Dixon, peering down the drive.

'How long does it take?'

'Three hours at most I'd have thought.' Dixon looked at his watch. 'C'mon, we're a bit early, but she's hardly going to turn us away, is she?'

Dixon followed the drive down towards the house and round a sharp bend at the bottom, where it opened into a large gravelled parking area hidden behind tall fir trees. A Jaguar and a Chrysler Crossfire were parked in a double garage, which was open, and an old Ford Fiesta was parked outside.

'D'you think that's Jean's?' asked Louise.

'Could be,' replied Dixon. 'Or it could be one of Mrs Painter's children.'

Dixon had learned a long time ago never to judge a person by the car they drive, more so if it was an old heap. He parked behind the Ford Fiesta and switched off the engine, wondering as he did so what an old Land Rover said about him. Still, it was bought and paid for.

'The Painters look well off, don't they?'

'They do,' replied Dixon. 'Assuming they own it all, but they might be up to their armpits in debt for all we know.'

Louise nodded.

Dixon was able to see right along the hall through the glazed front door to the kitchen at the far end. There was a desk in the bay window to his right: the office, probably; but the door on the left of the hall was closed. He had banged the door knocker twice before the barking started and Mrs Painter appeared in the kitchen door, closely followed by a Border Terrier, its feet skidding on the floor tiles. She turned and said something over her shoulder before walking towards the front door.

'Looks like that is Mrs Fletcher's car,' said Dixon.

'You're early, Inspector,' said Mrs Painter. 'We were just having lunch.'

'We could always . . .'

'No, don't bother. It's cold anyway. Come in.'

'This is Detective Constable Willmott.'

They followed Mrs Painter along the hall and into the kitchen.

'Jean, this is the policeman I was telling you about.'

Jean Fletcher was tall, with the grey hair and wrinkles that come with age, but Dixon recognised her from the wedding photograph. She was wearing black jeans and a cream pullover. A set of wooden beads around her neck jangled when she stood up. No make-up either, but then this was not the occasion for it perhaps. She forced a smile when she shook Dixon's hand.

'Is there somewhere private we can talk?' asked Dixon, turning to Mrs Painter.

'Yes, of course. Use the living room. Follow me.'

'Where's Mr Painter?'

'At work, Inspector. He's an orthopaedic consultant at the Nuffield.'

'Both cars are in the garage.'

'He took the Bentley this morning.'

The living room was large, taking in both bay windows at the side of the house and giving views right across east Somerset. A table and chairs at one end and two brown leather sofas at the other, one in front of the fire and the other opposite a wall mounted flat screen TV.

'On a good day you can see King Alfred's Tower,' said Mrs Painter, looking out of the window.

Dixon nodded.

'We'll sit here I think,' he said, gesturing to the table and chairs.

'I'll leave you to it,' said Mrs Painter, backing out of the room and shutting the door behind her.

Dixon sat down opposite Mrs Fletcher with his back to the view and waited for Louise to take out her notebook.

'I'm very sorry for your loss, Mrs Fletcher.'

'Don't be. He's not my loss. I'm here for Eve really.'

'When did you divorce?' asked Dixon, nodding.

'We didn't,' replied Mrs Fletcher.

'You're still married?'

'Yes. We separated, but never divorced.'

'Why not?'

'There didn't seem much point. We were both too old, and there was nothing to fight over. Not that we had any fight left in us.'

'What does Ian make of that? It is Ian, isn't it?'

'Ian Newby. He doesn't mind. He's divorced himself, so he understands.'

'Let's start at the beginning then. When did you marry?'

'Nineteen seventy-eight. Good it was too. To begin with.'

'What changed?'

'He did. In the Falklands. He came through a tour in Northern Ireland the year after we married and seemed fine, but the Falklands was different . . . He was never the same after that.'

'Mrs Painter said he witnessed the attack on the *Sir Galahad* from the shore.'

'He did, but I never really got him to open up about it.'

'Then he was injured in a fire on an armoured personnel carrier.'

'There were no APCs on the Falklands, Inspector. If there had been, the boys wouldn't have had to yomp across the island, would they?'

'I suppose not.'

'And the Guards wouldn't have been on the *Sir Galahad* either,' continued Mrs Fletcher, her eyes glazing over for a split second.

'What was it then?' asked Dixon.

'A common or garden Land Rover. The ambulance conversion. Eve always says it was an APC, but it wasn't. I don't know where she got that from. Not that it matters. What matters is he got everyone out.'

'And was decorated for it.'

'That and other things. He won the DSO. That was the last really good day, getting that from the Queen.'

'What went wrong?'

'He started drinking. Got himself overlooked for promotion when the second in command moved on, and a few years later he was ushered quietly out of the army. That was just the start though.'

'Was he ever diagnosed with post traumatic stress disorder perhaps?'

'Saw a shrink, you mean?'

'Yes.'

'God, no. That wasn't the done thing in those days.'

'Tell me about the guest house then.'

'That was our first disaster,' replied Mrs Fletcher, shaking her head. 'It was good to begin with; then the recession got us. Bookings were down, and we were into negative equity before we knew it. Interest rates at fifteen per cent too. You'll be too young to remember that I expect.'

'Just about,' replied Dixon.

'Anyway, it was the bank that pulled the plug. We both ended up doing IVAs and spent the next few years paying off what we could when we could, which wasn't often. I worked as a secretary, and he got a job managing a fleet of vans. Hated it though. We both did.'

'Where were you living?'

'We rented a cottage in Dorchester, then Bridport. Then my mother died and I inherited her house in Weymouth. Till we lost it.'

'What happened?'

'We borrowed against it to set up the letting agency. This was the late nineties, and interest rates had gone down by then, so it was affordable. Just.'

'But the letting agency failed?'

'Yes. It took a few years though, and everything we had. We sold the house first and used the equity to prop the company up. Ended up losing the bloody lot. It was wound up and Alan taken to court. It was very messy and led to more drinking.'

'Did he hit you?'

'No. Never. We rowed a lot, as you can imagine, but he never laid a finger on me. I'll give him that.'

'Was that when you separated?'

'After a couple of years, yes. I was working as a secretary again, and every penny I earned went on rent and drink. In the end I'd had enough and just left.'

'What did he do?'

'He stayed where he was, until the landlord got fed up with him not paying the rent, and then he moved in with Lillian.'

'And you?'

'I went to my sister's, in Telford. One suitcase. That's all I had to show for . . .' Her voice tailed off.

'When was this?'

'Ten years ago now.'

'There's a lot of stuff online about the collapse of the letting agency. Lots of angry landlords and tenants.'

'It wasn't him.'

'What wasn't?'

'The missing deposits,' said Mrs Fletcher. She was looking down at the nail varnish on her right index finger, flicking at the edge with her thumbnail. 'He did that by the book, and everything was in a separate client account.'

'Where did the money go then?' asked Dixon.

'I don't know.' She looked up and stared at Dixon.

'And Alan?'

'He never mentioned it.'

'How much are we talking about?'

'Not a huge amount. Eight thousand or so. A drop in the ocean when it came to it. The average rental deposit was only four hundred pounds back then don't forget, one month's rent.'

'We're looking for a motive for his murder, Mrs Fletcher. Can you think of anyone who might wish to harm Alan?'

'Not really. I can't believe it's a former client. That was ten years ago.'

'Did they get any money back?'

'No. There was nothing left.'

'What about you? Were you very bitter after the separation?'

Dixon's question came out of the blue and took Mrs Fletcher by surprise. She shifted in her seat, crossed and uncrossed her legs.

'You're not serious?' she asked, shaking her head.

'Where were you in the early hours of Saturday morning?'

'At Ian's house.'

'You don't live together?'

'I rent a flat in Oakengates.'

Dixon nodded. 'Has he travelled down with you today?'

'No.' Mrs Fletcher stood up and walked over to the window. 'Look, why would I want to kill him after all this time?'

'How much did you know about his mother's failing health?'

'Eve told me she didn't have long, but I shouldn't think for a minute I'm a beneficiary in her will, if that's what you're getting at. Or his for that matter.'

'No, but if Alan was dead you'd be able to claim against his estate, wouldn't you? You are still married after all.'

'That's not the reason we're still married.'

'What is?'

'I told you.' Mrs Fletcher hesitated. 'There was no point in divorcing. I don't want his bloody money.'

Dixon stood up.

'Right, thank you for your time, Mrs Fletcher. We may need to have another word with you, and with Mr Newby at some point, but that's all for now.'

◆　◆　◆

'She cleared out the client account, didn't she?' asked Louise as Dixon drove up the drive to the main road.

'Probably.'

'And what was all that stuff about the will? Alan needed to survive his mother surely. Otherwise he'd have had nothing for her to claim against. And he didn't.'

'Yes, but she doesn't know that, does she? We haven't released the order of death yet.' Dixon was looking left and right before turning out of the drive.

'There's another reason they didn't divorce, which she forgot to mention too,' said Louise.

'His army pension?' asked Dixon.

It was just before 4 p.m. by the time Dixon slumped into an office chair at a vacant workstation in the window at Bridgwater Police Centre. He swivelled round and watched DCI Lewis walking towards him in the reflection. The street lights were just coming on outside, although the nights were starting to draw out a bit at last as winter gave way to early spring, the first shoots from daffodil bulbs just visible through the thin layer of snow on the grass verges.

'How are you getting on?' asked Lewis.

'It's bloody ridiculous,' replied Dixon, turning around. 'I've gone from a case where we couldn't find a motive to one where everybody's got one.'

'Any good?'

'Probably not. The sister was bitter about their mother's will, and the wife was either preserving her chance of an inheritance or her army pension. Or both.'

'Ex-wife, surely.'

'Separated but not divorced, so she'll get the widow's benefit – half, probably. Conveniently failed to mention it too.'

Louise walked over and placed a mug of coffee on the desk in front of Dixon.

'How are the others doing?'

'Nothing yet, Sir.'

'Find out everything you can about the army pension, will you? How much is the widow's benefit? And let's see if the landlord had to take Fletcher to court to get him out of that last place they were living.'

'Yes, Sir.'

'There's nothing like a court case to stoke up a bit of angst,' said Lewis.

'He's had a few of those in his time has our victim.'

'What about the mother?' asked Lewis.

'Coincidental. There's no sign of foul play, and she was terminally ill too,' replied Dixon.

'Is that official?'

'Not yet. The timing of her death might be relevant to the sister's motive, but that's it.'

'To ensure he didn't inherit under her will?'

'That's right. I'm not convinced though. The sister is married to a consultant orthopaedic surgeon and doesn't look short of a bob or two. We'll have a close look at their finances, but they don't seem to need the money. The wife on other hand . . .'

'Skint?'

'Hasn't got a pot to piss in. There's plenty of bitterness there too.'

'Well, keep me informed,' said Lewis, checking his watch.

'Yes, Sir.'

Dixon switched on the computer on the desk in front of him and then turned back to the window. Shame. It was a perfect evening for a walk on the beach. Cold, crisp and the sky on fire as the sun set.

He logged on and began scrolling through his emails, deleting most without opening them, and had almost finished when he heard the soft ping sound of a new email arriving. It came from Donald Watson, forwarding the lab results on the brown powder found around Alan Fletcher's mouth and in his lungs. This one he opened.

Silica 60%, aluminum oxide 30%, iron oxide 6%, calcium oxide 4%, magnesium oxide trace.

Dixon jabbed the off button on his computer, holding it in until the screen went blank. Then he jumped up. Louise was standing by his workstation with a piece of paper in her hand.

'What does it all mean?'

'Sand, clay and lime. Ring SOCO and get a photographer to meet us at the pillbox. Then get your coat.'

'I don't understand. What is it?'

'Dust,' replied Dixon. 'Red brick dust.'

Chapter Five

'You haven't forgotten Valentine's Day, have you?' asked Louise as Dixon sped north towards the motorway roundabout. It was a bit of a detour, but a mile north, then one junction south was going to be far quicker than trying to negotiate Bridgwater town centre at rush hour.

'What did SOCO say about the photographer?'

'He's on the way, but he may have to go back in the morning if he needs daylight.'

Dixon nodded.

'So, you reckon the brick dust came from the pillbox?' asked Louise.

'Where else could it have come from?' replied Dixon. 'But let's check. Ring SOCO and get them to test for a match with the brickwork at the scene.'

Dixon waited for Louise to finish her call to Donald Watson.

'The other question you have to ask yourself is why,' he continued.

'I dunno.'

'Neither do I, but it must be significant. The dust, or the fact that it was red brick, or that he inhaled it.'

'Or all three?'

'We're looking for fresh marks in the brickwork,' said Dixon. 'It might be random scratches or it could be sending a message.'

'Who to?'

'Alan Fletcher. Perhaps it's his epitaph.'

'Or us?' asked Louise.

'Exactly. And we won't know until we find it.'

'Are the lights on full beam?'

'Yes.'

'I can't see a bloody thing,' muttered Louise.

Dixon had parked at the end of the lane, facing the pillbox with his headlights pointing straight at it, although they only illuminated one side of the hexagon, the side he was examining. Louise was using the light from her phone and peering at the adjacent section of brick wall, to the left of the entrance.

'Here, take this,' said Dixon, passing her his torch. 'And keep an eye on where you're treading.'

Louise shone the torch at her feet and breathed a sigh of relief that her footprints had missed the two piles of dog mess just visible under the snow.

'What about inside?' she asked, stepping back on to the path.

'It's lined with concrete.'

'This looks recent.' Louise was pointing at several areas where slivers had flaked off, revealing fresh brick underneath.

Dixon peered around the corner of the pillbox.

'Shine the torch at it, will you?'

He was looking at an area the size of a large oval dinner tray where the brickwork appeared new, or at least not weathered and dirty like the rest. There were faint traces of black spray paint, but the message was no longer legible.

'Looks like it's been cleaned with a pressure washer to me, to remove graffiti I expect. Probably brought the outer layer of these bricks off at the same time. Check for any scratch marks.'

Dixon turned back to the side of the pillbox and shook his head. Almost every brick had a message etched into it, except those where the brick itself had crumbled away. It was almost impossible to tell whether a message was fresh too, unless the scratches were shallow, in which case they appeared to weather more quickly. The deeper they were, the more recent they appeared, or so it seemed. In some cases lichen had grown over some or all of the message, and that would have taken months, so Dixon could ignore those. But that still left too many to count. And this was only one side of the pillbox.

Just below the machine gun slit was a message that the author had clearly taken some time and trouble over.

DAVE SOLOMON 22/6/81

He had even bothered to underline it. The carving was deep into a dark brick and appeared bright orange. Was it fresh though? Had Dave been there recently and etched his date of birth into the brick, or had he been there on that day in June 1981? If the latter, then it had not weathered at all and still looked fresh. As did several more messages.

KEV P; DAISY 9.6.68; PHIL H; MANDY; ADAM 17/10/91

It looked as though Lisa had forgotten the year she was born: *LISA 7/8/*

Lots of people '4' someone else, but that was hardly a suitable epitaph for a murder victim, unless it was a crime of passion perhaps. Dixon grimaced. And someone called ME, although it might have been MEL, had etched his or her postcode into a brick, TA8 2HE. What the bloody hell was all that about? Several names had been scratched out too.

'We're wasting our time here,' muttered Dixon.

'I can't tell what's new and what isn't,' said Louise.

'Neither can I.'

'Some look old, but lots of them look like they could be new.'

'And that's assuming no attempt has been made to disguise it.'

'How would you do that?'

'Rub mud into it?'

Louise nodded. She stepped back and shone the torch at the top corner of the pillbox.

'Looks like it's going to fall down soon anyway.'

There was a large crack along the top of the wall, wider at the corner and with grass growing out of it.

'It'll take more than that,' replied Dixon. 'These things were designed to take a direct hit from a high explosive shell don't forget, and the walls are three feet thick.'

'D'you mind if I wait in the car? My feet are freezing,' asked Louise.

'Switch the engine on,' replied Dixon, handing her his car keys. 'The heater's on full blast.'

'Thanks.'

Dixon turned back to the pillbox and brushed the long grass away from the base with his foot, revealing more bricks and a few more etchings. He crouched down and peered at them, but it was more of the same. The blue tape – POLICE LINE DO NOT CROSS – that SOCO had left wrapped around the pillbox had been torn down and was lying in the snow at his feet.

The headlights of his Land Rover flickered as Louise started the old diesel engine. He could hear the fans over the rattle of the engine and watched Louise sitting in the driver's seat, rubbing her hands together.

Where the bloody hell's that photographer?

Dixon reversed his Land Rover into the field gateway to allow the Scientific Services van to get closer to the pillbox.

'Cold, innit?' said the photographer, blowing on his hands.

'You haven't been sitting here for half an hour twiddling your thumbs,' said Dixon, slamming the door of his Land Rover.

'Sorry about that.'

'What's your name?'

'Scott Pilling.'

'Well then, Scott, we need you to photograph this pillbox.'

'That's easy enough.'

'Each and every brick. Separately.'

'You're kidding?'

'Nope,' said Dixon, shaking his head. 'I want a separate photo of each brick with any writing on it, and I'd like the album on my desk by the end of tomorrow.'

Pilling sighed. Dixon watched him walk around the pillbox and back again.

'I can do these three sides, but there's not enough room for the spotlamps the canal side. I'll need to come back and do those in the morning.'

'And the album?'

'I'll see what I can do.'

'Don't clean them off before you photograph them,' said Dixon, walking over to his Land Rover. 'Just as they are will do.'

'Wait a minute,' said Pilling. 'You're not leaving me here on my own, are you?'

It was just after 7 p.m. when Dixon dropped Louise back at Express Park after a miserable hour and a half spent watching Scott Pilling photographing the pillbox brick by brick. Dixon had run the engine of his Land Rover from time to time for warmth, but both of them were cold and fed up, although not as cold and fed up as Pilling.

Dixon had arranged a briefing for 8 a.m. the following morning, and as he sped north on the M5, Louise's advice was ringing in his ears.

'Not the Zalshah!'

Odd that, thought Dixon, shaking his head. It seemed the perfect venue for a romantic Valentine's Day dinner for two.

There were no lights on in the cottage, so he turned into the car park of The Red Cow and spotted Jane, Monty at her feet, sitting by the fire with a gin and tonic in one hand and her phone in the other. He was walking towards her with a pint in his hand when the text message arrived, his phone bleeping in his pocket.

'Don't tell me; you're in the pub,' said Dixon.

Monty began jumping up at him.

'You look cold,' said Jane, standing up. 'Here, sit by the fire.' She kissed him and then dragged another chair out from under the adjacent table.

'Have you eaten?' asked Dixon.

'I was waiting for you.'

'Fish and chips'll do me.'

'Me too. I'll go.'

Dixon was standing with his back to the fire, as close as he could get to it without treading on Monty, who had stretched out on the rug, when Jane got back from the bar.

'It'll be about twenty minutes,' she said.

'How was Child Protection and Internet?'

'An eye opener,' replied Jane. 'You wouldn't believe what people get up to online. And if you know what you're doing, you can be almost impossible to find.'

'Almost?'

'We're catching up.'

'Pleased to hear it.'

'What about you? Where have you been?'

'Sitting in the cold watching someone photographing every brick of that pillbox.'

'Every brick?'

'The victim had been forced to inhale brick dust, so I'm hoping there's something written on the wall.'

'Yes, but it—'

'I know,' interrupted Dixon. 'It could just be random scratches, of course it could, but I can't ignore it.'

'What about a motive?'

'Two so far, tenuous at best and I'm not convinced by either. A will—'

'You're obsessed by wills,' said Jane, grinning.

'Comes from being a solicitor I suppose,' replied Dixon, taking a swig of beer. 'And besides, wills mean money, and that's a powerful motive as we know.'

Jane nodded.

'Both the wife and sister could be interested in that though,' continued Dixon. 'And then there's his army pension. The wife gets a half or two thirds of that.'

'How old was he?'

'Sixty-five. He'd only just started drawing the damn thing.'

'Nice income for the wife then.'

'Better than nothing. She tried to hide it too. Made out they hadn't got round to divorcing because there was nothing left to fight over. But she could just have been preserving her pension entitlement.'

'Sounds plausible,' said Jane.

'Maybe, but you can split a pension on divorce these days,' replied Dixon. 'So why wait?'

Dixon's eyes glazed over. He was staring into what was left of his beer, swilling it around in the bottom of the glass.

'Thank you for that,' he muttered.

'What?'

'You've just driven a coach and horses through my motive.'

'I knew it would be my fault.'

'If they'd divorced, chances are the pension would've been split and she'd have got half. Right?'

'Yes.'

'So now he's dead her widow's entitlement is what? Half or two thirds?'

'Half is more likely.'

'Louise is checking, but if it's a half, then she's no better off, is she?'

'I suppose not.'

'I never liked it much anyway,' muttered Dixon.

'You've still got the will,' said Jane.

'It left everything to my victim, but he died first, so it goes to the daughter's children.'

'What's wrong with that?'

'Nothing on the face of it. The daughter's well off anyway if appearances are anything to go by, so it must be unlikely she killed her brother for it. It's convenient for her family he died before his mother though, otherwise my victim would've inherited the lot.'

'The lot?' asked Jane.

'Well, the house anyway. Not sure there's much else,' replied Dixon. 'And if he'd inherited . . .' His voice tailed off.

'Has he got a will?'

'We haven't found it yet if he has.' Dixon sighed. 'If he hasn't got one, then his wife would've inherited under the intestacy rules, which might be the reason why she never divorced him I suppose. And she could claim against his estate, as his spouse anyway. But, and here's the real flaw in this one, she would've needed him to survive his mother first and inherit her estate.'

'Why?'

'Because without that he had nothing for the wife to inherit or claim against. As it is he's died penniless.'

'That just leaves the sister then?' asked Jane.

'She's the only one who needed him to die before the mother, that's right,' replied Dixon. 'But this isn't about that, is it? I mean, one of her cars is worth more than you and I earn in a year. Put together. And why the pillbox? Why the brick dust?'

Jane nodded.

'Thank you, Sergeant,' said Dixon, standing up.

'What for?'

'Clearing my mind. Another drink?'

Chapter Six

'What've we got then?' The following morning had dawned cold and crisp, and Dixon was waiting in meeting room 2 when the others arrived. He'd even found time for a walk on the beach first.

'We've had a call from someone in Fordgate who was out when we did the house to house. They saw lights about oneish,' replied Pearce.

'What sort?' asked Dixon.

'Car headlights. I'm going over there later on to get a detailed statement.'

'Better try the other houses where we got no reply before while you're there.'

'Yes, Sir.'

'On both sides of the canal,' continued Dixon.

'I've got the files from the Insolvency Service too,' said Pearce, nodding. 'I'll copy them for you.'

'Good.'

'Anything on his mobile phone?'

'Nothing,' replied Pearce.

'Nothing yet from the Boat and Anchor either,' said Harding. 'Nothing that stands out anyway.'

'How many people have you spoken to?' asked Dixon.

'Twenty or so. No one saw anything unusual, but it was a busy night and there were people coming and going all the time.'

'What about the taxi firms?'

'I've spoken to their passengers. They're regulars and the landlord remembers them too. Nothing sinister,' replied Harding, shaking his head.

'Widen the search. Let's speak to the landlords of any pub between North Curry and Fordgate. If I was meeting someone to kill him, I doubt I'd stop for a beer in the nearest pub first, but I might have one a few miles away.'

'Yes, Sir.'

'What about the North Curry house to house?'

'Nothing,' replied Pearce. 'But there were a few empties to follow up.'

'Louise can give you a hand. Let's try roadblocks on Friday night too, all routes into North Curry, and see if any motorists remember seeing anything.'

'Yes, Sir.'

'What about the army pension, Louise?' asked Dixon.

'The widow gets a half.'

'Well, that's that motive out the window.'

'Why?'

'If they'd divorced, then the pension would have been split and she'd have got half anyway, which is the same as the widow's benefit, isn't it?'

'I wonder why she didn't mention it then,' said Louise.

'Probably thought it made her look bad,' replied Dixon.

'And why didn't she divorce him and go after it?'

'How much is it?'

'Not huge. He was a captain and he'd only been in the army sixteen years or so.'

'There's your answer then.'

'Wouldn't he have lost it when he went bankrupt?' asked Harding.

'He didn't go bankrupt, did he, Mark?' asked Dixon.

'No. He did an IVA when the guest house failed, and the letting agency was a limited company. It went into liquidation, but he never went personally bankrupt.'

'It would depend when anyway,' said Dixon. 'Since May 2000 a workplace pension is protected from bankruptcy. I checked.'

'Do we still need to speak to her partner, Ian Newby?' asked Louise.

'Get the Shropshire lot to do it.'

'That still leaves the will though.'

'Yes, but for the wife to have any chance of getting any money, Fletcher needed to survive his mother and inherit her estate.'

'So if it was her, she'd have made sure the mother was dead first.'

'Precisely. It may be a reason they didn't divorce I suppose, but that's it.'

'That still leaves the sister, surely,' said Pearce.

'I checked the Land Registry website,' replied Dixon, 'and there's no mortgage on her house. What do we think that's worth, Louise?'

'Dunno. Seven hundred thousand, something like that?'

'And her husband uses the Bentley to commute to work,' said Dixon, raising his eyebrows.

'What about her children?' asked Harding.

'Both are in London,' replied Louise. 'One's a doctor and the other works in the City. A broker of some sort.'

'Where does that leave us then?' asked Harding.

'We've got the possibility of a message etched into the brickwork at the scene,' replied Dixon, 'and the failed businesses, plus anything else we can dig up.'

'So keep digging,' muttered Pearce.

'We still need to find Fletcher's will, if he's got one,' said Dixon. 'Louise, can you ring round the local solicitors and see if you can find one? Try Dorset too. Bridport, Dorchester and Weymouth.'

'Yes, Sir.'

'Then start going through the address book. Check every entry. Friends, family, anything. All right?'

'Where are you going?'

'On a wild goose chase.'

Dixon sat down in the corner of the canteen with a cup of coffee and opened a web browser on his phone. He typed 'Welsh Guards Museum' into Google and glanced down at the results, the third of which caught his eye. 'The Guards Museum – Family Research . . . Many of these people ring the museum to ask us to search the archives . . .' It even gave a phone number, so he clicked on it.

The page turned out to be a request not to contact the museum, but instead the regimental headquarters at Wellington Barracks, London, which held the service records on individual soldiers. It also gave a different telephone number for each of the Guards regiments.

'Welsh Guards archivist. Can I help?'

'My name is Detective Inspector Dixon, Avon and Somerset Police. Who am I speaking to, please?'

'Tom Cuthbert.'

'I'm trying to get in touch with the commanding officer of the 1st Battalion during the Falklands War and was hoping—'

'I'm not sure I should be giving that sort of information out really.'

'His name then. That'll be in most history books on the subject, won't it? I can find the rest on the police computer.'

'Colonel Huw Byrne it is. That's Huw with a "w". Retired now of course. Lives in Pembroke he does.'

'Whereabouts?'

'A little place on the coast there. Stackpole.'

'Thank you.'

'Are you going to see him?'

'Yes, I hope to.'

'Tell him RSM Cuthbert sends his regards.'

'D'you know him?' asked Dixon.

'Served under him, I did,' replied Cuthbert.

'On the Falklands?'

'Yes, I was just a lance corporal then. B Company.'

'D'you remember the adjutant, Captain Alan Fletcher?'

'I do. Four times he went into that burning ambulance. It was a bloody marvel, it was. I was there,' said Cuthbert. 'A fine man and a crying shame he never became the CO. A crying bloody shame.'

'Why didn't he?'

'Colonel Byrne'll know. He would've written up his reports.'

'What happened to the ambulance?'

'It was an engine fire. Two medics and two Royal Engineers in the back. They'd been clearing landmines and . . . Anyway, Mr Fletcher had got them clear by the time me and the lads got to him.'

'I may need to speak to you again, Mr Cuthbert,' said Dixon. 'Can I get you on this number?'

'Tuesdays and Thursdays. But I'll give you my mobile.'

'Thank you,' replied Dixon, scribbling the number on the back of his hand.

'Is Mr Fletcher all right?'

'He's dead I'm afraid.'

'I am sorry to hear that. How did he die?'

'I'm afraid I can't say.'

'Oh, like that, is it?'

'I'll be in touch, Mr Cuthbert. Thanks again.'

Dixon rang off, drained his coffee and went in search of Louise.

'Get on to the Pembrokeshire lot and get me an address and phone number for Huw Byrne, will you? Lives in Stackpole. That's Huw with a "w".'

'Er, yes, Sir,' replied Louise. 'Who is he?'

'Fletcher's commanding officer.'

'Oh right.'

'Can you remember how long Mrs Fletcher said she was down here for?'

'A couple of days I think. Why?'

'If he did die without a will, then she's his next of kin and inherits his estate.'

'But there is no estate. We've already established that.'

'What about Nimrod?'

It was a three hour run to Stackpole, an hour to the Severn Bridge and then two hours from there. Dixon had left Express Park just after 9.30 a.m. and arranged to meet Colonel Byrne at 2.30 p.m. That would give him time to get there, eat and then take Monty for a walk on Broad Haven South beach first. He might even have enough time for a look along the clifftops at St Govan's Head and a visit to Huntsman's Leap. A trip down memory lane.

Jane would be pissed off if she knew what she was missing. Still, he had left a note in the kitchen when he'd picked up Monty – *Gone to Wales. Back later. Nx* – and would take a photograph or two on his phone, so she shouldn't feel too left out.

The view from the Second Severn Crossing was spoilt by the need to keep his eyes on the road, but he was able to pick out Steep Holm to the south. Driving was usually premium thinking time, but Dixon found himself dwelling on the past, remembering the many sea cliff climbing trips he had made with Jake, his old and now dead climbing partner, killed in a fall in Cheddar Gorge the previous October.

Not a lot had changed on the M4 heading west. It was still a dual-carriageway, stop start most of the way and slower than ever before past the steelworks at Port Talbot thanks to a lane closure, but Dixon arrived in the car park above the beach just after 1 p.m. The sky was blue and the view along the coast to Caldey Island was clear. Dixon could even make out the line of *Always the Sun* at Stackpole Head, a steep arête that had almost cost Jake a broken ankle when he hit the ledge from thirty feet up. Still, he'd got up it a week later for the second ascent.

It was a weekday during school term and the beach was deserted, so Dixon left the remains of his sandwich on the passenger seat and let Monty out of the back of the Land Rover. Monty set off down the stone steps to the beach, with Dixon following, to make the first footprints in the wet sand as the tide went out.

The waves were bigger than at Burnham and Berrow. A strong south-westerly wind was sending huge breakers crashing on to the beach, even on the ebb tide, but Monty soon got used to them and only got soaked once.

An hour later and they were sitting in Dixon's Land Rover outside the Old Post Office in Stackpole, Monty curled up on the passenger seat. Both had their coats on, and the heater was on full blast too. Dixon thought about his meeting with Colonel Byrne. He hoped to learn more about Fletcher the man and Fletcher the soldier. What sort of man came back from the Falklands, and why did his career falter? It might go some way to explaining the failed businesses, although that might have been pure bad luck.

The Old Post Office was the largest house in the village, right in the middle, opposite the Stackpole Inn. The pub looked to have been refurbished since Dixon was last in there, his climbing equipment strewn all over the beer garden drying in the sun. He parked outside the pub and walked across the road. The curtain twitched and then the door opened before Dixon was halfway along the garden path.

'You've come a long way, Inspector.'

Colonel Huw Byrne was in his mid-seventies, with short white hair, and stood tall, as you would expect of a Guards officer. Dixon remembered his days in the cadets being shouted at on the parade ground: 'Shoulders back, arms straight, look to your front. You're slouching, boy!' He blinked and the vision was gone.

'Yes, Sir. Thank you for seeing me.'

'Only too happy to help if I can.' Colonel Byrne allowed his spectacles to slide off the end of his nose, to be caught by the cord around his neck. He was wearing an open neck check shirt, brown wool cardigan and corduroys. 'You'll have to forgive my appearance. I've been tying flies all morning.'

'Trout?' asked Dixon.

'Sea trout,' replied Byrne. 'D'you fish?'

'Used to. Pike mainly, out on the Somerset Levels.'

'C'mon through. Can I get you a drink? Tea, coffee, something stronger perhaps?'

'Yes, tea would be nice thank you.'

'Make yourself comfortable,' said Byrne, opening the door to the living room. 'The fire's lit.'

Dixon looked at the photographs on the wall either side of the fireplace and recognised a young Alan Fletcher standing in the back row of one marked 'Officers, 1WG, 6th September 1979'. Colonel Byrne was sitting in the middle of the front row of course.

The older photographs, in black and white, showed a younger Huw Byrne, starting in officer training at Sandhurst and rising through the ranks, until the photographs switched to colour when he was a major.

Dixon recognised the terrain in the background of another set of colour photographs that were mounted in a single large frame to the left of the fire. Some had been taken at night, the scene lit up by flares and tracer fire visible slicing through the darkness, but it was the faces that told the story; camouflaged with boot polish, eyes red and wide, mouths open – a mixture of fear, anxiety, anticipation. He squinted at a small brass plaque on the frame: 'Mount Harriet, June 1982'. There was no sign of Alan Fletcher in any of them.

Dixon was looking at the photograph of Fletcher from September 1979 when he heard footsteps behind him.

'That one was taken just after we got back from Northern Ireland,' said Byrne. 'That was a quiet tour, mercifully. Well, comparatively anyway.'

'Where were you?'

'Belfast. North Howard Street,' replied Byrne, handing Dixon a mug of tea. 'We all came home though; that's the main thing. Not all of us in one piece, sadly, but we all came home.'

'What happened?'

'Mortar attack on the barracks that time if I remember rightly. Have a seat.'

'Thank you.'

'You wanted to talk to me about Alan Fletcher, you said?' asked Byrne.

'I'm investigating his murder.'

'Murder?'

'He was killed in the early hours of Saturday morning in an abandoned World War Two pillbox on the banks of the Bridgwater and Taunton Canal.'

'Good God.'

'It's purely general enquiries at this stage. I'm just trying to build a picture of him, and a number of witnesses have said that he came back from the Falklands a changed man.'

'We all did, Inspector,' replied Byrne. 'We lost a lot of men on the *Sir Galahad* – men we knew: colleagues, friends.'

'Were you on the ship?'

'No. If I had been, it wouldn't have bloody well happened. I'd have got everybody off. They were sitting ducks out there.'

'Where were you?'

'I was in Fitzroy, just along the coast.'

'And what about Alan Fletcher?'

'He was in Bluff Cove on the shore. Watched the whole thing unfold. We'd lost the *Atlantic Conveyor*, and that took all the helicopters bar one to the bottom. The *Sir Galahad* was supposed to be a shortcut along the coast to Port Stanley. It was either that or walking.'

'Was Fletcher's best man on the ship?'

'Charlie Booth, yes,' replied Byrne, nodding. 'Didn't make it, sadly.' The nod became a shake of the head.

'Were they close?'

'Yes. Both were good men.'

'What about on Mount Harriet then?' asked Dixon. 'Only I can't see Fletcher in any of the photos over there.'

'Those were taken at the battalion command post.'

'Shouldn't he have been there with you, as adjutant?'

'Yes, he should.'

'Isn't that odd?'

'He was there I think. I can't remember,' replied Byrne, taking a swig of tea. 'He may just have been out of shot.'

'Are there any other photographs with him in?'

'No.'

'So was he there or wasn't he?'

'I really can't remember.'

'Did you ever ask him?'

'Not that I recall. It was in the middle of a battle, Inspector. You have to understand . . .'

'When was the last time you remember seeing him that night then?' asked Dixon. He balanced his tea on the arm of the sofa and took out his notepad and pen.

'I remember him on the march in. We approached from the west through a minefield, and the attack went in from the east. The walk in took hours, and it was pitch dark. He was there when we set up the CP definitely, but I don't remember seeing him after the battle started—42 Commando moved forward when the barrage lifted, and all hell broke loose.'

'What about your second in command? Where was he?'

'Major Hardcastle went forward to the start line with A and B Companies. We were in touch by radio.'

'Didn't you think it odd that Alan Fletcher wasn't there?' asked Dixon.

'Not really,' replied Byrne, shaking his head. 'Look, I'm not sure where this is going, but if you're asking me whether I investigated my adjutant for deserting the battlefield, I did not. There was never any suggestion that he did. He was a good man, a dedicated officer, and there were a whole host of reasons he might have needed to leave the CP.'

'When was the next time you saw him?'

'The next morning I think. And don't forget he won the DSO a few days later, pulling those chaps out of the burning ambulance.'

'RSM Cuthbert told me about that. He asked to be remembered to you,' said Dixon.

'One of the best, Tom Cuthbert.'

'Who recommended Alan for the DSO?'

'I did.'

'Is the incident mentioned in the battalion war diary?'

'War diaries were phased out in the seventies, Inspector. Now it's the quarterly report. But yes, it's in there.'

'Is he mentioned during the battle?'

'Not that I recall.'

'Who wrote the report?'

'Major Hardcastle, subject to my scrutiny as CO of course. You can find them at regimental HQ, but they're not terribly enlightening.'

'Tell me about Fletcher when you got back from the Falklands. Why was he never promoted again, for example?'

Byrne sat back in his armchair and sighed.

'You'll find my reports on his service record,' he replied. 'He became surly, insubordinate. We had to pull him off ceremonial duties for being drunk. D'you know I think he was drunk the day he got back off sick leave? It was a bloody shame because he was a high flyer, destined for the top.'

'Did you take him to task about it?'

'Tried to. Never got anywhere. I think it was the guilt, that he hadn't been on the ship when it was hit. That he'd somehow been spared. He never said so, but I do believe that was behind his complete disregard for his own safety when that ambulance caught fire. He was badly burnt and came home on a hospital ship. It was almost as if it was his penance.'

'What about his wife?'

'I spoke to Jean about it, but she was at her wits' end too. He never paid his mess bill either. Then there was a car accident in Camberley. An allegation of drink driving was made.'

'Was he prosecuted?'

'No. I dealt with it.'

'Disciplined?'

'No. The reputation of the regiment was at stake, Inspector. A scandal like that . . . It was unthinkable. A Welsh Guards officer being prosecuted for drink driving? The regiment comes first. Always.'

'When was this?'

'Not long before he left the army. He wasn't really given a choice if the truth be told. It was a sad end to what had been a promising career,' said Byrne, shaking his head.

'Was he offered counselling when he got back from the Falklands?'

'Yes, but he refused it. We all did. It was something officers just didn't do. And it was a long time ago. Less enlightened times, shall we say? Things are different now, thankfully.'

Dixon nodded.

'Well, thank you, Colonel Byrne. You've been most helpful.'

'Doesn't feel like it, but if there's anything else I can do, please let me know,' replied Byrne, standing up.

'I will.'

Dixon parked in the car park at St Govan's Head and walked down the steps to the old chapel, keeping Monty on his lead. The waves were just visible in the last of the daylight, crashing on to the rocks below, the spray being whipped on the wind and into his face as he stood in the doorway. It was too late for a walk along the clifftops to Huntsman's Leap, even if he was minded to ignore the red flag fluttering in the wind by the sentry post.

He wondered whether Alan Fletcher and the Welsh Guards had ever visited the range for live fire training, although it was mainly tanks and artillery that used the Castlemartin and Manorbier ranges.

He took out his phone and sent Louise a text message.

Get on to MOD and get Fletcher's service record pls

It struck him as odd that Colonel Byrne had no recollection of Fletcher being at the command post during the battle of Mount Harriet. Still, that really was 'in the heat of battle', so perhaps he could be forgiven. And it was an interesting take on Fletcher's determination to pull those injured men from the burning ambulance. Penance.

Guilt, Byrne had said. Maybe he felt the same.

Dixon took a couple of photographs of the chapel for Jane and then sent another text message to Louise.

Fletcher arrested drink driving rta camberley 1990 or 91 see what you can find pls

He was learning more about Fletcher the man. There was no doubt that the *Sir Galahad* had changed lives, and not just for those on the ship. But was it possible that Fletcher had returned to the burning ambulance time and again as some form of penance for escaping the carnage on the *Sir Galahad*? Byrne had concluded that it was, and Dixon had to agree with him.

He checked his watch: 4.45 p.m. Just enough time for a cup of tea in Ye Olde Worlde Cafe in Bosherston before the long drive home.

Chapter Seven

Dixon was sitting in the window at Express Park, waiting for a computer to start up and thinking about the time he and Jake had run into the St Govan's Inn and put someone's severed thumb in an ice bucket. The climber had been airlifted to Chepstow Hospital, and they never had found out whether his thumb had been sewn back on or not.

He had arrived home just before 9 p.m. the night before, having stopped at the Little Chef at Carmarthen, to find Jane had scribbled a note on the bottom of his own note to her.

Gone to see parents. Back later. Jx

She hadn't been too impressed with the photographs when she got home, and the picture of Monty on the beach had rubbed salt into the wound, but she had been placated by the promise of a trip to Pembrokeshire in the summer. Climbing was not on the agenda.

Dixon logged in and scrolled down through his emails, deleting all except one from Donald Watson and another from the photographer, Scott Pilling. Watson confirmed that the dust matched the bricks used in the construction of the pillbox. The best that could be said was that it came from the same batch, the remainder of which could have been used anywhere of course.

Pilling had photographed 412 bricks, too many to print off and put in an album, so he had uploaded them to a secure server. His email gave Dixon the link, which he followed.

He began scrolling through the pictures. Some were obviously old marks and some were illegible, all or part of the message obscured by paint or lichen, or crumbled away. That left a hundred or so that warranted closer scrutiny. He was noting down the reference number of each when Louise arrived.

'You're early.'

'Couldn't sleep,' replied Dixon.

'Mark asked me to give you this,' said Louise, fishing a file out of a filing cabinet. 'He'll be in later.'

'What is it?'

'The insolvency papers. Copies.'

'Did you find a will?' asked Dixon, nodding.

'Nope. I tried every firm I could find.'

'What about the address book?'

'The mother's friends mainly, and she seems to have outlived most of them.'

'Anything interesting from the house to house?'

'Not really. There was a bloke from Fordgate who'd been out with his dogs and heard an engine. He was in his back garden and saw the headlights going off down the lane.'

'Is that it?'

Louise nodded.

'What was he doing out at that time?'

'He goes out with the dogs when he lets them out apparently. They bark and wake the neighbours.'

Dixon rolled his eyes.

'Time?'

'Just after one,' replied Louise. 'Mark's still got some others to follow up. Empties on the other side of the canal.'

'Did you get my message about Fletcher's service record?'

'It's on its way.'

'And the RTA?'

'Nothing. There's not even a record of a road traffic accident, let alone an arrest for drink driving.'

'I suppose we could try going a bit further back; 1989 perhaps,' said Dixon.

'I did,' replied Louise, switching on the kettle. 'Anything useful from his CO?'

'Background stuff, that's all.'

'Coffee?'

It was mid-morning by the time Dixon had finished going through the photographs. He emailed a list of reference numbers to Scott Pilling of those he wanted printed off and put into an album. The rest could remain in digital format. He had selected only those that looked recent, or could not have been old due to weathering or growth of lichen.

He closed his eyes and let out a long sigh. He was making two assumptions, and he hated those at the best of times. Yes, the dust came from a brick in the same batch that was used to build this pillbox, but it could still have come from somewhere else. Another pillbox built with bricks from the same batch, for example. There were two within a couple of hundred yards of it for a start. Not only that, but he was assuming the dust had been collected on the night of the murder. He grimaced. What if the killer had collected the brick dust months or even years before? Then the mark would appear old and weathered, perhaps even obscured by lichen. Still, that was unlikely. They were reasonable assumptions, and the search could always be widened if he drew a blank.

And then there was the very real possibility that there was no message at all, just simple scratch marks. And why had Fletcher been forced to inhale the dust?

Dixon fished his phone out of his pocket and sent Roger Poland a text message.

Was Fletcher asthmatic?

Then he picked up the landline and was dialling Mrs Painter's number in Ilminster when Poland's reply arrived on his mobile. It was short and to the point.

No.

'Mrs Painter, this is DI Dixon. I was hoping to speak to Mrs Fletcher. If she's still there?'

'Hang on.'

Dixon waited. He clamped the phone tight to his ear and listened: footsteps, muffled voices, nothing of interest.

'Yes.'

'Mrs Fletcher, we've been unable to trace Alan's will, which leaves you as the administrator of his estate.'

'There isn't an estate to administer.'

'Well, there's Nimrod.'

'I thought he'd been put to sleep.'

'Not yet. He's here in the kennels.'

'Well, you'd best get on with it. I don't want him.'

'So, you're content for me to do whatever I see fit?' asked Dixon.

'Yes.'

Mrs Fletcher rang off, leaving Dixon staring at his phone. He shook his head.

'Some people,' he muttered, replacing the handset.

He looked around the CID area, which was deserted, apart from Louise, who had a telephone clamped to her ear. Mark Pearce had gone to complete the house to house enquiries, and Dave Harding was no doubt in a pub somewhere between North Curry and Bridgwater.

The insolvency files made interesting reading for different reasons. The guest house had been repossessed by the building society, but when it was finally sold at auction for less than the Fletchers had paid for it, the proceeds failed to cover the mortgage, arrears and costs.

The building society had not pursued them for the shortfall, having insisted that the Fletchers take out a mortgage guarantee indemnity policy, so the insurance had covered the loss. That left the Fletchers owing various local traders and suppliers. They had consulted a local insolvency practitioner in Poole, and an IVA had been agreed quickly and without much protest from their creditors.

The sums of money involved were small by today's standards, and it was difficult to imagine anyone involved bearing a sufficient grudge over it to kill Fletcher after all these years.

The letting agency, on the other hand, had been a much more acrimonious affair. Fletcher had continued trading whilst insolvent for over six months, pocketing rents along the way. Several landlords with multiple properties or properties in multiple occupation had lost large sums of money. Not only that, but the client account, containing the deposits paid by tenants, had been cleared out, although Dixon suspected who was behind that. It had been Mrs Fletcher's escape fund.

Several landlords had been taking debt recovery proceedings against Fletcher, and at least two had commenced court proceedings when HM Revenue & Customs stepped in and served a winding up petition on the company in pursuit of unpaid tax. The company had been wound up in the High Court on 14 March 2006.

The Official Receiver had begun the winding up, before appointing an insolvency practitioner in Exeter to conclude it, but that was only after Fletcher had been disqualified from acting as a company director. Dixon glanced down the list of creditors, most of whom received nothing. What little money there had been after the mortgages were paid off had gone to the taxman as a preferred creditor.

The biggest losers were the landlords, and the more properties they had, the more they lost. Most of the tenants had lost their deposit, but got that back easily enough by failing to pay their last month's rent. That had added to the landlords' losses and bitterness at the outcome.

The biggest losers were both companies, Weymouth Developments Ltd and Ziatabari Property Services Ltd. Both had lost over thirty thousand pounds, more than the other landlords put together. A Mrs Jessica Kelsall was next in line at twelve thousand pounds.

Dixon closed the file. The investigation needed a direction, and perhaps this was it. He had known people killed for less.

He dropped the file on to Louise's desk.

'Have you read this?' he asked.

'No.'

'Just the papers on Fletcher Lettings. Then let's set up a meeting with the insolvency practitioner in Exeter for tomorrow. Company searches on the two corporate landlords too, and we'll pay them a visit at the same time.'

'Yes, Sir.'

'What about Fletcher's own landlord before he moved in with his mother . . . Where was it?'

'They were renting in Bridport,' replied Louise. 'Can't find the landlord. He sold it a few years ago, according to the Land Registry, but I checked with the local county courts and can't find a record of possession proceedings against Fletcher.'

'Have we had High Tech's report on his laptop yet?'

'No.'

'Chase it up, will you?' said Dixon. 'I'll see everybody back here at five o'clock. I'm off to church.'

Dixon parked across the lychgate and looked up at the Church of St Peter & St Paul, North Curry. It seemed unusually large for such a small village and looked more like a cathedral in miniature, with an oblong tower and huge stained glass windows. A service was unlikely at 2.30 p.m. on a Wednesday afternoon, so he left his Land Rover where it was and walked up the path towards the church.

The path had been swept clear of snow, and the piles either side were all that was left now that it had clouded over and warmed up a bit.

The front door was open, so Dixon walked in and stood in the middle of the aisle looking up at the altar and the huge chandelier hanging from the vaulted ceiling.

'Can I help you?'

Jeans, pullover, beard, but no dog collar.

'I'm looking for the vicar,' said Dixon.

'That's me, Julian Comley. How can I help you?' A big smile and an outstretched hand.

'Detective Inspector Dixon. I'm investigating the death of Alan Fletcher.'

'Ah, so you don't need saving.'

'I wouldn't say that.'

'But perhaps not now, eh?'

Dixon smiled.

'I heard about Alan. Shame,' continued Comley. 'And Lillian. Less of a shock perhaps, but still . . .'

'Did you know them well?'

'Lillian had been a regular here before I came to the parish. Lovely lady. I only went in to see her last Thursday, as it happens.'

'What did she say?'

'Nothing of interest to you, Inspector. She knew her time was coming.'

'And Alan?'

'Odd fellow,' replied Comley. 'Lived in the parish for years, then suddenly starts coming to church twelve months or so ago.'

'Did he say why?'

'Something from his past came back to haunt him, he said. He never elaborated though.'

'Was that when his mother was taken ill?'

'No, I don't think so. She'd been ill on and off for years. I don't know why, I really don't. One day he was just there,' said Comley, shaking his head, 'sitting at the back.'

'Did he have any friends in the congregation? Anyone he spoke to, chatted with?'

'Not really. Always sat at the back. Came in last thing and was first out, even before I got there to thank everyone for coming.'

Dixon shook his head.

'And what about you, Inspector? Do you believe?'

'It's difficult, Father, when you see what I see,' replied Dixon. 'D'you mind if I sit for a while?'

'Not at all. So, you do believe in God?'

'Let's just say we have an understanding.'

The last of the snow had melted by the time Dixon arrived at the pillbox. It was just after 4 p.m. and he had a bit of daylight left, but not much.

He walked around the pillbox and noticed at least three piles of dog mess with footprints in them. Scott Pilling would have needed to clean his van.

The grass around the base had been flattened, revealing the bricks previously hidden, but Dixon recognised those with writing on them from the photographs. Pilling had been thorough.

He checked for traces of brick dust in the grass, but found none. What dust there may have been would have been snowed on and then washed away when the snow melted. Still, it was worth a try. There were several patches of exposed brickwork that looked fresh, but the outer layer had crumbled rather than been scratched away. Dixon took out his car keys and began scratching at a brick near the entrance, with his left hand underneath to catch the dust. It worked, and he soon had a small pile of red dust in the palm of his hand. The mark left by his key was quite obvious too, so he began looking for scratch marks rather than legible writing. He looked at the names and dates that had been scratched out too, but saw nothing that looked fresh.

He went back to his own mark in the brickwork and rubbed a small amount of mud into it with the tip of his finger. He grimaced. Looking old and being old were clearly two different things.

The briefing at 5 p.m. had not lasted long. Dave Harding gave Dixon a file of thirty-three witness statements, all of them short and containing, in Dave's words, 'bugger all'. The statement from the witness at Fordgate, out with his dogs at 1 a.m. on the night of the murder, was just as thin, and the address book had turned up nothing of interest.

The report on Fletcher's ancient laptop had arrived from High Tech and was in the file sitting on Dixon's passenger seat as he drove north on the M5. He also had the insolvency file to go through again, two company searches, and the photograph album from Scott Pilling to pore over.

One last call and then it was home for an evening with his feet up in front of the telly, if Jane hadn't got there first.

It was a large bungalow in Warren Road, Brean, that backed on to the beach, the back garden giving way to sand dunes and then the sea. Perfect for dogs, as evidenced by the barking when Dixon turned into the drive.

He walked up the steps and knocked on the door.

'Yes.' She was in her early sixties, with her grey hair tied back in a ponytail, and spoke from the porch behind the glazed front door. Her black pullover was covered in dog hair.

'You don't remember me?' asked Dixon.

'The big white Staffie,' she said, squinting at him.

'That's me. Monty.'

'I may forget a face, never a dog. Is everything all right?'

'Yes, he's fine.'

'Good,' she replied. 'D'you want to come in?'

Dixon looked down at her feet. She was surrounded by an indeterminate number of dogs, all different shapes and sizes and all of them jumping up at her.

'No, this won't take long,' replied Dixon. 'I'm a police officer and we have a Jack Russell, Nimrod. His owner's died and I was wondering if you'd be able to take him in.'

'Is he in the car?'

'He's in the kennels at Bridgwater.'

'Yes, we'll take him. How old is he?'

'Four, we think.'

'I'm sure we'll find him a home. Drop him over whenever.'

'Thank you. It'll be tomorrow or Friday if that's OK.'

'Fine.'

'I thought you'd had enough of war films.'

'It's a classic.'

'What is it?' asked Jane, rolling her eyes.

'*Ice Cold in Alex*. Haven't you seen it?'

'No, I haven't.'

Dixon hit the pause button on the TV remote control, closed the file of papers on his lap and stood up. 'I'll start it again when you're ready. Lasagne all right with you?'

'Yes, thanks.'

'Good day?'

'I'm back in Bridgwater from Monday. They're short staffed at the SCU, so I'm transferring as soon as my training's over.'

'That's a stroke of luck, isn't it?'

Jane threw her coat over the bannister at the bottom of the stairs. 'And my adoption file arrived today.'

'You applied for it then?'

'I said I was going to.'

'Yes, but I never thought you'd go through with it.'

'Why not?'

'You seemed so nervous about it.'

'Well, I applied a couple of weeks ago and it came today.'

'Have you told your parents?'

'Not yet.'

'You really need to do that before you do anything else.'

'I know.'

'What does it say?' asked Dixon, appearing in the doorway of the kitchen holding a bag of garlic bread.

'Dunno. I haven't opened it yet.'

Jane pulled a sealed envelope from her handbag, unfolded it and handed it to Dixon. 'I don't know if I can.'

'Why not?'

'I'm not sure I want to know. What if I don't like what I find?'

'You need to be sure you want to know. Whatever it is. If you're not sure, don't open it.'

'Not today then.'

'You will when you're ready. Unless you want me to.'

'No.'

'Well, here. This'll take your mind off it for a while,' said Dixon. He reached into his file on the sofa and pulled out the Scientific Services photograph album. 'Flick through that lot and see if anything leaps out at you.'

'You're not supposed to be bringing this stuff home, you know.' Jane sat down on the sofa and began leafing through the pictures. 'Anything else come up today?'

'Not really.' Dixon was shouting from the kitchen. 'I've found a home for the Jack Russell at least.'

'Good.'

'And High Tech found his Christmas card list on the hard drive of his laptop. It'd been deleted, but they restored it.'

'That'll give you a few more names and addresses to follow up.'

'It will. I'm still without a plausible motive though. Or a suspect.'

'You'll get there.'

'You haven't forgotten we're out to dinner on Friday night?' asked Dixon.

'Where are we going?'

'It's a surprise.'

'Is it the Zalshah?'

Chapter Eight

Dave Harding was waiting for the kettle to boil when Dixon arrived in the CID area at Express Park. It was just gone 8 a.m. and no one else was in.

'Dave?'

'Yes, Sir.'

'Traffic cameras.'

'Bloody hell, why is it always me?'

'Because you're good at it.'

Harding sighed long and loud.

'We've got a time from the bloke out with his dogs at 1 a.m., and that fits with what Roger's telling us, so start with Junction 24. Try the number plate cameras in Bridgwater too.'

'Yes, Sir.'

'And let's see what mobile phone numbers are registering on the nearest base station at that time too.'

Harding nodded.

'Let me know how you get on,' said Dixon, dropping his file on to a workstation and switching on the computer. He made himself a coffee while the computer powered up and then began looking through the photographs of the pillbox that had not been printed off and included in the album. There were just over three hundred of them, and he was halfway through when Louise arrived.

'What've we got for today?' asked Dixon.

'The insolvency practitioner in Exeter at ten. Then we're over to Weymouth. We're seeing the MD of Weymouth Properties at two o'clock, and then Mr Ziatabari after that. He works from home and will be in all afternoon, he said.'

'Good. It'll be interesting to see if Mark's tracked down anyone off Fletcher's Christmas card list by the time we get back too,' said Dixon. 'If he can get himself out of bed.'

Baker Endfield was a firm of accountants and insolvency practitioners on Southernhay in Exeter. Dixon followed the tree lined one-way system up Southernhay West and down Southernhay East, looking at the bewildering array of gold plates on almost every door. Once elegant Georgian townhouses, they were now occupied by law firms, accountants, estate agents, surveyors, stockbrokers, financial advisers, architects and dentists. He noticed several modern office blocks being converted into flats too, victims of businesses moving to out of town office parks no doubt. He grimaced. Spaceships on ring roads, just like Express Park.

'What was the address again?'

'Curlew House, Southernhay West,' replied Louise.

'That's the other side,' muttered Dixon. 'We'll go round again.'

He parked in a loading bay and they walked back to Curlew House.

'Mr Endfield's expecting you,' said the receptionist. 'Go through into the boardroom. I'll let him know you're here.'

Dixon waited in the window, which was at the back of the building and looked straight out at Exeter Cathedral.

'Quite a view, isn't it?'

Dixon spun round. Endfield was in his late fifties perhaps and dressed in his professional uniform: regulation grey suit, black shoes, matching shirt and tie. Dixon had worn it every day too until he had escaped the legal profession.

'I've been looking at the file to remind myself,' said Endfield, dropping a blue folder and a lever arch file on to the table. 'Do sit down.'

'That's the file we've seen?' asked Dixon.

'Yes.'

'What do you remember about Alan Fletcher?'

'Nice chap actually. Just got in over his head as far as I can recall,' replied Endfield. 'It was an unusual one because it came to me after the Official Receiver had already wound up the company. They went after him personally too and had him disqualified as a company director.'

'So, why did the business fail?'

'Usual reasons really. The company wasn't making enough money, pure and simple. And he was taking too much out. He'd got his clients by undercutting his competitors, and his margins were ludicrously tight. Most letting agents charge ten or twelve per cent commission, but he was doing it for five per cent for the bigger clients with several properties. It was unsustainable.'

'How much money was he taking out?'

'More than he should have done, but then he had to just to keep up with his mortgage payments. He'd mortgaged their house twice come the end. I remember Mrs Fletcher got a job elsewhere to bring some money in, but that just about covered their living expenses, and there wasn't enough coming into the company each month to enable him to pay the mortgages. It's a classic situation.'

'So what'd he do?'

'He started robbing Peter to pay Paul. He was able to keep that going for months before it all came crashing down.'

Endfield noticed Dixon frowning.

'Let me explain. He'd taken too much out of the company, he continued. 'So he couldn't pay the rent due to Mr Smith. The tenant paid it to Fletcher, and he was supposed to pass it on to Mr Smith less his commission, right?'

Dixon nodded.

'So, he used the money paid by Mr Jones's tenant to pay Mr Smith, then the rent from another landlord's tenant to pay Mr Jones, and so it went on. Round and round, which was fine until he lost a couple of tenants. Then he couldn't pay anyone and it all came crashing down like a house of cards.'

'Is that it?' asked Dixon.

'Well, there was a bit more to it than that, and it went on longer because he propped it up with a second mortgage, but that's basically it. I felt sorry for him really. Once he'd got himself into it, he couldn't get out, and it must have been incredibly stressful.'

'Then HM Revenue & Customs stepped in?'

'They did. He couldn't pay his tax either. It was almost a relief to him when that happened.'

'Was it incompetence or dishonesty?' asked Dixon.

'It started out as pure incompetence I think,' replied Endfield. 'I remember him saying once, "I'm a bloody soldier, not a businessman," which was true of course. He was no businessman. Then he started lying to people to keep it afloat, stringing them along.'

Dixon shook his head.

'Did he cooperate with you?'

'Oh yes. The only thing we never got to the bottom of was where the client account had gone. The whole lot just disappeared.'

'What did he say about it?'

'Just that it must have got swallowed up.'

'What about his creditors then? Did they turn nasty?'

'One did, certainly. There were one or two sets of court proceedings ongoing,' said Endfield, nodding, 'but they were discontinued when the company was wound up. The creditors' meetings were pretty ugly too.'

'Who were the biggest losers?'

'Weymouth Developments nearly went bust themselves, from memory. They'd grown by debt and all of their properties were heavily mortgaged. As you can imagine, when the rents stopped coming in from Fletcher it nearly tipped them over the edge.'

'Anyone else?'

'There were a couple of smaller fry who instructed solicitors, and there was a lot of piss and wind – pardon my language – but it never came to anything.'

'And the unsecured creditors got nothing?'

'Nothing at all. It all went to secured and preferred.'

'What about Mrs Fletcher?' asked Dixon. 'Did you ever interview her?'

'She was a shareholder, director and the company secretary, but according to him that was in name only. He did everything. I did speak to her, but she pleaded ignorance.'

'Did Fletcher ever say he'd been threatened?'

'Not to me. I've had several cases where threats have been made, Inspector, but the sums of money have always been much larger. I don't think . . .'

'Well, somebody did, Mr Endfield,' said Dixon. 'Somebody did.'

Dixon was surprised to find the offices of Weymouth Developments Ltd above a letting agency in Portland Road. He parked on the forecourt next to a powder blue Maserati and closed his eyes. It had been over two and a half hours in the Land Rover, but they had at least found a decent pub for lunch.

'What's this fellow's name?'

'Dean Maynard,' replied Louise.

'What did you tell him?'

'Just that we wanted to ask him some questions about Alan Fletcher.'

'Not that Fletcher's dead?'

'No.'

'Good,' said Dixon. 'Let's go and see what he's got to say for himself then.'

'There's someone waving at us from the letting agents,' said Louise.

Dixon opened the door.

'We're looking for Dean Maynard.'

'That's me. Come in.'

'We wanted to have a word with you about Alan Fletcher,' said Dixon, showing Maynard his warrant card.

'Ten years too bloody late . . .'

Maynard was in his mid-forties. His shirt was open at the neck, with the collar turned up, blue jeans and brown leather winkle pickers. Dixon suspected the tan was fake.

'Is there somewhere private we can talk?'

'We'll go upstairs. Follow me.'

They followed Maynard along a corridor, through a narrow door and out into a courtyard at the back, where a flight of metal stairs led to another door and Maynard's office.

'Do I need a solicitor?' asked Maynard, grinning. He sat down behind his desk, watching Dixon examining the pictures on the wall.

'Only if you killed him,' replied Dixon without turning around.

'He's dead?'

'Tell me about the other shareholders in Weymouth Developments.'

'What the hell's it got to do with us?'

'I'm trying to find out who and what it's got to do with, Mr Maynard. That's why I'm here.'

'My wife and mother are the other shareholders,' replied Maynard. 'Why?'

'What about your father?'

'He died ten years ago. Heart attack.'

'How many properties do you own?'

'Twenty-seven.' Maynard picked up a biro and began flicking it around his thumb. The first attempt failed, sending the pen spinning across his desk.

'And how many did you have ten years ago?'

'Seventeen or so, something like that. Look, what's this all about?'

'We're investigating Alan Fletcher's murder, Mr Maynard.'

Maynard smiled and slumped back into his chair, shaking his head.

'What goes around comes around.'

'Where were you on Saturday night between midnight and 2 a.m.?' asked Dixon.

'Now, hang on a minute. You can't seriously think I did it?'

'We have questions we have to ask, Mr Maynard.'

'Well, I didn't do it. There was a time I might've done if I'd had the bottle, but not now.'

'You were Royal Marines karate champion I see,' said Dixon, picking a frame off the mantelpiece. 'Two years in a row.'

'That was a long time ago.'

'When did you join?'

'In 1989. I was eighteen.'

'And you left when?'

'I did ten years.'

'Where were you on Saturday night?'

'At home with my wife.'

'What happened when Fletcher Lettings went bust?'

'Twat,' said Maynard, shaking his head. 'He took us for right bloody mugs. We almost lost the lot. But I blame myself really. We got greedy, grew too far too fast, all of it funded by borrowing.'

'You borrow against a property as the value goes up and use the money to buy another.'

'Yes. It's fine as long as property prices keep going up and the tenants keep paying the rent.'

'And as long as your agent keeps passing it on.'

'Bastard. He popped up offering to manage all the rentals for five per cent or whatever it was, and I jumped at it. My old man said it would end in tears.'

'Was your father a shareholder?'

'Yes.'

'Your mother has fifty per cent, so I'm guessing she inherited his share when he died.'

'That's right. Me and Debs have the other half. How do you—?'

'We did a company search,' interrupted Dixon. 'How much did you lose when Fletcher Lettings went bust?'

'Thirty grand or so, but we nearly lost everything. We had no income to pay the mortgages, so my father remortgaged their house to bail us out. My mother blames his heart attack on the stress of it.'

'When was it?'

'A few months after it all kicked off.'

'Was your father a marine?'

'Yes. He left just after the Falklands. He was a sergeant. How did you know that?'

'Father and son, it's not unusual.'

'Was your old man a copper?' asked Maynard, his eyes narrowing.

'No,' replied Dixon. 'You were suing Mr Fletcher, weren't you?'

'That was a waste of time. What's the point of suing someone who hasn't got any money?'

'None,' replied Dixon.

'Shame our bloody solicitor didn't tell us that. Anyway, we dropped it when the taxman got involved.'

'And what about now?' asked Dixon. 'You use the letting agency downstairs I suppose.'

'We own it. We decided to set up our own. It's safer. And we've got other clients too now, as well as our own properties to manage, so it's making good money these days.'

'And what about Alan Fletcher personally? How well did you know him?'

'He seemed all right to begin with. Ex-army and all that. We met at a Dorset Business Club lunch I think.'

'And when did you find out his business was in trouble?'

'Not for months. The first inkling we got was when the excuses started. The cheque's in the post, that sort of crap. Then he'd pay and it'd be OK for a few months. Then all of a sudden the payments stopped altogether. That's when we took legal advice.'

'Was your mother involved in the decision to remortgage her house?'

'Yes. I think she argued with my father about it, but there wasn't a lot of choice in the end. It was either that or we went bust as well.'

'Where does your mother live?'

'Burton Bradstock. Why?'

'We may need to speak to her I'm afraid.'

'Now, hang on. I don't want my mother upset by this. She had nothing to do with it.'

'Routine enquiries, Mr Maynard,' replied Dixon. 'That's all.'

Dixon and Louise arrived back at Express Park just before 5.30 p.m. They had stopped off in Bridport to meet Koorosh Ziatabari, who lived in a large house not far from the golf course, and had seemed genuinely saddened by the news of Fletcher's murder.

Yes, he had lost a lot of money when Fletcher's company had gone bust, but he could afford it and had even offered to help Fletcher out, albeit too late. With nineteen properties, none of them mortgaged, Mr Ziatabari had taken the whole sorry affair in his stride.

'We're still not really any closer, are we?' asked Louise as they walked across the top deck of the car park.

'No.'

'Maynard's mother possibly, but I don't think he had anything to do with it.'

'You believed him?' asked Dixon.

'I did.'

'Me too,' muttered Dixon as he wrenched the security door open.

Dave Harding and Mark Pearce were waiting for them in the CID area, although Harding had the look of a man whose eyes had glazed over several hours ago.

'Anything, Dave?'

'I'm checking the details of twenty-one cars on the camera at Junction 24. The town cameras are far too busy to get anything meaningful without knowing what we're looking for.'

'What about you, Mark?'

'I've traced two from his Christmas card list so far. Both ex-army. They hadn't heard from him for years and thought he may have died.'

'Who are they?' asked Dixon.

'Major Redhead and his wife. They live in Cardiff. And a Lieutenant Colonel Collis. He's in France. Both retired.'

'Is that it?'

'That's it,' replied Harding.

'Are the roadblocks fixed for tomorrow evening?'

'Five till seven.'

'Good. Well, you might as well bugger off for the night.'

'And me?' asked Louise.

'And you.'

Dixon sat down at a workstation and swivelled round on the chair to look out of the window. He thought about another visit to the pillbox, but it was far too cold for that so settled on another scroll through the photographs on the system. The brickwork had to hold the key, and if he stared at it for long enough he felt sure it would come to him. It was a tactic that had always worked in the past, although it was being well and truly tested this time.

'Where is it we're going tomorrow night?' asked Jane as Dixon walked in the back door of the cottage.

'I told you, it's a surprise.'

'I need to know what to wear.'

'Posh.'

'Really?'

'And warm.'

'Eh?'

'We've got roadblocks underway at North Curry from five till seven, so we need to check on them on the way.'

'You are kidding.'

'Table's booked for seven, so I thought we could just look in.'

Jane sighed.

'You can stay in the car,' continued Dixon.

'Thanks.'

He noticed the sealed envelope containing Jane's adoption file still sitting on the side exactly where she had left it last night.

'I was waiting for you,' she said. 'Supper'll be ready in five minutes.'

'What about the envelope?'

'I thought I'd open it at the weekend.'

'Whatever you say,' replied Dixon.

He slumped down on to the sofa and began flicking through the photograph album again.

'How many times have you been through that?' asked Jane, handing him a can of beer.

'God knows.'

'Well, I couldn't see anything.'

'We're probably looking straight at it, only the significance of it hasn't hit us yet.'

'Yet?'

'It will.' Monty jumped on the sofa and curled up next to Dixon. 'It always does,' he said, scratching his dog behind the ears.

Chapter Nine

'OK?'

Dixon looked up from his screen to find DCI Lewis standing over him. Either Lewis was getting better at creeping up on people, or Dixon had been so engrossed in the photographs that he hadn't seen him coming. He'd try a workstation facing the window next time. Perhaps the reflection would offer some sort of early warning system.

'Only we're into Friday, nearly a week now,' continued Lewis, 'and the chief con's wondering what's going on.'

'We're making progress,' replied Dixon.

'That sounds like flannel.'

'We've ruled out the sister and wife. So we're digging into his past . . .'

'The failed businesses?'

'Yes. The letting agency has potential, but nothing concrete yet.'

'Why the brick dust then?'

Lewis had done his homework.

'Rip someone off in a property transaction and they make you inhale brick dust?'

'Is that it?'

'It's possible.'

'Bollocks.'

'We've got the roadblocks tonight,' said Dixon.

'Well, if they come up with nothing we'll have to try a TV appeal.'

Dixon winced.

'Just make it happen, Nick. You haven't let me down yet.'

Dixon was about to respond when Lewis turned on his heels and walked away. Lewis was right though. Nearly a week in and the investigation was floundering. No sensible motive. A few tenuous ones and several people who either gained from Fletcher's death or celebrated it. But no real motive or suspect. Or even any sense of direction for that matter.

He had spent the afternoon trawling through Fletcher's army service records, which included the reports from his commanding officers, first Colonel Owens and then Colonel Byrne. All were glowing in the years leading up to the Falklands War. After that they made uncomfortable reading. Dixon looked for any reference to a car accident and a charge of drink driving but found none.

A highlight was finding Fletcher's DSO citation. The recommendation for the award had been signed by Colonel Byrne on 31 July 1982.

For conspicuous gallantry and devotion to duty. In rescuing four seriously injured men from a burning ambulance, he saved their lives. He insisted on returning to the ambulance although suffering from severe burns, displaying a complete disregard for his own safety. He then directed efforts to put out the fire, setting a fine example of endurance and leadership.

Dixon was showered, changed and ready to go by the time Jane arrived home from Portishead.

'You're wearing a tie?'

'Yes.'

'Crikey, it must be posh. Good day?'

'Not really. Lewis crept up on me and gave me an earwigging.'

'Really?'

'He was nice about it, but the chief con's getting impatient, apparently.'

'Ignore it.'

'And I dropped Nimrod over to the foster home on the way back.'

'Well done.'

'Oh, and these came for you.'

'I wonder who they're from,' said Jane.

'No idea,' replied Dixon, grinning as he handed her a bunch of red roses.

'Have we got a vase?'

'Somewhere. I'll find it. You go and get ready.'

He fed Monty and was standing in the field at the back of the cottage when Jane appeared in the doorway. Her blonde hair was flowing over her shoulders, released from its ponytail, and she was wearing a black dress and high heeled shoes. Dixon walked over and put his arms around her waist.

'You look—'

'I know.'

'Blimey, where are you two off to?'

'Behave yourself, Cole,' said Dixon through the open window of Jane's car.

'Sorry, Sir.'

'Have you found anything?'

'Not yet, but we've still got half an hour or so.'

'What about the others?'

'Not that I know of.'

'Where's Mark Pearce?'

'He said he'd be over on the Taunton road.'

'Thanks.'

'Shall I let him know you're on the way, Sir?'

'No need.'

Dixon drove into the centre of North Curry and then south on the Taunton road, coming across the roadblock a few hundred yards outside the village. He was flagged down by a uniformed officer he didn't recognise.

'Excuse me, Sir, we're asking—'

'It's all right, Dan, this is the DI.' It was Mark Pearce's voice, coming from behind the constable, who was leaning on the car door.

'Oh, sorry, Sir.'

'Well?'

'Nothing,' said Pearce.

Dixon grimaced.

'We'll give it until 7.30 p.m., but it's very quiet. And those we have had say they saw nothing.'

'Let me know if you get anything.'

'Will do,' replied Pearce. 'Going anywhere nice?'

'The Little Chef,' muttered Dixon, winding up the car window.

Exposed beams, Somerset willow chairs, a single candle, more red roses in a vase and a bottle of champagne on ice. Jane squeezed Dixon's hand as they looked down at the table in a quiet corner of The Willow Tree in Taunton.

'You never said we were coming here.'

'I've been saving up,' said Dixon, grinning.

'And champagne?'

'I can have one glass, but you'll have to have the rest.'

'I'm sure I'll manage,' replied Jane, smiling. 'I was convinced we'd end up at the Zalshah.'

'Well, we could always . . .'

'Don't even think about it.'

'I'll have to give myself a few extra units as it is,' said Dixon. 'Have you seen the dessert menu?'

They watched the waiter opening the champagne.

'I'll have the cork, please,' said Dixon.

He passed it to Jane.

'Here, a memento. The first of many.'

'I like the sound of that.' Jane smiled as they clinked champagne flutes in the middle of the table. 'I've never really thanked you properly for saving my life last year,' she said, her eyes welling up with tears.

'You don't have to,' replied Dixon. 'It's what you do, isn't it? When you love someone.'

'I'd do the same for you. You do know that, don't you?'

'I do.'

'For the same reason.' Jane reached across the table and held Dixon's hand.

'I know.'

'Just as long as you do.'

'It's a shame we're not still working together, isn't it? We made a good team.'

'We still do,' replied Jane.

'That we do. And the chief con is married to one of the assistants, so who knows?'

'I thought you said you'd dump me when you became chief constable,' said Jane, grinning.

'Probably will come to think of it.'

Dixon winced. Then he reached down and rubbed his shin.

'I'd rather refuse the promotion, honestly, Officer.'

'I should bloody well think so,' said Jane.

Dixon smiled. His foray into the murky world of local politics had been a welcome distraction after finding Fran's killer and dealing with the fallout from that, both emotional and disciplinary. But Fran was gone, and now it was Jane's time. And he would see to it that it stayed that way.

'Tell me about Child Protection and the Internet then,' said Dixon.

'We're not talking shop, are we?'

'Good point.'

And they managed to avoid it until the coffee arrived, just after 10 p.m.

'Where will you be this weekend?' asked Jane.

'No idea,' replied Dixon. 'Sitting in front of that damn pillbox I expect, staring at the walls.'

'You could just sit at home in the warm and look at the photographs.'

'I suppose I could.'

'You could even take them on the beach when you go for a walk.'

'You're taking the piss now, aren't you, Sergeant?'

'Listen, I was thinking. You've been looking at the names.'

'Yes.'

'But what if it's the date that you'll recognise?'

'What d'you mean?'

'Apart from the "Jane loves Nick" scribblings and the obscenities, a lot of the others have dates with them, don't they? Maybe that's the significant part.'

Dixon nodded.

'That's assuming any of it is significant of course,' said Jane, standing up. She looked down at Dixon, stirring his coffee. 'I'll just be a couple of minutes.'

Dixon was still stirring his coffee when Jane got back, although most of it was in the saucer. He was staring at the flame of the candle, flickering in the draught from the door, and she knew better than to interrupt his train of thought.

He looked up, tipped the coffee from the saucer back into his cup and drank it in one go.

'You finished?' he asked, snuffing out the candle between his index finger and thumb.

'Not yet,' replied Jane.

'I'll get the bill.'

'Where are we going?'

'I thought you might fancy a bit of fresh air.'

'Dressed like this?'

'You can wait in the car if you like,' said Dixon, fumbling in the glove box of his Land Rover for his torch. He had parked with the headlights shining straight at the pillbox.

'Why don't you just look at the photos when we get home?'

'It won't take a minute. I know what I'm looking for. And besides, it's on the way.'

A light dusting of snow had fallen while they had been in The Willow Tree, but it had only settled on the wet grass. Dixon left the engine running and jumped out.

'Be careful where you're treading,' he said, spinning round when he heard footsteps behind him. Jane was tiptoeing towards him, her arms folded tightly around her, and the collar of her coat turned up as far as it would go.

'What are we looking for then?' she asked, sighing loudly.

'It's this side I think,' replied Dixon. 'I'll know it when I see it.' He was on the canal side of the pillbox, where the bank narrowed to no more than a foot or so.

'If I tread in anything, you're cleaning my shoes.'

Dixon shone the torch at the ground in front of Jane.

'Don't worry if you fall in. It's not frozen over.'

'This is not how I imagined Valentine's Day ending.'

'Look for anything with a date.'

'I thought I had a date,' muttered Jane.

The light from the Land Rover was shining directly in their faces, casting a shadow over the side of the pillbox. Jane was holding her phone in front of her and squinting at the brickwork.

'What about this one?'

'What's it say?' asked Dixon.

'Dave, two, twelve, eighty-four.'

'That's not it.'

'Not what?'

'The right date.'

'I'm sure there's one . . .'

'How about this one?' said Jane. 'A Kandes, eleven, six, eighty-two.'

Dixon tucked the torch under his arm, took his phone out of his pocket and switched it to camera mode.

'Where is it?'

'Here,' replied Jane, pointing to a spot just above a machine gun slit.

'Hold this a second.' Dixon handed Jane the torch and then reached up, holding his phone in both hands, to take a close up of the mark.

A KANDES 11/6/82

'Is that it?' asked Jane.

'That's it,' replied Dixon, dropping his phone back into his pocket.

'Is it the date that's significant?'

'The Falklands War. The Battle of Mount Harriet.'

'And your victim was there?'

'He was.'

'It could be a—'

'No, it couldn't. I don't believe in coincidence.'

'Where are we going now?' asked Jane as Dixon turned off the M5 at Junction 23.

'Express Park. I need a phone number off the file.'

'It's too late to ring them now, whoever it is.'

'Have you got a data signal?'

Jane fished her phone out of her handbag.

'Yes, 4G,' she replied.

'Google something for me, will you?'

'What is it?'

'Try "Falklands War, A Kandes".'

'Give me a sec.'

'Well?'

'How about this?' said Jane. 'Palace Barracks Memorial Garden. The meta-description says Sergeant A Kandes.'

'Click on it. Maybe he died in the battle.'

'It's listing the Royal Navy.'

'Scroll down,' said Dixon. 'You don't get sergeants in the navy.'

'Royal Fleet Auxiliary?'

'No.'

'Royal Marines?'

'Yes.' Dixon turned into Express Park and parked in the visitors' car park.

'Here he is. Sergeant A Kandes,' said Jane.

Dixon nodded.

'You coming in?'

'How long will you be?'

'Two minutes.'

'No, just leave the engine on, will you?'

Dixon leaned across and kissed Jane on the cheek. Then he opened the door and climbed out of the Land Rover.

'Still think it's a coincidence?' he asked, leaning in the driver's door.

Roll-of-honour.com gave a full name, but apart from that confirmed what Dixon either knew or had guessed.

Kandes, Adrian A; Sergeant; 42 Commando; Royal Marines; Age, 38; Date of Death, 11 June 1982; Manner of Death, Killed during the Battle of Mount Harriet

It also gave his place of residence as Guildford, Surrey.

Dixon closed his laptop when he heard Jane opening the bedroom door.

'What time is it?' she asked, walking down the stairs.

'Eightish.'

'How long have you been up?'

'A couple of hours.'

Dixon opened the back door of the cottage and let Monty out.

'Coffee?'

'Yes, pl—' The rest was lost in a yawn.

The rattle of dog biscuits in his tin bowl soon had Monty scratching at the back door, although how he heard it from the other side of the yard and over the kettle was a mystery to Dixon.

'What are you up to today?' asked Jane.

'I've got a call to make first,' replied Dixon, handing Jane a mug of coffee. 'Then I'll be able to tell you.'

'Have we got time to take these back to bed then?'

It was just before 9 a.m. when impatience got the better of Dixon and he dialled Tom Cuthbert's mobile number.

'Yes.'

'Mr Cuthbert, this is DI Dixon. We spoke the other day.'

'Did you get hold of Colonel Byrne?'

'I went to see him actually. He sends his regards.'

'How can I help you?'

'I told you Alan Fletcher was dead, but what I didn't tell you was that I am investigating his murder.'

'Murder?'

'Yes. He died of a heart attack during a particularly vicious assault, and we're treating it as murder.'

'He didn't deserve that.'

'No one does, Mr Cuthbert.'

'True enough.'

'Does the name Adrian Kandes mean anything to you?'

Silence.

Dixon waited.

'His name and date of death were etched into the brickwork where Mr Fletcher's body was found,' continued Dixon.

Silence.

'Look, whatever it is, it's going to come out. A man is dead, and you said yourself he didn't deserve it.'

Dixon had his phone clamped to his ear and heard a long, faint sigh.

'Would it help if I came to see you?' he asked.

'There's no need for that,' replied Cuthbert. 'Oh shit, shit, shit . . .'

'I've got Colonel Byrne telling me he can't recall Fletcher at the battalion CP during the battle and the name of a man who died in it at the scene of Fletcher's murder. You don't need to be a rocket—'

'This needs to be off the record,' interrupted Cuthbert. 'You didn't hear this from me. All right?'

'Agreed.'

'This is all rumours mind you. I wasn't there and saw none of this.'

'I understand.'

'Mr Fletcher was moving up to the start line. I was there with A and B Companies and the second in command, Major Hardcastle. We were in support of 42 Commando, so we were just waiting, ready to go if needed. And we weren't, thank God.'

'Go on.'

'42 Commando had gone in with fire support from HMS *Yarmouth*, and it was a right bloody mess, the sky lit up by flares and explosions, screaming and shouting.'

'Did Mr Fletcher make it to the start line?'

'Well, that's just it, isn't it? No, he didn't.'

'What happened to him?'

'He was found at first light on the southern slope, unconscious.'

'Was there an investigation?'

'Informal, like,' replied Cuthbert. 'The shit hit the fan it did. Remember, you didn't hear this from me.'

'I know.'

'Anyway, Mr Fletcher said he'd intercepted a marine doing a runner.'

'Doing a runner?'

'Fleeing the battlefield. Deserting in the face of the enemy. He's there, pointing his sidearm at this marine, and the marine's pointing his rifle at him. Stand off it was. Then wham! He's hit from behind and wakes up the next day.'

'And this marine was Adrian Kandes?'

'Yes, only Kandes was already dead by then. He went back and stormed a machine gun position single handed, then got hit by a sniper. Holding up the whole advance from the south it was. He should've got a posthumous Victoria Cross for it, but it was blocked because of the allegation made by Mr Fletcher.'

'And what did the informal investigation conclude?'

'You'd have to ask Colonel Byrne that, but the whole thing was swept under the carpet. Kandes never got his VC, and you know about Mr Fletcher.'

'I do.'

'Cause of a lot of bitterness it was. On both sides. But neither regiment wanted the scandal. The regiment always comes first.'

'I've heard that somewhere before,' said Dixon.

'I never told you any of this.'

'I get it,' said Dixon.

Cuthbert rang off and Dixon turned to Jane, sitting on the arm of the sofa.

'Fancy a weekend away?'

'Lovely. Where are we going?'

'Pembroke.'

Chapter Ten

Dixon left Jane sitting in the Stackpole Inn with Monty and walked across the road to the Old Post Office. Lights were on inside, which was a relief because he'd decided not to make an appointment. Better to catch Colonel Byrne on the hop.

He spotted the spyhole in the front door just in time and turned his back. Better still to give Colonel Byrne no time to compose himself.

Dixon turned around when he heard the door opening.

'You?'

'Yes, Sir.'

'Well, you've had a wasted journey. There's nothing more I can tell you.'

Dixon watched Byrne swallow hard. He looked down, unable to meet Dixon's stare. Byrne was obviously not someone to whom lying came easily.

'We could continue this down at the station, Sir, if that would assist.'

'Pembroke?'

'Bridgwater, Sir,' replied Dixon, matter of fact.

'You'd better come in.'

Dixon stepped into the hall.

'Follow me,' said Byrne.

Colonel Byrne's office was at the back of the house, overlooking a walled garden.

'Drink?' Byrne asked, pouring himself a large Scotch from a decanter on the side.

'No, thank you, Sir.'

Dixon used the opportunity to look at the pictures on the walls. There were two large bronze figurines of British soldiers standing at either end of the mantelpiece and yet more photographs from a long and distinguished military career. Dixon recognised Colonel Byrne laying a wreath at the war memorial in Port Stanley.

'What do you want to know?' asked Byrne, slumping down into the chair behind his desk.

'Whatever you're prepared to tell me,' replied Dixon. 'I'll find out the rest and then come back and arrest you for obstruction.'

Byrne sat up. 'You can't speak to me like that.'

'A man is dead, Colonel. One of your officers.'

'I know that.'

'Let's start with the night of the battle.'

'It was chaos—'

'You said you didn't investigate Alan Fletcher for deserting the battlefield.'

'That's correct.'

'But you did investigate his allegation that he had encountered two or more marines deserting the battlefield. There must have been at least two because he was pointing his sidearm at Sergeant Adrian Kandes when he was hit from behind.'

'Ah,' said Byrne, taking a swig of Scotch. 'You know about that.'

Dixon nodded.

'It was one of those situations when nobody wins,' continued Byrne. 'Kandes was a good man. He'd just flipped by all accounts. But he got himself together, went back and should've won the VC by rights. Albeit posthumously.'

'And what about Fletcher?'

'He was a good officer; did what he thought was right, and look where it got him. Neither regiment wanted any scandal, so I persuaded him to drop it, and Adrian Kandes went without his medal.'

'Who conducted the investigation?'

'I did, with the CO of 42 Commando. Can't remember his name now.'

'Is there a file?'

'Long gone,' replied Byrne. 'There was nothing official. No mention made in any quarterly reports.'

'And what about the marines? Were the others ever identified?'

'There were five of them. They spotted Kandes making a run for it and went after him to bring him back. Only Alan Fletcher got in the way.'

'Were they ever identified?'

'Never formally, but the marines knew who they were, I have no doubt about that.'

'And the one who hit Mr Fletcher?'

'Got away with it. Look, I've no criticism to make of the marines, Inspector. We were waiting in support, and even though they were heavily outnumbered we weren't needed. What does that tell you?'

'How long was he unconscious?'

'Not long. He was back on duty in a couple of days.'

'And how did he react to your arrangement?'

'I think he was left feeling he wasn't believed, or that he'd somehow let the regiment down. Maybe it explains why he went into the burning ambulance all those times.'

'Is there anything else I need to know?' asked Dixon.

'He had a run-in with a group of marines on the road outside Port Stanley,' replied Byrne, shaking his head. 'It was about a week after the ceasefire. There were allegations of insubordination made, but the risk of everything else coming out was too great, so Alan dropped it.'

'Voluntarily?'

'I persuaded him.'

'Were these the same marines? From 42 Commando?'

'Alan thought so, but it was his word against theirs.'

'How did he know?'

'From remarks they made. Look, you have to understand the British Army was on the crest of a wave. We'd just won a famous victory thousands of miles from home and against the odds. The last thing we needed was a scandal like this, investigations and disciplinary action. Brigade HQ were terrified the media might get hold of it. I had my orders. This was not going to be the story.'

'Were there any witnesses to this incident?'

'Two Royal Engineers, from memory. They'd been ordered to arrange the shipment of captured Argentinian radar cabins back to Malvern.'

'What's at Malvern?'

'RSRE. The Royal Signals and Radar Establishment. At least it was. Never too sure any more with all these damn cuts.'

'Thank you, Colonel Byrne. If you think of anything else, please ring me. I really don't want to have to come back again.'

'Of course, Inspector.'

Once out into the porch, Dixon turned to Colonel Byrne, ignoring his outstretched hand.

'You said Captain Fletcher thought he'd let the regiment down.'

'Yes.'

'Maybe the regiment let him down. Did you ever stop to think of that?'

◆　◆　◆

'I've found a B and B that takes dogs,' said Jane. 'Over in Bosherston.' She was still sitting by the fire in the Stackpole Inn, with Monty asleep at her feet.

'We'd better get back.'

'Oh no you don't. I've packed an overnight bag, and I intend to use it now we're here. And besides, I want to see Huntsman's Leap and the other places you used to go climbing.'

'A beer first then,' said Dixon, smiling. It was just after 2.30 p.m. Plenty of time for a pint, followed by a walk along the clifftops.

'How did you get on with the colonel?' asked Jane.

'He took a bit of prodding.'

'But he confirmed it?'

'Fletcher was in the wrong place at the wrong time,' replied Dixon, shaking his head. 'It blighted the rest of his life and God knows how many others too. And then decades later he's killed for it.'

'Poor bloke.'

'And his wife don't forget. It trashed her life too.' Dixon took a large swig of beer. 'Still, there'll be time enough for that. D'you want cliffs or the beach?'

'Cliffs.'

'OK.'

'We can do the beach tomorrow before we go.'

Two hours later they were sitting by the gas fire in Ye Olde Worlde Cafe enjoying a piece of sponge cake and a cup of tea. It had been freezing cold along the clifftops, a strong south-westerly blowing straight in off the Atlantic, and the shivering, coupled with the added exertion of walking into the wind, had caused Dixon's blood sugar levels to drop dangerously low. At least that had been his excuse, and Jane had fallen for it.

'You can't come to Pembroke and not have tea with Mrs Weston,' said Dixon, grinning.

Jane nodded.

'We used to come every Easter, and this place'd be heaving with climbers. The campsites packed, people queuing for the best routes. Those were the days.'

'You and Jake?'

'I never really climbed with anyone else. We were always off the beaten track too, Jake trying something desperate.'

'And you'd abseil into Huntsman's Leap?'

'Abseil in, climb out. Great fun. There's nothing like sea cliff climbing, unless a wave catches you,' said Dixon.

'I'll take your word for it.'

It couldn't have been the fresh air and exercise, because Dixon got plenty of that at home, but he woke late for him, just after 8 a.m., to find Monty sitting by the bedroom door, tapping it with his paw. Maybe it was the fact that he hadn't got to sleep until gone two in the morning.

He threw on his clothes and tiptoed downstairs with Monty. The gate on the large grass car park next to the B and B was locked, so Dixon lifted him over the drystone wall and left him to it.

It was a cold morning, clear and crisp, with not a single cloud in the sky. A perfect climbing day. He noticed a car drive past with two rucksacks on the back seat and a rope on the parcel shelf.

Lucky buggers.

Still, a full English breakfast and a walk around the Lily Ponds to Broad Haven South was not to be sniffed at. Then it was back to the real world. And the hunt for Alan Fletcher's killer.

A Sunday afternoon rugby international at the Millennium Stadium had brought the M4 past Cardiff to a standstill, and Dixon arrived at Express Park twenty minutes late for the briefing he had called for 4 p.m.

DCI Lewis spotted him through the glass partitioning and stormed out of meeting room 2.

'Where the hell have you been?'

'Stuck on the M4.'

'This'd better be good.'

'Give me five minutes and I'll be in,' said Dixon, switching on a computer. He printed off four colour copies of the relevant photograph, made himself a cup of coffee and then sat down at the head of the table in meeting room 2.

'Well, what've you got then?' asked Dixon.

'Nothing, Sir,' said Harding. 'Not on any of the cameras. And the vehicles we have got all check out. Locals mainly.'

'What about you, Mark?'

'Only the two on the Christmas card list. They thought he was dead anyway,' replied Pearce, shrugging his shoulders.

'Louise?'

She shook her head.

'Right, well, I got lucky at least,' said Dixon, passing the copies around the table.

'Thank God for that,' muttered Lewis.

'This is a photo of a brick from the pillbox. The name A Kandes is etched into it, and the date you can see is his date of death. It explains the brick dust inhaled by our victim.'

'Who is A Kandes?' asked Louise.

'Sergeant Adrian A Kandes, F Company, 42 Commando, Royal Marines, killed during the Battle of Mount Harriet on 11 June 1982.'

'And Fletcher was there?' asked Lewis.

'Not only that, but he came across Kandes fleeing the battlefield. I've been to see his CO in Pembroke. Fletcher stopped Kandes at gunpoint and was then struck on the back of the head by another marine, who'd gone after Kandes to bring him back. Fletcher was found unconscious the next morning.'

'What happened to Kandes then?' asked Harding.

'He went back and was killed taking an Argentinian machine gun position single handedly. He should have won the VC for it but it was blocked, given the allegations made by Fletcher.'

'Gits,' muttered Harding.

'For once I agree with you, Dave,' replied Dixon. 'He confronted his fear and overcame it, which makes him more of a hero in my book, not less of one.'

'Was there an investigation?'

'An informal one. But it was all swept under the carpet,' replied Dixon. 'Fletcher had a run-in a few days later with a group of marines on the road outside Port Stanley. There was a good deal of bitterness apparently. Then he was wounded himself rescuing four men from a burning ambulance, and came home on a hospital ship.'

'So, what do we do now?' asked Lewis.

'Let's start with Kandes. I want his service records and details of his family and friends. Everything you can find, with background checks on them all. Mark?'

'Yes, Sir.'

'And contact details for the CO of 42 Commando during the Falklands War. If he's dead, get the second in command's.'

Pearce nodded.

'Dave, we need service records for all members of F Company during the conflict too.'

'All of them?'

Dixon treated it as a rhetorical question.

'That'll be over a hundred men,' muttered Harding.

'We'll come at it from the other end, Louise. Get on to the Royal Signals and Radar Establishment at Malvern, or whatever it is these days, and find out what you can about Argentinian radar cabins. They were dismantled and shipped back to Malvern for examination after the war. The run-in with the marines after the battle was witnessed by two Royal Engineers who'd been tasked with getting them on a ship back to the UK. See if you can find out who they were and where they are now.'

'Weren't Maynard and his father marines?' asked Louise.

'They were.'

'Who's Maynard?' asked Lewis.

'The biggest loser when Fletcher's letting agency went bust,' replied Dixon. 'Weymouth Properties. The father served in the Falklands.'

'It would be interesting if the father was in F Company,' said Lewis. 'Wouldn't it?'

'It certainly would,' said Dixon.

'That's good work, Nick,' said Lewis when the others had left meeting room 2.

'Thank you, Sir.'

'You've made two trips to Pembroke?'

'Colonel Byrne failed to mention any of this the first time, so I had to jog his memory.'

Lewis shook his head.

'For the good of the regiment apparently,' continued Dixon. 'They didn't want the scandal then and they don't want it now.'

'Well, they've bloody well got it,' said Lewis. 'Will he complain about you?'

'Little old me?' asked Dixon, smiling. 'If he does, remind him he withheld information in a murder investigation.'

'It'll be my pleasure,' replied Lewis.

'Not looking good on the Royal Signals and Radar Establishment,' said Louise. 'I just googled it. It became part of the Defence Research Agency in 1991, then the Defence Evaluation and Research Agency in 1995. Then it split in 2001. Half became the Defence Science and Technology Laboratory, and the rest was privatised.'

'Privatised?'

'You could always take it up with your local MP,' said Pearce, grinning.

'Shut up, Mark.'

'It's now part of a company called QinetiQ,' continued Louise.

'Well, try the Defence Science and Technology Lab first and see what you can find out. You never know, they may still have the records.'

'I'll call them tomorrow.'

Dixon spent the next ten minutes surfing the 42 Commando website, before turning to Louise, who was sitting at the adjacent workstation.

'See if you can get me a phone number for Bickleigh Barracks, just outside Plymouth. All there is here is an email, and it's not monitored outside office hours.'

'OK.'

'I'll be back in ten minutes.'

Dixon got back from the canteen, his blood sugar levels restored by a bar of chocolate, to find a scrap of paper with a phone number on it on his keyboard.

'I got it from the MoD Police in Plymouth. It's the guardhouse number. They use it when they've got drunk and disorderlies and someone comes and fetches them.'

Dixon winced. The idea of meeting a group of drunk and disorderly marines on a night out was too horrible to contemplate. He dialled the number.

'Bickleigh Barracks, guardhouse.'

'I'd like to speak to the commanding officer, please.'

'Who's calling?' The voice was just audible over a loud sigh, although the change of tone when Dixon identified himself was immediate. He pictured the person on the other end of the line standing to attention.

'He's off duty I'm afraid, Sir. He'll be in tomorrow.'

'Are you able to contact him today?'

'In an emergency, Sir.'

'Good. Would you be so kind as to ring him now and give him my number. I need to speak to him about a murder investigation. And it is urgent.'

'I'll call him straightaway, Sir.'

'Thank you.'

Dixon rang off.

'I need to go, Sir, if that's all right.' Mark Pearce was standing by his workstation.

'You carry on. And you, Louise. We're not going to get much done on a Sunday now, are we?'

'I'll just finish this.'

'Where's Dave?'

'Already gone I think.'

'Be back here at eight tomorrow,' said Dixon, standing up.

He was halfway along the landing when his mobile phone rang.

'Dixon.'

'Lieutenant Colonel Hatfield, Inspector. I gather you wanted to speak to me.'

'Yes, Sir. Thank you for calling me back. I'm investigating the murder of a Falklands veteran and was hoping to come down to Bickleigh.'

'Yes, of course. We're just back from a month's training in Norway as it happens, but I'm in Whitehall until Tuesday night I'm afraid. Was he one of ours?'

'The murder victim isn't a marine, Sir, but I wanted to talk to you about Adrian Kandes.'

Silence.

'Wednesday at ten?' asked Dixon.

'Er, yes, that'll be fine. I hope I can help.'

'So do I, Sir.'

◆ ◆ ◆

Bullets ricocheted off the rocks behind him, sending sparks flying into the air above his head. He followed the phosphorous glow of the tracer rounds high into the night sky, until they fizzled out and fell to earth hundreds of yards away in the sparse covering of heather.

He closed his eyes to preserve his night vision when a flare went up. The man lying next to him was shaking but making no sound. Not that he would have heard much anyway over the noise of the machine guns and the artillery barrage hitting the Argentinian positions further up the hill. First the flash, then the bang. And then the debris landing on him; they were that close.

Away to his right three lads were lying behind a boulder, their faces camouflaged, the whites of their eyes visible in the eerie glow, until the flare fell to earth and they were shrouded in darkness again. If only just for a second, until the next one went up, or until the flash of another shell landing on the hill above them.

Then the barrage stopped. He closed his eyes.

This is what you trained for, for fuck's sake. No. More. Running.

Breathing hard now.

He glanced to the east and watched a small group of marines moving forward, tracer fire snaking across the hillside towards them.

Then he noticed Lieutenant Burton in front of him, lips moving, shouting, but there was no sound. Burton crawled across to the others and began shouting at them too, his fist clenched.

'Let's go. Let's fucking go!' No one needed to hear it to get the message.

They stood up as one and followed Burton, weaving up through the boulders, the last of the heather brushing against their legs and clawing at their feet. Then it was out on to open hillside.

Two machine guns opened up on them from the base of the rocks just below the summit.

'They must have NV.'

Night vision – that's all we fucking need.

On the ground now, he crawled across to Lieutenant Burton.

Dead.

Blood seeping from a gaping wound in his neck.

'Where's the fucking radio?'

The shout came from his left.

'What do we do, Sarge? We're pinned down.' The marine was lying in front of him, shaking him. And shouting. He looked down at the marine's hand on his arm, blood soaking into his sergeant's stripes. Less than an hour ago this same marine had whacked that woodentop too. And he'd done it for him.

'What've we got?'

'Two geeps at the base of the rocks,' came the reply.

He reached over and pulled Burton's sub-machine gun from his lifeless hand. Then he waved at the marine carrying the 66 mm anti-tank launcher, who crawled over to him.

'Give it to me.'

A shallow gully led diagonally up to the base of the summit rocks, perhaps eighty yards away. A boulder halfway along would offer some cover from which to fire the AT. Then it was open ground all the way.

Fuck it.

He closed his eyes while he waited for the flare that was floating down to hit the ground. He thought about his family and hoped they would understand. Then he was up and running for the base of the gully, bullets kicking at the ground behind him.

Crawling now, AT in his left hand, rifle in his right, bayonet fixed, SMG slung over his shoulder, he made it to the comparative safety of the boulder. The enemy machine guns would be trained on it, waiting for the slightest movement, so he crawled past it, only a yard or two, then sat up and fired the AT at the first geep to open up at him.

Direct hit.

He dropped the empty rocket launcher and picked up his rifle. Then he jumped up and ran towards the remaining machine gun, straight across the open ground below the summit of Mount Harriet.

The first bullet hit him in the left shoulder, the second in his right thigh.

He fell twenty yards short of the enemy machine gun post and lay still, searing pain in his leg. He reached down and felt blood, but not that much. Artery missed. That gave him another few minutes.

The bones in his shoulder grated when he moved his arm, but it moved, and he was beyond feeling pain now.

He waited until the machine gun began firing again before he took the pin out of a grenade, ever so slowly. Then he threw it and scrambled to his feet, lurching forward, dragging his right leg. The grenade detonated as the machine gun was swinging towards him, killing the gunner.

Firing from the hip, he killed one enemy soldier as he came round the base of the rocks, two shots to the face; then another ran at him, bayonet fixed. He shot him in the legs and lunged at him with his bayonet. The serrated blade stuck in the man's eye socket, so he dropped the rifle and reached for the sub-machine gun that was still over his shoulder.

He felt a hammer blow to his chest. Then another. He pulled the trigger as he dropped to his knees and watched the two remaining enemy soldiers fall backwards in slow motion. Others above him on the summit had their arms in the air.

Silence.

Either he was beyond hearing or the battle was over.

He tried to focus on a man kneeling over him, silhouetted against a flare lighting up the night, a green beret and a dog collar just visible in the light that was fading fast, despite more flares going up.

Redemption.

Chapter Eleven

The snow was settling on Monty's red coat and on the line of seaweed left along the high tide mark, but not on the sand. It had last settled on the beach in 2010, although back then even the seawater puddles had frozen, and it had to be pretty damn cold for that.

Dixon thought about his days ice climbing with Jake, turning back from the summit of Ben Nevis, their tracks in the snow being covered over as fast as they made them. And the summit of Mont Blanc. The sky had been clear that day, which had made the long slog worth the effort.

He had parked on the beach and was walking towards Brean Down. He had until the sun came up; then it would be home to drop Monty off and down to Express Park for 8 a.m. Jane didn't have to be there until 9 a.m., so they had agreed to go in separate cars to be on the safe side.

Sergeant Adrian Kandes VC. Dixon shook his head. It had a certain ring to it.

Colonel Byrne had been adamant that the other marines had gone after him when he left the battlefield to bring him back, which meant they must have been identified and spoken to at some point and by someone. Five of them, he had said. It would be very interesting to find out where Maynard's father had been during the battle as well, but too good to be true perhaps, if he was one of the five. Dixon was never that lucky.

And what of the bitterness Tom Cuthbert talked about? On both sides. From the Welsh Guards that a marine had struck one of their officers no doubt. But if that was the case, why would one of them kill Fletcher?

No, the greater anger would have come from the marines, surely. That one of their number had been denied the Victoria Cross. Even Lieutenant Colonel Hatfield was familiar with the story, judging by his reaction on the phone, and he would have been no more than a boy in 1982. But would the anger and bitterness fester this long?

And why now?

Then there was Kandes's family. A father's bitterness that his son had missed out on a VC? Kandes would have been nearly seventy now, making his father over ninety perhaps. Wife and children then, brothers and sisters possibly. It would be interesting to see what Mark Pearce came up with.

Dixon kicked Monty's ball along the sand and watched him tear off after it in the first light of dawn. He had found his motive at last. The only problem was that it fitted God knows how many people.

Dixon sat down at a workstation and switched the computer on.

'Adrian Kandes was single,' said Pearce, craning his neck over his monitor. He was sitting at the workstation in front of Dixon.

'No girlfriend?'

'There was one, but they broke up just before he went to the Falklands.'

'Find her.'

'Yes, Sir.'

'Parents?'

'Neither alive. There's a sister though. Living in Guildford.'

'What about the CO?'

'I'm working on it.'

'I've been on to the Defence Lab,' said Louise, 'and they've got a radar cabin in storage still.'

'Where is it?' asked Dixon through a mouthful of bacon and egg sandwich.

'Porton Down. That's Wiltshire, isn't it?'

'Can we go and see it?'

'It's in an old hangar apparently,' said Louise. 'I've spoken to the site manager, and he can take us out there at midday if that's any good.'

'That'll do,' replied Dixon. 'Let me have the sister's address, Mark. We'll be halfway there already, so we'll pay her a visit.'

'D'you want me to ring her?'

'No.'

'What'd he say we should do?' asked Dixon.

'He said he'd meet us at the gate,' replied Louise.

They had gone in Dixon's Land Rover on the assumption that a four wheel drive might be more useful if it didn't stop snowing, and he had stopped in the middle of the road opposite the police control point at the entrance to Porton Down. Both barriers were down either side of the guardhouse, and they had already attracted the attention of the officers inside, who were watching their every move.

'What do they think we're going to do?' asked Louise.

'We could be terrorists,' replied Dixon. 'Or animal rights activists.'

'They do animal testing here?'

'Amongst other things.'

'Like what?'

'Chemical and biological weapons testing.'

'I wouldn't have come if I'd known,' muttered Louise.

'I don't like it any more than you do, but we've got a job to do. All right?'

Louise nodded.

Dixon drove up to the barrier and wound down the window.

'Can I help you?'

Dixon was relieved that the officer armed with the machine pistol had stayed in the guardhouse.

'We're here to see the site manager,' he said, passing his warrant card to the officer standing by the driver's door.

'Wait here.'

Dixon watched him walk back into the guardhouse and pick up the telephone.

'Can you wind the window up?' asked Louise, shivering.

The officer came back out and lifted the barrier.

'Park over there,' he said, gesturing to a small car park just inside the entrance. 'He's on his way.'

Dixon reversed into a parking space and left the engine running.

'What's his name, this fellow?'

'Keith Draper,' replied Louise.

Dixon took his phone out of his pocket, intending to send Jane a text message while he waited.

'No signal,' he muttered. 'You got one?'

'No. Maybe there's a blocker on it.'

'You've been watching too many James Bond films.'

'Is this him?' asked Louise, pointing to a dark green Land Rover coming down the access road.

'Good taste in cars if it is.'

The Land Rover pulled up next to them, and the driver wound down the window.

'You here to see the radar cabin?'

'Yes. We're—'

'Hop in then.'

Dixon switched off the engine and climbed out of his Land Rover.

'It's in an old hangar on the other side of the complex,' continued the driver, watching Dixon and Louise climb into his Land Rover and slide across the bench seat.

'Are you Mr Draper?'

'No. I'm just maintenance. He took one look out of the window and sent me I'm afraid. Tosser.'

Dixon looked at Louise and raised his eyebrows.

'What's your name?'

'John.'

The driver was wearing blue overalls underneath a parka, one of the old blue ones with the orange lining and fake fur around the hood. He was in his early sixties, with fingerless gloves and grey hair poking out from under a black bobble hat.

'How long have you been here?' asked Dixon.

'Forty-two years. Retiring next year, and I can't bloody wait.'

'Were you here when the cabin arrived?'

'Yes. It came over from Malvern when RSRE was closed down.'

Dixon looked out of the window as they drove past various buildings, all with large and full car parks in front of them. It reminded him of the police HQ at Portishead, the original buildings of red brick with the old metal windows, and the newer ones all concrete and glass.

'Where are the biological warfare labs?' asked Dixon.

'Over the other side. You're quite safe.'

Then they were out into the country on an old concrete road.

'There are the hangars,' said John. 'Left over from the days when we had aircraft here. Now they're just used for storage.'

John turned the Land Rover into the empty car park in front of the first hangar. There were three, two large ones and a smaller one at the far end.

'As you can see, not many people come out here these days.'

Theirs were the first tyre tracks in the fresh snow.

'Which one is it?' asked Dixon.

'This one,' said John, pointing to the first hangar.

Two huge steel doors towered over them, perhaps forty feet high and wider still.

'We don't have to open those, do we?' asked Louise.

'No,' replied John, holding up an old key and grinning. 'There's a side door.'

It took him several minutes to switch on all the lights and even longer for them to come on, the old strip lights flickering in protest.

'Follow me.'

They weaved their way through high metal shelving units, all packed to the top with boxes, each labelled and assigned an archive number.

'What's all this lot?' asked Dixon.

'Can't tell you,' replied John. 'I'd have to kill you.'

Dixon wondered how many times John had used that line. Thousands possibly, but he still appeared to enjoy it all the same.

'Here it is.'

The shelving on the far side of the hangar opened out to reveal an area the size of at least two tennis courts. There were boats on trailers, motorbikes, two MoD Land Rovers, two skips full of old computers and an old tank.

'What's the tank for?'

'Chemical weapons testing,' replied John. 'See if the men inside would survive an attack. It's an old Scimitar.'

'Where's the cabin?'

'At the back.'

They followed John through the piles of junk to the back of the hangar.

'It's basically just a cabin on wheels,' he continued. 'I'm not sure what use it'll be to you.'

'Is there a light back here?'

'Somewhere.'

Another set of strip lights flickered into life, revealing a dark green cabin mounted on a trailer. There was a set of steel steps at the back and various boxes on the roof.

'No windows,' said Dixon.

'There are a couple of skylights in the roof.'

'Can we go in?'

One of the tyres was deflated, giving the cabin a list to one side.

'There's not a lot to see, except a few radar screens and desks.'

'We've come this far . . .'

'And it's full of shit.'

'Really?'

'I'm joking. When it was captured, they found a turd in one of the drawers, or so the story goes.'

Dixon shook his head.

'Is it locked?'

'No.'

Dixon walked up the steps at the back and opened the door. He fumbled for a light on the wall, but the switch was dead, so he waited for his eyes to adjust to the gloom.

'It stinks like an old caravan,' said Louise, standing behind him.

'It is an old caravan. And so would you if you'd been dumped in a damp warehouse for thirty years.'

Desks had been built in around the walls, with radar screens set into them, four in total, presumably to cover north, south, east and west. A radio set was still there, but everything else had been stripped out, leaving exposed cables and gaping holes in the panelling.

'I wouldn't open the drawers if I were you,' said Dixon.

'I won't.'

Dixon heard footsteps on the stairs behind him and turned to see John leaning on the railings.

'What's going to happen to it?'

'Nothing I expect,' replied John. 'It'll probably be here long after I've gone. More of an effort to remove it I shouldn't wonder.'

'Really?'

'Yeah, very costly. It's lined with asbestos. We tried the Imperial War Museum, but they didn't want it. Neither did the RAF Museum, so it'll just stay here I expect.'

'Were there any others?'

'Three, but they were broken up in the Falklands and shipped back in pieces. They're long gone now.'

'Has anyone else been in here recently?'

'I dunno. Why?'

'Fingerprints in the dust,' replied Dixon, pointing at a hole in the panelling.

'I'll check,' said John, reaching into his pocket for his phone.

'What d'you make of it?' asked Dixon, turning to Louise.

'Nothing to be honest.'

'Me neither.'

'It was some bloke about a year or so ago,' said John. 'Something to do with the asbestos.'

'I wonder what that was about?'

'Probably just pricing up its disposal we think. We've had several quotes in the past, according to Mr Draper.'

Dixon nodded.

'I've seen enough, thank you.'

'How far's Guildford?' asked Louise once they were back in Dixon's Land Rover.

'An hour or so.'

He was on the M3 before he spoke again.

'What's the address?'

'It's Shalford actually, just outside Guildford on the A281—33 Shillingbourne Road.'

'Have you got satnav on your phone?'

'No.'

Dixon reached down behind the passenger seat and handed a map book to Louise.

'Over to you, Constable.'

Twenty-five minutes later they were parked across the drive of a large semi-detached house. It had stopped snowing just east of Porton Down, although it was cold enough to snow and would no doubt start again before they left.

Dixon looked up at 33 Shillingbourne Road. Lights were on inside, the narrow shafts of light just visible through the jungle in the front garden. The property itself appeared tidy and well maintained. Maybe they just hated gardening.

'I hope she's in,' said Louise.

'Let's go and find out.'

Dixon rang the doorbell and waited, peering through the stained glass panels in the large solid oak front door. The rails of a stairlift were fixed to the wall at the bottom of the stairs, but the chair was out of sight, presumably at the top. Apart from that not much was visible in the hall.

'Yes.'

Dixon looked up to find a woman leaning out of an upstairs window. Sixty-five or so, long hair swept back under a band, cigarette in the corner of her mouth.

'We're looking for Mrs Glenda Campbell.'

'What do you want?'

'Police.'

'What's he done now?'

'Mrs Cam—'

'I'll come down,' she said, slamming the window.

'One day somebody's going to be pleased to see us,' said Louise.

'I doubt that.'

It took several minutes for the stairlift to bring Mrs Campbell down the stairs.

'How do I know you're police?' she asked, her face pressed to the stained glass.

Dixon pushed their warrant cards through the letterbox. She bent down, picked them up and then opened the front door.

'What's who done now?' asked Dixon.

'My stepson,' replied Mrs Campbell. 'Useless loafer. He's supposed to do the garden for a start.'

'Are you married?'

'My husband's dead, and he left me with Sam. Comes and goes as he pleases, when he needs money usually.' She handed back the warrant cards.

'What can I do for you then if it's not about Sam?'

'Can we come in?'

'Er, yes.'

They followed her into the lounge. 'Just shift that lot on to the floor,' she said, gesturing to the cats asleep on the sofa.

Dixon watched her slump down into the armchair.

'Multiple sclerosis, Inspector. I have the occasional medicinal joint, but you've not come all the way from Somerset for that, have you?'

'No.'

'So, what can I do for you?'

'We wanted to talk to you about your brother.'

Mrs Campbell closed her eyes and took several deep breaths. Then she struggled to her feet and shuffled across to the mantelpiece. She smiled at a photograph as she picked it up and passed it to Dixon.

'Adrian. He died for Queen and country. This is the last picture of him, taken just before they left for the Falklands.'

Dixon looked at the picture of a man perhaps his age, maybe a year or two older, sitting astride a motorcycle on a seafront somewhere.

'It's his birthday today,' she said, her eyes welling up with tears.

'Would you like a cup of tea, Mrs Campbell? Constable Willmott can . . .'

'No, I'm fine. What d'you want?'

'D'you have a photograph of him we can keep?'

'Take that one. I've got another copy. Just leave me the frame.'

'How much d'you know about what happened on the night of the battle?' asked Dixon, handing the photograph to Louise.

'Everything. I know everything.'

'Tell me.'

'Look, what's this about?'

'We're investigating the death of Captain Alan Fletcher.'

'Him? He's dead?'

Dixon nodded.

'Good.'

'He was murdered, Mrs Campbell.'

'Who did it?'

'That's what we're trying to find out.'

'Well, when you do, thank them for me, will you?' She lit a cigarette.

'What happened on the night of the battle?'

'The marines were pinned down, so Adrian went for reinforcements and bumped into Fletcher. The bastard tried to say Adrian was a deserter, and they took away his VC.' Mrs Campbell's cheeks were flushed, and she spoke as she exhaled the smoke. 'He should've won the VC.'

Dixon watched the ash fall off the end of her cigarette on to the carpet.

'Who told you this?'

'I went down to Bickleigh for the parade when they got back, and I was told it by men who were there. I met the padre who knelt over him when he was dying. And the men he saved. They all said he should've got the VC.'

'And before that?'

'We just got a telegram and then a visit from some liaison person, that's all. They knew nothing.'

'Do you still keep in touch with any of his fellow marines?'

'No. I get the occasional invitation to parades and memorials and things like that, but I never go. I can't travel.'

'Have you still got the telegram?'

'My mother burnt it.'

'Were you ever given any official explanation of what happened in the battle and why he wasn't awarded the VC?'

'No. He just wasn't. I wrote a few times, but they never gave a reason. I was just fobbed off.'

'Was Adrian married?'

'No.'

'Girlfriend?'

'Not at the time. He had one up until just before they left, but she dumped him and went back to Canada.'

'Can you remember her name?'

'Ginette Lundy. That's "gin" as in gin and tonic.'

'Did he have any children?'

'No.'

'What about your parents?'

'Both died in the nineties.'

'Any other brothers or sisters?'

'Just me,' replied Mrs Campbell. 'Just me to keep his memory alive.'

They had been in the Land Rover for nearly half an hour before Louise broke the silence.

'You didn't tell her the truth,' she said as Dixon drove down the slip road on to the westbound M3.

'It's not my place to do it. And besides, how do we know what's true and what's not?'

'I suppose so.'

'All we've heard so far is the Welsh Guards' version of events, and as we know, there are three sides to every story.'

'Three?'

'The two sides and then the truth, which is usually somewhere in the middle.'

Louise smiled.

'She may have convinced herself her brother was wronged all those years ago,' continued Dixon. 'People have an amazing ability to block out what they don't want to hear.'

'You can't blame her.'

'I don't. Or maybe she really was told that by the marines. One thing's for sure: I intend to find out.'

Dixon dropped Louise back at her car at Express Park just after 7 p.m. and was relieved to find Jane's had gone. He took his phone out of his pocket and sent her a text.

where r u? Nx

The reply came as he was heading north on the M5.

red cow Jx

Dixon smiled. It had been a long day, most of it spent behind the wheel of his Land Rover, and he wasn't convinced it had been that productive. But he could think of no better way to end it than with his feet up in the pub.

He arrived ten minutes later to find Jane sitting by the fire, staring at the envelope on the table in front of her. It was still sealed. Monty was asleep on the floor as usual.

'What time did you get home?' asked Dixon.

'Five. Mark said you were out, so I left early.'

'I'll take Monty with me tomorrow now it's getting a bit milder.'

'I hadn't noticed,' said Jane.

'The snow's melting. How was the SCU?'

'I'll get used to it.'

'Don't try. Learn to live with it, but don't get used to it.'

'Maybe.'

Dixon knew better than to press the point.

'Not opened the envelope yet I see.'

'No.'

'How about some food and another drink then?'

Chapter Twelve

'Well?'

Dixon had been up since 5 a.m., and what little sleep he had got had been broken by a hypo that had sent him scurrying down to the kitchen in search of sugar. Biscuits and a banana usually did the trick. And it would remind him to check his blood sugar levels before he went to bed. Still, at least he always got plenty of warning when his blood sugar was dropping too low. Unlike some.

Now he was standing by a workstation in the CID area at Express Park stifling a yawn.

'The service records are on the way, Sir,' replied Harding. 'They kicked up a bit about releasing them all, but I sorted it out.'

'Well done.'

'And here's the old CO's name and address,' said Pearce, handing Dixon a piece of paper. 'There's a phone number too.'

'The girlfriend's name was Ginette Lundy, Mark. "Gin" as in gin and tonic. She went home to Canada, so see what you can do.'

'Yes, Sir.'

'Louise, you follow up the Royal Engineers. You know what we're after.'

'What are you doing?' asked Louise, nodding.

'I'm off to . . .' Dixon looked down at the piece of paper in his hand. 'Dartmouth.'

Lieutenant Colonel Christopher Wood OBE MC RM Retired was standing in a first floor window watching Dixon park in the drive below. It was a large detached and timber clad property on Above Town, Dartmouth overlooking the quay, a grandstand view, which explained the huge windows and double balcony.

Dixon climbed out of his Land Rover and looked up just in time to see Wood turn away from the window. No need to knock on the door.

'Good trip down?'

'Yes, Sir, thank you,' replied Dixon.

Wood had opened the front door and was leaning on the frame watching as Dixon peered in the back window of his Land Rover. Dixon reckoned he was almost eighty, and yet his hair was black. Dyed, surely. And he winced at the slightest movement in his left leg.

'What've you got in the back there?' asked Wood.

'My dog.'

'I would say bring him in, but I'm not sure our cats would appreciate it.'

'That's fine, Sir. He's asleep.'

'What is he?'

'A Staffie,' replied Dixon.

'I'd have another, only I'm too old now, and this damn hip slows me down. Still, I'm having it done next month, so we'll see.'

'Maybe something a bit smaller?'

'Good idea,' replied Wood. 'Come in. We're upstairs. Bedrooms only on the ground floor.'

'Do you need to see my ID?' Dixon was fumbling in his pocket for his warrant card.

'Oh, don't bother with that.'

Dixon followed Wood up the stairs and into the lounge.

'Shouldn't you be using a walking stick, Sir?'

'Over my dead body, young man,' replied Wood, grinning.

Dixon walked over and stood in the window.

'What's that place over there?'

'Kingswear,' replied Wood. 'You can get over on the ferry; then you come in the back end of Torbay.'

Dixon nodded.

'Coffee?'

'No, thank you, Sir,' replied Dixon.

'I would suggest we sit out on the balcony, but it's a bit nippy today.'

'It is.'

'Well, what can I do for you?' asked Wood. 'You mentioned the death of a Falklands veteran.'

'Yes, Sir. A Welsh Guards officer by the name of Alan Fletcher.'

Wood folded his arms and sat back in his chair, looking down at the floor.

'He's dead, is he?'

'Yes, Sir. He was murdered.'

'Well, I'm not sure how I can help.'

'He was found in an old World War Two pillbox on the Bridgwater and Taunton Canal.' Dixon was staring at Wood as he spoke. 'And etched into the brickwork, along with the other graffiti, was a name and a date: "A Kandes 11/6/82".'

Wood smiled and shook his head.

Dixon waited.

'He was a good marine. A fine marine,' said Wood. 'Volunteered to go, you know. He was right at the end of his twenty years and could've stayed behind. Have you seen his sister?'

'Yesterday.'

'How is she?'

'She has MS, but seems to get by.'

'Tell her to contact the benevolent fund if she needs anything, will you?'

'I'll pass that on, Sir.'

Wood was struggling to lift himself out of his chair, leaning on the arm.

'Can I get you anything?' asked Dixon.

'Pour me a Scotch, will you?' replied Wood, gesturing to a bottle on the sideboard. 'And help yourself while you're about it.'

'Thank you, Sir.'

Dixon watched Wood in a gilt mirror on the wall above the sideboard while he poured the drinks. A large one for Wood and a small one for himself.

'We never told her the truth,' said Wood as Dixon handed him a glass.

'Why not?'

'She didn't need to know. No one did.'

'And what was the truth?'

'He broke. The last one you'd expect to run, but he did. He came back though and redeemed himself.'

'What about the marines who went after him?' asked Dixon. 'Were they ever identified?'

'Yes. There were five of them.'

'Names?'

'I can't remember now. Not all of them anyway.'

'How many do you remember?'

'Three.'

Dixon took his notepad and a pen out of his pocket while he waited.

'They were all F Company men,' said Wood. 'Corporal Absolon was one. And I remember Hagley was there too. But we never did find out who bashed Fletcher.'

'And the third?'

'Foster. But the others have gone, sorry. There were definitely five though.'

'And you conducted an investigation with Colonel Byrne?'

'Yes, informally. I kept some notes but destroyed them when we finished. We came into Southampton on a troop ship, Inspector, bands playing, flags waving. No one wanted an investigation.'

'What reason did you give for not recommending Kandes for a VC?'

'I did recommend him. But I was ordered to withdraw it.'

'What reason did they give?'

'Lack of witnesses, confusion of the battlefield, risk of a scandal. It was a travesty. He turned the battle. The whole of F Company on the left were pinned down by two geeps at the base of the rocks . . .'

'Geeps?'

'GPMGs – general purpose machine guns,' replied Wood. 'Manned by regulars too, not conscripts. He saved us all that day, including the Guards in reserve.' Wood drained his whisky.

'Can I get you another?'

'I'd better not.'

'These five marines – were they the same marines who had a run-in with Fletcher a few days later on the road outside Port Stanley?'

'You're well informed, Inspector. Yes, they were.'

'And what happened then?'

'There was an allegation of insubordination, but it wasn't pursued after Fletcher was injured in the fire.'

'Why not?'

'The rest of it would have come out. And no one wanted that.'

'So, tell me what happened.'

'This was over thirty years ago.'

'Try.'

'Well,' said Wood, shaking his head, 'Fletcher ordered the lads to dismantle some enemy radar cabins. Two sappers were trying to get them on a ship back to the UK. As you can imagine, it turned nasty pretty damn quick and would probably have got out of hand if the military police hadn't turned up.'

'So, they dismantled the cabins?'

'Yes, they did. Took them three days. We should've countermanded the order but didn't. Couldn't really in the circumstances I suppose.'

'And now all these years later Fletcher's been murdered. What d'you make of that?'

'Wounds fester, Inspector. I'm not excusing it, but Kandes was well respected, and a lot of men were very angry he didn't get the medal he deserved. Myself included. But I didn't kill him, before you ask.'

Dixon kicked Monty's tennis ball along the sand at Broadsands Beach and watched Monty take off after it, although he lost interest before he had gone halfway, distracted by a large pile of rotting seaweed.

The ferry across the River Dart had seemed a reasonable way to get home, via a beach, although Dixon's last visit to Torbay had not ended well. Two people had died that day.

He thought about what he had learned from Colonel Wood. Not much, except that Fletcher had ordered the marines to dismantle the radar cabins. Or tried to anyway. From the sounds of it the military police had been needed to enforce the order. No doubt he would have learned some new words if he had been a fly on the wall.

He took his phone out of his pocket and rang Louise.

'Got anywhere with the Royal Engineers?'

'Not yet, Sir. Just waiting to hear back.'

'What about the service records?'

'Dave's sorted that and they're on the way.'

'Good.'

'There are some missing though.'

'How many?'

'Five.'

'Have you got a list of names?'

'Dave has.'

'Get it.'

'Hang on.'

It was just after 4 p.m., and Dixon wouldn't get back until gone 6 p.m. even if he cut short his walk on the beach.

'Here it is,' said Louise.

'Don't tell me,' interrupted Dixon. 'Absolon, Hagley and Foster.'

'Yes, that's right. And Jones and Hampton.'

'Where have their records gone?'

'They're finding out.'

'Make sure they do.'

'Yes, Sir.'

'Let's have everybody in for an 8 a.m. sharp. Then we're off down to Bickleigh, all right?'

'Yes, Sir.'

Dixon rang off. Shame. If he'd had his night insulin with him, he could have stayed over in Devon.

'She was sixteen.'

'Who was?' asked Dixon, closing the front door behind him.

'My mother,' replied Jane. She was sitting on the sofa with a glass of red wine in her hand.

'You opened the envelope?'

Jane nodded.

'What about your father?'

'There's no name given, but she wasn't raped or anything like that. He was just a boy she was in a relationship with.'

'Do you know your mother's name?'

'Sonia.'

'Where?'

'It's Carlisle social services.'

Dixon dropped on to the sofa next to Jane and took her free hand in his. Monty jumped up and sat on her lap.

'What d'you want to do?'

'Nothing. For a while. Then I'll see.'

'Can I read it?'

'If you want to,' replied Jane. 'It's on the side over there.'

'How was work?'

'Who was it who said never work with children and animals?'

'It was an actor I think,' replied Dixon.

'Should've been a police officer.' Jane took a large swig of wine.

'You eaten?'

'No.'

'I'll bung something in the oven.'

Monty followed Dixon into the kitchen.

'Yes, yes, and you, I know.'

'I don't know whether I can risk her dumping me again,' said Jane. 'She's done it once.'

Dixon was putting Monty's bowl on the floor and looked up to see her standing in the kitchen doorway, tears streaming down her cheeks. He walked over and put his arms around her.

'What've you got to lose?'

'Nothing I suppose.'

'Exactly. D'you think your parents will love you any less?'

'No.'

'Or me?'

'No.'

'Then if she doesn't want to know, you've lost nothing, and at least you'll know.'

'What if I hate what I find?'

'Then you cut her loose. It'll be your decision, and you'll be dumping her.'

'I suppose I just need to toughen up a bit.'

'Bollocks,' replied Dixon. 'Why should you change because of her? If you've got a wasp in your car, you don't toughen up; you wind down the window and get rid of it.'

'A wasp? Where the bloody hell did that come from?'

'Oh, I dunno. Maybe it got in through the air vent.'

'You know what I mean.'

'Look, you owe her nothing. If you don't like what you find, wind down the window and let her go.'

'And you'll be there?'

'Yes.'

Jane smiled. 'Tell me about your day then.'

'Getting close I think. Lots of jigsaw pieces on the table, and I've got the edges all nicely laid out. Trouble is I haven't got the lid with the picture on it.'

'Any pieces missing?'

'Dunno.'

'Have you been drinking?'

'No. Why?'

'You're talking crap.'

'Thank you, Sergeant.'

◆ ◆ ◆

Dixon had never questioned why it was that he did his best thinking when he was doing something else – in the shower, walking his dog, driving. There was no pattern to it, and it was best not to analyse it. Just go with the flow. And if all else failed, stop dwelling on it and put on a good film.

Tonight it had been Jane's choice, and Dixon had got off lightly thanks to a screening of *12 Angry Men* on Channel 4. Back in the old days a police officer was excused jury service, but not any more. That all changed in 2004, and the prospect sent shivers down his spine. He closed his eyes and tried to go to sleep. Again. But each time the same picture appeared of him sitting in the jury box, watching himself giving evidence. Still, at least Henry Fonda wasn't on the jury.

He woke just after 7 a.m. to find the bed empty next to him. The familiar sound of a tin dog bowl scraping along a tiled floor was coming from downstairs, soon drowned out by the kettle and closely followed by the smell of coffee. It was enough to get anyone out of bed.

'What's the plan for today?' asked Jane.

'I'm off down to Plymouth to begin with,' replied Dixon. 'After that it's anyone's guess.'

'Are you taking Monty?'

'Yes.'

'Good.'

Twenty minutes later Dixon was leaning on a fence post watching Monty wandering around the field behind the cottage. It was milder, and the last traces of snow on the ground had gone. He closed his eyes and took a deep breath, allowing the air to fill his lungs and holding it in for as long as he could before letting it out.

Oh shit.

He bundled Monty into the back of the Land Rover and then flung open the back door of the cottage.

'Gotta go, sorry.'

'But you haven't had your toast.'

'I've got it,' said Dixon, climbing into the driver's seat of his Land Rover. 'My jigsaw puzzle lid.'

'Have you done your jab?' shouted Jane from the back door, but it was lost in the revving of the old diesel engine.

He ignored Junction 23 on the M5 and sped past Bridgwater, heading south, a diesel stop at Taunton Deane giving him the chance to ring Louise.

'Where are you?'

'Meeting room two, Sir. Where are you?'

'Taunton Deane. I'm going straight down to Plymouth, but I'll get back as quick as I can. Tell Dave to sort the service records into companies and then troops. I want to know who was in Kandes's troop.'

'Yes, Sir.'

'And let Mark chase the engineers. I want you to ring that Draper chap at Porton Down and find out exactly who has been to see that radar cabin in the last two years. I want names and addresses, the lot.'

'Yes, Sir.'

'They'll have the records. And I need them before I go in to see the lieutenant colonel at ten. All right?'

'I'll see what I can do.'

Dixon rang off. It was going to be an interesting meeting with Lieutenant Colonel Hatfield.

Chapter Thirteen

Another guardhouse, this time inside high steel gates with a roll of barbed wire along the top. A sign on the grass verge – a red cross on a yellow background with a crest in the centre: 42 Commando, Royal Marines. Dixon was in the right place.

He parked opposite the entrance and rang Louise.

'You said you wanted two years?'

'I did.'

'He's got two so far, but he thinks there was a third before that. He's ringing me back with it.'

'Give me the ones you've got.'

'Simon Taylor from Asbestos Solutions Limited. They're in Salisbury. He visited last July and quoted for disposing of it.'

'Yes,' replied Dixon. He had his phone trapped between his ear and his shoulder and was scribbling in his notepad.

'And Anthony Fripp. Just says Bangor. Draper says he doesn't know why he was there, but it wasn't to quote for getting rid of it. Or if it was, he never gave a quote. That's all he can remember.'

'When?'

'January last year.'

'OK,' replied Dixon. 'I'm going in now, so text me when you get the other one.'

'Will do.'

Dixon rang off and opened a web browser. He typed 'Anthony Fripp Bangor' into Google and hit the 'Search' button. The first result came from the UK Register of Expert Witnesses. He clicked on it.

'Dr Fripp in Bangor; industrial lung disease, occupational asthma, asbestosis, respiratory diseases, lung injury, mesothelioma, pulmonary function testing, Certificate of Expert Witness Accreditation.'

Dixon smiled. He was looking at his jigsaw puzzle lid.

'Park there, Sir. That's the HQ building over there.'

'Thank you.'

It was an odd looking building for a Marines headquarters – not that Dixon had seen one before. Dark red, almost black bricks at ground floor level, with the first floor clad in light green corrugated iron.

'Detective Inspector Dixon to see Lieutenant Colonel Hatfield,' he told the marine on duty at reception.

'Take a seat, Sir. I'll let him know you're here.'

Dixon was flicking through a loose leaf folder of newspaper clippings, '42 Commando in the News', when the inner doors flew open.

'Inspector Dixon?'

'Yes.'

'This way, Sir. The CO's expecting you.'

He followed the marine along the corridor, trying not to get in step, and into a meeting room at the back of the building, overlooking the war memorial.

'Can I offer you a coffee, Sir?'

'No, thank you.'

'Colonel Hatfield will be along in a minute.'

'Thank you.'

Dixon was still staring at the memorial when the door opened behind him.

'Rather puts it all in perspective when you see that, doesn't it?'

'It does, Sir,' replied Dixon, recognising Hatfield from his picture on the Internet. They shook hands.

'Do sit down.'

'Thank you.'

'Look, I don't think there's any harm in me telling you that I've spoken to Colonel Wood. He rang me.'

Dixon nodded.

'We're both benevolent fund trustees,' continued Hatfield. 'And I'm not sure there's much I can usefully add to what he's told you.'

'You've heard of Adrian Kandes?'

'Every marine has. Certainly everyone in 42 Commando.'

'And is there much bitterness about it?'

'Not these days. All of his contemporaries have long since retired, and we've lost too many men in Iraq and Afghanistan since then, Inspector. I guess you could say he's passed into corps legend.'

'Are there regular meetings of veterans?'

'Oh yes. There's a veterans' association, a magazine and regular get-togethers. I can let you have a copy of the magazine before you go.'

'Thank you.'

'Are you saying that you think a marine killed Fletcher?' asked Hatfield, frowning.

'Not a serving marine, no,' replied Dixon. 'But a Falklands veteran possibly.'

Hatfield nodded.

'One of the men Kandes gave his life to save,' continued Dixon.

'That would give you a lot of suspects. Although some might say they saved him rather than the other way round.'

'What from?'

'A court martial, dishonourable discharge.'

Dixon nodded.

'Have you looked at their service records?' asked Hatfield.

'We're doing that now, Sir,' replied Dixon.

'Well, you've got your work cut out I think.'

'Can you tell me whether there are any records of the investigation carried out by Colonel Wood in the days after the battle?'

'There aren't, I'm afraid. I had someone look after we spoke on the phone.'

'Are there any sets of court proceedings going on involving 42 Commando?'

'That's an odd question.'

'Humour me,' said Dixon.

'We've got a couple of speculative claims from Iraq and Afghanistan, but I don't usually get involved in that. They're made against the Ministry of Defence, and the Government Legal Department deals with them. The old Treasury Solicitor as was.'

'Who deals with them here?'

'My adjutant, David Shaw.'

'Can I speak to him?'

'Er, yes. He's here today. Give me a minute.'

Hatfield left the room and returned a few minutes later with another officer. Dixon was back in the window, looking at the war memorial.

'Does it have names on it, the memorial?' asked Dixon, turning around.

'Yes, Inspector,' replied Hatfield.

'And is Adrian Kandes on it?'

'He is.'

Dixon nodded.

'Inspector, this is Major Shaw. You were asking about court proceedings.'

'Yes. Are there any, Sir?'

'We've got several claims under investigation,' replied Shaw. 'But only one set of court proceedings at the moment. That dates back to the Falklands.'

'Asbestosis?' asked Dixon.

'Mesothelioma to be precise. How could you possibly know that?'

'Dismantling Argentinian radar cabins lined with asbestos?'

Shaw nodded.

'Five of them?'

'One's died, sadly, so it's down to four now. There's a hearing next week at Bristol County Court.'

Chapter Fourteen

Cars flashed past the lay-by on the A38 as Dixon switched his engine off and clamped his phone to his ear.

'Government Legal Department. How can I help you?'

'My name is Detective Inspector Dixon, of Avon and Somerset Police. I'm investigating the murder of Captain Alan Fletcher, a retired Welsh Guards officer and need to speak to the solicitor dealing with a mesothelioma claim against the MOD. It'll be Absolon, Hagley and Foster versus the Ministry of Defence.'

'Er, I'll see if I can track them down. Please hold.'

'And I need to speak to them now.'

'Yes, Sir.'

Dixon waited. He checked his watch. It was just after 11 a.m. and it would be lunchtime before he was back at Express Park, teatime before he could get to London.

'It's Mr Sharma, but he's in a meeting I'm afraid. He'll be free just before lunch if that's any good?'

'Get him out of it.'

The receptionist sighed.

'This is a murder investigation. Please get him out of the meeting. Now.'

Dixon was drumming his fingers on the steering wheel. He took a deep breath.

'Please hold.'

He watched a lorry approaching in his rearview mirror and then pass him, slowing as it began to struggle up the hill.

'This is Virat Sharma.'

'Mr Sharma, my name is—'

'I know who you are. How can I help?'

'Are you dealing with mesothelioma claims dating back to the Falklands War? Five marines dismantling Argentinian radar cabins.'

'Yes. There's a hearing next week. It's four and the executors of the fifth.'

'Is Captain Alan Fletcher a witness?'

'Yes, although his statement's been agreed.'

'He's dead and I'm investigating his murder.'

'What happened?'

'What time are you going to be there until tonight?' asked Dixon.

'I usually finish at 5.30 p.m.'

'I'm going to travel up to London now. Please do not go home before I get there.'

'Of course.'

Dixon gave Sharma his mobile phone number.

'How many files are you running?'

'Two,' replied Sharma. 'Four of the claimants are represented by one firm of solicitors, and the fifth by another.'

'I'll need two copies, please,' said Dixon. 'Correspondence, pleadings, expert reports, witness statements, the lot.'

'Bloody hell.'

'It is a murder investigation, Mr Sharma.'

'Yes, of course.'

'Have you got their service records?'

'They're on the file.'

'Them too then, please.'

'That'll take two people all afternoon. And two photocopiers,' muttered Sharma.

'And don't tell anyone either.'

'I need to notify the other side.'

'Not before I get there. Do you understand?'

'You've got me worried now.'

'What d'you mean?' asked Dixon.

'Well, that's two now, isn't it?'

'Two?'

'I took over the case at the end of last year when a chap here was murdered.'

'What was his name?'

'Robert Fryer.'

'What happened to him?'

'He was pushed under a train at Wimbledon station.'

'Get us on a fast train to London. Not before 1.30 p.m.,' said Dixon, looking at his watch.

'Yes, Sir,' replied Louise.

'Let me know the time, and line up a traffic car to get us to the station. If we go from Taunton, we can get a direct train to Paddington.'

'I know.'

'And get DCI Lewis to speak to his opposite number at Wimbledon. I need a meeting with whoever's dealing with the murder of Robert Fryer. He was pushed under a train at Wimbledon station last year. All right?'

'Who was he?'

'A solicitor at the Government Legal Department.'

'What's his—?'

'I haven't got time to go through that now.'

'OK.'

'Are you all right for an overnighter?'

'Yes, should be. My husband can look after Kate.'

'Book us two rooms at a cheap hotel. We should be out at Wimbledon by then.'

'Dog friendly?'

'No, he can go home with Jane.'

'What about the Royal Engineers?'

'Leave that with Dave and Mark.'

Dixon rang off and turned on to the A38. He floored the accelerator in third gear, but it would probably have been quicker to hitch a lift on that lorry that had crawled past.

We're on the 1.35. Wimbledon SIO is DCI Gresham, expecting your call

Hannah Gresham a DCI? A lot had changed at Wimbledon in the six months since he'd worked there. He checked his watch, deleted the text message and then rang Louise.

'I'm still south of Exeter and not going to make it in time, so I'll meet you at Taunton. Make sure there are two officers with you and one of them can drive my old bus back to Express Park.'

'Yes, Sir.'

'They'll need to give the keys to Jane so she can sort Monty out.'

'Leave it with me.'

Then Dixon rang Jane.

'What's up?'

'Got an overnighter in London I'm afraid.'

'But you haven't got your night insulin or your blood testing kit. Not to mention a toothbrush.'

'I'll be all right for one night. I'll have to be.'

'What's going on?'

'I'll tell you when I get back. Look, I'm picking up the train at Taunton, so someone's going to drive my car back to Bridgwater and give you the keys. Don't forget Monty!'

'I won't. And be careful.'

'Yes, Mother.'

Dixon and Louise were sitting in the window of an InterCity 125 watching the Somerset Levels flash by, some of the fields and houses still underwater. Louise was deep in thought, digesting the briefing she had just received. The train carriage wasn't crowded and they had sat at the far end, but Dixon had still whispered, which hadn't helped. She had got the gist of it all the same.

'And you got all of that from the radar cabin?'

'That and Colonel Wood telling me Fletcher had ordered the marines to dismantle the others. That's when it all dropped into place. And Dr Fripp of course. But they confirmed it at Bickleigh this morning.'

'How?'

'I am a solicitor, don't forget.'

Louise shook her head.

'Fletcher was forced to inhale the brick dust, remember? A hand over his mouth,' continued Dixon. 'And mesothelioma is a lung disease, as we know.'

'Actually, it's the lining of the lung,' replied Louise. 'A form of cancer caused by exposure to asbestos. My grandfather died of it.'

'Really?'

'He was an electrician. Died when I was four.'

'I'm sorry to hear that.'

Louise smiled.

'Well,' continued Dixon, 'if you dismantle three asbestos lined cabins without the proper equipment and you inhale the dust, chances are you'll be seeing a solicitor decades later.'

'How d'you know they didn't have the right equipment?'

'Stands to reason, doesn't it?'

'Why?'

'If they did, they wouldn't be dying now, would they?'

'No, I suppose they wouldn't.'

'And court proceedings wouldn't have got off the ground.'

Louise nodded.

'What lawyer would take it to trial on a no-win, no-fee agreement?' asked Dixon.

'I can think of a few.'

'They shipped tons of equipment to the Falklands: weapons, ammunition, food. But equipment for dealing with asbestos? Somehow I doubt it.'

The taxi dropped them outside the offices of the Government Legal Department in Kemble Street just after 4 p.m., and Virat Sharma was waiting for them in reception, Dixon having rung ahead. More concrete and glass, this time arranged like a honeycomb.

'Don't say it,' said Louise, watching Dixon looking up at the building and frowning. 'You're starting to sound like Prince Charles.'

Dixon smiled. At least there was someone else who shared his disdain for modern architecture.

'Inspector Dixon?'

'Yes.'

'Virat Sharma.' He was tall and thin, dressed in a grey suit with trousers too short in the leg, although he was young enough that he may have just grown out of them.

'This is Detective Constable Louise Willmott.'

They shook hands.

'We're on the fifth floor. The lift's this way,' said Sharma, gesturing to the back of the reception area. 'I've got the copies ready, but it's two boxes I'm afraid.' He pressed the button and the doors opened.

'That's fine,' said Dixon, stepping into the lift. 'We'll take a cab.'

'Would you like a cup of tea?'

'Yes, please.'

'Follow me.'

The lift doors opened, and they followed Sharma through large double doors marked 'Litigation Department' and into a glass panelled meeting room.

'These are the boxes,' said Sharma. 'I'll just get my secretary to organise the tea.'

He returned a minute or so later to find Dixon flicking through the witness statements.

'Right, well, what do you want to know?' asked Sharma, sitting down at the table.

'Tell me about the case,' said Dixon. 'Are they going to win?'

'No.'

'You sound sure.'

'Section 10 of the Crown Proceedings Act 1947. A member of the armed forces can't sue the Crown for personal injury. It was repealed in 1987, but still applies to injuries suffered before 1987, which covers the Falklands of course.'

'Why have they commenced court proceedings then?'

'They're relying on Article 6 of the European Convention on Human Rights. In the determination of his civil rights, everyone is entitled to a fair and public hearing. I'm paraphrasing, but that's the gist of it. They say the Crown Proceedings Act denies them a fair and public hearing.'

'So they're taking it all the way to the European Court?'

'They're threatening to. No one's ever done it before, so it'll be a test case. They also have to show they've got a winnable case, but the exposure was short-lived and our expert says it wouldn't have caused mesothelioma on its own. The exposure needs to be more prolonged. That's our defence anyway.'

'The European Court will take years though, surely.'

'It will, by which time they'll all have died, sadly.'

'Can't you settle it?'

'I had a go when I first took the case over. I offered them the chance to discontinue the proceedings, with each side paying their own costs, but that wasn't good enough.'

'Why would they consider that?' asked Louise.

'Because when they lose they'll have to pay all our costs as well as their own. They've backed themselves into a corner and commenced proceedings in a case they can't win, and I was offering them a way out before the costs ramped up. But she was adamant she wanted compensation for her clients.'

'Who was?' asked Dixon.

'The solicitor acting for the claimants. I can't remember her name.'

'And you won't pay?'

'Why would we? It would open the floodgates to other claims, and the court was satisfied that we had a defence,' said Sharma, shrugging his shoulders.

'What d'you mean "the court was satisfied"?' asked Dixon. 'The trial's next week, surely.'

'That's just a hearing of the preliminary issue, of whether the Crown Proceedings Act applies. If it does, then the claims are dismissed and off we go to Europe, assuming they actually go that far. I'm talking about the case management conference last October. The court fast-tracks mesothelioma cases where the claimants are still alive, for obvious reasons, and the defendant has to show that he has a defence to the claim at the case management conference. If he can't, the claimants win at the first hurdle, and get an immediate interim payment of fifty thousand pounds, with the rest of their damages at the end of the case.'

'So they didn't get the interim payment?'

'No.'

'What happened to Mr Fryer?' asked Dixon.

'He lived over at Berrylands on the Waterloo line. He was on his way home from work. Anyway, he's standing on the platform when someone comes up behind him, and the next thing he's on all fours across the tracks in front of the Woking train. Still, he wouldn't have known much about it I suppose.'

'Has an arrest been made?'

'Not as far as I know. There's CCTV, I've seen it on the local news. But they haven't got anyone yet I don't think.'

'Has any connection been made with this case?'

'No. Not yet anyway.'

'What can you see on the CCTV?'

'Nothing really. He's wearing a hood. A beard possibly, but that's it.'

'How well did you know Fryer?'

'Not that well. I've only been here a year and there's thirty of us. He kept himself to himself.'

'When was this?'

'November thirtieth. It was a Monday. I came in on the Tuesday, and they were allocating his files.'

'So, what will happen without Captain Fletcher?'

'His witness statement is agreed, so it won't make much difference.'

'When did you first get in touch with him?'

'Fryer did about a year ago, when it first started. He needed a witness statement from him.'

Dixon nodded.

'You haven't got a death certificate by any chance, have you?' asked Sharma.

'You'll need to contact the Somerset coroner. There's only an interim death certificate at the moment.'

'Thanks,' replied Sharma, scribbling a note on the pad in front of him.

'What stage was the case at when you took it over?'

'It was already listed for hearing on the preliminary issue. Two days at Bristol County Court. I've just served witness summonses and lined up a barrister. Feels like it's jinxed though.'

'Why?'

'She returned the brief and now this,' replied Sharma.

'Why?'

'I never asked. We've had the same barrister all the way through, and then it's returned when it comes to the hearing. I was going to complain to the head of chambers, but there didn't seem a lot of point, and they offered us someone more senior for the same fee.' Sharma was shaking his head. 'It's odd though, because she gave her available dates after the CMC, and now all of a sudden she's not available.'

'What was her name?'

'Miss Alison Crowther-Smith.'

'Which chambers is it?' asked Dixon.

'St Luke's in Bristol.'

'Tell me about the claimants then. Who are they?'

'Four marines and the executors of the fifth. He died last August. Mesothelioma.'

'What about the others?'

'They've all got mesothelioma, some more advanced than others, and the medical evidence points to asbestos.'

'And what does your expert say?'

'Now you're asking,' replied Sharma, raising his eyebrows. 'That's Dr Fripp. Basically, that there wouldn't have been enough in the three cabins to do it, so there must have been exposure to asbestos elsewhere in their employment history, which is not the liability of the MOD.'

'Have the claimants got their own expert?'

'Yes. He says the opposite of course. It's not disputed that they were tasked to dismantle the cabins, or that they were lined with asbestos. And their evidence is that they have never been exposed to asbestos anywhere else. They've still got to get past the Crown Proceedings Act though.'

'What sort of asbestos was it?'

'The worst sort I'm afraid.'

'What are the claims worth?' asked Dixon.

'Damages have been agreed on a without prejudice basis. They range from ninety thousand pounds through to one hundred and fifty thousand, depending on their loss of earnings. Hagley's is the biggest award. If he wins.'

'Who's acting for them?'

'The four are represented by Lings in Bristol. And the fifth by Holt Burton in Reading.'

'Were the four always represented by one firm?'

'Yes.'

'And how are they funding the claim?'

'Lings are doing it on a conditional fee agreement – no-win, no-fee – and Holt Burton are private.'

'No-win, no-fee on a case that's likely to go to the European Court?'

Sharma nodded. 'Lings are on a bit of a crusade I think, and once they'd commenced court proceedings, they had to keep going.' He shrugged his shoulders. 'And I sort of hope they win, between you and me. The Crown Proceedings Act was designed to protect the government from claims by soldiers injured in battle due to the negligence of their commanders. Not from this type of claim. And there are sixty or so veterans with mesothelioma that predates 1987 – navy, army and

RAF – all of them being denied compensation. They just get a war pension instead.'

'Where do the claimants live?'

'God knows. Their addresses will be in their witness statements.'

'Well, thank you, Mr Sharma. It seems we've got a lot of reading to do.'

'Yes, sorry about that.'

'Where d'you live?' asked Dixon, standing up.

'Maida Vale.'

'And how do you get to and from work?'

'Underground usually. Sometimes I cycle. Why?'

'Are you married?'

'No.'

'What about family?'

'My parents are in Barnes.'

'Can you go there?'

Sharma nodded.

'Do so,' replied Dixon. 'And take a cab.'

'You're not saying . . . ?'

'I'll alert the local police, and they'll keep an eye on you, all right?'

'Yes, thank you.'

'Don't leave tonight until someone's made contact,' continued Dixon. 'D'you need me to speak to your supervisor?'

'No, I can deal with it,' replied Sharma, thrusting his hands in his pockets to hide their shaking.

Chapter Fifteen

'Brace yourself.'

'Eh?'

'You're about to enter a parallel universe,' continued Dixon, walking up the yellow painted steps at the front of Wimbledon Police Station.

'I forgot you used to work here,' said Louise, still struggling with a box of papers. Dixon was carrying the other, but instead of taking a taxi they had walked down to Temple tube station and got on the District line out to Wimbledon. Something about not having time to waste sitting in traffic.

'Seven years,' replied Dixon. 'Before I moved back to Somerset last year.'

He dropped his box down on the counter in reception.

'DI Dixon and DC Willmott to see DCI Gresham.'

The duty sergeant leaned over the counter and looked down at their feet.

'What?'

'Just checking you haven't got any cow shit on your wellies,' he said, grinning.

'I forgot to warn you, Louise,' said Dixon, rolling his eyes. 'Everyone's a bloody comedian.'

The sergeant picked up a telephone and dialled a three-digit extension number.

'Worzel Gummidge is here to see you.'

Dixon sighed and turned away.

'She's on her way.'

Dixon paced up and down in the reception area, trying to avoid eye contact with two lads sitting in the corner. Answering bail no doubt. Louise used the opportunity to send her husband a text message. Both of them turned when the security door opened behind them.

'Nick, it's good to see you.'

'And look at you,' replied Dixon. 'A DCI.'

Hannah Gresham was tall with long black hair, recently brushed. Dixon noticed the fresh squirt of perfume too. So did Louise.

'It would have been you if you hadn't left,' said Hannah.

Dixon shrugged his shoulders. He knew that, but had left anyway.

'You're dealing with the Fryer case?' asked Dixon.

'Let's go through,' replied Hannah. 'I've got Sunny and Fred on it, so I've asked them to join us if that's OK.'

'Fine.'

'We're in my office.'

They followed Hannah up the stairs to the first floor and along the corridor, past the open plan CID area and into her office. Dixon frowned. It was large enough for a desk at one end and a small conference table at the other. Maybe he shouldn't have left.

'Louise, this is Sunil Kohli, Sunny, and Gary Piper,' said Dixon.

'I thought you said his name was Fred?' asked Louise.

'He looks like Fred Astaire and dances like Fred Flintstone,' said Sunny, grinning.

'The old ones are always the best,' muttered Louise.

'What've you got on Robert Fryer?' asked Dixon.

'We've got an e-fit from the CCTV, but not a lot else,' replied Sunny. He opened a file and slid a colour print across to Dixon, who was sitting opposite him. 'Five feet ten or so, mid-thirties, carrying a yellow rucksack. There's a beard, so we've got the hair colour from that. In the film he's got a bobble hat on under a hoodie, so you don't see his hair.'

Dixon stared at it. Dark hair, sharp blue eyes, trimmed beard.

'Witnesses?'

'Some, but he never spoke and got clean away in the confusion,' replied Gary.

'Is that it?' asked Dixon.

'What about you?' asked Hannah. 'What's your interest?'

'I'm investigating the murder of a retired Welsh Guards captain,' replied Dixon. 'Just after the fall of Port Stanley in 1982 he ordered five marines to dismantle some enemy radar cabins, which were lined with asbestos. Those same marines are now dying of lung cancer and suing the MOD. Robert Fryer was the solicitor at the Government Legal Department conducting the case, and my victim was a witness in the same case.'

'Fucking hell,' said Sunny.

'The case goes to trial on a preliminary issue next week,' continued Dixon.

'We'll need access to the case file,' said Hannah.

Dixon leaned over and lifted a box off the floor, placing it on the table. 'Yours,' he said, sliding it across to Sunny.

'Thanks.'

'What else have you got?' asked Hannah.

'Nothing yet,' replied Dixon. 'Can we see the CCTV?'

Sunny looked at Hannah, who nodded.

'Follow me.'

Dixon stood up and handed a note to Hannah. 'Someone needs to make contact with this guy. He took over the case from Fryer and he's shitting himself. I've told him to go to his parents' in Barnes. He's going to take a cab.'

'I'll see to it.'

Dixon and Louise followed Sunny to his desk in the CID area and stood behind him.

'Ready?'

'Yes.'

The film was grainy and showed a railway station from above, the glare from the lights obscuring parts of the platform.

'There's Fryer,' said Sunny, pointing to a middle-aged man in a grey suit reading a tabloid newspaper. He was standing just behind the white 'Do Not Cross' line on the edge of the platform. Several commuters were in the shot further down.

'He'd walked to the front of the platform,' said Sunny, 'presumably to try and get a seat.'

'And he was heading to Berrylands?'

'Yes. He was waiting for a stopping train.'

'Have you picked him up at Waterloo?'

'Yes.'

'Anyone following him?'

'Not that we can see, and certainly not his killer.'

'Have you tried other stations?'

'His killer arrived and left on foot,' replied Sunny. 'We've got him on CCTV leaving the station, then we lose him heading on to Wimbledon Common.'

'He knows his CCTV then,' muttered Dixon.

'Oh yes. You'll see in a minute. He knows exactly where the cameras are.'

Dixon watched Fryer flicking through the pages of his newspaper. Then he folded it up and tucked it under his arm.

'He caught the first train out of Waterloo, a fast train to Wimbledon,' said Sunny. 'Now he's waiting for a train that stops at Berrylands.'

Dixon folded his arms across his chest. He was about to watch a man die, and there was nothing he could do to stop it. He glanced across at Louise, who was breathing hard.

'Here he is.'

Sunny was pointing at the bottom left hand corner of the screen. A man wearing a green anorak with the hood pulled up had just come into shot. The rucksack was yellow and appeared shiny. He paused and then edged further left into the shot, revealing black jeans and trainers. He stopped behind Fryer, keeping his head down.

'Here comes the train,' said Sunny, pointing to lights in the distance.

At the last second the man stepped forward and pushed Fryer in the small of his back with both hands. Fryer was thrown forward, landing between the railway tracks, and was just visible on all fours in the split second before the train hit him. Dixon thought Fryer looked up at the last moment, but couldn't be sure.

Then the screaming started – that much was obvious despite the footage having no sound; passengers running in all directions on the platform, some vomiting. Two collapsed.

Dixon looked but the killer was gone, having crept back out of shot the way he came in.

'I've seen enough,' said Dixon. He looked at Louise, who was wiping her eyes with a tissue.

Sunny stopped the film.

'Can you email that to me?'

'Yes.'

Dixon gave Sunny his address and watched while he attached the film to an email and clicked 'Send'.

'D'you want the e-fit too?'

'Yes, please. And any other footage you've got.'

'Give me a minute.'

'Where does the e-fit come from?'

'The camera in the ticket hall.'

'Can we see it now?'

'Yeah, sure.'

Again the shot was from above. The angular jaw was visible and the dark beard, but not much else.

'Where did the eye colour come from?'

'A witness,' replied Sunny. 'But she couldn't be sure.'

Once back in Hannah Gresham's office, she handed Dixon an envelope. 'These are the witness statements. Fred's getting you a set of photographs.'

'Thanks. I can let you have what we've got when I get back tomorrow.'

'Are you staying over?'

'We're in a hotel somewhere. Cheap and cheerful,' replied Dixon.

'You could come back to mine,' said Hannah, smiling. 'I'm sure Louise wouldn't mind.'

'Er, no.'

'It's fine, thanks,' said Dixon. 'We've got to be away early in the morning.'

'OK.' She sat down behind her desk.

'How long would it take us to get another e-fit done?'

'Ten minutes,' replied Sunny, appearing in the doorway behind them. 'Why?'

'Let's have one without the beard.'

'Without the beard? Why?'

'If he takes the time and trouble to learn where the cameras are, chances are he'll take the time and trouble to change his appearance. Grow a beard, dye it.'

'Yes, but if you suddenly grow a beard people are going to notice, aren't they?' asked Sunny.

'What was the date of the murder?'

'November thirtieth.'

'Half the adult male population is growing a beard or moustache in November,' continued Dixon. 'So you grow one, dye it, commit the murder on the last day of the month and then shave it off the next morning.'

'Fuck, yes, it's Movember,' replied Sunny.

'And you can even raise money for charity while you're doing it.'

'An old flame?' asked Louise as they waited for a taxi outside Wimbledon station.

Dixon had his hands in his pockets and was standing astride the remaining box of papers.

'A long time ago.'

'D'you think he's our killer then, the same bloke?'

'He's too young to be one of the surviving four marines, but he'll be connected with them in some way,' replied Dixon, nodding. 'Bound to be.'

A black cab pulled up in front of them, and Dixon opened the back door.

'The Holiday Inn, Merton High Street.'

'The Express,' said Louise.

'There's a good curry house just along from there too,' said Dixon. 'I need to eat something.'

It was gone 2 a.m. by the time Dixon finally fell asleep. The witness statements in the Fryer murder case had taken no more than ten minutes to read and told him nothing he didn't already know. But the photograph album had been something to behold. The train driver had braked hard, coming to a halt just outside Raynes Park station, meaning that Fryer's remains had been scattered over a distance of almost two miles.

A left hand, lying on the brown stained gravel between the tracks, wedding band still on the finger; the wrist with the watch still on it, the time matching the stamp on the photograph; a foot with a short grey sock and black brogue – all of them photographed in the bright glare of an arc lamp and gone by rush hour the next morning.

But by far the most shocking of the photographs was the last one in the album, of Robert Fryer on the slab in the mortuary after the pathologist had pieced him back together.

Dixon wasn't sure what he had learned from the photographs if anything, but they had kept him awake long enough to read most of the litigation file. The medical reports made grim reading. All five claimants had been smokers, which increased the risk of damage from asbestos exposure. Otherwise they confirmed what he already knew. Not only were the surviving four claimants too old to be Fryer's killer, they were also far too ill, each with a life expectancy of no more than two years. And the reports were already over a year old.

Fripp's report was interesting, if only for his conclusion that three radar cabins, dismantled in the open on an exposed hillside in the Falkland Islands, might not have been sufficient to cause the injury of which the claimants complained. The fourth had been shipped back to the UK intact of course.

The claimants' witness statements, on the other hand, said that it took them three days to dismantle the cabins and that the dust inside them had been overpowering. They had, they said, been left coughing for months afterwards. Not one of them mentioned Adrian Kandes.

Fletcher's witness statement was purely factual and confirmed he had ordered the marines to dismantle the cabins under the direction of the Royal Engineers. A good deal of insubordination had resulted, and order had only been restored at the intervention of two military policemen. The insubordination itself was unspecified. There were also statements from the two Royal Engineers and one of the military policemen, which Dixon would look at more closely on the train home.

They were standing on the concourse at Paddington station by 8 a.m. the following morning, Dixon watching the steam rising from a cup of coffee.

'What time's the train?'

'Twenty minutes,' replied Louise. 'Did Jane remember to get Monty out of your car?'

'She had him up in the SCU office all afternoon apparently,' replied Dixon, rolling his eyes. 'Asleep under her desk.'

'And no one spotted him?'

'Not until she was leaving.'

'I spoke to Mark,' said Louise. 'They've identified the Engineers and want to know what you want them to do.'

'There are statements from them on the file, so tell him to wait until we get back. Just concentrate on the claimants and their families. All five of them.'

'I'll ring him now.'

Dixon watched Louise pacing up and down with her phone to her ear. Then he glanced up at the departure boards.

'C'mon, that's us,' he said. 'Platform Four.'

Once on the train he passed the witness statements to Louise, both in the Fryer murder and the litigation, but spared her the photographs.

'What d'you notice about Fletcher's?'

Louise flicked through the bundle of statements, pulling one out and looking at it.

'I dunno. What?'

'It's dated last March. Around about the time he suddenly became a churchgoer.'

'You spoke to the vicar?'

Dixon nodded.

'The guilt?' asked Louise.

'Probably,' said Dixon. Then he started on the pleadings.

The Statements of Claim, each marked 'Living Mesothelioma Claim', alleged the usual stuff he had seen umpteen times before: failure to provide training; failure to provide any or any adequate personal protective equipment; failure to conduct a risk assessment properly or at all; breaches of the Health and Safety at Work etc Act 1974. The list went on.

In response the Government Legal Department had filed a Defence that alleged the claims were statute barred by virtue of Section 10 of the Crown Proceedings Act 1947. It then went on to deny each and every allegation individually, before continuing, 'If, which is not admitted, the Claimants were exposed to asbestos when dismantling the radar cabins, then the Defendant will say that the exposure was not prolonged and/or sufficient to have resulted in the alleged injury.'

The Defence had been drafted by a barrister, and Dixon found the fee notes on the correspondence pin. Miss Alison Crowther-Smith of St Luke's Chambers, Bristol, had drafted the Defence, and a Request for Further Information. She had represented the MoD at the case management conference on 17 October, showing cause why the defendant should be allowed to defend the claim and defeating the interim payment application. After that she had provided her available dates to the court for the listing of the preliminary issue. Odd then that she had returned the brief.

Dixon jumped up from his seat and walked along the aisle to the gap between two carriages. He looked up St Luke's Chambers on Google and then dialled the number.

'St Luke's Chambers.'

'This is Detective Inspector Dixon of Avon and Somerset Police. I was hoping to speak to Miss Crowther-Smith.'

'She's no longer with us I'm afraid.'

'Where is she?'

'Well, actually, I'm sorry to say she's dead.'

'When?'

'Last October. She drowned in a caving accident.'

Chapter Sixteen

Dixon rang off and then dialled Mark Pearce's number.

'Yes, Sir.'

'Dr Anthony Fripp. He's an expert witness, based in Bangor. Find him. Tell him to stay where he is and then get the local police to send someone.'

'What's going on?'

'He's an expert witness in a case in which two, and possibly three, people have been murdered.'

'I'll get on to it now.'

'And ring me when you've spoken to him.'

'Yes, Sir.'

Jane was waiting for them in Dixon's Land Rover when they walked out of Taunton railway station just after 10.30 a.m.

'Good trip?'

'Very enlightening,' replied Dixon. 'What are you doing here?' Monty jumped over on to the front seat and started licking his ears.

'I needed to get out for a bit,' replied Jane, shrugging her shoulders. 'Where to?'

'Is everything all right?'

'I'll tell you about it later.'

'Coroner's office then,' said Dixon.

Jane looked at Louise and raised her eyebrows.

'Don't look at me,' said Louise. 'He's hardly said a word all morning.'

Jane parked in the car park behind The Winchester Arms, switched the hazard lights on and left the engine running.

'I'll go round the block if a traffic warden comes.'

'We won't be long,' said Dixon, opening the passenger door.

Old Municipal Buildings in Corporation Street, Taunton was an ornate granite building with sandstone mullion windows. Until 1870 it had been home to Taunton Grammar School, but it now served as the Somerset Register Office, as well as the offices of the Somerset Coroner, Michael Roseland.

'Coroner's officer, please,' said Dixon.

'Up the stairs, first door on the right along the landing.' The receptionist spoke without looking away from her screen.

The carved oak staircase led to a wood panelled corridor.

'You have to like wood to work in a place like this,' muttered Louise.

Dixon knocked on the door with the 'Coroner's Officer' sign on it and walked in. Both desks were occupied, but Dixon recognised the coroner himself sitting on the window ledge.

'Ah, Inspector Dixon, isn't it?' said Michael Roseland, standing up.

'Yes, Sir. And this is Detective Constable Willmott.'

'What can we do for you?'

'I need to see the file on the death of Alison Crowther-Smith, Sir. She was a barrister from Bristol who died in a caving accident.'

'That'll be the Mendips probably, so that's East Somerset, Tony Williamson's patch. We should have the file here though. Ken?'

'Yes, Sir,' replied the man at the desk on the right. 'The inquest's not been fixed yet, so the file should be . . .' He opened the top drawer of a filing cabinet and then the next one down. 'Here it is.'

'What d'you need?' asked Roseland.

'Witness statements and the medical report, please.'

'Copies?' asked Ken.

'Yes, please.'

Roseland nodded.

'I'll be back in a minute,' said Ken, opening the office door.

'Is there anything we need to know?' asked Roseland.

'Miss Crowther-Smith was a barrister defending a mesothelioma claim against the MOD, Sir,' replied Dixon. 'The solicitor conducting the defence and a witness have been murdered, so I'm guessing that Miss Crowther-Smith was also murdered.'

'How did she die?'

'Drowning as far as I know, but I've only spoken to her clerk so far.'

'I'll tell Tony, and we'll sit tight on the inquest.'

'Yes, please, Sir.'

'Here are the statements and medical report,' said Ken, handing an envelope to Dixon.

'Thank you.'

'Keep us informed, Inspector, please,' said Roseland.

'Yes, Sir.'

They arrived back at Express Park a few minutes late for the briefing Dixon had called for 11.30 a.m. DCI Lewis was sitting in meeting room 2 with Dave Harding and Mark Pearce, drumming his fingers on the table.

It took Dixon no more than twenty minutes to bring everyone up to date with the investigation. He was interrupted only once, when Mark's phone rang.

'That was Birmingham, Sir,' said Pearce, dropping his phone back into his jacket pocket. 'They've got Fripp at a hotel in the city centre. He's giving evidence this afternoon at Birmingham County Court, then they'll move him to one out of town.'

'Good.'

Dixon slid the box across the table.

'Copies of the witness statements for everyone, please. Let's focus on the families of the claimants.'

'Including the dead one?' asked Harding.

'Especially the dead one,' replied Dixon. 'Look for brothers and sisters, children. We'll need to have a look at the solicitors acting for them too. You take them, Louise. Lings in Bristol and Holt Burton in Reading. I want to know who's dealing with the cases. And any barristers they've instructed.'

Harding looked at Pearce and raised his eyebrows.

'It's a lot of work,' continued Dixon. 'And we haven't got a lot of time. There's a hearing next week.'

'Next week?'

'This is an e-fit of Fryer's killer, with and without beard.'

'Can you email us the CCTV footage?' asked Harding.

'Yes, Dave. Right, well, we know what we've got to do?'

'Yes, Sir.'

Lewis waited until the others had left the room.

'If we're in a race with the Met, it's one the chief constable would no doubt like us to win, Nick.'

'I'm sure he would,' said Dixon. 'We'll let them handle the Reading end. Three of the claimants and the executors of the other all live down here, so we'll focus on them.'

'We may find a Major Investigation Team is put together when Portishead get wind of it.'

'Bollocks. It's a Bridgwater case, and we're going to deal with it.'

'You're on the MIT anyway,' said Lewis.

'That's not the point.'

'I'll see if I can stall it.'

'Thank you.'

'And keep up the good work.'

◆ ◆ ◆

Dixon spent the next half an hour sitting in the canteen reading the witness statements and post mortem report on the death of Alison Crowther-Smith. Recently divorced, she had left behind two young children, who were now living with their father.

He started with the statement from Sean Toms. He had met Alison at a party several months earlier and had finally persuaded her to go caving with him. She had hired a wetsuit and oversuit from Cave and Rock in Cheddar, and then they had gone down Swildon's Hole, near Priddy, intending to go as far as Sump One and no further. It was a good beginner's cave apparently, and Toms knew it well, having been a member of Wessex Cave Club for several years.

Alison had been hesitant at first, although had taken some comfort from Toms's assurances that the entrance was the narrowest section, and once in the cave she had been fine, apart from a few tears on the wire ladder at the Thirty Foot Pot.

When they arrived at Sump One, Toms had explained that it was a short crawl underwater, seven feet at most, pulling on the white nylon rope, and then it opened out into another cavern. He had even been through the sump and back again to show her how easy it was. She assured him she would have a go at it, so he went back through and pulled on the rope three times, the standard signal. After a short pause, which he took to be her summoning up the courage, the rope began to move as if she was pulling on it.

Her light was visible in the clear water, so he knew she was in the sump, but then the rope began jerking from side to side. She was taking too long. Far too long. That was when he went back in and tried to pull her out. He said that he had hold of her wrists and was pulling as hard as he could but she was stuck fast.

He had to let go and back out for air, and she was dead by the time he was able to get back in.

He tried again and was able to pull her lifeless body through the sump. He tried CPR, but to no avail, so he left her where she was and came back out of the cave to raise the alarm.

The post mortem had been fairly straightforward. Drowning. But none of the witnesses could shed any light on how it happened. No one had ever drowned in Swildon's Hole before, according to the secretary of the Wessex Cave Club, although there had been a near miss a few years before when the rope became tangled around a caver's headlamp. She had been pulled back out of the sump by someone behind her and lost her torch in the process.

Andrew Kemp of the Mendip Cave Rescue team could also not recall a caver drowning in Sump One before. There had been deaths due to hypothermia, natural causes and even rockfall, but never drowning.

Dixon took out his phone and dialled Roger Poland's number, draining his tea while he waited for Poland to answer.

'What's up?'

'I need you to have a look at a PM for me. It was done by somebody over at Weston.'

'When?'

'Last October.'

'Probably been cremated by now,' said Poland. 'Or buried.'

'I just need you to look at the photos to begin with. All I've got is the PM report, and it says drowning, but I need to know whether there are any injuries consistent with her being held under the water. She was in a sump, and if someone came up behind her they could've grabbed hold of her feet.'

'Name?'

'Alison Crowther-Smith. I'll scan the report and email it over to you now.'

'All right. I'll get on to Weston.'

'Thanks, Roger.'

Dixon rang off and went in search of Louise.

'Scan this and email it over to Roger, will you?' he said, handing the PM report to her.

'Will do.'

'I'm off. Give me a ring if anything comes up, but I doubt I'll get a signal.'

'Where are you going?'

'Down a hole.'

Dixon found Cave and Rock in a small industrial unit on the outskirts of Cheddar. The large door was open, and a man was throwing bags into the back of a Land Rover that had been backed into the unit.

Dixon parked outside and walked down the side of the Land Rover. He looked in and noticed that each bag contained a helmet, red caving suit, wellington boots and various pads, presumably for knees and elbows.

'You hire caving kit?' asked Dixon.

'Where are you going?' The man was tall, with a closely cropped beard. He was wearing jeans and a blue fleece jacket with a Cave and Rock logo on it.

'Swildon's Hole.'

'It's closed. The landowner closed it after the accident. It may reopen in the spring.'

'What's your name?' asked Dixon.

'Andy Kemp.'

'Cave rescue?'

'Yes. Who wants to know?'

Dixon passed him his warrant card.

'Oh,' said Kemp, handing the warrant card back. 'How can I help?'

'You referred to an accident?'

'Yes. A woman drowned in Sump One last October. Took us hours to get her out. It was nearly midnight by the time we finished.'

'What makes you think it was an accident?'

'What else could it be?'

Dixon raised his eyebrows.

'You're joking?' asked Kemp.

'No,' replied Dixon. 'Now, I need to go down there, so can you hire me the kit?'

'You'd never find it. And if you did, you'd never find your way out again.'

'I need a guide then.'

'You want to go now?'

Dixon nodded.

Kemp looked at his watch and sighed. 'I'll take you.'

'Thanks.'

'How tall are you?'

'Five eleven.'

'Didn't you used to climb with Jake?' asked Kemp, looking Dixon up and down.

'A long time ago.'

'I thought I recognised you.'

Dixon followed Kemp up to the Wessex Cave Club hut on top of the Mendips, just beyond Priddy.

The hut itself looked more like an old farmhouse that had been converted, but either way, rendered in grey pebble dash, it made a dark and foreboding place. It didn't help that it was an overcast and freezing cold February day.

Kemp walked over to a scaffolding tower with a wire ladder hanging from it.

'Climb it like so,' he said, 'hands round the back of the ladder. And keep your weight over your feet.'

Dixon nodded. He felt sick, but he wasn't going to admit that to anyone, let alone Kemp.

'First things first. We'd better write our names on the board.'

Kemp unlocked the front door and peered along the corridor to the back of the hut.

'Quiet, isn't it?' said Dixon.

'It's busier in the spring and summer.'

The lounge smelled damp. A huge open fire, stone cold, with the embers spilling out on to the hearth; two leather sofas held together by duct tape; caving magazines lying everywhere. It reminded Dixon of a climbing club hut in winter.

Kemp picked a piece of chalk off the mantelpiece and started writing on the blackboard above the fireplace.

Thursday 20 Feb Swildon's One Kemp +1 2.30 pm

'We'd better get changed.'

The changing rooms were filthy, but then most cavers left clean and arrived back covered in mud, so that was to be expected. Next to the showers were two drying rooms, full of caving equipment.

'They just leave it here?'

'The locals do. They'll be back at the weekend.'

'Are you sure I don't need a wetsuit?' asked Dixon. He was sitting on the bench pulling a fleece undersuit on over his ankles.

'No, you'll be fine as long as you keep moving. And the ground's freezing up here, so there shouldn't be too much water down there.'

'Won't it be cold?'

'Not too bad. The temperature only fluctuates a degree or so between summer and winter.'

'You mean it's bloody cold all the time?'

'Freezing,' replied Kemp, grinning. 'Are you going through the sump?'

'I'll let you know when I get there,' replied Dixon, pulling the elasticated ankle bands of the oversuit over his feet. 'These are tight.'

'Got a quid?'

'Are there lockers?'

'No. It's for access. We bung it in the tin here for the landowner.'

Dixon sighed. Getting cold, wet and miserable was one thing, but paying for the privilege?

There was a large sign on the wall above the tin. "Swildon's Hole closed until further notice by order of the landowner."

'It's all right,' said Kemp. 'We're on official business.'

'What's in these sheds?' asked Dixon as they walked out towards the stile at the bottom of the garden.

'That one's a store, and that one's an air compressor.'

'For the cave divers I suppose.'

'We've got a few,' replied Kemp, slinging an orange rucksack over his shoulder. 'You can go as far as Sump Twelve these days, but you need oxygen tanks to do it. The aim is to connect with Wookey Hole one day.'

They walked out across the fields, over three drystone walls and then along a track that followed the edge of a wood.

'There it is,' said Kemp.

Dixon looked down at the entrance to Swildon's Hole. A small blockhouse built of grey stone that looked more like an outside toilet cubicle stood in the bottom of a hollow, with a large tree stump next to it and a stream disappearing into the ground under it. For once Dixon was grateful for the cold weather, which had reduced the stream to a trickle under a layer of ice.

'The cave follows the stream I suppose,' said Dixon.

'That's it,' replied Kemp. 'They put some dye in it once and it came out at Wookey. That's how we know the systems connect.'

They scrambled down the rough track to the blockhouse and went inside, further progress blocked by a triangular drain cover set into a concrete floor.

'It's not locked?'

'No point. We've all got keys anyway, but if he says it's closed, it's closed.'

'Is it too late to change my mind?' asked Dixon.

'Yes.'

Kemp lifted the cover clear and Dixon peered into the hole – a narrow gap down between the dark limestone rocks, just enough to squeeze through. The sound of running water echoed all around him.

'Plenty of people turn back at this point,' said Kemp, frowning at Dixon.

'I'll be fine.'

'Down you go then.'

Dixon sat with his feet dangling in the hole and then lowered himself down until he was standing on the rock below, his head now the only part of him above ground.

'What's that smell?'

'Metallic, isn't it?' replied Kemp. 'It's all the minerals.'

Dixon slid his legs forward until he was sitting on the rock and shone his torch into the darkness. A narrow gap under a huge block lay in front of him, his first real test.

'We'll go straight on instead of through the Zig-Zags,' said Kemp.

'We go under this boulder?' Trying not to sound nervous.

'Yes. It shouldn't fall on you.'

Dixon could picture the grin on Kemp's face.

He slid on his back, his face turned away from the rock above him, until his feet were flailing in the clear. Then he felt for the rock below with his heels, finding a foothold just before he slid off the rock. He was able to lower himself into a sitting position and look up at the boulder, one corner perched on a ledge no more than a few inches wide.

'One day that's going to go,' he muttered.

'Yeah, but the chances of you being under it when it does are pretty bloody small.'

Everything in climbing had been a risk – assessed, calculated and then taken. It was like gambling. Check the odds and then go for it. Some people, like Jake, had taken bigger risks than others. And the same applied to caving.

Kemp was right. The chances of Dixon being under that rock when it collapsed were small, but maybe somebody one day would take the same gamble and lose.

Dixon crawled clear of the boulder, grateful for the knee pads, and waited for Kemp to appear.

'Which way now?'

'Follow me.'

The rock fell away beneath them, but the cave roof was only two foot above. Dixon watched Kemp slide down on his back with his hands and feet braced against the rock above. Anything to stop himself sliding to the bottom – knees and elbows even. Dixon winced. Style marks had been all important in climbing, but clearly played no part in caving. Jake would be turning in his grave.

Once at the bottom of the slab, Kemp stopped and waited for him.

'Switch off your light.'

'What for?'

'Just try it.'

They both switched off the lamps on their helmets.

'Absolute darkness it's called,' said Kemp. He was sitting no more than a few feet away, but Dixon couldn't see him. At all.

'I can't even see my hand.'

'Touch your nose,' said Kemp.

'I am.'

'There's no external light source at all, so the darkness is total.'

'What happens if we run out of batteries?'

'That's why we carry spares,' replied Kemp.

Dixon felt the breast pocket of his undersuit and breathed a sigh of relief. Zipped up inside were two sets of spare batteries and a bar of chocolate.

'C'mon, let's get moving,' said Kemp, switching on his lamp. 'And try to keep up.'

Dixon followed Kemp's light along the stream bed, a gravel cleft in the rocks towering over them on either side.

'Usually this is a raging torrent,' said Kemp. 'You're getting off lightly.'

'Thanks.'

After twenty minutes of crawling, wriggling, ducking and banging his head, Dixon caught up with Kemp when he stopped at the end of a narrow passage.

'What's up?'

'The Thirty Foot Pot,' said Kemp, pulling a wire ladder out of his tackle sack. He clipped one end into the bolt on the rock wall to his right and then let it uncoil over the edge.

'Did it reach the bottom?' asked Dixon.

'It's a thirty foot ladder. Don't panic.'

Kemp took a rope out of his tackle sack and handed one end to Dixon, which he clipped on to his caving belt.

'Right, down you go, and remember: hands behind the ladder.'

Dixon made short work of it, even taking the time on the way down to admire the rock formations behind the waterfall. He looked up at the side walls, crystals glinting in the light from his lamp, searching for foot and handholds, his old climber's instinct getting the better of him.

Kemp abseiled down the rope, leaving it in situ with the ladder, and five minutes later they were moving again, Dixon struggling to keep up with him. Not that he would have let on.

They arrived at a double waterfall, each no more than a four foot drop into a pool beneath, although very little water was cascading over the edge.

'The Double Pots,' said Kemp. He grinned at Dixon and then jumped in, landing in water up to his waist. Then he waded across the pool and jumped over the next waterfall. Dixon listened for the splash and heard no scream after it, so Kemp must have landed safely.

The water was cold, Dixon knew that, and the prospect of jumping into it filled him with dread. He looked at the side walls, spotting a narrow ledge no more than a few inches wide and several handholds on the wall above. Perfect.

He climbed over the edge and around the side wall, doing the same at the next waterfall and arriving on the rocks the far side bone dry.

'You won't get past the Washing Machine,' said Kemp, grinning. Then he turned and set off along the passage again.

'This bit's the Inclined Rift.'

It reminded Dixon of a narrow alleyway between two tall buildings, no more than two feet wide, and then tipped at an angle of forty-five degrees or so. He watched Kemp wriggling down it, bracing himself against the rocks on either side.

Next came the Washing Machine, and Kemp had been right: Dixon would not get past it. He tried but fell back into the water, the cold taking his breath away. Nothing for it but to keep moving.

They stopped for a short break at Tratman's Temple, Kemp insisting that Dixon admire the vast cavern, and it was worth it. Huge waterfalls of cascading crystals glistening in the lights of their headlamps, hundreds of stalactites and stalagmites too, although Dixon couldn't remember which was which. And what looked like small waves of red rock frozen as they broke over the rock walls.

'We call that flowstone,' said Kemp. 'It's mineral deposits left behind by the water running down the walls.'

'How much further is it?'

'Ten or fifteen minutes. We're making good time.'

The passageway ended in a small boulder strewn cavern, the only clue to the way ahead a white nylon rope that disappeared into the water under the back wall.

Dixon was sitting on a boulder, eating his chocolate. He was shaking, but that was probably a combination of cold and fear. Either way he wasn't taking any chances with his blood sugar.

'So, this is where it happened?'

'This is it. We found her body on the other side though.'

'How far is it?'

'Seven feet.'

'And what's on the other side?'

'Another cavern, with a small beach believe it or not.' Kemp was sitting in the water, feeling along the roof of the sump with his hand. 'There's nothing she could have snagged her suit on. It's weird.'

'It's my belief someone came up behind her and held her feet,' said Dixon.

'So, you do think she was murdered?'

'That's why I'm here.'

'D'you want me to go through?'

'Yes, please.'

He watched Kemp lie down in the water, duck down and begin kicking with his feet. The water was churned up by all the kicking and splashing, and the noise echoed around the chamber.

Dixon started counting.

It took eleven seconds from the time his head went under the water until his feet disappeared. More than enough time for someone hiding in the rocks behind her to switch on their lamp, jump out and grab hold of Alison Crowther-Smith's feet. And she no doubt took longer than Kemp to scrabble her way into the sump.

Dixon was standing on a boulder at the back of the cave when Kemp emerged from the sump, panting hard.

'Fuck, it's cold.'

'There's a place here he could've hidden,' said Dixon, shining his lamp behind a large rock, the gravel on the floor of the cave beneath it revealing no telltale footprint.

'Are you going through?' asked Kemp.

'I've seen enough, thanks.'

It was pitch dark by the time Dixon stuck his head out into the fresh night air. He pulled back the elasticated wristband of his oversuit and looked at his watch: 7.30 p.m.

They trudged back across the fields, snow falling in the lights of their headlamps, and arrived at the hut to find a light on upstairs.

'What's that?' asked Dixon.

'It's a bunkhouse,' replied Kemp. 'Five pounds a night for visitors; three fifty for club members. We've got reciprocal rights at other clubs too. It's not bad.'

Dixon nodded. It reminded him of the summers he'd spent climbing with Jake, moving from one bunkhouse to the next.

Kemp hosed himself down using the tap on the side of the shed.

'You'll need another quid for a hot shower,' he said.

'I'll go straight home I think. Have a hot bath.'

'So, what happens now?'

'That'll be for the coroner to decide,' replied Dixon, dodging the question.

He changed clothes and then threw the bag of wet caving equipment into the back of Kemp's Land Rover.

'I'd better scrub our names off the board, or I'll be getting a call-out later I expect,' said Kemp.

'One last thing,' said Dixon. 'How many ways are there in and out of that place?'

'Two. The way we went, and there's another entrance on the village green at Priddy, but you really need to know what you're doing to go that way.'

Chapter Seventeen

The snow turned to sleet and then to rain as Dixon drove down through Cheddar Gorge, the heater in his Land Rover on full blast. In different circumstances he may have enjoyed his first caving trip, but he doubted there would be another, and certainly not if the stream was a raging torrent.

He allowed his mind to wander back down Swildon's Hole, although that made the metallic smell in his nose seem stronger if anything. Dazzling cascades of crystals and waves of flowstone left behind by water running down the walls for millions of years. It had been a sight to see. And Dixon had stayed dry, apart from one dunking in the Washing Machine, and warm for most of the time, making for an interesting and enjoyable experience.

Would he do it again? Maybe one day.

And the sump? No bloody fear.

He might pop down there on his own one day, or take Jane. He smiled. Idiot. What were the chances of him finding Sump One again? And getting back out? Kemp had said it was a maze of passages and caverns. No, you needed to know what you were doing and where you were going down there.

Dixon stamped on the brakes and screeched to a halt in the middle of the mini-roundabout at the bottom of Cheddar. He reached into his jacket pocket and took out the still from the CCTV footage, looking down on to the killer standing behind Fryer on the platform at Wimbledon station, and squinted at the rucksack in the weak glow from the interior light of his Land Rover. It was yellow and shiny, waterproof no doubt, with a black flap and straps and a handle on the side. Not your ordinary rucksack.

And just like Kemp's caving tackle sack.

He took his phone out of his pocket and checked for a data signal. 3G. That would do.

He opened Google, typed in 'caving sack' and hit 'Enter'. Then he selected 'Images'. And there it was. He clicked on the link below the image, which took him to caving-gear.co.uk, and seconds later he was looking at a Petzl thirty litre Portage Tackle Sack, perfect for approaches and all caving use apparently.

Mark Pearce answered his phone at the second ring.

'Yes, Sir.'

'Where are you?'

'Still at the nick.'

'What about Louise?'

'She's here.'

'I want you to drop everything and focus on caving, Mark,' said Dixon. 'The rucksack he was carrying when he killed Fryer is a specialist caving tackle sack. A Petzl. You can see it on the CCTV footage. And remember he got down to Sump One and back out again on his own, so he knows Swildon's Hole like the back of his hand.'

'Makes sense.'

'It does.'

'What do we do then?'

'We're looking at anyone connected with the five claimants, aren't we? So go through their social media profiles again. Facebook and Twitter, and look for any caving pictures. All right?'

'Yes, Sir.'

'Instagram too,' continued Dixon. 'Any reference to caving even. And get Louise to help you.'

'OK.'

'Get on to the caving clubs as well. We'll need a list of members from them. And a list of anyone Cave and Rock hired kit out to last October.'

'Which caving clubs?'

'All of them.'

'Anything else?'

'Go back through the service records and see if any of the marines went caving. I bet they had a caving club.'

'They're a bit past it now.'

'But their children and grandchildren aren't.'

'No, Sir.'

'He's a bloody caver,' muttered Dixon as he slid his phone into his pocket.

'How'd you get on?'

'I might have enjoyed it,' replied Dixon. 'If I hadn't been investigating a murder.'

'I can't imagine anything worse,' said Jane, shuddering. 'Makes my skin crawl just thinking about it.'

'I can see the attraction.'

'Would you go again?'

'In the middle of a drought perhaps.' Dixon was stripping off in the kitchen, leaving his clothes in a pile in front of the washing machine.

'Maybe leave it till the summer next time,' said Jane.

'Yes. It depends on the rain though. It doesn't make a lot of difference to the temperature. That stays pretty much the same whatever's going on above ground.'

'Freezing cold I suppose.'

'Without the right kit you wouldn't last long.'

'And was she murdered?'

'She could've been,' replied Dixon, standing in the kitchen doorway, dressed in his underpants. 'He'd need to have been an experienced caver, that's for sure, which gives us a new line of enquiry. But unless we catch him and he confesses, we'll never really know.'

'You eaten?'

'Not yet. I'll have a quick shower, then we'll nip over to the pub?'

'Hurry up then,' said Jane.

Dixon leaned over the sofa, put his arms round Jane and kissed her on the cheek.

'What was the matter this morning?' he asked. 'When you came to collect us from the station.'

'I just need to toughen up a bit. I'll get used to it.'

'Safeguarding children?'

'It's not easy,' replied Jane, shaking her head. 'Now, go and have that shower. You stink.'

Monty was barking when Dixon stepped out of the shower, so he wrapped a towel around his waist and went downstairs to find Jane and Roger Poland in the kitchen, unpacking various silver trays from a carrier bag.

'I got you a biriani. I hope that's all right,' said Poland.

'Yes, thank you.'

'Well, don't just stand there dripping water all over the place.'

It took Dixon less than five minutes to get dressed.

'I put yours in the oven,' said Jane as he came running down the stairs.

'This is a pleasant surprise, Roger,' said Dixon.

'Call it a working supper.'

'Eh?'

'I've looked at the PM on the caver, Alison Crowther-whatsit.'

'And?'

'She was wearing a wetsuit and boots, with a caving suit over the top. That's got tight elasticated ankle bands.'

'I could hardly get mine on over my feet, and they've left red marks around my ankles.'

'Quite.'

'Still, it stops the water getting in,' continued Dixon, tearing off a piece of naan bread.

'And makes finding any other marks almost impossible,' said Poland.

'Oh, so does that mean . . . ?'

'I said almost.' Poland grinned. 'You'd never see them if you weren't looking for them, the faintest impressions in amongst the other bruising.'

'Finger marks?' asked Jane.

'Possibly. That's the best I can say really. But they're definitely different from the others, and on both legs, just above the ankles. Exactly where the elastic would've been.'

'Makes sense,' said Dixon through a mouthful of vegetable curry.

'Jane said you'd been down there.'

'It's a small cavern, about the size of a tennis court, smaller perhaps. Boulders everywhere and then a pool in the far corner. That's the entrance to the sump. There's a rope; you lie down in the water, pull on it, duck down and through you go.'

'Did you go through?' asked Jane.

'Too bloody cold for that.'

'Wimp.'

'So, you hide amongst the boulders, jump out when she ducks down and grab her ankles,' said Poland.

'That's about it,' replied Dixon. 'Or clamp them to the roof of the sump. No one would ever see you hiding, particularly if you were wearing a black wetsuit.'

'What about her partner?' asked Jane.

'He'd already gone through, and with her in the sump there was no way for him to get back.'

'D'you go through first if you're leading a novice?' asked Poland.

'I suppose so. He did anyway.'

'Well, there are faint marks, although the best I can say is that they're consistent—'

'But she would've been banging her ankles and lower legs for a couple of hours already by the time she reached the sump,' interrupted Dixon. 'Tripping and stumbling over rocks in the dark, would she not, Doctor?'

'Yes.'

'Climbing down wire ladders, jumping over waterfalls, wriggling through narrow gaps, over ledges and boulders.'

'Yes.'

'And the marks are consistent with that, are they not?'

'Well, there's a pattern to them. It's faint, but consistent with fingertips.'

'But equally consistent with a trip here, a stumble there regularly over several hours.'

'Possibly.'

'Case dismissed.'

'You should've been a bloody barrister,' muttered Poland, through a mouthful of mushroom bahjee.

'Let's run through the five claimants,' said Dixon the next morning. He was sitting in meeting room 2 with Dave Harding, Mark Pearce and Louise Willmott.

'The dead one is Grant Foster,' replied Pearce. 'Died in August. Mesothelioma. His claim's marked "dead" but stays with the others because they're linked. They're fast-tracked as "living claims".'

'Where did he die?'

'Bristol Royal Infirmary, but he'd been in Weston until a week or so before the end. He lived in Weston.'

'Solicitors?'

'Lings.'

'What about his executors?'

'That's his wife and daughter.'

'Who's next?'

'Richard Hagley,' replied Pearce. 'He's in Bristol with days to go. Mesothelioma.'

'Family?'

'He's a widower. One son in Australia, but the other's local. No grandchildren.'

'Where does the son live?'

'Yatton. He goes in to see his father every day, apparently.'

'Lings?'

'Yes.'

'Lawrence Hampton is next on the list, Sir,' said Louise. 'He's the one in Reading, and the Met are going to see him today and Holt Burton on Monday.'

'Family?'

'A wife and four children. The Met are going to speak to them too.'

'And what's his prognosis?'

'Two years, but that was given a year ago. He's housebound now, on oxygen.'

'Then we've got Harry Jones,' said Harding. 'Divorced and lives in Bristol. One son, in Abingdon, and one grandson.'

'And the last one is Raymond Absolon,' said Pearce. 'Lives in Bath. Divorced and recently married again.'

'Children?'

'Two,' replied Pearce, looking down at his notepad.

'Any reference to caving?' asked Dixon.

'Nothing yet, Sir. We're waiting for the membership lists from the clubs though.'

'Well, keep an eye out for it,' said Dixon. 'Whoever killed Alison Crowther-Smith must have been an experienced caver.'

'If she was murdered.'

'Quite.' Dixon rolled his eyes. 'What about Maynard?'

'He was a member of Naval Party 8901,' replied Louise. 'They were the small detachment on the Falklands when the Argentinians invaded. They were flown home after the invasion and then went back as part of 42 Commando.'

'Did he go back with them?' asked Dixon.

'No, Sir. He was wounded, medically discharged six months later and then set up Weymouth Properties with his wife.'

'But he was 42 Commando and would've known Kandes.'

'Yes, Sir.'

Dixon nodded.

'What about the solicitors?'

'Lings in Bristol. They're behind the Hippodrome. Brett Greenwood is the solicitor dealing with the case, and the partner in charge of the department is Fiona Hull. Their photos are on the firm's website, with short bios. We're leaving Holt Burton to the Met, aren't we?'

'Yes.'

'Anyway, it's Michael Adcock there. Again, his photo's on the Holt Burton website.'

'Anyone get anywhere with the Royal Engineers?' asked Dixon.

'I've spoken to them on the phone,' replied Pearce. 'There were only the two of them because the rest were clearing minefields. That's why Fletcher got the marines to do the donkey work. They can't really add anything to the statements they gave to the MoD in the civil claim though.'

Dixon nodded.

'What about F Company?'

'The Order of Battle lists a hundred and eight men, and we've got a complete set of service records now,' replied Harding. 'Kandes was in 3 Troop, so I've separated their service records out for you to have a look at.'

'Anything leap out at you?'

'Not really.'

Chapter Eighteen

'Where are we going?' asked Louise. She was sitting in the passenger seat of Dixon's Land Rover, speeding north on the M5.

'Drop Monty off at home, then Bristol. It seems to me that we need to speak to Richard Hagley before it's too late.'

Dixon parked in the multistorey car park and they walked down the hill to the Bristol Royal Infirmary, dodging the puddles on the pavement. Once inside they took the lift up to the third floor and found Richard Hagley in a private room opposite the nurses' station.

Dixon peered in through the small window in the door. Hagley's eyes were closed and he had an oxygen mask over his mouth. A man, aged thirty or so, was sitting in the armchair beside his bed. His son probably.

'Can I help you?'

Dixon turned to face the nurse in the dark blue uniform behind him. 'Matron' it said on her badge.

'I need to have a word with Mr Hagley,' he replied, taking his warrant card out of his pocket.

'He's not really in a fit state to—'

'It's a murder investigation. And we won't be long.'

'He's on morphine.' The matron hesitated and then shrugged her shoulders. 'Give me a minute.'

Dixon watched her through the window, leaning over and speaking directly into Hagley's ear. The younger man in the armchair was craning his neck to hear what was being said. Then he jumped up.

'For fuck's sake, I've already told them to leave him alone.'

Hagley nodded his head on the pillow and pointed at the door.

'His son says—'

'I'm not interested in what his son says,' interrupted Dixon as the matron closed the door behind her. 'I'm interested in what Mr Hagley says.'

'He'll see you. But do bear in mind he's very short of breath and will find it difficult to speak for any length of time.'

'I will.'

Dixon opened the door and walked in.

'I've already told you lot to fuck off,' said the younger man.

'And you are?'

'Philip Hagley. His son.'

'And who did you speak to?' asked Dixon.

'The Metropolitan Police. Someone rang this morning.'

'We're from the Avon and Somerset force, Sir,' said Dixon matter of fact. 'And you can rest assured that we wouldn't be troubling a man in your father's condition unless it was absolutely necessary.'

Philip Hagley slumped back into his chair.

'Is there somewhere you could wait, Sir?' asked Dixon. 'The canteen perhaps.'

'I'd rather stay.'

'Forgive me. I framed it as a question, but I do need to speak to your father alone.'

Philip Hagley sighed loudly and left the room.

Dixon leaned over Richard Hagley, lying in his hospital bed.

'Mr Hagley, can you hear me?'

Hagley nodded. Dixon showed him his warrant card and he nodded again.

'I'm investigating the death of Alan Fletcher, Mr Hagley.'

Hagley reached up slowly and slid the oxygen mask to one side.

'Did you say death?'

'Yes.'

Dixon watched the smile turn into a grin, then a laugh, all of it lost in the bout of coughing that followed. He waited.

'I know it was Captain Fletcher who gave you the order to dismantle the radar cabins,' said Dixon.

'It wasn't an order,' said Hagley, gasping. 'It was a . . . a fucking death sentence.' He slid the oxygen mask back across his nose and mouth, breathing deeply.

'What happened when Adrian Kandes ran?'

Hagley closed his eyes, still panting into the mask, the condensation appearing and then disappearing inside with each shallow breath. Then he pulled the mask away from his mouth to speak.

'You know about that?'

'We do.'

'Me and the lads went after him.'

'Who?'

Dixon glanced over at Louise. She was sitting in the armchair taking notes.

'Ray, Grant, Harry and me.'

'That's four. I was told there were five of you.'

'And Loz.'

'Lawrence Hampton?'

'Yes.'

'Raymond Absolon, Grant Foster, Harry Jones and you?'

Hagley nodded.

'And who hit Fletcher?'

Hagley let the mask snap back over his nose and mouth, the elastic round the back of his head holding it in place. Dixon noticed the grin, before it was obscured by more condensation. He watched Hagley's right hand moving slowly until he was pointing at the centre of his own chest with his index finger.

'You hit him?'

Hagley nodded, then moved the mask again. 'And what're you going to do about it now, eh?' He grinned, revealing yellow broken teeth.

Dixon shook his head.

'What did he think he was going to do, shoot Adrian?' continued Hagley. 'The twat.'

'And the next day?' asked Dixon.

'We all swore Adrian was there all the time . . .' More coughing. 'And it was his word against ours.'

'Tell me what happened when you ran into him again outside Port Stanley.'

'It's all in my statement. It was his moment of . . .' Hagley's voice tailed off and he retreated behind the oxygen mask again.

'So, who killed Captain Fletcher?'

Hagley shook his head on the pillow.

'And now you're suing the marines?' asked Dixon.

'We're suing the MOD. And it's not about the money, it's about justice.' Hagley allowed the oxygen mask to cover his mouth before he grinned again. 'You'll never catch him,' he spluttered.

'Your son?'

'He knows nothing.'

'Who then?'

Hagley tilted his head back and closed his eyes.

'How many more people have to die, Richard?' asked Dixon. 'For your justice.'

Hagley's right hand moved slowly, his index finger reaching for the red alarm button in the clip on his bedside table.

'How many?'

Coughing and spluttering broke the silence.

'Do the right thing, Richard, before it's too late.'

Dixon waited.

'These are innocent people, with families, children. Just doing their jobs. Think about it, Richard.'

No response.

'Alison Crowther-Smith was thirty-six years old, with two young children. You think about that.'

'She stopped us getting our money.' More coughing. 'Now it's too late.'

'She was just doing her job, Richard.'

Hagley's voice was muffled behind the oxygen mask, but Dixon recognised his reply all the same.

'Fuck you.'

'So, it was about the money, until you realised you wouldn't live long enough to see it. Is that it?'

'What else is there?'

Hagley finally reached the alarm button.

'I fought for my country,' he gasped, falling back into his pillow. 'Fuck all of you.'

'C'mon, Louise, let's leave him to it,' said Dixon, standing up.

Philip Hagley was waiting for them outside the private room.

'What the hell was all that about?'

'We're investigating a murder, Mr Hagley, and Detective Constable Willmott here has a few questions to ask you. I suggest using the day room. It was empty when we came in.'

'Follow me, Sir,' said Louise.

Dixon turned and watched through the small pane of glass as two nurses attended to Richard Hagley.

Hagley knew the who and the why; he had made that clear enough. But he would be dead within forty-eight hours. And for what? He'd served his country and stood by his friends, another victim of a freak set of circumstances that started when an otherwise exemplary marine fled the battlefield. A set of circumstances in which everyone had thought they were doing the right thing and yet no one had escaped unscathed. And now they were all either dead or dying. And more innocent people besides.

An old soldier would no doubt say that such were the fortunes of war.

'He knows. He bloody knows who's doing it, and he's going to take it to his grave,' said Louise, shaking her head.

'Well, we can hardly arrest him in his condition, can we?'

They were sitting in Dixon's Land Rover in the car park at Brent Knoll motorway services.

'Let's check his phone. Mobile and the one by his bed,' he said.

'Yes, Sir.'

'Focus on what he did tell us,' muttered Dixon, ripping open a sandwich carton, 'instead of what he didn't.'

'Like what?'

'Well, first off, we're in a race with the Met,' replied Dixon through a mouthful of egg and cress sandwich.

'They were supposed to leave Hagley to us,' said Louise.

'They were. Still, the son saved us the job of telling them where to go.'

'What else?'

'He knows who it is, so it's someone he knows, someone connected to him in some way. To all of them possibly.'

'Not the son though,' replied Louise. 'He was in Tenerife when Alison Crowther-Smith was murdered and has an alibi for Fletcher's too. It's only his girlfriend, but—'

'Check it.'

'I will.'

Dixon screwed up the sandwich carton and dropped it into the carrier bag in the footwell.

'Disgusting.'

'Anything else?' asked Louise.

'That it's about the money,' replied Dixon.

'The damages?'

'It must be. If it was just about Kandes, then killing Fletcher would've been enough, wouldn't it?'

'I suppose.'

'The rest are lawyers defending their claims, denying liability,' said Dixon. He was staring in his rearview mirror, watching a dog running about on the grass area behind the car park.

'So, the lawyers are being killed because they're defending the claims?' asked Louise.

'Let's say your father was dying of cancer and you knew it was caused by someone else,' continued Dixon. 'It was their fault. But he's being denied compensation by some smart lawyer dragging the case out until after your father died. Would you be angry?'

'Yes.'

'Enough to kill?'

'No.'

'And there's a very good reason for that.'

'What?'

'You're not a psychopath,' said Dixon, starting the diesel engine.

'DCI Lewis was looking for you, Sir,' said Pearce as Dixon walked past his workstation.

'Where's he gone?'

'No idea.'

'Louise, see if you can fix us up with Foster's executors tomorrow, and Absolon too if you can. Not too early.' Dixon was leaning against a filing cabinet, waiting for the kettle to boil.

'Yes, Sir.'

'Where's Dave?'

'He had to go,' replied Pearce.

'Find anything?'

'We're putting together family trees with profiles. Hagley was easy. There's just him and his two sons – Philip, and Jim in Australia,' replied Pearce. 'I spoke to Jim on the phone and he's coming over on Monday apparently.'

'He'll be too late,' muttered Dixon.

'That bad, is it?'

'How did you know it was Jim you were speaking to?'

'Er, he's over for two weeks and he gave me his mobile number. He sounded legit.'

Dixon nodded.

'Anything else?'

'Jones's son's got previous. GBH and affray. A while ago now though. And Absolon's stepson is a known drug dealer. That's it really.'

'Any of them cavers?'

'No, Sir. Not that we can find anyway.'

Dixon spent the next half an hour glancing through the service records of 3 Troop. Some ended on 11 June 1982 – those who had been killed in action on Mount Harriet. There were seven of them, including Kandes. He had joined the Royal Marines at the age of eighteen and risen to the rank of sergeant after almost twenty years unblemished service, and he had only months left of his twenty when he died.

His reports were always good, if not spectacular, describing him as a hardworking, committed marine. Dixon shook his head. Why then had he broken on the night of the battle?

Dixon switched on a computer and then fished the medical reports from the filing cabinets. There were five sets, one for each claimant, and they included psychiatric as well as medical, occupational therapists and employment consultants' reports. The investigation of each had been thorough and had not been challenged by the defence, which explained why the amount of the damages in each case had been agreed.

Dixon ignored the medical reports from the consultant physicians setting out the previous medical history and diagnosis in each case and instead turned to the psychiatric reports. These documented the psychological effect on the claimants and their concern for those left behind. Hagley hadn't mentioned his sons once, or at least Dixon could find no reference to them in the report. Absolon, on the other hand, was very concerned, because his second wife did not get on with his children and he knew there would be arguments after he died. About money of course.

Hampton had painted a picture of a happy marriage being cut short, and his bitterness was obvious, although at two years, his life expectancy was longer. Jones was divorced and talked about his son, who was an alcoholic. There would be no one to look after him when

Jones died, which caused him great distress. Grant Foster had died before a psychiatric report had been prepared.

The employment reports set out their working histories since leaving the marines and, for those below retirement age – all except Absolon – gave a forecast used in their future loss of earnings claims.

All of their previous employers were listed, matching the statements from each confirming that they would not have come into contact with asbestos.

'We're seeing Mrs Foster in Weston at ten and then Raymond Absolon in Bath at two. All right?' asked Louise.

'Meet me at my place at nine then,' said Dixon.

'Will do.'

He put the file of medical reports back in the filing cabinet and took out the pleadings in the civil claim. Then he turned to Louise.

'Right, I'm off. See you in the morning.'

The sound of waves breaking greeted him as he climbed on to the top of the dunes and looked down at the beach. He was surprised to see the tide still thirty yards or so away and the waves small, although there was very little wind and the sound was carrying more than usual. Still, it left some beach for a decent walk, and Monty was already making the most of it.

Jane had been two thirds of the way through a bottle of wine when Dixon arrived home, and the idea of getting cold, and possibly wet too, had not appealed to her. Monty, on the other hand, had needed no persuading.

Dixon had still not managed to get the metallic smell out of his nostrils from his caving trip the day before, and a good blast of sea air might just be enough to get rid of it. And the cobwebs.

He checked his watch. He had an hour or so of daylight left and set off towards Brean Down, although there was no chance of getting there and back before dark.

Hagley's admission that he knew the killer had taken Dixon by surprise. Or had it? Perhaps not. After all, what had Hagley got to lose? But it had given Dixon a direction, a focus.

Another question was bugging him, and no amount of walking on the beach was going to help him with this one. Alison Crowther-Smith had been killed by an experienced caver, drowned in Sump One down Swildon's Hole. He was as sure of that as he could be with no real evidence. But how the hell did her killer know she'd be down there?

Chapter Nineteen

Jane was fast asleep by the time Dixon got home just after midnight, the empty bottle of Pinot Grigio on the floor by the sofa explaining why she didn't wake up when Monty ran down the stairs, barking.

Dixon had gone back to Express Park, spending the evening going through the service records of F Company, 42 Commando, looking for any reference to caving and finding none. But standing at the end of the bed, looking down at Jane asleep, he wondered whether he should have spent the evening at home. Jane understood 'the job'; of course she did. She was struggling all the same, and Dixon needed to be there for her. Struggling to adjust to one of the most difficult jobs demanded of a police officer, and struggling to adjust to the reality that her mother – her birth mother – was out there somewhere. And all the questions and uncertainty that went with that.

He couldn't do much about the job, but he could do something about her mother. Perhaps he should.

He stifled a yawn before tiptoeing out of the room. Then he went downstairs and cracked open a can of beer. Nothing for it but to go through the pleadings. Again.

The Statements of Claim, Defence, Request for Further Information, and Reply to Request for Further Information. Legal jousting, reciting the same allegations made in thousands of cases, followed by the same denials, with the added extra of the Crown Proceedings Act thrown in for good measure. Then came the case management conference, when Alison Crowther-Smith had shown cause why the MoD should be allowed to defend the claims. The standard interim payment in 'Living Mesothelioma Claims' had also been dismissed at the same hearing. Fifty thousand pounds. Dixon nodded. He could understand the bitterness.

The case was then listed for a trial on the preliminary issue within sixteen weeks, with a time estimate of two days.

It was enough to put anyone to sleep.

'What time is it?' asked Dixon, yawning.

'Eight,' replied Jane. She was standing in front of Dixon with a mug of coffee in each hand. 'You should've come to bed.'

'You all right?'

'Fine.'

'Only—'

'I'm fine. Really. How're you getting on?'

'Good I think. Making progress anyway. We've got the caving thing to work on. He's wearing a caving sack when he kills Fryer.'

'Pushes him under the train?'

'Yes.' Dixon took his jacket off the back of the sofa and handed Jane the photograph. 'From the CCTV.'

'You told the Met?'

'Not yet.'

'Why not?'

'I didn't think,' replied Dixon, grinning.

Jane shook her head.

'What about you?' asked Dixon.

'I'm doing all right. It's difficult to . . . You just wanna knock the door down and beat their brains in, but you can't. It's really not easy.'

'Can you apply for a transfer?'

'That's admitting defeat, isn't it?'

Dixon shrugged his shoulders.

'I guess I'm just not cut out for it,' continued Jane. 'But I can't apply for a transfer.'

'What about your mother?'

'I haven't done anything about that. I want to, but I can't face it at the moment.'

'It might help.'

'Yeah, but it might not.'

'What are you up to today?'

'I'll go and see my folks if you're busy.'

'Louise'll be here in a minute, I'm afraid. Weston then Bristol again.'

'What's the address?' asked Dixon, driving along Marine Parade, Weston-super-Mare. He was turning in his seat to get a look at the north side of Brean Down, where he had been plucked from the sea by the Burnham lifeboat only a few short weeks before. He winced when he remembered the taste of the seawater, which had repeated on him for days afterwards, until he had seen it off once and for all with a visit to the Zalshah.

'Severn Road. It's right off the seafront just up there,' replied Louise. 'Number 71B, so that's a flat I expect.'

'Upstairs probably.'

Dixon parked across the drive of the property next door and looked back at Number 71, Severn Road. It was built of grey stone, with sandstone cornicing around the red front door and windows. The original sash windows were rotting and the sandstone was stained black, the ornate carving above the bay windows crumbling away. Unlike next door's, where the stone had been restored, and the sash windows replaced with PVC.

Next to the red front door were two door bells.

'That's the one,' said Dixon.

'Are you going to leave this here?' asked Louise, climbing out of the Land Rover.

'Can you see anywhere else to park?'

Dixon rang the top doorbell and waited. The click of heels on stairs; then the door opened.

'Yes.'

'You'll be Mrs Megan Hanbury?' asked Dixon. She was in her mid-thirties, with her long blonde hair in dreadlocks, and clearly had a high pain threshold, judging by the number of piercings.

'Ms Hanbury. I'm divorced. You've come to see my mother?'

'Yes.'

'Come in.'

They followed her to the upstairs flat and along a narrow corridor into the front room, where an elderly lady was sitting in a chair by the window.

'Mrs Foster?'

'Call me Mary, please.'

'Mary, we're—'

'I know who you are.'

'You're not here to talk about the court case, are you?' asked Megan.

'Indirectly,' replied Dixon. 'Only, the defence solicitor, the defence barrister and one of the witnesses have been murdered.'

'Oh my God,' said Mary, putting her hand over her mouth. 'Why?'

'We don't know. Yet.'

'Does this mean the hearing will be adjourned?' asked Megan.

'Possibly,' replied Dixon, 'but you'll need to speak to Lings about that.'

'Who would do such a thing?' asked Mary.

'I was hoping you might be able to shed some light on that, Mary.'

'Me?'

'Richard Hagley made it painfully clear that he knew who was behind the murders.'

'But he wouldn't tell you.'

'No. He'll take that information to his grave, sadly.'

Dixon watched both mother and daughter for any signal passing between them.

'Well, I'm sure I can't help you, Inspector. The last thing we want is the case adjourned. We just want it sorted out so we can move on.'

'It's been hanging over us for months,' said Megan. 'And it's not as if it'll bring Dad back, is it?'

'But it'll take years if it goes all the way to the European Court.'

'We're just hoping the government will settle it,' said Mary.

'Richard Hagley said it was about justice, what do you think he meant by that?' asked Dixon.

'It may be about justice for him, but it's about the money for Mum. You wanna try living on a widow's pension. And the war pension is peanuts.'

'They're the same thing, aren't they? Justice is money for the victims I suppose,' said Mary, glaring at her daughter.

'But your husband getting mesothelioma wasn't the lawyers' fault, was it?'

'No, but they didn't have to defend the claim, did they?' said Megan. 'They could've admitted liability and let my father have an interim payment before he died.'

'Would it have made a difference?'

'To him, yes. To know that Mum was going to be looked after.'

'He had a bad death, Inspector,' said Mary. 'He was very bitter, and there was a lot of anger, kicking and screaming.'

'How well did he know the other claimants?'

'Very well. They served together . . . fought together. That creates a bond that can't be broken. Even stronger than marriage it is, as I found out to my cost. They always came first.'

'Does the name Adrian Kandes mean anything to you?'

Mary smiled.

'He was a good lad was Adrian. Joined up the same day as my Grant. Good mates they were after that.'

'Why do you think Adrian fled during the battle?'

'He was mixed up. His girlfriend had broken up with him just before they left for the Falklands and gone back to Canada. Carrying his child she was. He fell apart after that, according to Grant.'

'His child?'

'Yes, she was pregnant.'

'How far gone was she?'

'No idea.'

'D'you know if it was a boy or a girl?'

'Don't know that either I'm afraid. When Adrian didn't come back, that was the end of it. We heard nothing more.'

'Your husband was one of the marines who went after him on the night of the battle?'

'He was. Adrian took the chance to put it right.'

'And saved your husband's life in the process,' said Dixon.

'He did his duty and he did it well. But my husband and the others saved his life, not the other way round.'

Dixon frowned.

'You have to understand the marines, Inspector. If Adrian had run, the shame alone would've killed him. He'd have been finished. No, they saved his life. And ended up paying for it with their own.'

'The asbestos, you mean?'

'Yes. Captain Alan bloody Fletcher. He was the one who gave the order. I'd like to get my hands on him one day.'

'He's dead, Mary. Murdered.'

Mary Hanbury sighed and shook her head.

'Can't say I'm sorry to hear that if I'm honest.'

'How?' asked Megan.

'I can't say at this stage,' replied Dixon.

'Well, I'm still not sure he deserved that,' said Mary. 'He was only doing what he thought was his duty, wasn't he? They all were.'

'Long, slow and painful if I had my way,' said Megan.

'You ever been caving, Megan?' asked Dixon.

'Once, years ago on a school trip. Why?'

'Where does that leave us with Hagley's justice I wonder?' asked Louise as Dixon turned on to the A370 and headed north-east towards Bristol.

'He said justice but he meant money, although it's the only way of compensating them now,' replied Dixon. 'It does make Fletcher's killing different, and that's got nothing to do with justice.'

'Why?'

'He was responsible for the deaths of the marines because he gave the order to dismantle the radar cabins, but there's no suggestion that he did so deliberately intending that they should die years later, is there?'

'No.'

'I bet he didn't even know the cabins were lined with asbestos.'

'Probably not.'

'So his murder is revenge. Pure and simple.'

'Yes, but for killing the marines with the order to dismantle the cabins or for blocking Kandes's VC?'

'Good point. Either way, it's different from the lawyers.'

'They're being killed because they're defending the claims,' said Louise.

'If Hagley can't have his compensation, then the lawyers must be to blame for that.' Dixon grimaced. 'I'm not convinced though.'

'Why not?'

'I've just got a feeling there's more to it than that.'

'Interesting that they didn't feel they owed their lives to Kandes like we thought. According to Mrs Foster, he owed his life to them. That's what she said.'

'She did, didn't she,' said Dixon, nodding. 'Or to be more accurate, he owed his death to them, which does give us a steer on who might be willing to give them their justice.'

'Does it?'

'Give Mark a call and find out where he got to tracing Kandes's girlfriend.'

'Raymond Absolon,' said Dixon as he looked at the terraced house in Jasper Street, Bedminster. It had been rendered in pink pebble dash, so you could hardly miss it.

'Odd that the houses on one side of the road have bay windows and this side they don't.'

'If you say so.'

The door was answered by a woman in her early sixties, keen to give up smoking but not having much luck, judging by the nicotine patches on her arm, gum in her mouth and cigarette in her right hand.

'We're here to see Mr Absolon,' said Dixon, holding up his warrant card.

'Follow me.'

'And you are?'

'His wife.'

They followed her through to a small conservatory at the back of the house. Dixon noticed a photograph montage on the wall in the corridor and stopped to look at the pictures. Various children, the same ones at different ages, all of them cut out and mounted behind a piece of glass. None taken down a cave, sadly.

The ashtrays in the kitchen and the conservatory were both full. That would be doing Mr Absolon's lungs the power of good.

Raymond Absolon was sitting in a bamboo chair in the corner of the conservatory, a thin plastic tube delivering oxygen up his nose and held in place by elastic over his ears. It was connected to a large black oxygen bottle on the floor behind his chair. On the small table next to him was an empty coffee mug and another ashtray.

'What d'you want?'

Dixon turned to Mrs Absolon, who had sat down on the small sofa next to Louise.

'Would you mind?'

'Ray wants me here, don't you, Ray?'

'Mr Absolon may do, but I do not,' said Dixon, matter of fact.

'What if I say no?'

'Then we'll continue this down at the station. And I'm sure you don't want to put Mr Absolon to that trouble.'

Dixon waited until Mrs Absolon had finished huffing and puffing and closed the door behind her.

'I'm sorry about that,' said Dixon.

'Don't mind me,' said Absolon. 'Nice to be shot of her for a bit.'

'You were a corporal in F Troop I understand.'

'Yes.'

'At the battle of Mount Harriet.'

'Let me save you the trouble,' said Absolon. 'Philip Hagley rang me, so I know why you're here.'

'Saves time,' said Dixon.

'It does. And there's nothing I can tell you that Richard hasn't.'

'Mr Absolon, innocent people are dying. The barrister had two children under five. Does that mean anything to you?'

'We were innocent people.'

'You were. But that doesn't explain why you are happy to see more die.'

'Look, I don't know who's doing it, all right?'

'Richard Hagley said he did.'

'He may do, but I don't. He just said he knew someone who'd fix it so we'd get our money.'

'And you didn't question that? Ask who or how?'

'No.'

'How well did you know Adrian Kandes?' asked Dixon, shaking his head.

'Very well. We were both NCOs, had been corporals together until he got promoted. He was a good lad.'

'How long was that before the Falklands?'

'A couple of years or so.'

'Tell me what happened on the night then.'

'They'd cleared a path through the minefields, and we were on our way up to the start line. The woodentops were—'

'Woodentops?'

'Guards. Welsh Guards. Anyway, they were supposed to meet us and guide us in, but they never appeared, so the whole thing started an hour late as it was. We were waiting, and then Harry spotted Adrian heading back down the slope, straight through the minefield, so we went after him. Me, Harry, Richard, Loz and Grant. Only we used the path, which took us the longer way round.'

Dixon nodded.

'Anyway, when we catch up with him there's this woodentop officer pointing his sidearm at him. Adrian was shaking and crying. So Richard belted him, and we grabbed Adrian and ran back to the start line. We couldn't have been gone more than fifteen minutes, and no one noticed.'

'Did the officer get a good look at you?'

'Adrian he did, and Harry and me. There were flares going up all over the place.'

'And during the battle?'

'I was right behind Mr Burton, our troop commander. He took the bullets that were meant for me. Then we were pinned down by two machine guns at the base of the rocks. Till Adrian sorted them out. You know about that I expect.'

'I do.'

'Adrian died a hero and it was a travesty, a fucking travesty, that he wasn't recognised for it. One mistake he made. That's all. Just one mistake.'

'What about on the Stanley Road?'

'It's all in my statement. Everything I can remember that is. We're talking about things that happened over thirty years ago.'

'Everything?'

'Except some of the choice language. We were minding our own business when the same officer spots us and orders us to dismantle the radar cabins. He even gets the sappers to bring the others on the island for us to do. Took three days in the end. And our lot couldn't countermand the order either.'

'Why not?'

'The COs did some deal I expect, to do with Adrian bolting and it being kept quiet.'

'And what about the asbestos?'

'Clouds of the bloody stuff. Terrible.'

'Who killed Alan Fletcher?'

'I dunno,' replied Absolon, grinning. 'But when you catch him, buy him a beer from me.'

'Richard Hagley said it was about justice.'

Absolon nodded.

'Who for?' asked Dixon.

'No idea. Him I suppose,' replied Absolon, lighting a cigarette. 'Or all of us maybe. I really don't know. I'm just in it for the money.'

'You're suing the MoD for mesothelioma and yet you're a smoker,' said Louise. 'How does that work?'

Absolon smiled.

'Asbestos is like tiny bits of glass that cut into the lining of your lungs over and over again. They lacerate it every time you breathe. As the cuts heal, it thickens the pleura, the lining of the lung, and that causes the cancer. The quacks can tell the difference between lung cancer caused by smoking and mesothelioma.'

Louise nodded.

'That's how it was explained to me anyway,' continued Absolon. 'And the biopsy wasn't very pleasant.'

'You said in your statement that you were worried about your wife and children falling out after you've gone,' said Dixon.

'She's a gold digger, and her son's up to no good. She's not getting the house. My son thinks she's just after the compensation. If there is any. If we lose, there's just going to be a big bill.'

'You're on a no-win, no-fee, surely?'

'Yes.'

'And you should be insured against defence costs if you lose.'

'No idea. I suppose so.'

'What about the house?'

'I gave that to my son and daughter years ago,' replied Absolon, whispering. 'Before I met her. It's in a trust for them.'

'She's going to love that,' said Dixon.

'I know.' Absolon grinned.

They were interrupted by the front door slamming. Then raised voices from the hall.

'They're here?'

'What did you let 'em in for?'

'That'll be my step-son.'

'We'll go, Mr Absolon,' said Dixon, standing up. 'You've been very helpful, thank you.'

'Have I?'

Dixon dropped Louise back to her car, which was parked outside his cottage, picked up Monty and then went down to Express Park. The place was deserted, apart from several uniformed officers on the ground floor, sheltering from the cold when they should have been out on patrol.

He kept thinking about Louise's question when they had come out of Absolon's house.

'He wasn't much help, was he?'

'Not really, but I wasn't going tell him that,' had been his answer, but the more he thought about it, the more he realised that Absolon had let slip one crumb of information that might prove useful. It really was just about the money.

Apart from that he was getting nowhere. Still, they wouldn't have to wait long. The hearing was just five days away now.

Dixon sat down at a workstation and switched on a computer. He opened his email and then deleted all of the new ones, including the one from DCI Lewis asking whether he had informed the Met of the caving line of enquiry. They were busying themselves interviewing witnesses it had been agreed would be left to Avon and Somerset. And would they tell him if it was the other way round?

Then he opened the police database enquiry screen. He typed in the name of Jane's mother as it appeared in the adoption file, Sonia Beckett, and his finger hovered over the 'Submit' button.

Could he really risk another disciplinary after his recent close shave, this time for abuse of the police national database? Perhaps not.

But he knew a man who could.

Chapter Twenty

'Where the bloody hell are you?'

'On the beach. Why?'

'Louise is here,' said Jane, yawning. 'Something about another body. Fripp. Does that mean anything to you?'

'Where?'

'Birmingham.'

'Tell her to pick me up at Berrow church.'

An accomplished lip reader would have been able to tell what Dixon was saying as he dropped his phone into his coat pocket, but the words themselves were lost on the cold north wind. Caught midway between the beach road and the church, heading for the church would at least mean he would be running downwind. He might even get there before Louise.

Running with his tennis ball in his mouth wasn't doing Monty any good, so Dixon stopped and put it in his pocket. Both of them were puffing, although Dixon put it down to the freezing dawn air.

'We were supposed to be on a diet,' he muttered as they scrambled over the soft sand of the dunes.

Fripp lived in Bangor and died in Birmingham. Staying away from home as instructed no doubt. He'd been giving evidence at a trial, hadn't he? So how the hell did his killer find him?

Dixon spotted Louise turning into the car park at Berrow church just as he ran down through the churchyard. He opened the back door of her car and let Monty jump in on the back seat. Then he jumped in the front.

'We're not taking Monty, are we?'

'We'll drop him off at home. It's on the way,' said Dixon. 'Why didn't you ring?'

'I thought I'd let you have a lie in.'

'Fat chance,' muttered Dixon.

They were heading north on the M5 ten minutes later, Dixon having dropped Monty off at home and picked up his insulin pen. Jane had been in the shower, but he had insisted on kissing her goodbye, and he was still flicking the water off his coat as they sped past Junction 21.

'What's the story then?'

'He was found last night, but we didn't get the call till this morning,' replied Louise. 'Single gunshot wound to the head. Right between the eyes apparently.'

'Where is he?'

'The mortuary at Birmingham City Hospital.'

'And where was he?'

'The Buckerell Lodge Hotel.'

'Do we know what he was still doing there?'

'The trial had gone into the Monday. And he'd been told not to go home, so probably just stayed the weekend to keep a low profile.'

'Not low enough.'

'No.'

'Do they know we're on our way?'

'I spoke to the SIO, DI Annie Kumari. She's notified the mortuary that we're on our way and said she'd meet us at the scene. I'll ring her when we get off the motorway.'

'Let's go to the mortuary first then.'

'Really?'

'Really.'

The pathology lab at Birmingham City Hospital was hidden away around the back and not well signposted, much like at Musgrove Park. Parking was equally tedious, and Dixon could not rely on Roger Poland baling him out if he got a ticket.

'Leave one of your cards on the dashboard,' said Dixon. 'It's a Sunday, and we won't be long.'

The front door was closed, so Dixon rang the bell and waited. It took three more rings before he heard footsteps, then a white-coated lab assistant appeared behind the glazed door.

Dixon waved his warrant card in front of the glass.

'Yes,' she said, looking up and sighing at the same time.

'You have the body of Dr Anthony Fripp here. I'd like to see it.'

'Well, I—'

'Now, please.'

'You're not local?'

'Avon and Somerset.'

'There are prop—'

'Look, I don't have time for proper channels. Ring DI Kumari if you need to. She should have told you we were coming.'

'All right, all right.'

Dixon felt sure he was being advised to 'keep his hair on' but couldn't be sure over the noise of the keys jangling and the door being unlocked.

'What's your interest in him?'

'I'm a police officer, and he has a bullet hole in his forehead.'

'Yeah, sorry,' replied the lab assistant. 'Follow me.'

'Thank you.'

A long corridor led to large double doors and then to a smaller steel door that reminded Dixon of the fridges in the school kitchens at Brunel, although this time he was unlikely to come away with a piece of fruitcake and a banana.

'When's the PM?' asked Dixon.

'Tomorrow, I expect.'

The lab assistant walked along a line of small doors, peering at the labels.

'Here he is,' she said, opening the door and pulling out a stretcher.

Fripp was still in a black body bag.

'Are you ready for this?'

Dixon rolled his eyes, so the lab assistant unzipped the body bag and stepped back.

Fripp's eyes were open. Wide open. But there were no black marks on his forehead around the entry hole.

'Not point blank at least,' muttered Dixon. 'Unless he had a silencer.'

'Dr Kent reckoned the shot was fired from about two feet away, maybe a bit more,' said the lab assistant.

'What about his hands?'

'Cable ties. We cut them off and bagged them up.'

Dixon nodded. Then he leaned over and squinted at Fripp's nose and mouth.

'What do you see, Louise?' he asked, stepping back.

She leaned over the side of the open body bag.

'It's not easy with his white beard, but there's a powder. White. You can see it in his nasal hairs.'

'Faint traces,' said Dixon. 'No bruises though.'

'I can't see any,' replied Louise.

'Still, if there's a gun to your head you're hardly going to need to be forced to inhale the powder.'

'Tested positive for cocaine,' said the lab assistant.

'Did it,' replied Dixon, nodding.

'Very clever,' muttered Dixon, watching the lab assistant locking the doors behind them.

'Using cocaine?'

'What better way to throw the local police off the scent?'

'I suppose so.'

'They'll treat it as a drug related killing. A drug buy gone wrong possibly. And even if it delays the investigation for a few days, that takes us up to the hearing on Thursday, doesn't it?'

'Why though?' asked Louise, opening her car door.

'Less chance of the hearing being adjourned.'

'I don't get it.'

'If the defence find out he's dead, they'll apply for an adjournment, won't they?'

'I suppose so.'

'We can't prove that any of these killings are connected,' continued Dixon. 'Fryer was pushed under a train in a random attack. And we've got no real evidence Alison Crowther-Smith was murdered. And then there's Fletcher, and the claimants have already agreed his evidence. But if the defence can show that these killings are part of a sinister plot to sabotage their case, a judge will almost certainly grant them an adjournment.'

'I should think so.'

'But if it looks like Fripp's death is random, a drug related murder, then it's just possible a judge may order the hearing to go ahead anyway.'

'How can it?'

'The defence have got four days to find another expert who supports Fripp's findings,' replied Dixon. 'These are living mesothelioma claims don't forget, and time is of the essence.'

'Seems a bit harsh.'

'If you think about it, it also undermines his evidence if it looks like he was on drugs, and that might force them to do a deal.'

'Settle it you mean?'

'Let's get over to the hotel.'

DI Anuja Kumari was waiting for them outside Buckerell Lodge, on the edge of Sutton Coldfield just north of Birmingham. It was a large country house hotel, covered in ivy, and with a new spa and swimming pool tagged on the side. How they got planning permission for that was a mystery.

It was part of the Best Southern chain and certainly looked upmarket if the cars in the car park were anything to go by.

'DI Kumari?'

'Call me Annie, please. This is Danny Maxwell. You've come a long way on a Sunday.'

'DC Willmott here needs the overtime,' said Dixon.

'Is Dr Fripp known to you?'

'He was due to give evidence in a mesothelioma claim at Bristol County Court next week. Now he's dead, to add to one of the witnesses, the defence solicitor and their barrister.'

'Shit,' said Kumari, shaking her head. 'We thought it was drug related.'

'It was made to look like that,' said Dixon. 'Where was he?'

'In the annex. This way.'

They followed Kumari into a small courtyard at the side of the hotel, all of the rooms single storey. A uniformed officer was standing in front of an open door.

'SOCO are still in there,' said Kumari.

'Did anyone see or hear anything?' asked Dixon, pulling a set of white overalls over his trousers.

'No.'

'No gunshot?'

Kumari shook her head.

'Is there any CCTV?' asked Louise.

'Up there,' replied Kumari, pointing to a camera mounted on the wall just beneath the guttering in the corner of the courtyard. 'Black leathers and a motorbike helmet. Only there's no motorbike showing up on any of the traffic cameras.'

'What time was it?' asked Dixon.

'Just after midnight.'

'So who found him?'

'A prostitute arrived at one. The door was open, and you can guess the rest.'

Dixon followed the line of metal plates, laid out like stepping stones, into the hotel room. The wall behind the cream sofa was spattered with blood, brain and skull fragments, and a large pool of congealed blood had soaked into the cushions and the carpet underneath.

A small area of wallpaper had been peeled back, and a hole in the plaster opened out to reveal the brickwork behind it.

'We recovered the bullet,' said Kumari.

Dixon nodded.

'Have you found his phone?' he asked.

'Yes.'

'Did he ring the prostitute?'

'We don't know yet. If he did, he didn't use the landline – we know that much.'

'The call will have been made on his phone,' said Dixon. 'But he didn't ring her.'

'Who did?'

'His killer. To discredit him. His body would've been found by the housekeeper in the morning, so why not have him found by a prostitute to add to the drama? Plant a bit of cocaine . . .' Dixon's voice tailed off.

'The cocaine was planted?'

'I'm guessing he was forced to inhale it at gunpoint.'

Kumari shook her head.

'Like I said, that's what you were supposed to think,' said Dixon. He was looking around the room. The bed hadn't been slept in, but the killer had taken the trouble to make it look like a burglary. Fripp's wallet was open on the table, his money and bank cards gone. All of the drawers were open and their contents dragged out on to the floor. Standard stuff, and it would have taken no more than sixty seconds.

'D'you wanna see the CCTV?' asked Kumari.

'Better had.'

They followed Kumari back to the hotel reception and stood behind the manager while he loaded the clip. They were crowded into a small room behind the reception desk, where there were three screens, each split into four.

'Would there have been anyone in here at that time of night?'

'No,' replied the manager. 'Reception closes when the bar closes, which is usually eleven, unless we've got something on.'

'Here we go,' said Kumari.

Dixon watched as a figure appeared around the corner. He or she was wearing black leathers, as Kumari had said, and a full-face motorcycle helmet. The figure approached the door to Fripp's room, knocked on it and then took a gun out from inside his or her jacket.

Fripp didn't stand a chance.

Dixon spent much of the journey south with his eyes closed. Louise had been warned about it by Jane and knew not to interrupt whatever was going on inside his head, although she could have been forgiven for thinking he had gone to sleep. She felt the same, and the rhythmic clunk of the windscreen wipers wasn't helping. That and the warm air from the fans.

She was coming over the Avonmouth Bridge when Dixon sat bolt upright in the passenger seat and opened his eyes.

'What's the single most important piece of information we learned today, Constable?'

Louise hesitated.

'He's got a gun?' she said, looking at Dixon out of the corner of her eye.

'That's a good point. All right, what's the second most important piece of information we learned today?'

'I don't know.'

Dixon took his phone out of his pocket and sent a text message to Mark Pearce, Dave Harding and DCI Lewis, Louise craning her neck to read it.

meeting room 2 5pm

'We still don't know who he is though, do we?' asked Louise.

'No,' replied Dixon, dropping his phone back into his coat pocket. 'But we do know where to find him.'

He closed his eyes and slumped back in the passenger seat before Louise could ask another question.

Chapter Twenty-One

'This'd better be good.'

Louise had dropped Dixon at home to pick up his Land Rover, and now he was sitting at a workstation at Express Park, flicking through the litigation file. Mark Pearce, Dave Harding and Louise were waiting in meeting room 2.

'It is,' replied Dixon without looking up.

'I've got the chief super breathing down my neck about putting together a MIT,' said Lewis. 'And I've had some twat on from the Met bending my ear about your lack of cooperation.'

'Mine?'

'Have you told them about the caving yet?'

'Not yet.'

'Well, I stalled them as long as I could. They're sending someone down here tomorrow. DCI Gresham, so you can brief them then.'

Lewis waited.

'All right?'

'Yes, Sir.'

'Well?'

'I'll be along in a minute,' said Dixon.

He watched DCI Lewis sit down in meeting room 2 and direct a question at Louise. He couldn't tell what it was, but her response was clear enough from the shrug of her shoulders. He turned back to the correspondence pin and flicked back to the previous October. There was a letter from Nuttalls in Bristol, who had acted as agent for the Government Legal Department at the case management conference, attending the hearing on their behalf, and their bill, but no attendance note. Next he tried the documents folder. And there it was.

'Right then,' said Dixon, closing the door of meeting room 2 behind him. 'What've we got?'

'Nothing,' said Harding.

'I've not come up with anything either,' said Pearce.

'What about Fripp?' asked Lewis.

'Single gunshot wound to the head,' replied Dixon. 'He was in a hotel in Birmingham, where he's been giving evidence in a trial at the local county court. He was due to finish on Monday, so he stayed over the weekend rather than go home. Bangor police had advised him to keep a low profile.'

'Anything else?'

'There were traces of a white powder around his nose, which tested positive for cocaine. It was staged to look like a drug related murder, but it wasn't.'

'So, where does that leave us?' asked Lewis.

'The defence will apply for an adjournment tomorrow and maybe get it, maybe not. It's a living mesothelioma claim, so the court will be reluctant to adjourn the hearing unless it absolutely has to. Assuming it doesn't, we've got until Thursday.'

'Before what?'

'Our killer disappears.'

'Eh?'

'It's about the damages claim. The money. It always has been.'

Harding looked at DCI Lewis and shrugged his shoulders.

'It all starts with the case management conference,' continued Dixon. 'That took place last October. There's a special procedure in living mesothelioma claims, and the burden is on the defence at that hearing to show why judgment shouldn't be entered for the claimants or, in other words, why they should be allowed to defend the claim. If they can't do that, then the claimants win at the first hurdle and get an immediate interim payment of fifty thousand pounds.'

'I thought civil claims took years,' said Harding.

'They usually do, but there's a special practice direction in mesothelioma claims. The court injects the urgency to try to get a resolution before the claimant dies. Anyway, in this case Alison Crowther-Smith turns up and satisfies the court there is a defence to the claims based on the Crown Proceedings Act and Fripp's report, defeating the interim payment application at the same time. And that's when the killings start.'

Lewis nodded.

'We've been looking at the claimants, their families and buddies in the marines, but it's not them,' said Dixon. 'It's the lawyers. Our killer is either a lawyer or connected to a lawyer.'

'Bloody hell,' muttered Lewis.

'First, Alison Crowther-Smith is drowned in the cave. So ask yourself: how did the killer know she'd be down there?'

Dixon waited.

Silence.

'Because he met her at the case management conference and they chatted,' he continued. 'Perhaps she was dreading it and mentioned it in passing. Perhaps she knew him. There'd have been plenty of time for a coffee and a chat once the formalities were out of the way, either before or after the hearing.'

'Do we know who else was there?' asked Lewis.

'The order made by the judge on the day is in the pleadings. It says 'on hearing counsel for the claimants and counsel for the defendant'.

That means barristers were instructed by all parties. I've got the attendance note from the agent acting for the GLD, and it names the barristers who were there, but it doesn't mention anyone else there with them.'

'How do we find out?'

'That's your job, Mark. Get on to Bristol County Court. Ask for the usher's records. They make notes on their copy of the daily list. Get the judge's notes too. He may have written it down.'

'Yes, Sir.'

'We know who the barristers were though, so let's start with them. Dominic Thorpe was instructed by Holt Burton, and Lings sent Ian Bullock. They're both from the same chambers in Bristol. Dave, you take them.'

'Yes, Sir.'

'Next comes Robert Fryer. The killer knows where he works, follows him home one day, pushes him under a train. He knows Fryer waits at the end of the platform, knows where the CCTV is. Easy.'

'Why though?' asked Lewis.

'To force the Crown to settle the case. There are tens of thousands of pounds in legal costs at stake don't forget.'

'What about Fletcher?'

'His murder was our starting point. And it was the wrong end of the case,' replied Dixon. 'His is the only killing that doesn't fit.'

'Why not?'

'His evidence had been agreed by the claimants. It wasn't controversial, so why kill him?'

'What d'you mean not controversial?' asked Louise.

'His witness statement is purely factual, and the facts are agreed. That he ordered the marines to dismantle the radar cabins. That it took them three days. OK?'

'Yes, Sir.'

'There's no financial motive for his killing. It makes no difference to the outcome of the case, does it?'

'So what are you saying?'

'If the other murders really are about the money, this one is about revenge pure and simple,' replied Dixon. 'Adrian Kandes's girlfriend, Mark. How far have you got?'

'Nowhere yet.'

'She was pregnant when she left, carrying Kandes's child. Find them.'

'Fuck me,' muttered Harding.

'What about Fripp then?' asked Lewis. 'How would the killer have known he was in Birmingham?'

'The order made at the case management conference listed the case for trial on the preliminary issue only within sixteen weeks on a date to be fixed. And then it said, "the parties to file dates to avoid within twenty-eight days".'

'Just like when we give our available dates for a trial,' said Harding.

'That's right. Within twenty-eight days of the case management conference, all parties had to provide the court with their complete calendars for the next sixteen weeks. That would have included Fripp, given that he was the key defence witness.'

'A complete list of where he would be and when,' said Lewis.

'Precisely.'

'Why now though? Why not kill Fripp first? If he was the key to the defence case.'

'Kill him too soon and the defence have plenty of time to find another expert witness. Kill him the night before the trial and the defence get an adjournment, but four days leaves them just enough time to find a replacement and makes an adjournment less likely. And that uncertainty might just be enough to make them settle the case.'

'What're you going to do?' asked Lewis.

'Louise and I will be dropping in on Lings and Holt Burton tomorrow. Meet back here fiveish. All right?'

'Why not interview them at home? Tonight?'

'I want to catch them off guard in the office in front of their colleagues.'

'The Met'll be here mid-afternoon,' said Lewis.

'Show 'em where the canteen is if I'm not back,' said Dixon, standing up. 'And be careful. We now know he's got a gun.'

'You're home early.'

'It's the calm before the storm,' replied Dixon, dropping his keys on the kitchen table.

He had asked Louise to meet him at his cottage at 8 a.m. the following morning, which gave him the night off, given that not much could be done on a Sunday anyway.

'How was Birmingham?' asked Jane, appearing in the kitchen doorway.

'Bullet hole in the forehead.'

'Nice.'

'What've you been up to?'

'Not a lot really. I watched one of your old films.'

'Which one?'

'*A Shot in the Dark*,' replied Jane, grinning. 'You're very like—'

'Don't you dare,' interrupted Dixon. He put his arms around her waist, pulled her towards him and kissed her.

'Wait a minute. That means he's got a gun.'

'I know, I know: be careful.'

'You eaten?' asked Jane.

'Not yet.'

'How about we get a takeaway from the Zalshah? Maybe a bottle of wine and an early night?'

'You read my mind.'

Chapter Twenty-Two

'Brett Greenwood, please.'

'Is Mr Greenwood expecting you?'

'No.'

'I'll see if he's free. Who may I say is here to see him?'

'Detective Inspector Dixon and Detective Constable Willmott, Avon and Somerset CID.'

'Oh, er, take a seat, please.'

Dixon walked over to the window and looked out into the small cobbled courtyard outside the office, the view obscured by the name 'Lings Solicitors' stencilled on the inside of the glass. It was a large building, tucked away behind the Bristol Hippodrome and accessed via a small alleyway between the pub next door and a newsagent.

Louise sat down and began flicking through a loose leaf folder of newspaper clippings.

'Here,' she said, passing the open folder to Dixon. 'Top left.'

Dixon read the headline out loud.

'Lings Solicitors raise five hundred pounds during Movember.'

The photograph was grainy. A photocopy of a newspaper article, but the names under the line-up of bearded suits were legible. Left to right, Daniel Sharp, Peter Walmlsey, Brett Greenwood. Dixon looked no further.

The article was dated 2 December, but the photograph was almost certainly taken several days before that. Most had gone for the moustache, but Greenwood had opted for the full goatee, just like the figure on Wimbledon railway station.

'Can I help you?'

'Brett Greenwood?' asked Dixon.

'Yes.'

An accent, American or Canadian perhaps. Mid-thirties, clean shaven with short brown hair and regulation suit and tie. He looked nothing like the e-fit, but then no one did.

'Is there somewhere we can talk?'

'Gina, are any of the interview rooms free?'

'I'd prefer to talk in your office, please,' said Dixon.

'Oh right. Yes, of course. I'm on the fourth floor though.'

'Is there a lift?'

'Yes.'

'There we are then,' said Dixon, smiling.

'Er, right. Follow me.'

The silence in the lift was punctuated by only one question from Greenwood, which Dixon ignored.

'What's this about then?'

He smiled and watched Greenwood watching himself in the mirror. And fidgeting.

Dixon sighed. The fourth floor of Lings Solicitors looked much like the fourth floor of most law firms in this modern age of open plan offices. The firm he had trained at had been open plan, and he thought he had escaped that nightmare, until he moved to Express Park.

There were glass partitioned cubicles around the outside for the lawyers, the area in the middle for the secretaries, each sitting at a workstation just large enough for a computer and separated from the next by red partitioning. Most of the desks were occupied by secretaries wearing headphones, their eyes fixed on the screens in front of them.

'This is my office,' said Greenwood, gesturing to an open door on the right as they stepped out of the lift.

He shut the door behind them. Louise sat down on a chair in front of the desk. Dixon busied himself looking at the various certificates on the wall.

'How can I help?' asked Greenwood, sitting down behind his desk.

He enjoyed a good certificate, did Greenwood, each of them mounted and framed. He was a member of the Association of Personal Injury Lawyers and even a registered first-aider. Dixon looked for his swimming certificates, but couldn't see them.

'You're acting for three marines and the estate of a fourth suing the MoD for asbestos related injury.'

'Yes. I took it over when court proceedings started. It's an unusual case that one. The government is hiding behind the Crown Proceedings Act, so it'll probably end up at the European Court. There's a hearing on Thursday.'

'And you're doing it on a no-win, no-fee.'

'We are. It's a bit of a flyer, but there's a massive injustice here, and it's a test case too. There are sixty service personnel suffering from mesothelioma, all of them exposed to asbestos before 1987. At the moment they get nothing except the war pension.'

'What will happen on Thursday?'

'The Crown will argue that we haven't got a claim and anyway it's barred by the Crown Proceedings Act. We'll argue that we have got a claim and we're being denied our rights under Article 6 of the European Convention on Human Rights.'

'And the outcome?'

'We'll lose. The only question is whether we get leave to appeal or not. If we do, we appeal, and if we don't it's straight off to the European Court.'

'Well, it's two marines and two estates now, sadly, Mr Greenwood,' said Dixon. 'Richard Hagley died just after 8 a.m. this morning.'

'Oh God, what a shame. I knew it was imminent. I think everyone was just hoping he'd live to see the hearing.'

Dixon spun round when the door opened behind him.

'Inspector, this is Fiona Hull, my head of department,' said Greenwood.

'What's going on?' she asked, allowing the door to slam behind her.

Fiona Hull was dressed for a court appearance: black trouser suit and white blouse. Mid-forties, with dark hair tied back in a ponytail and clamped to the side of her head with hairpins.

'I was just telling the detective inspector about the marines,' said Greenwood.

'What about them?'

'That it's a test case,' said Dixon.

'It's a bloody travesty, that's what it is,' said Mrs Hull. 'The Crown Proceedings Act was designed to stop a soldier injured in battle suing the government. Not in this situation. And there are sixty others being denied compensation too.'

Dixon sat down in the vacant chair in front of Greenwood's desk.

'And you'll take the case all the way to Europe?' he asked.

'If we have to,' replied Mrs Hull. 'No one's taken it that far before. So we'll see.'

'Hagley's dead,' said Greenwood.

'Oh no,' said Mrs Hull. She bowed her head and sighed.

'When I spoke to him, he said the case was about justice.'

'It's always about justice, Inspector. We deal with asbestos related injury, mesothelioma, and what good is money to them? Unless it's for the families they leave behind.'

'Quite.'

'The diagnosis is invariably terminal, and no amount of money can compensate for that.'

Dixon nodded.

'Is this why you're here?' asked Greenwood. 'To tell us Hagley's dead?'

'No.'

'Why are you here then, if I may ask?' Mrs Hull was standing behind Greenwood's desk, leaning against a filing cabinet.

'You may, Mrs Hull. Four people involved in the case are dead and—'

'Are they?'

'Yes.'

'Who?'

'Does the name Alison Crowther-Smith mean anything to you?'

'She was a barrister,' replied Greenwood. 'We met at the case management conference last October. But she died in an accident, surely?'

Dixon raised his eyebrows.

'Bloody hell,' muttered Greenwood.

'How did you know she was dead?'

'Ian Bullock told me at a conference, but I thought it was an accident. That's what he told me anyway. We don't use her chambers, so our paths rarely cross.'

'What about Robert Fryer?'

'Who's he?' asked Mrs Hull.

'The solicitor at the Government Legal Department who was handling the case.'

'You never speak to the same person twice there,' said Greenwood, shaking his head. 'I'm afraid his name means nothing to me. I couldn't tell you who's dealing with it now either. Whoever it is, they're just a reference on a letter.'

'What about Alan Fletcher?'

'He's one of the witnesses, isn't he?'

'Yes,' replied Dixon. 'He ordered the marines to dismantle the cabins.'

'We agreed his evidence,' said Mrs Hull, 'so he's not required for the hearing.'

'And what about Dr Anthony Fripp?' asked Dixon.

'Is he dead?' asked Greenwood.

'Yes.'

'When?'

'Yesterday.'

'That means the defendants will be after an adjournment,' said Greenwood, looking up at Fiona Hull. 'Bugger it.'

'Will you agree?' asked Dixon.

'No. Our clients are dying and don't have the luxury of time, Inspector,' replied Mrs Hull. 'It's going to be a long haul as it is, and we'll keep the pressure on. Sounds unhelpful I know, but that's the way it is. They've got time to find another expert.'

'Let's talk about Alison Crowther-Smith then. You met at the case management conference, Mr Greenwood?'

'Yes. I was there with Ian Bullock.'

'How long was the hearing?'

'An hour or so. Mesothelioma claims are classed as living or fatal, and the court treats them differently. I don't expect you to understand.'

'I am a solicitor as well as a police officer, Mr Greenwood.'

'Oh really? Sorry. That sounded awful, didn't it?'

Dixon smiled.

'Have you done mesothelioma work?'

'No.'

'Well, at the CMC in a living claim the defence have to show they've got a defence, and Alison Crowther-Smith did that. Anyway, that's why the hearing was a bit longer.'

'And how long were you kept waiting?'

'I don't recall. Half an hour or so.'

'What did you talk about?'

'I was with Mr Bullock, and Richard Hagley's son was there too.'

'What about after the hearing?'

'Look . . .' Greenwood was staring out of the window, shifting in his seat. 'We went for a coffee. She was a pretty lady. All right?'

Fiona Hull sighed.

'What did you talk about?' asked Dixon.

'Caving,' replied Greenwood. 'She said she was going caving that weekend. I'd hardly forget that, would I? After what happened.'

'What else?'

'Small talk really.'

'And how did you leave it with her?'

'She gave me her phone number, but when I tried it the following week it was unobtainable. I just thought she'd just given me the wrong number deliberately and left it at that.'

'Where did you write it down?'

'On my attendance note I think. Why?'

'Can I see it?'

'That's part of a confidential file,' said Mrs Hull. 'Solicitor–client confidentiality applies.'

'I would like to see the note, please,' said Dixon.

'It's privileged.'

'This is a murder investigation, Mrs Hull,' replied Dixon. 'And you can either show it to me, or I'll be back with a warrant and take the whole file. Take your pick.'

Hull turned to Greenwood. 'Can you print one off?'

'I need to see his handwritten note, not the dictated attendance note, please.'

'Why?'

'It's likely to contain additional information not relevant to the case.'

'Really?' Hull looked down her nose and frowned at Greenwood. He shrugged his shoulders.

'Zoe's got the file.'

'Get it,' said Mrs Hull.

Dixon watched Greenwood through the glass panel, walking over to his secretary's workstation. She was sitting at the first desk, with her back to him, several piles of files on the floor next to her chair.

She glanced in Dixon's direction, rolled her eyes and muttered 'For fuck's sake.' He'd never been the best of lip readers, but that much was obvious. Then they wrestled a thick green file from the bottom of the larger pile and Greenwood brought it back to his office.

'It'll be on the correspondence pin, with the typed note.'

'Is that all you need, Inspector?' asked Mrs Hull.

'For the time being.'

'Good. And it would be nice to have a bit of notice next time. This is a busy office.' She turned on her heels and walked across the open plan office.

'Here it is,' said Greenwood. 'I'll get Zoe to photocopy it. D'you need anything else?'

'No, thank you. That'll be all for now.'

Dixon and Louise followed Greenwood out to Zoe's desk and waited while he dispatched her to the photocopier.

'Zoe will show you out.'

'Thank you,' replied Dixon.

He looked down at her desk. It was identical to that of thousands of secretaries in thousands of law firms across the country, and just like those where he had trained. It sent shivers down his spine. Maybe Express Park wasn't that bad after all. At least he could come and go as he pleased. But a legal secretary? Audio typing all day and taking messages from angry clients, their only distraction a few photographs pinned to the partitioning.

Dixon looked down at the handwritten note Zoe handed to him, relieved that Greenwood's handwriting was legible. Just.

At the bottom of the first page, written at right angles to the rest, was the note 'Alison C-S', followed by a mobile phone number and then the words 'Sunday, Swildon's Hole'.

Dixon walked back over to Greenwood's office, a few short paces from his secretary's desk.

'Why did you write this bit about the caving?'

'To remind me to ask her about it. She was dreading it. You've got to appear interested, haven't you?'

Twat.

Chapter Twenty-Three

The conversation with the receptionist at Holt Burton Solicitors in their posh new office on the outskirts of Swindon was almost identical to the one Dixon had had only three hours earlier at Lings.

'Spaceships on ring roads,' he muttered, watching the traffic speeding past on the M4 in the distance.

'Mr Adcock will be down in a moment.'

'Thank you.'

'Here, see if they did Movember,' said Dixon, passing Louise the ever-present folder of newspaper cuttings. He watched her flicking through the pages.

'Here it is.'

'Adcock?'

'No.'

'Law firm marketing by numbers. Grow a beard, photo in the paper, raise profile.'

'How d'you know that?'

'Don't ask,' replied Dixon, rubbing his chin.

He turned when he heard footsteps behind the double doors and watched through the glass as Michael Adcock strode along the corridor towards him. Dixon recognised him from the firm's website. Tall, bald, Marks & Spencer suit, but no tie. Holt Burton were obviously a modern, forward-thinking firm. At least that's what their brochure said.

'Look, what's this about? We had the Met in here on Friday.'

'Mr Adcock?'

'Yes.'

'Do you have an office where we can talk, please, Sir?'

'No, we're all open plan upstairs. We'll have to use a meeting room.'

Dixon nodded.

'This way,' said Adcock, gesturing to the double doors behind reception. 'I'm assuming you're here about the MoD case.'

'Yes, Sir.'

'I'll get my trainee to bring down the file.'

'Thank you.'

Dixon was pacing up and down in the window when Adcock returned with the file and someone who must have been his trainee – he was wearing a tie.

'This is Ian Farrell,' said Adcock.

'Tell me about Lawrence Hampton.'

'He has mesothelioma. Not as advanced perhaps as Richard Hagley, but the prognosis is the same. It's just a matter of time for him.'

'Richard Hagley died this morning.'

'Shame. It doesn't come as a surprise though . . .' Adcock's voice tailed off.

'And what did the Met want?'

'They were asking about the murder of Robert Fryer. He was the Treasury Solicitor acting for the MoD and got pushed under a train. They seemed to think it was connected to this case.'

'Isn't it?'

'Not as far as I'm aware, no. There wasn't a lot I could tell them though. I'd met him a couple of times at CMCs in London, but that was it.'

'Did they mention anything else?'

'Alan Fletcher, of course, but they seemed to think his death wasn't connected. Something to do with an incident during the Falklands War, they said.'

'Did they?' muttered Dixon.

'Is it connected?'

'Does the name Alison Crowther-Smith mean anything to you?'

'No, I'm afraid not.'

'Did either of you attend the CMC?'

'No, we put counsel in and sent an agent to sit behind him,' replied Adcock.

'Who was it?'

'I don't recall. Ian?'

'Someone from Buckinghams I think.'

'Alison Crowther-Smith was the defence barrister at the CMC,' said Dixon. 'She died three days after the hearing. Drowned in a cave.'

'An accident?'

'We think not, Mr Adcock.'

'Oh God.'

'Puts Mr Fryer's murder in a different light, wouldn't you say?'

'Yes.'

'And the killing of Alan Fletcher.'

Adcock nodded.

Dixon opened his mouth to speak, but was stopped by a knock at the door.

'Come in,' said Adcock.

It was the receptionist, peering around the door.

'I'm sorry to bother you, Mr Adcock, but this fax has just come in. It's marked urgent.'

Adcock snatched the papers from her.

'Thank you, Dawn.'

Dixon watched his eyes scanning the pages.

'The defence have applied for an adjournment. Bugger it.' Adcock sighed. 'The hearing's at four this afternoon.' He passed the papers to Farrell. 'You'd better get on to St Mark's and see if they've got someone who can go.'

'Will you oppose it?' asked Dixon.

'Yes.'

'The grounds of this application are,' said Farrell, reading aloud, 'the sudden death of Dr Anthony Fripp in the early hours of Sunday, 22 February.'

'That was yesterday,' said Adcock.

'I was coming on to that,' said Dixon. 'Single gunshot wound to the forehead. Right between the eyes.'

He watched Adcock and Farrell for any reaction. There was none.

'May I see the attendance note of the CMC, please?' continued Dixon. 'I'm assuming Buckinghams prepared a note and it's on your file.'

'Er, yes, I don't see a problem with that,' replied Adcock.

Farrell opened the correspondence pin at a note typed on pink paper and slid it across the table to Dixon. He checked for any reference to caving, but there was none.

'Will they get their adjournment?' asked Dixon.

'Possibly,' replied Adcock. He spoke without looking up.

'Surely there's not the same urgency now that Mr Hagley's dead.'

'They'll all be dead before it gets to the European Court. They may get it, they may not, I really don't know.' Adcock was shaking his head, his cheeks flushed. Dixon watched him clenching and unclenching his fists. 'Yes, probably.'

'How is Mr Hampton's claim funded?'

'He's paying privately,' replied Adcock, looking up. 'Why?'

'Any insurance against paying the defendant's costs if he loses?'

'No. We couldn't get it, but he decided to go ahead anyway. He said he couldn't let his mates down.'

'Why didn't he go with Lings then?'

'They wouldn't take him on. Said he came in too late. He couldn't get anyone else to do it on a no-win, no-fee either. Lings are running the case. We're just tagging along really.'

'And your arse is covered?' asked Dixon.

'Oh yes. I wrote him a long letter setting out the risks and the sums that might be involved. He signed one copy and sent it back. It's sitting on our file.'

Dixon nodded.

'We've taken up enough of your time, Mr Adcock, thank you.'

'Happy to help, but I'm not sure I have.'

Dixon was walking through reception when Louise took his elbow and pulled him over to the seating area. She picked up the folder of newspaper cuttings, opened it and handed it to him. He looked down at the bearded faces, all of them grinning at the camera; front row, left to right, Simon Hart, Mark Dawson, Ian Farrell.

'We're getting close, aren't we?' asked Louise, climbing into Dixon's Land Rover.

'Closer.'

He switched the engine on and slumped back into the driver's seat, sliding his phone out of his jacket pocket at the same time.

'What're you going to do?'

'Interfere.'

He tapped out a text message, Louise craning her neck trying to read it.

Richard Hagley died this morning in Bristol Royal Infirmary

The reply came as he was turning out of Holt Burton's car park.

Thank you. Virat Sharma

'Ring Mark and find out where he's got to finding Kandes's girlfriend, will you?'

'OK.'

They were east of Bristol on the M4, heading west, Dixon deep in thought listening to the windscreen wipers trying to keep up with the rain as Louise made the call. Still, at least it had warmed up a bit.

'Ginette Lundy, right. Died last year in Toronto,' said Louise, turning to Dixon, her phone still clamped to her ear. 'Breast cancer.'

Dixon nodded.

'Twins?' continued Louise. She nodded. 'A boy and a girl. Joel and Tamsin. They'd be in their thirties now, right?'

'They did what?'

'I'll tell him.'

Louise rang off.

'They crossed the border into America at the end of last year and then disappeared. There's no record of them leaving the States.'

'No, but they did,' said Dixon, swerving on to the M32, heading south towards Bristol city centre.

'They're sending over pictures.'

'They'll have changed their appearance,' replied Dixon. 'Wouldn't you?'

Louise nodded.

'What's the time?'

'Twenty to four,' replied Louise.

'Plenty of time.'

'Where are we going?'

'Bristol County Court.'

Dixon parked on the pavement outside the Bristol Civil Justice Centre. All red brick and glass, which made a change from concrete and glass. Two uniformed officers were waiting for them at the front entrance, Louise having rung ahead and asked for backup.

'You two, with us.'

'Yes, Sir.'

Once past the security guards at the entrance, Dixon headed for the daily lists on the noticeboards in the foyer.

'Will it be before a district judge?' asked Louise. 'There are loads of cases listed.'

'Circuit judge probably,' replied Dixon. 'But it may not be on the list at all.'

'I can't see it.'

'What are we looking for?' asked one of the uniformed officers.

'Foster, Hagley and others versus the Ministry of Defence.'

'Here it is.'

Dixon leaned over. Scribbled on the bottom of His Honour Judge Ormerod's list in black ink was the hearing he was looking for.

'Where's Court One?' asked Dixon, turning to the nearest security guard.

'Up the stairs, along the corridor on the right.'

'Thanks.'

The usher intercepted them at the door of the court, his black gown flowing behind him as he ran along the corridor towards them.

'You can't go in there.'

'Let me see your list, will you?' asked Dixon, snatching the usher's clipboard. At the bottom was the name he was looking for, against the relevant parties to the case.

'There's a back door to the court, isn't there?'

'The judge's entrance, yes, but it's behind the bench.'

'Show this officer to it, please, and then let me know when he's in position.'

'What's going on?'

Dixon's warrant card and reference to a murder investigation silenced any further objection.

He turned to the uniformed officer. 'Wait behind the door and arrest anyone who tries to come through it.'

'Yes, Sir.'

'Unless he's wearing a red robe and a wig,' continued Dixon.

'Who are we after?' asked Louise.

'Let me see if he's in there,' said Dixon, opening the outer door.

He peered through the glass panel in the inner door. There were three lines of benches facing the judge, who was sitting on a raised bench at the back of the court directly beneath the royal crest, his wig on the desk in front of him. In front and below him was another desk, occupied by the court listing officer, if the frown was anything to go by.

The lawyers occupying the front desk had their backs to Dixon. The defence counsel on the left was on his feet, no doubt asking the judge for the adjournment, and the two lawyers for the claimants were sitting side by side at the right hand end of the desk. Holt Burton had put counsel in for the hearing, Dixon knew that. Brett Greenwood was sitting next to him.

Dixon stepped back out on to the landing and turned to the remaining uniformed officer. 'We're after the man sitting down at the right hand end of the desk. All right?'

'Yes, Sir.'

'Who is it?' asked Louise.

'Brett Greenwood,' replied Dixon. 'Remember the certificate on his wall, Member of the Canadian Bar Association?'

Louise shook her head.

'The red maple leaf?' continued Dixon.

'I didn't see it.'

'You didn't look. You can learn a lot about people from the pictures on their walls.'

Dixon opened the door of the court and stepped inside. Louise followed. He looked along the back wall and waited for the uniformed officer, with the usher following, to enter by the other door.

Greenwood was standing now, objecting to the adjournment.

'Time is of the essence, Your Honour, and this remains a living mesothelioma claim, despite the sad death of Mr Hagley. Three of the claimants remain terminally ill, as you know—'

'Excuse me, Mr Greenwood,' interrupted the judge. 'What's going on?'

Dixon stepped forward. Greenwood saw him coming, the blood draining from his face. He jumped up on to the desk in front of him, leapt across to the listing officer's desk and then up on to the judge's bench. Judge Ormerod stood up and tried to grab hold of his legs, but Greenwood lashed out with his foot, catching him in the side of his face and sending him crashing to the floor behind his chair.

Then Greenwood jumped down and wrenched open the small door.

Dixon was right behind him, having followed him across the desks and up on to the bench. He heard a shout, several grunts and a thud, arriving to find Greenwood face down on the floor in the private corridor behind the court, his hands being cuffed behind him.

'Good work.'

'Thank you, Sir,' replied the uniformed officer.

'Brett Greenwood, I am arresting you on suspicion of the murder of Anthony Fripp. You do not have to say anything, but it may harm your defence if you do not mention when questioned something that you later rely on in court.'

Dixon stepped back as the uniformed officer dragged Greenwood to his feet.

'Anything you do say may be given in evidence.'

'I didn't kill him. I didn't kill anyone.'

'Get him out of here.'

'Yes, Sir.'

'Louise, you go with him. Get him processed and down to Express Park as quick as you can. I'll see you down there.'

'Yes, Sir.'

'Are you all right, Sir?' asked Dixon, helping the judge up.

'A bit dazed. It was a glancing blow, but my glasses have had it. There's a spare pair in my chambers.' He was feeling the bridge of his nose between his thumb and index finger.

'I'll go, Your Honour,' said the usher.

'Thank you, George.'

Dixon picked up the red leather chair, and the judge collapsed into it.

'Well, that's a first for me,' he said, shaking his head. 'I've known defendants jump the bench in criminal trials, but never a solicitor.'

'I'm sorry about that, Your Honour,' said Dixon.

'He killed Fripp, you say?' asked the judge.

'I've arrested him on suspicion of it, yes, Sir.'

'And you are?'

'Detective Inspector Dixon, Sir.'

'Bloody good thing you know your way around a court.'

'Thank you, Sir.'

'Ah, thank you, George,' said the judge, putting on his spare glasses. 'Right, will somebody please telephone Lings and get them to send someone to represent their clients? They've got fifteen minutes. Then we'll finish this adjournment application.'

Chapter Twenty-Four

'There you are.' The voice came from the staff canteen as Dixon crept past the door. He kept walking, pretending not to have heard it.

'Dixon!'

'Yes, Sir,' he replied, craning his neck around the door.

'You know DCI Gresham and DC Kohli I gather?'

'I do.'

'Where have you been?' asked Lewis.

'Bristol. We've made an arrest. He's on his way down here now. Louise is bringing him.'

'Who is he?'

'Brett Greenwood, the solicitor acting for four of the claimants in the civil litigation.'

'Which firm?'

'Lings.'

'Has he said anything?' asked Hannah Gresham.

'Only that he didn't kill anyone, but that was after he jumped the bench in Court One and kicked the judge.'

'I've been tempted to do that many times,' said Sunny, grinning.

'Well, I've had a go at briefing them, but you'd better fill 'em in properly. Then DCI Gresham can sit in with you when you interview him. All right?'

'Yes, Sir. Whenever you're ready.'

Dixon's phone bleeped in his pocket, announcing the arrival of a text message.

Hearing adj to 1st open date after 28 days. Defence to disclose expert's report not later than 7 days before. Thanks again. VS

Dixon smiled. Now time was on his side too.

It was just after 7 p.m. when Louise arrived from Bristol with Brett Greenwood. He was held downstairs in the custody suite, while she went upstairs to find Dixon. Instead she found Jane peering around a pillar at the far end of the CID area.

'What's up?'

Jane nodded towards a workstation on the far side, where Dixon was sitting with his back to her.

'Who's that?' she asked.

Louise peered over her shoulder. DCI Gresham was sitting on the corner of Dixon's desk, her legs crossed, her short skirt having ridden up even higher.

'Some DCI he used to work with in Wimbledon. He gave her the brush off when we were in London.'

'Is that it?'

'There's ancient history, he said.'

'What're the Met doing here?'

'Come to find out what we know I expect. You've nothing to worry about. Really.'

Jane smiled.

'Besides, he's not the type,' continued Louise.

Jane walked over and tapped Dixon on the shoulder.

'Are you staying late?'

'We've got an interview. Couple of hours at most,' replied Dixon, smiling. 'Meet Hannah Gresham. We used to work together at Wimbledon. Hannah's here to take the credit.'

'Piss off.'

'Jane and I live together.'

'Oh, sorry, are you two—?' asked Hannah, sliding off the corner of the desk and straightening her skirt.

'Yes,' interrupted Jane.

'He's downstairs, Sir,' said Louise, changing the subject.

'Has he asked for a lawyer?'

'No. He said he is one.'

'What's that old saying?' asked Hannah.

'A solicitor who acts for himself has a fool for a client,' muttered Dixon. 'C'mon, let's get this over with. You'll have to sit this one out, Louise. DCI Gresham's going to sit in.'

'Yes, Sir.'

'I'll see you at home, Jane.'

'Right then, Brett, you're still under caution.'

Greenwood nodded.

'For the tape, Mr Greenwood nodded his head.'

Dixon was sitting next to Brett Greenwood in one of the new interview rooms at Express Park. Hannah Gresham was sitting to his left, and they were all sitting opposite the tape recorder. Dixon would never get used to it. The layout had taken Hannah by surprise too, if her 'What the fuck?' was anything to go by. Dixon felt the same.

'And you've declined a solicitor?'

'Yes.'

'OK, Brett, let's cut to the chase if you'll pardon the pun. Why did you run?'

Greenwood closed his eyes and sighed. Long and slow.

Dixon waited.

'I'm here illegally.'

'What?'

'My visa expired last year.'

'Is that it?'

'I'm employed as a paralegal, unqualified staff, but paid the same as a solicitor because I'm qualified in Canada. Only I'm not. The certificate is a forgery.'

'So you're not actually a lawyer?'

'Not a qualified one, no.'

'What qualifications do you have?'

'None.'

'Experience?'

'I worked in a law firm in Ontario for eight years, then decided to do a bit of travelling. Pitched up in the UK and got a job with Lings.'

'When was that?'

'Last May.'

'So why did you lie?'

'Paralegals get paid bugger all. So I forged the certificate from the Canadian Bar Association and told Lings I'd sit the exams in this country so I'd be dual qualified.'

'And they paid you the same as a solicitor?'

'Near enough.'

'What's the difference?' asked Dixon.

'A paralegal gets maybe fifteen to eighteen thousand a year. With my experience perhaps twenty-five. They paid me forty.'

'Section 2 of the Fraud Act 2006,' muttered Hannah.

'Fraud by false representation, I know,' replied Greenwood.

'Weren't checks done?' asked Dixon.

'There are checks for solicitors, but not paralegals. They asked for copies of my driver's licence and a bank statement, but that's it.'

'What about your visa or a work permit?'

'They never asked.'

Gresham looked at Dixon and raised her eyebrows.

'Lings are in trouble then,' she said.

'They've been good to me. It's not their fault.'

'I'm sure the Border Agency will take that into account,' said Hannah. 'What's the fine these days?'

'Twenty thousand pounds,' replied Dixon. 'Let's talk about Alison Crowther-Smith, Brett. Had you met her before the CMC?'

'No, never.'

'What about after that?'

'No. I told you, I rang the following week and got "number unobtainable".'

'So, you didn't follow her down Swildon's Hole and drown her?'

'No, I didn't!' Greenwood's voice had jumped an octave.

'Or wait for her down there perhaps.'

'No!'

'Have you ever been caving before?'

'No,' replied Greenwood, slumping back into his chair.

'Where did you meet Alan Fletcher?'

'I've never met Alan Fletcher.'

'But you knew Dr Fripp would be in Birmingham because you'd seen his dates to avoid.'

'I didn't kill Fripp. I've never even fired a gun before.'

'Before what?'

'Before! I've never fired a gun before!'

Greenwood was staring at the wall above the tape machine, breathing deeply.

'What's your father's name?'

'Mike. Why?'

'And your sister?'

'I haven't got a sister. I'm an only child.'

'And your mother?'

'Hazel Greenwood.'

'Is she still alive?'

'Yes.'

'Does the name Adrian Kandes mean anything to you?'

'No,' replied Greenwood, shaking his head. 'I've never heard of him. Look, I've told the truth. I'm in the UK illegally, I lied to Lings about my qualifications and I kicked the judge. But I'm not a killer, and I haven't murdered anyone. All right?'

'You can take the credit for that one I think,' said Hannah, smiling at Dixon.

They were standing in the lift waiting for the doors to close, Dixon jabbing the first floor button.

'Thank you,' he said, his teeth gritted.

'When I catch the killer, I'll let you know.'

Dixon rolled his eyes.

Hannah waited until the lift doors closed. 'You and Jane then – is it serious?'

Dixon hesitated.

'Yes, it is,' he replied, nodding.

'I envy you.'

'Really?'

'A relationship with someone who understands the job? Mine never last.'

'We certainly didn't.'

'How long was it?'

'A month,' replied Dixon. 'I wasn't ready for anything serious. Too many ghosts.'

'But you're ready now?'

'Yes.'

'Well, Louise has booked us into The Walnut Tree, if you change your mind.'

'I won't, but thank you for the offer.'

DCI Lewis, Sunny and Louise were waiting for them when the lift doors opened.

'Well?'

'He'll be charged with fraud by false rep and common assault,' replied Dixon. 'We'll leave the Border Agency to decide about any immigration offences.'

'I'm not interested in that. What about the bloody murders?' asked Lewis.

Dixon shook his head.

'So it's back to the drawing board.'

If we had one.

'How'd it go?' asked Jane.

'Not good,' replied Dixon, letting Monty out of the back door.

'Oh.'

'It's not him.' The crack of a can of beer being opened punctuated the conversation. 'Have you fed Monty?'

'Yes.'

'Where's Hannah Gresham?' asked Jane.

'At The Walnut Tree. She goes back to London in the morning, full of hilarious stories about how bloody useless we are I expect.'

'And where d'you go?'

'Square one.'

'There's a curry in the fridge. D'you want me to bung it in the microwave?'

'No, I'll do it, ta.'

Dixon set the microwave going and then walked into the lounge. Jane was stretched out on the sofa in front of *Doctor Zhivago*, paused at the final scene with Zhivago's lifeless body lying in a snow-covered Moscow street.

'Press "Play". I need cheering up.'

'It's all right, I can start it again when you're ready.'

'This arrived today,' said Dixon, taking an envelope out of his jacket pocket. 'I've not opened it.'

'What is it?'

'Your mother's address.'

'You found her?' Jane sat bolt upright.

'I used an enquiry agent. It's yours if you want it.'

'Have you contacted her?'

'Oh no,' replied Dixon, shaking his head. 'You've got to take it from here.'

'Are you sure you didn't look it up on the PNC?'

'With my disciplinary record? I'm hardly going to abuse the police national computer.'

'So you got someone else to do it.'

'I don't want to know how he did it. Now, d'you want it or not?'

'Yes.' Jane lurched forwards and snatched the envelope from Dixon's hand. 'Thank you.'

She folded it in half and stuffed it in the pocket of her jeans.

'Aren't you going to open it?'

'When your case has finished.'

Joel and Tamsin Kandes, born in 1982, but that was unlikely to be the surname on their birth certificates. Joel and Tamsin Lundy probably.

Dixon had assumed that the marines owed their lives to Kandes for dealing with the machine guns on Mount Harriet, but that was the wrong way round. Kandes owed the five marines who fetched him back to the battlefield and then lied for him. They had enabled him to die with honour and pass into Royal Marine legend, as Lieutenant Colonel Hatfield put it. So, were his children repaying the debt? It seemed a reasonable theory.

The drizzle was turning to powder snow as Dixon climbed Hill Lane, deep in thought. He was following the fluorescent band on Monty's coat, which was just visible on the end of the extending lead, as Monty sniffed his way along the grass verge.

So if it was Kandes's children, where the hell were they? Brett Greenwood wasn't the son, that was for sure. But then that would have been too easy. The real Joel Kandes would hardly have left a Canadian Bar Association certificate on his office wall, if he had an office at all.

Random thoughts popping into Dixon's head. What the hell was he doing walking up Brent Knoll in the snow at one in the morning for starters?

Their mother dies of breast cancer and they come to England to find their father, or to learn more about him, assuming they know he's already dead. Then what happens? They meet Richard Hagley, who tells them the whole sorry tale and demands their help. Maybe they offer it.

Fletcher's death was about revenge pure and simple. Dixon could understand that perhaps. But the others? Would they really embark on a series of killings just because someone asked them to? Or to repay a debt owed by a man they had never met, even if he was their father?

And why the gaps between each killing? Alison Crowther-Smith in October, Fryer at the end of November, then Fletcher in February. The timing of Fripp's to inconvenience the defence as much as possible was plausible, and it was probable that they were only granted the adjournment because Hagley had died, removing the immediate urgency, given the longer life expectancy of the others.

Dixon stopped at the gap in the hedge and looked at the path leading off across the fields to the summit of Brent Knoll. Night climbing in the snow. The last time he'd done that was on the Matterhorn, and it hadn't ended well, lightning striking the rocks all around them. He and Jake had turned for home that night, and Dixon would do the same now, although Brent Knoll was hardly in the same category.

What if they were buggering off back to Canada after each killing? To let the dust settle. That would explain the gap between each of them. It would also mean that they were in Canada now, after killing Fripp.

Note to self: check flights to Canada after each murder. If the same names appear . . .

He hoped he had done the right thing finding Jane's mother. And why she had insisted on watching *Doctor Zhivago* all over again was beyond him, not that he minded. He had ignored her protestations that his film selection was limited. 'Crap' was the word she used.

Bloody cheek. And what's wrong with watching the same film over and over again? People listen to the same music all the time, don't they?

It wasn't just because Brett Greenwood was Canadian. It was because he knew that Alison Crowther-Smith was going caving and no one else did. Or did they?

Dixon pulled Monty towards him, reeling in the extendable lead, and squatted down.

'What would I do without you, old son?' he asked, scratching him behind the ears.

Then he started to run.

Chapter Twenty-Five

'Don't you miss this?' asked Harding, yawning.

'Strangely enough I do,' replied Jane. 'Coffee anyone?'

Louise, Mark Pearce and Dave Harding had arrived at Dixon's cottage just before 3 a.m. Jane was standing in the kitchen, waiting for the kettle to boil.

'Yes, pl—'

'No time for that,' said Dixon, appearing in the doorway. 'Have you got an address?'

'Yes, Sir,' replied Louise. 'It's owned by a Sarah Witheridge.'

'Backup?'

'Meeting us there.'

'Right, let's go.'

'You haven't forgotten you're giving me a lift home from work tomorrow?' shouted Jane from the back door of the cottage, but it was lost in the rattle of Dixon's diesel engine.

◆ ◆ ◆

Vernon Court was a large block of flats in St Paul's Road, Clifton. It was built over eight floors of red brick, with metal windows and squared off balconies. You didn't need to be an architect to know it was built in the twenties.

Dixon parked across the drive of a house opposite, and Dave Harding parked alongside him.

'Where's the backup?'

'I'll check,' replied Louise.

Dixon climbed out of the Land Rover and looked up at Vernon Court. Lights were on in two of the flats, but apart from that it was pitch dark, the streetlights not due to come back on for an hour or two. He turned the collar up on his coat and blew on his hands, watching his breath hanging in the air in front of him. It had stopped raining as they drove north, but was colder if anything.

'Armed response will be here in five minutes,' said Louise, getting out of the car.

'Body armour, everyone,' said Dixon.

'Is he likely to be in there?' asked Harding.

'You wanna take the chance?'

'No.'

'Here they come,' said Louise, turning to watch two patrol cars driving towards them. They pulled up in front of Harding's car.

'What've we got then?' asked a uniformed police sergeant.

'We're looking for a brother and sister. Four murders, the last used a firearm. This is the sister's address, and we don't know who else is in there.'

'Battering ram,' said the sergeant, turning to another firearms officer. 'We'll give them the warning when we're in there. All right?'

'Fine by us,' replied Dixon. 'It's Flat 27.'

Each of the flats had its own door, accessed by a long covered landing at the back of the block. Flat 27 was on the second floor.

Dixon followed the four armed response officers along the landing, with Dave Harding, Mark Pearce and Louise behind him.

'Here it is,' whispered the sergeant. He had stopped outside a blue door, with a frosted glass panel. No light was visible inside.

'Ready?'

Dixon nodded.

'We go on three,' said the sergeant. 'One, two, three.'

The firearms officer swung the battering ram at the lock. The glass shattered, the wood splintered and the door swung open.

'Armed police!'

The sergeant was first through the door, his machine pistol at the ready, closely followed by the constable who had dropped the battering ram. Two more followed behind, and then Dixon.

'Armed police! Stay where you are!'

The sergeant kicked open a door on the right of the corridor. A woman screamed. She was sitting up in a single bed with the duvet pulled up around her.

'Hands!'

She dropped the duvet and put her hands up.

A loud crash behind him, and Dixon spun round to see an officer kick open a door on the left. Another scream.

'Hands!'

The other officers headed through to the room at the far end of the corridor, an empty sofa against the far wall.

'Clear.'

'Lounge and kitchen clear.'

'Clear,' said the sergeant, emerging from the bedroom behind Dixon.

'He's not here?'

'No.'

'Fuck it.'

'Who's this?' asked Louise, peering over Dixon's shoulder into the bedroom on the right.

'Sarah Witheridge probably. Find out, will you?'

'Yes, Sir.'

'This, on the other hand,' said Dixon, pushing past the firearms officers blocking the corridor, 'is Miss Zoe Tremblay, Brett Greenwood's loyal, hardworking, downtrodden secretary. Isn't that right, Zoe?'

'Fuck you.'

'People keep offering to do that lately.'

She spat at him, but missed.

'Or should I call you Tamsin Kandes?'

Just before 8 a.m. Dixon was waiting in the courtyard outside the offices of Lings Solicitors with Mark Pearce and three uniformed officers. Several police cars were parked on the pavement outside and in the lane at the back, with other officers covering the back door.

A search of the flat had turned up nothing of interest, and Sarah Witheridge and Zoe Tremblay were on their way down to Express Park to await interview.

'See if you can chase up the photos from Canada,' said Dixon.

'They'll all be asleep over there,' replied Pearce.

'Wake them up.'

'Yes, Sir.'

Dixon watched Pearce pacing up and down with his mobile phone to his ear. He turned when he heard footsteps in the alleyway behind him.

'Can I help you?'

'Who are you?'

'John Tuckett, the practice manager.' He was flicking through a large set of keys.

Dixon identified himself and showed Tuckett his warrant card.

'What's going on?'

'We have two members of your staff in custody, Mr Tuckett, one on suspicion of murder and the other has been charged with fraud and assault.'

'Who?'

'Zoe Tremblay and Brett Greenwood.'

'I'm going to need to make a few phone calls.'

'You do what you have to do. In the meantime we need access to Brett Greenwood's files and Zoe Tremblay's computer. Here's a warrant.'

Tuckett opened the front door of the office and allowed Dixon and the other officers into the reception area.

'Can you wait here?'

'No,' replied Dixon.

'Well, just let me make a phone call then,' said Tuckett, dialling a number on his phone. 'Peter, where are you? Look, come straight to the office. The police are here with a warrant, and they've got Brett Greenwood and his secretary locked up.'

'What's going on?' A woman's voice from the doorway.

'Thank God, Fiona's here,' said Tuckett. 'Yes, and make it quick.'

He rang off and handed the warrant to Fiona Hull. She looked at Dixon and then back to the warrant.

'I think you know which file we're interested in, Mrs Hull. Shall we?' asked Dixon, gesturing to the lift. 'What time does your IT manager get in?'

'Anytime now,' replied Tuckett.

'We'll need him when he does.'

'I'll text him to come and find us.'

'Thank you.'

Once out of the lift Dixon walked straight across the deserted fourth floor to Greenwood's office, Tuckett trailing behind him. He opened the first filing cabinet inside the door and pulled out the 'Hagley and

Others' files, two correspondence files and three documents. The pile was about a foot thick in total.

He opened 'Correspondence 2 of 2' and looked at the departmental summary sheet on the inside flyleaf. The file had been reviewed by Greenwood's supervisor, Mrs Hull, twice. Once in August, before the case management conference, and then again in January, after Alison Crowther-Smith's murder.

'Are you taking the whole file?' asked Tuckett.

'No,' replied Dixon. 'Just the attendance note.'

'We can print off another if that's any good.'

'I need the handwritten one,' said Dixon, flicking through the correspondence pin. 'The original.'

'Can we keep a copy?'

'Yes.'

'Thank you.'

'Is your IT manager here yet?'

'He's downstairs,' replied Tuckett, looking at his phone.

'We'll need the password to Zoe Tremblay's machine.'

'I'll ring him,' said Tuckett.

Dixon picked up a pair of scissors and cut the treasury tag on the correspondence, releasing the attendance note. Then he passed it to Mark Pearce.

'Make a copy of that for Mrs Hull, will you?'

'Yes, Sir.'

'I'll switch the copier on,' said Mrs Hull, walking over to the other side of the floor.

Zoe Tremblay's workstation was just like any other in the office. Neat and tidy, a wire basket in the corner for that day's typing, a pile of files on the floor, and a selection of stationery in plastic tiered shelves. Dixon sat down and opened the desk drawers one by one. Paper handkerchiefs, sachets of soup, a box of paracetamol, fruit tea bags, elastic bands. The next drawer down was no more exciting: padded envelopes, plastic document wallets, memos from someone with the initials PJC and the minutes of the last departmental meeting. The bottom drawer contained shoes and empty carrier bags.

He was looking at the photographs pinned to the partitioning when the door slammed behind him.

'What the bloody hell's going on?'

'This is the senior partner, Peter Cotter,' said Tuckett.

'Do you want to explain it to him or shall I?' asked Dixon, swivelling round on the chair. 'Oh, and we'll need their personnel files too.'

Tucker took Cotter to one side. The discussion was animated – lots of arm waving, the odd expletive carrying across the room – but Tuckett seemed to calm him down. Cotter strode over to where Dixon was sitting at Zoe Tremblay's workstation.

'Don't think you've heard the last of this, Inspector.'

'Well, you certainly haven't, Mr Cotter. Brett Greenwood was in this country illegally. And you employed him.'

Dixon turned back to the photographs on the partitioning and listened to yet more animated discussion, this time with Fiona Hull joining in.

He thought he recognised Thailand amongst the pictures, and Australia was obvious enough. Then he focused on the people. A mixture of young and old. Friends with their children, boyfriends too perhaps, all smiling at the camera. Some taken during the day, others at night. Fireworks over Sydney Opera House, a young man smiling at the camera.

A young man carrying a yellow rucksack.

'What d'you notice about that photo, Mark?'

Pearce stared at it for several seconds.

'Oh shit.'

'Bag 'em up,' said Dixon.

'Yes, Sir.'

'This is James Hubert, Inspector, our IT manager,' said Tuckett.

'What d'you need?' asked Hubert.

'The digital dictation schedules for Thursday, 17 and Friday, 18 October. You have daily backups?'

'Yes, on tape.'

'And the dictation itself?'

'The voice files, yes.'

'Good.'

'Anything else?'

'I need you to get me into this machine.'

'As administrator?'

'As Zoe Tremblay.'

'OK, I've got a list of passwords. Can I sit down?' asked Hubert, gesturing to the chair Dixon was sitting on.

'Yes, of course.'

The door opened and two secretaries walked in, laughing loudly.

'Wait downstairs, please, Gina,' shouted Tuckett. 'And tell anyone else to wait in reception.'

'Er, OK.' Gina noticed the police officers for the first time.

'There you go,' said Hubert, standing up. 'You're in.'

'What was her password?' asked Dixon.

'Tamsin82.'

'A daily reminder,' muttered Dixon. 'Where do I find the client folders?'

'On the N drive. Here, let me.' Hubert leaned over and took the mouse. He clicked on 'My Computer', selected 'N Drive' and then scrolled down to 'Litigation Department'. 'Now you just go to Brett's folder and go into "Clients".'

'Thanks.'

Dixon clicked on the Hagley folder and then the subfolder 'Attendance Notes'. Then he selected the note of the case management conference, right clicked on the mouse and selected 'Properties'.

It had been created on 18 October by Document Author Zoe Tremblay.

'I need the backups of this folder for 17 and 18 October.'

'That's easy enough.'

'Presumably this is all on a server.'

'Yes, why?'

'We may need to take it, but I'll check with our High Tech team first.'

'What?' screamed Cotter. 'You can't do that! We've got a business to run.'

'And I've got a murder to investigate, Mr Cotter,' said Dixon.

Chapter Twenty-Six

'What did she have to say for herself?' Dixon asked.

'Not a lot really. She advertised a room to rent in the *Bristol Post* last year and Zoe answered the ad,' replied Louise. She was standing by the corner of Dixon's workstation with Dave Harding, the two of them having just interviewed Sarah Witheridge.

'Is that it?' asked Dixon.

'She said Zoe was a good lodger,' replied Harding. 'Quiet, clean, didn't go out much.'

'When did she move in?'

'Last May.'

'Where was she living before?'

'She told Sarah she'd just moved to Bristol for work and was in a bed and breakfast,' replied Louise.

'Where from?'

'London.'

'Is she in a relationship?'

'No. Not according to Sarah anyway.'

'Any sign of the brother?'

'No,' replied Louise, shaking her head.

'Did she know Zoe was Canadian?'

'Yes. From Toronto originally, she said.'

'Well, that's something I suppose.'

'She stayed in most nights watching telly,' said Harding. 'She did go back to Canada in December though. First two weeks.'

'Right after Fryer's murder,' said Dixon.

'Yes.'

'Better check the passenger list, but I bet they travelled on separate flights. Probably from different airports too.'

'If they did, we've got no chance,' said Harding.

'Just check if the person she sat next to flew to Canada after Alison Crowther-Smith's murder too.'

'Yes, Sir.'

'When are you going to interview Zoe?' asked Louise.

'Now,' replied Dixon, looking at his watch.

'Is it her?'

'Yes, Sir,' replied Dixon, handing DCI Lewis a black and white copy of the photograph that had come over from Canada. They were standing in front of a monitor, watching Zoe Tremblay waiting not so patiently in the adjacent interview room. Her solicitor was scribbling in a notebook.

'Can't really see from this angle,' said Lewis. The camera was mounted on the wall just under the ceiling and they were looking down on Zoe.

'She's changed her hair colour and had it cut, but that's it.'

'What was it before? You can't tell from this.'

'Brown.'

Her hair was short and jet black, the flowing hair in the photograph long gone.

'What about the brother?'

Dixon handed Lewis a photograph. Light brown hair, shaved at the sides, longer on the top and swept over; piercing blue eyes and a square jaw. He was wearing a sleeveless white T-shirt, revealing the whole of his right arm, tattooed from the shoulder to the wrist.

'Is this a mugshot?' asked Lewis.

'His previous,' said Dixon, holding up several pages of A4 paper.

'How the hell did he get into this country with this lot?'

'Illegally.'

Lewis grunted as he flicked through the pages of previous convictions. 'Nasty piece of work, isn't he?'

'His sister's not much better,' replied Dixon. 'I managed to dodge the gob when we picked her up.'

Lewis shook his head.

'Shame the Met didn't stay for this one.'

'I'll send them an email later.'

'Can I have a cigarette?'

'No, you can't,' said Dixon, sitting down next to Zoe in the interview room. Her solicitor was to her right and Louise to Dixon's left.

He leaned forward and switched on the tape.

'My name is Detective Inspector Dixon. To my left is . . .'

'Detective Constable Louise Willmott.'

'The time is 12.15 p.m. on Tuesday, 25 February, and this is the first interview of Zoe Tremblay. Zoe, you've been rearrested on arrival here on suspicion of the murders of Alison Crowther-Smith, Robert Fryer and Anthony Fripp. You've also been reminded that you are still under caution. Is that correct?'

'Yes.'

'We'll stick with Zoe for the time being, shall we?' asked Dixon without looking up.

She tilted her head to one side and smirked at him.

'Sitting to Zoe's right is her solicitor . . .'

'Thomas Cable.'

'When did you come to the UK, Zoe?'

'Last year. May.'

Any pretence at an English accent had gone, replaced by Canadian.

'What for?'

'A holiday. I decided to stay on.'

'So you're here illegally?'

'Yes.'

'And working illegally?'

'Yes.'

'Did Lings check your immigration status?'

'They asked to see a bank statement and my driver's licence. I'd opened a bank account by then and used a fake licence.'

'What about a visa or a work permit?'

'They didn't ask.'

'Why Lings?'

'I came to Bristol and saw an advert in the *Bristol Post*.'

'Why Bristol then?'

'It seemed like a nice place. London was too big and too busy for me.'

'Your full name is Zoe Tremblay. Is that correct?'

'Yes.'

'When were you born?'

'September 12, 1982.'

'Where?'

'Toronto.'

'Do you have any brothers and sisters?'

'No.'

'Any previous convictions?'

'No.'

'Does the name Tamsin Jayne Lundy mean anything to you?'

'No.' She sat on her hands and began rocking backwards and forwards on her seat.

'Really?'

'No. Why? Should it?'

'Well, it's your real name, so I suppose it should, yes,' replied Dixon. Zoe shook her head.

'Tamsin Jayne Lundy: date of birth 12 September 1982, mother Ginette Lundy, father unknown.'

'Never heard of her.'

'This is a copy of your birth certificate,' said Dixon, handing her a piece of paper. She glanced at it and then passed it to Cable.

'I've never seen that before.'

'Do you have any criminal convictions in Canada?'

'Like what?'

'Oh, I don't know, you tell me.'

'No.'

'Well, let's start with theft and forgery of a credit card, contrary to Section 342, Subsection 1 of the Criminal Code of Canada.'

Zoe shook her head.

'January 2001 that one,' said Dixon. 'Let me make it easy for you, Zoe. When you were arrested, your fingerprints were taken. D'you remember that?'

No reply.

'Anyway, when you arrived here, your fingerprints were taken again. Now, you must remember that, surely.'

'Yes.'

'They match, Zoe.'

'Look, Inspector, I think my client has made her position clear.'

'Your client has lied, Mr Cable. Zoe Tremblay doesn't exist, does she, Tamsin?'

Dixon waited.

No reaction.

'OK, let's move on to the last time you were arrested, shall we? March 2011. Possession of Stolen Property, Section 355, and Unauthorized Possession of a Firearm, Section 91. Remember that?'

'No.'

'Well, that time a DNA swab was taken. A cotton wool bud inside your mouth. Ring any bells?'

'No.'

'The fingerprints are conclusive, but DNA is better still and we're going to check the sample we've just taken with the sample from 2011. Call it a transatlantic DNA test. It's one of the wonders of modern science.'

She looked up at the ceiling, breathing heavily.

'That's going to prove your real name is Tamsin Jayne Lundy, isn't it?'

Her reply was lost in a loud sigh: 'Yes.'

'Repeat that for the tape, please, Tamsin.'

'Yes, all right, fucking yes.'

'Tamsin it is then,' said Dixon. 'You'll need to amend your legal aid application form, Mr Cable.'

'Thank you,' replied Cable, rolling his eyes.

'Right then, let's start again, shall we? Why did you come to the UK, Tamsin?'

'For a holiday.'

'Not to find your father?'

'No.'

'Or to find out about him?'

'I don't know who my father is.'

'Really?' said Dixon. 'I do.'

'My mother never told us anything.'

'Us?'

No reply.

'By "us" I assume you mean you and your brother.'

'I don't have a brother.'

'You do have a father though. Sergeant Adrian Kandes, killed in action during the Battle of Mount Harriet, 11 June 1982.'

'Never heard of him.'

'And he's got a sister, which makes her your aunt. Still alive and kicking. So here's what we're going to do. Another DNA test. This time between you and her, checking for a familial match. And what d'you think we'll find?'

'I have an aunt?' asked Tamsin.

'You do.'

'What's her name?'

'Glenda.'

'Where does she live?'

'I'll need her permission to tell you that.'

Tamsin nodded.

'Where's your brother?' asked Dixon.

'You'll never find him.'

'If you say so. Why did you come to the UK then?'

'To find out about my father. My mother told me about him before she died.'

'What did she tell you?'

'All she said was that he was a Royal Marine and that he'd been killed on the Falklands.'

'Nothing else?'

'That he should've won the VC, but it was taken away from him.'

'So you know how he died?'

'Yes.'

'What did you do when you got here?'

'I got in touch with the Royal Marines Association, and they put me in touch with some people who knew him.'

'Richard Hagley?'

'Yes.' Beads of sweat were starting to appear on her forehead. 'Can I have a tissue?' she asked, turning to Cable.

'And what did Hagley tell you?' asked Dixon.

'Everything.'

'What did you think when you found out your father was a hero?'

'That he was a fucking idiot.' Her face was flushed, nostrils flaring. 'What did he die for? What? Nothing, that's what.'

'Well, he—'

'Queen and country? Don't give me that crap. A small piece of rock thousands of miles away? He knew my mother was pregnant. He knew . . .' Her voice tailed off and she began wiping her face with the tissue Cable had given her.

'And he volunteered to go,' said Dixon.

'Why would he do that? And why did he have to die like that?'

'If you could ask him, I reckon he'd tell you he did it for his mates. For the man standing next to him and those behind him.'

'What the fuck d'you know about it?'

'Nothing, luckily,' replied Dixon.

'Well, shut up then!'

'Why did you get the job at Lings?'

Silence.

'Was it to help Hagley, to make sure he won?'

'No, it wasn't.'

'Why then?'

'To find Alan bloody Fletcher. He was the one. If it hadn't been for him, my father would've got away.'

'He'd have been caught and court-martialled, Tamsin.'

'But he'd have lived. They don't shoot deserters any more.'

Tears were streaming down her cheeks now.

'So you get a job at Lings. How?'

'I met Brett and he put in a word for me.'

'And whose idea was that?'

'Hagley's.'

'Then you find Fletcher, but he's not killed until a couple of weeks ago, is he?' asked Dixon. 'Why not just kill him and leave, go back to Canada?'

'No comment.'

'What happened?'

'Nothing.'

'Alison Crowther-Smith. Defence barrister, drowned in a caving accident in Swildon's Hole two days after defeating the interim payment application at the case management conference.'

'No comment.'

'She was just doing her job, Tamsin. If it hadn't been her, it would've been someone else. And she had two young children.'

'I . . . I didn't know that.'

'Know or care?' asked Dixon, shuffling the papers in front of him.

'Know.'

'She didn't drown in an accident though, did she? We both know that. Your brother crept up behind her at Sump One and held her feet, drowning her.'

'You can't prove that.'

'I can prove you knew that she would be down there. I can prove that. You found out after the case management conference and before she died.'

'How?'

'I've got Greenwood's handwritten note. You photocopied it for me,' replied Dixon, handing her a copy. 'See, there, next to her phone number.'

'That doesn't prove anything.'

'It proves you knew, because he dictated his attendance note of the hearing that afternoon, and you typed it up the next day. You'd have had the file open on your desk, Tamsin.'

No reply.

'Alison C-S. Caving, Sunday, Swildon's Hole.' Dixon was reading aloud from the handwritten attendance note.

Silence.

'And Dr Fripp. Killed in a hotel room in Birmingham, where he was giving evidence in a trial at the county court. You knew that from his dates-to-avoid, which were sitting on the file.'

'You can't prove a thing.'

'Catch your brother and I can.'

'I don't have a brother. Check my phone calls if you don't believe me.'

'A few minutes ago you said I'd never find him,' said Dixon. 'Don't call me, I'll call you.'

'What's that supposed to mean?'

'We found these taped to the back of the drawer in your bedside table.' Dixon held up a bag of pay-as-you-go SIM cards. 'There are eight of them, Tamsin.'

'So?'

'You ring him, fresh SIM card every time. Different network. Very neat.'

Zoe shook her head, her stare fixed on the floor in front of her.

'Your phone is unlocked. I checked,' continued Dixon. 'And it's being looked at now by our High Tech team.'

'That's ridiculous.'

'How else d'you explain a bag of new SIM cards?'

She shifted in her chair and then folded her arms tight across her chest.

'I still don't get it,' said Dixon. 'You get the job at Lings to find Fletcher and kill him, but you don't. You kill Alison Crowther-Smith first. And then there's the Treasury Solicitor too don't forget. I can't get used to calling it the Government Legal Department. Your brother probably followed him home from work one day. But why?'

'I didn't kill Alison Crowther-Smith or Fripp or Fryer.'

'You know who Fryer is though,' said Dixon, raising his eyebrows. 'Or was.'

Silence.

'I'm using "you" collectively, Tamsin. I mean you and your brother. You found out who was conducting the defence, told your brother and he did the rest.'

'I told you, I don't have a brother.'

'How much did Hagley offer to pay you?'

'Nothing.'

'Who then?'

Cable leaned over and whispered in Tamsin's ear.

'No comment,' she said.

'Was it one of the others? Lawrence Hampton perhaps? Or were you working on a no-win, no-fee deal like Lings?'

She smirked at Dixon.

'That's it, isn't it? You were working on a no-win, no-fee.'

'No comment.'

'Force the Crown to settle the case and take a cut of the damages,' said Dixon, nodding. 'Is that it?'

'No comment.'

'Whose damages?'

'Nobody's.'

'We'll find Joel, Tamsin,' said Dixon, handing her copies of the mugshot from Canada and the photo from her workstation. 'How long's he had that yellow caving sack? He's wearing it in this photo too. It's a still from the CCTV at Wimbledon station. That's Robert Fryer there, right in front of him.'

She looked down at the photograph, tears starting to fall down her cheeks.

'Oh Joel, Joel.' She shook her head.

'Where is he, Tamsin?'

'So far off the grid you'll never find him.'

'Off the grid? You've been watching too many Hollywood films.'

'You'll never take him alive.'

'And I've heard that somewhere before,' muttered Dixon.

Chapter Twenty-Seven

'Did you see that?'

'We were watching on the monitor,' replied Lewis, who was standing by Mark Pearce's workstation in the CID area. Dave Harding was waiting by the kettle.

'Well, that's a first for me. Killers working on a no-win, no-fee,' said Dixon. 'Make mine a strong one, please, Dave.'

'Yes, Sir.'

'What makes you think someone was paying them?' asked Lewis.

'I get why Fletcher was killed. I can see the motive for that. But why else were the others killed?'

'If it wasn't for money, you mean,' said Louise.

'That's right. You heard what she said about her father's death. That's the one bit that was probably true. And if that's right, then she sure as hell didn't see herself as beholden to Hagley and the others for what they did for her father.'

Lewis nodded.

'So, what now then?'

'We drop everything and find her brother.'

'Where do we start?' asked Pearce.

'I'll get the usual alerts out,' said Lewis. 'We can use this mugshot.'

'Thank you, Sir,' replied Dixon. 'Anything from High Tech on her phone?'

'Not yet,' replied Pearce.

'Let's get the guest houses checked, bed and breakfasts, and hostels. In and around Bristol. He won't have gone far from Tamsin.'

'Yes, Sir.'

'What about her flights to and from Canada?'

'Nothing, but then we don't know what name he's using,' said Harding. 'There was no one called Joel on the flight and the passenger sitting next to her was female.'

'Off the grid, she said,' muttered Dixon through a yawn. 'Whatever the hell that means.' He sat down at a vacant workstation in the large windows at Express Park and switched on the computer.

'Is it worth checking the CCTV at the airport?' asked Louise. 'When she flew home.'

'Good idea. He may be there with her, checking in on a different flight perhaps.'

'I'll check DVLA and see if there's a car registered in her name.'

'Good thinking, Mark.'

Another yawn.

'When was the last time you slept?' asked Lewis.

'I'm fine,' replied Dixon.

He waited until Lewis had gone, then leaned back in the chair and closed his eyes.

'Nick, Nick.' Someone was shaking his arm.

'What the . . . ?'

He opened his eyes to find Jane sitting on his desk, smiling at him.

'Was I . . . ?'

'Yes, you were. You didn't sleep at all last night, so it's hardly surprising.'

'What time is it?' asked Dixon, yawning.

'Twoish,' replied Jane. 'You need to get to bed.'

'Later,' muttered Dixon, reaching for his coffee.

'That's stone cold.'

Dixon grimaced.

'Where are the others?' He was looking around the CID area, which was empty, apart from Louise, who was on the phone.

'Lewis sent them home. They were up all night too don't forget.'

Dixon yawned.

'How'd you get on?' asked Jane.

'We've got the daughter. We'll hold her overnight and charge her tomorrow morning. We've got enough. Now we just need to find her brother. Him.' Dixon handed Jane a copy of the mugshot.

'Any idea where he might be?'

'Off the grid apparently. We're checking all the usual places. I shouldn't think he'll be far from Bristol.'

'Have you tried the YMCA?'

'Funny, isn't it,' said Louise, her hand over the mouthpiece of her phone, 'we thought it was one of the lawyers and it turned out to be a secretary.'

Dixon nodded. Then he jumped up and ran over to the filing cabinet. He pulled out the copy of Sharma's correspondence file and began flicking through it. Louise replaced the handset on her phone and glanced across at Jane, who shrugged her shoulders.

'Looking at these telephone attendance notes,' said Dixon, 'someone was desperate to settle this case at the outset. First they'd accept fifty grand plus costs, then thirty.' Dixon flicked through the pages. 'It dropped to twenty just before the court proceedings started.'

'What are you saying?' asked Louise.

'Then the file's transferred to Greenwood and the killings start.' Dixon snapped the file shut. 'Let's go.'

'Where?'

'Back to Bristol.'

Dixon double parked in the road outside the Hippodrome behind two patrol cars that had been waiting for them. It was just after 4 p.m., the afternoon cold and clear, the snow visible on the tops of the Mendips as they had raced north on the M5.

He climbed out of the driver's seat and walked across the pavement towards the alleyway leading to Lings Solicitors.

'Give a lawyer a financial interest in the outcome of a case,' he muttered.

'No-win, no-fee,' replied Louise.

Once through the alleyway, he pushed open the glass front door.

'Is Mrs Hull in?'

'Let me check,' said the receptionist. She walked over to her desk and looked at the open notebook on the counter. 'She went out at lunchtime and hasn't come back yet.'

'Is she due in?'

'I'll ask her secretary,' she replied, picking up the phone. 'Wendy, is Fiona due back this afternoon?' She nodded. 'Oh right, thanks.'

'Well?'

'She's supposed to be in the office.'

Dixon grimaced.

'Would you like me to try her on her mobile?'

'No, thank you. Who's dealing with Mr Greenwood's files?'

'There's a locum. Mr Atkins.'

'Tell him we're on our way up to see him.'

'You can't just . . .'

Too late. Dixon, Louise and two uniformed officers were already on their way up the stairs, the receptionist's frantic voice just carrying over their footsteps.

'Mr Cotter, the police are here, and they're on their way up to the fourth floor.'

Dixon burst through the double doors on the fourth floor and spotted Atkins sitting at Greenwood's desk, on the phone. He stood up when he saw Dixon and Louise heading towards him across the open plan office. Dixon glanced at Tamsin's desk, which was already occupied by another secretary.

'I need to see the conditional fee agreement for Hagley, Absolon and others against the MOD,' said Dixon, holding up his warrant card.

'Er, yes, all right,' replied Atkins, glancing over Dixon's shoulder.

'What the bloody hell is going on?'

Dixon spun round to find the senior partner, Peter Cotter, steaming towards him with John Tuckett close behind.

'I need to see the no-win, no-fee agreement, Mr Cotter,' replied Dixon. 'Then I need a word with Fiona Hull.'

'Let's go in here, shall we?' asked Tuckett, gesturing to a vacant office.

'Who's this?' asked Cotter.

'Greg Atkins,' replied Tuckett. 'He's a locum filling in for Brett Greenwood.'

'You'd better come too. And bring the file.'

Atkins nodded.

'Now, what's this all about?' asked Cotter, closing the door behind them.

'I need to speak to Mrs Hull in connection with the murders of Alison Crowther-Smith, Robert Fryer and Dr Anthony Fripp,' replied Dixon.

'Oh good God.' Cotter sat down on the corner of the vacant desk.

'May I see the agreement?'

Cotter waved at Atkins, who pulled a document from the file and handed it to Dixon. He turned straight to the back page.

'It's signed by Mrs Hull.'

'That's perfectly normal. She's the head of department,' replied Tuckett.

'Is it perfectly normal for Lings to take a case to the European Court on a no-win, no-fee agreement?'

'No, it bloody well isn't,' said Cotter.

'And without insurance against paying the defence costs if you lose?' asked Dixon.

'Is that right?' asked Tuckett, looking at Atkins.

He nodded.

'Bloody hell,' said Cotter. 'Not again.'

'You're going to need to explain that last remark, Mr Cotter,' said Dixon.

'You can go, Greg. Leave the file,' said Tuckett.

'She's, er . . .' Cotter was waiting for Atkins to close the door behind him. 'She's taken on some thin cases in the past and lost us a lot of money, Inspector. Always on a no-win, no-fee basis, and we've been left tens of thousands of pounds down. She's on her last warning. It's not just the lost fees, you understand, but there's the expenses we pay out too – court fees, experts' fees. We fund the expenses, and if we don't win we don't get them back.'

'She assured me the Crown would settle,' said Tuckett. 'She's a good lawyer. Her heart's in the right place and she wants to help people. She just forgets this is a business.'

'What will happen now?'

'We'll need to go through her files, but if what you say is right, she'll be dismissed,' replied Cotter.

Dixon turned to watch one of the uniformed officers step outside, his mobile phone ringing in his coat pocket. The officer stared at Dixon through the glass partition, nodding from time to time. Dixon was no lip reader, but he recognised the words 'We're on our way' before the officer rang off.

'Can I have a word, Sir,' said the officer, leaning in through the door of the office.

Dixon and Louise stepped out on to the landing.

'We've got a jumper,' whispered the constable. 'Female, mid-forties, fits the description of Mrs Hull.'

Dixon shook his head.

'There's a briefcase with letters in it. And a Lings case file.'

'Is someone on the way to her house?'

'Yes, Sir.'

'All right, let's go.'

A cold north wind was whistling down the Avon Gorge as Dixon stood on the parapet and looked down on to the cars speeding along the Portway below; commuters racing home from work probably. He turned up the collar of his coat and sunk his hands deep into his pockets.

'Cold enough for you?' he asked, turning to Louise.

She grimaced.

The tide was out 240 feet below, and the River Avon had receded to reveal thick grey mud. Two coastguard officers wearing yellow helmets and orange lifejackets were crawling out from the bank on mats, trying to reach the body, a red coat just visible in the mud.

A flat bottomed boat was resting on the mud at the water's edge a few yards away, the tide having gone out before it could reach the body.

The road was closed, but their warrant cards had got them past the patrol car, and they walked out across the Clifton Suspension Bridge, the huge supporting cables towering above them. The bridge was moving in the wind, but then it was supposed to, Dixon reminded himself.

They walked towards a group of fluorescent jackets huddled around a briefcase on the pavement just inside the railings, a third of the way across on the north side.

Dixon stepped over the crash barrier on to the pavement and looked at the suicide fence that had been placed inside the old railings. It had five strands of wire along the top and was overhanging, designed to be difficult to climb over no doubt.

Not difficult enough.

'Detective Inspector Dixon?'

'Yes.'

'Sergeant Edmunds, Sir.'

'What time was it?'

'Just after 3.30 p.m.'

'We were still out on the M5, Sir,' said Louise, shaking her head.

'She stood on her briefcase, then jumped up and over,' continued Edmunds.

'Have you looked in it?'

'Yes, Sir. There's a file and some other papers. And a sealed envelope addressed to her husband.'

'Have you informed the coroner?'

'Yes, Sir.'

'I'd like a copy of the letter when you open it, please.'

'Yes, Sir.'

Dixon nodded.

'C'mon, Louise, let's get back. We've still got to find Joel Kandes.'

Chapter Twenty-Eight

Dixon arrived back at Express Park just before 6 p.m., having picked up Monty on the way and dropped Louise at home, remembering just before he got back on the M5 that he was supposed to be giving Jane a lift home from work.

'How'd you get on?' she asked, pulling her handbag out from under her desk.

'She jumped off the Clifton Suspension Bridge half an hour before we got there,' replied Dixon. 'It's a sod of a long way down. I never really noticed it when I used to go climbing in the Avon Gorge.'

'She must've known you'd make the connection when you picked up Tamsin.'

'It was just a matter of time.'

'Did she leave a note?'

Dixon nodded.

'Four murders,' said Jane shaking her head.

'Three,' replied Dixon. 'She had nothing to do with Fletcher's, not that it makes much difference now.'

'Did she have children?'

'Two.'

'Poor buggers,' muttered Jane, opening the door of Dixon's Land Rover. 'That just leaves Joel then.'

'If you were going off the grid, where would you go?'

'Oh, I dunno. It's too cold for camping. A guest house perhaps, paying cash. What about you?'

Dixon's reply was lost in a yawn and a shake of the head.

'What?' asked Jane.

'Nothing.'

One junction north on the M5 and then home. Dixon would be in bed within fifteen minutes and unlikely to wake up until the morning.

'Switch your phone off when you get home.'

'I can't do th—' Dixon stopped mid-sentence and turned to Jane. 'I know exactly where I'd go to get off the grid.'

'Where?'

'Climbing bunkhouses. Five quid a night, cash in the tin, no names, false names. Who cares?'

He reached forward and opened the glove box.

'Check the torch is all right, will you?'

Jane took it out and switched it on.

'It's fine, why?'

'Fancy a trip up to Priddy? We could have a bite to eat at the pub.'

'What's up there?'

'The Wessex Cave Club hut.'

'How d'you know he'll be here?'

'I don't, but it's got to be worth checking. The place is deserted with Swildon's Hole closed, and as far as he's concerned everybody thinks

Alison Crowther-Smith's death was an accident. He won't know about his sister and Fiona Hull yet either.'

'Well, be careful,' said Jane.

'I'm just going to see if anyone's there, that's all. Don't panic.'

'He's got a gun you said.'

'If he's there, we'll call for backup. All right?'

'OK.'

'If not, we can try the Mendip Caving Group place further along the top.'

Dixon switched his headlights off as he turned into the drive, which followed the back of a farmyard on the left before opening out into the car park. Snow was settling on the bonnet of his Land Rover, but he was able to pick out the line of the concrete drive by following the post and rail fence on his right.

'There's a light on upstairs,' said Jane. It cast an eerie glow across the field, but was just enough.

Dixon switched off the engine and allowed the Land Rover to coast into the car park, the crunch of the gravel beneath his tyres the only sound. He turned and parked on the left, under a large tree and next to an old camper van.

'I wonder who that's registered to?' he whispered.

'D'you want me to check?'

'Yes. And wait here.'

Dixon opened the driver's door and slid out of the Land Rover. He closed the door behind him, making only the faintest click as he leaned against it, and then tiptoed across the car park towards the entrance to the changing rooms. It was locked.

The upstairs light had gone out by the time he came round the corner, but he remembered the scaffolding tower on the grass in front of the hut just in time. He paused, hoping his eyes would adjust to the darkness a bit more. Then he crept up the garden path and tried the front door. It was open.

He reached in and switched on the light in the hall. The door was open into the lounge, but the light was off, although the dying embers of a fire were still glowing in the hearth. The smell, a mixture of log fire and curry, was welcoming. There was even an empty can of beer on the table in front of the sofa.

Dixon looked along the corridor to his left, which led to the stairs and then the changing rooms, both in darkness, so he stepped into the hall and closed the door behind him.

He was standing in the hall when the light on the landing came on. He turned to look at the noticeboard in front of him and listened to the footsteps coming down the stairs.

'Hello,' said Dixon, turning when the footsteps reached the bottom step.

Short brown hair, a full growth of beard and a long sleeved fleece. It could be. It just could be.

'I just popped in to see if there were any meets coming up,' continued Dixon, turning back to the noticeboard.

'Cancelled,' said the man. 'Swildon's is closed.'

Was that a Canadian accent? Well disguised if it was. Mid-thirties, the right age bracket.

'Where are you going?' asked Dixon.

'Eastwater.'

Definitely an accent there, but what?

'On your own?'

'No, my mate's coming tomorrow.'

'What's your name?'

'Joel Kandes, but then you knew that.' The movement was quick, smooth, almost rehearsed, and Dixon found himself looking down the barrel of a gun. 'I've used it before. And I'll use it again.'

'I have no doubt about that, Joel,' replied Dixon. 'D'you prefer Lundy or Kandes?'

'Kandes.'

Dixon nodded. He looked at Kandes's right wrist, the tattoo revealed now his arm was extended holding the handgun.

'Give me your phone,' said Kandes.

Dixon took his iPhone out of his pocket and threw it to Kandes. He caught it and turned it over in the palm of his hand.

'What's the code?'

Silence.

'What's the code?' he screamed, jabbing the gun at Dixon.

'Three-two-seven-five.'

Dixon watched Kandes tap in the code, checking for recent calls.

'I was expecting to see 999 in there,' said Kandes, shaking his head. He dropped the phone on the floor and stamped on it, shattering the glass with his heel. 'You won't need that where you're going.'

'I'm curious,' said Dixon.

'What about?'

'I can understand why you killed Fletcher, but why the lawyers?'

Kandes smirked. 'They should've settled the case, shouldn't they? They had the chance.'

'The brick dust was a nice touch, but if you hadn't done that I wouldn't be here now and you'd have got clean away.'

'Would I?'

'Yes.'

'You're assuming I want to.'

'Did you know you had an aunt? Your father's sister. Only Tamsin seemed a bit surprised when I told her.'

'Happy families, eh?' asked Kandes, grinning.

'Well . . .'

'Shut the fuck up!'

Kandes was becoming agitated now, the gun waving from side to side.

'This way,' he said, gesturing along the corridor with the barrel. 'Go in front. One wrong move and it ends.'

Dixon nodded and walked along the corridor slowly.

'Hands where I can see them.'

Dixon put his hands behind his head, interlocking his fingers.

'In there,' said Kandes.

Dixon kicked open the door of the changing room and switched on the light. It looked much the same as before. Dirty caving equipment piled up everywhere. The floor was at least dry this time.

Kandes took a coat off a hook and put it on one arm at a time, careful to keep the gun pointed at Dixon. Then he picked up his yellow caving sack and slung it over his shoulder.

'Out.'

Dixon turned to face the back door, his back to Kandes.

'Aren't you going to put a quid in the tin?'

He heard the crack before he felt the pain explode across the back of his head. He pitched forward, stumbling on to a large cardboard box full of wetsuits, warm fluid trickling down the back of his neck. His head was spinning, but the first searing pain had gone, replaced by a dull ache.

'Get a move on.'

Dixon opened the back door and stepped out into the snow, his hands back behind his head, if only to stop the bleeding. Kandes put on a helmet and switched on the lamp. He also switched on a handheld torch.

'Over that wall,' he said, slamming the door behind him.

Dixon glanced across to the Land Rover without turning his head. Monty was standing up at the rear window, snarling and butting the glass with his head, but there was no sign of Jane.

'I'll deal with him when I get back,' muttered Kandes.

Dixon stepped over the wall at the bottom of the garden and walked along the track behind the hut, Kandes behind shining the torch at the ground in front of him and pointing the gun in the middle of his back, with the occasional prod to remind Dixon it was there.

'What had Alison Crowther-Smith ever done to you?' asked Dixon as he climbed over the first drystone wall.

'Nothing.'

'She had young children.'

'Whatever.'

'She was just doing her job.'

'And I was doing mine.'

'What's that supposed to mean?' asked Dixon.

'She was advising the Crown to fight the case. It was business, purely business.'

Another prod in the back with the gun barrel, more of a jab this time, catching Dixon right on the spine.

'No-win, no-fee,' he said, wincing.

Silence.

'Whose idea was that?'

'Mine. Like it, do you?' asked Kandes.

'Very inventive,' replied Dixon. 'And Fryer?'

'His replacement wanted to settle. Now that was progress.'

'So, when did you find out about your father?'

'My mother told me about him before she died,' replied Kandes.

'Tamsin didn't have a good word to say about him.'

'She doesn't understand. Blames him for dying. He knew how to die. And so do I.'

'What about Fletcher then? Tamsin wanted him dead because he stopped her father from getting away. But you, why did you kill him?'

'My father should've won the VC for what he did. He was a fucking hero. And it was that twat's fault he didn't.'

The snow was settling fast as Dixon trudged across the fields, and their footprints were inches deep.

'Not business then?' asked Dixon, waiting for Kandes to climb over the next drystone wall.

'Strictly pleasure that one,' said Kandes, grinning. 'Till he went and had a heart attack on me. Useless tosser. He got in touch with Hagley, would you believe it? Wanted to know what he could do to help them win the case.'

'And what did Hagley tell him?'

'To meet me at the pillbox. I'd got it all mapped out too. Two in the chest, one in the leg and one in the shoulder. Just like my old man.'

Dixon nodded.

'You liked the brick dust then?' continued Kandes. 'I thought it had a sense of irony.'

'You were doing all right up to that point. A caving accident and a random killer pushing someone under a train. No one had made the connection.'

'I'm still doing all right.'

'Not really. Your sister's in custody.'

'She won't say a thing.'

'What d'you think I'm doing here?'

'But how many people know you're here? Eh?'

'And Fiona Hull's dead. So you won't be getting any money now, will you?'

Silence.

'She jumped off the Clifton Suspension Bridge, Joel.'

The beams of light illuminating the way ahead stopped and Dixon turned round. Kandes was standing in the snow, breathing hard, the gun in his right hand pressed to his forehead.

'You.' Kandes pointed the gun at Dixon. 'You fucking . . .'

'She had two children, Joel.'

'Just keep walking.'

Dixon arrived at the wall at the end of the track leading to the entrance to Swildon's Hole. He hesitated.

'Go!'

'Another caving accident, is it?' asked Dixon.

'Three lawyers and a copper. I'm the one who should get the damn medal.'

'Posthumously?'

'Keep moving,' replied Kandes, shaking his head.

Dixon watched the beam of Kandes's headlamp lighting up the woods above them, the snow settling now on the branches. A scene from a Christmas card perhaps. Then the hedgerow on the right. Barbed wire and brambles – no way through even if he could get away.

'Down you go,' said Kandes, pushing Dixon in the small of the back with the gun barrel. Below them was the stone blockhouse at the entrance to Swildon's Hole.

A second caving trip had not been on Dixon's agenda, and certainly not with a gun in the small of his back. Nor was it how he expected his life to end. A fall from the north face of the Eiger perhaps, not that he had ever gone anywhere near it, or Cheddar, like Jake. But down a hole?

Fuck that.

'I want you a couple of yards ahead of me. Any closer and it ends with one in the back of your head. Understand?'

Dixon nodded.

'All right,' said Kandes, nodding towards the entrance. 'Get in there.'

'I won't be able to see where I'm going.'

'Tough.'

Dixon sat down on the edge of the hole in the concrete floor with his feet dangling over the stream below. Still a trickle, mercifully. Then he felt a solid blow to his lower back and he fell feet first into the hole, landing on the rocks below.

'Keep going!'

There was just enough light from Kandes's headlamp and the torch in his left hand, although the beam of that was dancing around all over the place as he climbed down into the hole himself.

'Not under the big boulder. We'll go in through the Zig-Zags so I can keep an eye on you.'

The rock wall dropped away to the left just before the large boulder that Dixon had squeezed under on his last visit, so he followed the narrow shaft, crawling on his hands and knees. Not easy without gloves and knee pads, but that was the least of his worries.

'Where are we going?'

'You'll know when we get there.'

'If you're hoping people will think I came down here on my own and got stuck, you're—'

'Will you just shut the fuck up!'

The same metallic smell invaded his nostrils. It had taken him days to shift it last time. His arms and legs were saturated, his knuckles bloody and bruised, and they'd only been in the cave a matter of minutes. And the cold? No fleece undersuit and caving suit this time. He gritted his teeth to stop the chattering; not that he could hear much over the running water echoing all around him.

He waited for the beam of Kandes's torch to light the way ahead and then moved, pausing until the beam swung back again, all track of time lost.

Then the Zig-Zags opened out into another passageway, and he was at the bottom of the slab that he had climbed down only a few days before. At least he knew where he was now. Twenty minutes to the Thirty Foot Pot, he remembered that. And it might give him a chance to jump Kandes.

'Stop.'

Dixon looked over the drop, but it was impossible to see much more than a few feet in the light reflecting from Kandes's headlamp.

The waterfall cascaded over the edge, but soon disappeared into the darkness, landing on the rocks thirty feet below.

'Here,' said Kandes.

Dixon turned just as Kandes threw him a coiled up wire ladder.

'Clip that into the bolt and then down you go.'

'But . . .'

'Get on with it.'

Dixon clipped the karabiner on the end of the ladder into the bolt that had been drilled into the rock at chest height, just above the waterfall. Then he dropped it over the edge, watching it uncoil into the darkness below.

'What about a rope?'

'Down!'

Dixon began climbing down the ladder, remembering to have his hands behind it to stop himself swinging out. Once he was over the edge there was more light as Kandes looked down into the void, his teeth glinting in the glare from his headlamp as he grinned at Dixon.

Then Dixon's legs were flailing.

'Sorry, I forgot: it's a twenty-foot ladder,' said Kandes, the sound of his laughter echoing around the chamber.

Dixon froze and waited until the ladder stopped swinging. Then he began climbing down hand over hand. Once dangling from the bottom rung by his right hand, he looked down and caught a glimpse of the gravel stream bed a few feet to his left in the light from Kandes's headlamp. Directly below him were rocks. He started to swing slowly, letting go when he was over the gravel and landing heavily in a heap in the shallow water.

'Well done,' said Kandes.

'What now?'

'You die. It won't take long. It'll look like you came down here with the wrong ladder, fell and died of hypothermia. Another tragic accident. Could be months too before the cave opens and they find you.'

'What about a torch?' asked Dixon.

'Good point,' replied Kandes. He switched off both his headlamp and the handheld torch.

'Ready?'

Then he dropped the torch over the edge.

'Oh, you missed it,' he said as the sound of breaking glass echoed around the chamber.

Chapter Twenty-Nine

The back door of the hut swung open, a shaft of light illuminating the snow falling on the path and the sheds along the drystone wall. Jane looked in the rearview mirror and gasped. Mesmerised, she watched Dixon step out into the night with his hands on his head.

Oh shit.

She threw herself across the driver's seat and listened for voices. Not easy over the noise of Monty barking and scrabbling at the back door of the Land Rover.

Craning her neck, she watched in the wing mirror as Dixon walked down the path towards the drystone wall at the bottom of the garden, a man behind him carrying a torch in one hand and a gun in the other, another lamp mounted on his helmet.

She reached into the back of the Land Rover, pulled her wellington boots out from under the bench seat and put them on. Then she took the torch from the glove box, slid across to the driver's seat and opened the door. She climbed down from the Land Rover and closed the door behind her, leaning against it just as Dixon had done only a few minutes earlier.

Click.

She locked it and followed Dixon's footsteps across the car park to the back door of the hut, careful to place her feet in his footprints. She tried the door. Locked.

The two lights were just visible through the snow and appeared to be climbing up and over a drystone wall in the distance. Jane ducked down behind the sheds and dialled 999.

'This is 3242 Detective Sergeant Jane Winter. I'm at the Wessex Cave Club hut east of Priddy. I need backup and Armed Response. Is that clear?'

'Er, yes, Sarge.'

'Detective Inspector Dixon has been taken hostage and is being led at gunpoint across the fields west towards Priddy.'

'Stand by,' replied the controller.

Jane waited.

'Armed Response are on the way, but the helicopter's grounded by the weather.'

'How long?'

'Twenty-five minutes.'

Shit.

Jane rang off. Then she climbed over the wall at the bottom of the garden and started following the footprints in the snow. She held her torch low to the ground and switched it off as she arrived at the first drystone wall, peering over it into the darkness. A faint glow was visible in the distance and then it disappeared.

She jumped over the wall and started running along the line of tracks in the snow, over the next drystone wall, sharp right turn and then over another. Now she was looking into the bottom of a dark hollow along the base of some woods on her left. A spooky place at the best of times.

She could just make out a light in the distance before it went out.

Where the hell are they going?

She ran along the bottom of the hollow until the tracks stopped abruptly, and turned down a steep path towards a small grey stone building the size of telephone box. A stream disappeared under the tree roots at the side.

It's a cave. A fucking cave.

She crept down to the entrance and read the sign nailed to the stonework outside.

'Swildon's Hole. In case of emergency, dial 999 and ask for Cave Rescue.'

No shit.

No signal. She ran back to the drystone wall and stood on top of it, waving her phone in the air above her head. Two bars. That would do. Then she dialled 999 again.

'This is 3242 Detective Sergeant Winter. DI Dixon has been taken down Swildon's Hole at gunpoint. Is that clear?'

'Understood.'

'We'll need Cave Resc—'

'Stand by.'

Come on!

'Under no circumstances should you foll—'

Jane rang off and ran back to the cave entrance. Why did it have to be a cave? She stopped and retched into the undergrowth.

Nice and quiet, easy does it.

Tears streaming down her cheeks, she peered into the hole in the concrete floor of the blockhouse, the sound of running water echoing in the darkness below. Then she dropped into the hole and slid down the rock into a small chamber, fumbling for the off button on the torch. She was shaking violently, but wasn't cold, so it must have been fear. At least she could control that. Or try to. She listened. Nothing.

But which way? Straight on under the huge boulder in front of her, or follow the narrow corridor to the left?

And what is that smell?

She retched again, trying to muffle the sound. She switched the torch back on and shone it under the boulder, but the beam was flickering all over the place.

Stop shaking!

The rock looked polished by years of cavers' backsides sliding across it.

That must be the way.

Torch off again, she wriggled under the boulder feet first, lying on her back. Fear was taking over and she was in danger of hyperventilating. She closed her eyes.

Control it!

Then her feet dropped clear of the rock, and she slid out on to the floor of a smaller chamber on the other side. Torch on for a quick look around and then off again. It was an odd sensation. No light source anywhere, and yet she could see her fingers as plain as day. She blinked and they were gone, pitched into the absolute darkness once again.

Which way now?

Nick had said the cave followed a stream down through the Mendips, so follow the water. That must be right, mustn't it? But which way? The sound of running water was all around her.

Down. It must be down.

Crawling now, no knee or elbow pads, but it wouldn't have been much fun with them anyway. Move, torch off and listen. Move, torch off and listen. Nothing over the sound of the running water and her own breathing. She was inching her way down now.

How far had she gone? Not far, and she was sure she could find her way back out again.

Move, torch off and listen. Nothing. Torch on. She was at the top of a slab that fell away beneath her, the cave roof only two feet above. She'd need to go down on her back, using her hands and feet to brace herself against the roof. Nothing for it. She opened her mouth and held the torch between her teeth like a big fat cigar.

A narrow corridor joined from the right at the bottom of the slab and another from the left, all meeting at the gravel stream bed. Which way now? Torch off and listen. Left was down, at least that was the way the water was going. It must be that way.

Then she heard it. The crunch of gravel. A boulder rocking over. Moving quickly, whoever it was, and coming from the left. She shone her torch into the narrow corridor on the right and ran into it, diving into a shallow cleft under the wall just as she switched off the light. She lay still and waited, soaked to the skin and still shaking, but not cold at all.

The crunch of the gravel was getting louder now, the footsteps faster. Then she saw the light. Only one this time. It paused at the bottom of the slab and then disappeared up it.

She waited, listening to the shuffling and scrabbling of feet on rock. No gunshot. Nick must still be alive.

Ninety-nine, one hundred. She had counted to a hundred three times to give him five minutes to get clear; then she slid out of her cleft in the rock and stood up. One last listen. Nothing. Torch on.

Holding the torch in her right hand, she followed the narrow streambed down, walking as fast as she could, always looking two or three paces ahead for places to put her feet. When the chamber opened out, she started to run, but it soon closed in, and she was crawling on her belly again, cursing the lack of knee pads and a helmet.

Then the path levelled off into a narrow corridor, the sound of running water closer now. She shone her torch along to the end, where a wire ladder followed the line of a waterfall into the darkness below.

'Nick?'

She crept towards the edge, fighting back the panic, the tears drying on her cheeks.

'Nick?'

Chapter Thirty

The sound of running water was getting louder, the metallic smell stronger. Odd how the other senses take over when you are plunged into darkness.

Dixon squatted down and felt the cavern floor around him. Gravel, boulders to the right, and shards of broken glass from the torch. The waterfall was in front of him, that much was evident from the sound and the spray hitting his face.

He put his left arm out and began shuffling towards the wall that he knew must be there. Somewhere in the darkness.

His hand touched the cold, wet rock.

He stopped and felt around with his foot. No rocks in the immediate vicinity, just gravel, so he started running on the spot, his hand still on the wall to his left.

Keep moving or die. It was as simple as that. But how long could he keep going?

Jane must've called for help by now, surely. That was assuming she saw him being led away at gunpoint. And assuming Kandes hadn't found her. Dixon shook his head and started counting. Anything to take his mind off what might be happening above ground.

A mouthful of fruit pastilles would help too.

Odd that. The waterfall seemed to pause and then start again. And again, as if the tap was being turned off and then on. Either that or someone was walking along the stream bed.

Dixon stepped to his left, his back to the wall, and looked up. A light coming along the passage. But who was it? Surely it wasn't Kandes coming back to finish him off.

'Nick? Are you down there?'

He closed his eyes and exhaled slowly.

'Nick?'

'Down here!'

Dixon opened his eyes and watched the beam of light searching for him in the darkness, squinting when Jane shone the torch in his face.

'Nick, thank God. Are you all right?' She was standing at the top of the waterfall, leaning over, one hand on the wire ladder to steady herself.

'Yes, I'm fine. Did you call it in?'

'Yes.'

'Where's Kandes?'

'He passed me in the passage back there. He's gone.'

'Did you lock the Land Rover?'

'Yes, why?'

'Doesn't matter,' replied Dixon. 'Do they know we're down here?'

'Yes. I rang again from the entrance and asked for cave rescue.'

'There's no time for that. In these clothes I'll be dead before they get here.'

'What do you want me to do?'

Dixon looked at the ladder hanging freely ten feet above him, swinging gently in the water pouring down. The walls on either side were overhanging, the one on his left drier than the one on the right, but the ladder was further away from that side.

'Shine the torch at this wall.'

Dixon looked at the overhanging wall above him. A large ripple of flowstone covered the first twenty feet or so – red or orange, it was difficult to tell in the light of the torch, but more importantly it had several pockets in it, where water cascading over the waterfall had eroded it.

He looked at the waterfall and thanked his lucky stars that it was just a trickle. A raging torrent would have been a very different matter.

'When I give you the signal, start swinging the ladder towards me. All right?'

'What're you going to do?'

'Climb as high as I can and reach for it.'

'We could wait for a longer ladd—'

'We don't have time, Jane. All right? Just believe me. We don't have time.'

Dixon turned to face the rock, Jane shining the torch just above his head.

'Keep it just above me.'

'OK.'

He reached up and took hold of the edge of the flowstone in his left hand and leaned over to his right. Then he put his right toe in the first pocket and stood up on it. Left hand a bit higher now, sliding it up the edge of the flowstone, searching for a decent handhold with his fingers.

The next pocket was just out of reach above him, his fingers no more than a few inches short. Nothing for it but to step up on his left foot and hope for the best. He looked for a foothold, but the best he could find was a small bump in the flowstone. Rock climbing boots would have been fine, but leather soled shoes?

Jake, where are you when I need you?

Dixon stepped up on to his left foot and reached for the pocket above him with his right hand.

Shit.

'Shine the torch on the ground!'

Dixon turned and jumped, landing in the stream bed with a splash.

'What's the matter?'

'My feet were slipping.'

He bent over and undid his shoelaces.

'What are you doing?' asked Jane.

'Taking my shoes off. It's the only way.'

He looped the laces through his belt and then tied them, before sliding the shoes around to his side, his socks, saturated though they were, he stuffed in his pockets.

Then he turned back to the overhanging rock.

He glanced down at his feet, shards of broken glass glinting in the light from the torch all around them. Turning and jumping was no longer an option, unless he wanted to cut the soles of his feet to ribbons.

This time his left foot held on the small bump, and he was able to reach the second pocket with his right hand. He slid his left higher still up the leading edge of the flowstone and searched for another pocket for his right foot, finding a small one, just enough for his toe.

He was almost level with the bottom of the ladder now, but needed to be higher. He turned back to the rock. The large pocket he had seen from the cavern floor was just above him now; it was large enough for both hands and he could reach for the ladder from there. He was sure of it.

Taking the strain on his left hand, he walked his feet up the wall until he was able to get his right toes in the same pocket as his right hand. Then he lurched upwards for the large pocket above.

Reach for it. Higher. Stop mucking about.

Is that you, Jake?

Dixon's fingers closed around the edge of the handhold and he pulled up, moving his left hand across at the same time.

Now for the ladder.

'Start swinging it towards me,' he shouted, watching the bottom rung. It would be that one or perhaps the next one up, leaving his feet flailing again.

'Make sure you let go when you see me go for it.'

'OK.'

Several deep breaths, the ladder swinging closer each time. Then he reached out with his right hand and caught the bottom rung. A good firm grip. Now for it. He let go of the rock with his left hand and swung out across the cavern, just missing the wall on the other side.

Both hands on the bottom rung now, he waited until the ladder stopped swinging, remembering all the years of rock climbing training he'd done with Jake. Pull-ups on door tops one handed.

He pulled up with both hands and reached for the next rung with his left. Then his right, gathering momentum. He stopped for a rest when he got his left foot on the bottom rung, his hands behind the ladder now, caving style.

'You've done it!' shouted Jane.

He made short work of the ladder, Jane grabbing his arm and pulling him across from the top rungs to the safety of the passageway.

'Thank you,' he said, gasping for breath.

Jane threw her arms around him and kissed him.

Dixon untied the shoelaces knotted around his belt and dropped his shoes on the ground in front of him. Then he slid his feet into them and knelt down to tie the laces.

'Right then,' he said, looking up. 'Let's go and find Kandes.'

Moving quickly, they were soon back at the base of the slab, Jane in front with Dixon behind, carrying the torch.

'What if he's locked us in?'

'He won't do that. He wants it to look like an accident don't forget,' replied Dixon. 'Up you go.' He was shining the torch up the slab.

Dixon went first under the large boulder and shone the torch for Jane to follow. Then he climbed out into the darkness and listened.

Sirens in the distance, but that was it.

'C'mon then,' he said, helping her out. They turned when two loud bangs echoed across the hillside.

'Is that—?'

'Gunfire,' said Dixon.

They were running along the bottom of the wood towards the first drystone wall when Dixon saw lights coming across the field from Priddy, off to their right. Blue lights were reflecting off the snow on the rooftops of the houses.

'That'll be the cave rescue team,' said Dixon.

'I'll go,' said Jane. 'I'll catch you up.'

Dixon crept up to the drystone wall at the bottom of the garden, breathing heavily. He had run all the way from the cave entrance, following Kandes's tracks in the snow, and had warmed up even if he hadn't dried off.

He peered over the wall. The scene was lit by the headlights of two marked police cars that were blocking the drive. Two armed officers were behind the wall on the far side of the car park, and another two were crouched behind the leading car.

An ambulance was waiting out on the road, with other police cars, judging by all the blue lights.

Dixon looked across and spotted Kandes behind one of the sheds, only a few yards away from him.

'Joel,' said Dixon.

The armed officers swung their guns towards the sound of his voice.

'Armed police. Stay where you are!'

'This is 3275 Detective Inspector Dixon.'

'How the fuck did you get out of there?' asked Kandes, shaking his head. He was still pointing the handgun at the armed response officers on the far side of the car park.

'It's over, Joel. Put the gun down.'

'It'll never be over.'

'You've got a sister, and an aunt. It doesn't have to end here.'

Kandes sighed, turned to Dixon and grinned.

'Like father like son, eh?'

Then he jumped up and ran towards the police cars, firing from the hip.

Dixon turned away, slumping down into the snow behind the wall as the shots rang out.

Chapter Thirty-One

'Is he all right?' shouted Jane from the other side of the car park.

'Fine,' yelled Dixon, peering in the window of his Land Rover and trying to make himself heard over Monty's barking. 'But he's torn his bed to shreds.'

Dixon turned and looked across at Kandes, lying on his back in the snow in the car park outside the Wessex Cave Club hut, a firearms officer doing CPR while others moved the patrol cars blocking the drive to allow the ambulance through.

The patch of red snow underneath him getting larger all the time.

Jane walked over and watched the paramedics working on Kandes.

'He's dead,' she said.

'Well, he got what he wanted.'

'Are you OK?'

Dixon turned to find a paramedic peering at the back of his head.

'Yes, I think so. He hit me with the gun butt.'

'We'd better have a look at it. Let's go inside.'

Jane made tea in the kitchen, warming her hands over the stove, while the paramedic attended to Dixon's head. He was wiping away the blood congealed in Dixon's hair with a medicated towel.

'Stings, does it?' he asked when Dixon winced.

'Yes.'

'You'll need stitches in it.'

'Can you just patch me up for now?'

'Yes, but—'

'I'll go to the hospital tomorrow.'

'They're in here, Mark.' Dixon recognised Louise's voice.

'Anything we can do, Sir?' said Mark from the doorway.

Dixon was sitting on the arm of the sofa.

'Light the fire?'

'Will do.'

'Is he dead?' asked Louise.

'Yes,' replied Jane, handing Dixon a mug of tea.

'What happened?'

'Like father like son,' muttered Dixon. 'Only not quite.'

'You'd better come and see this, Sir,' said Pearce. 'They've opened that camper van in the car park.'

'Who's it registered to?'

'An elderly lady in Nailsea. The buyer paid cash, said he'd fill in the V5 and send it to DVLA.'

'Description?'

'It's Kandes.'

Dixon nodded.

'Well?' he asked, trudging across the car park in a pair of wellington boots and a fleece undersuit he'd found in the changing rooms.

Dixon looked into the back of the camper van, where a firearms officer was kneeling down, holding open a bag.

'Cocaine, cable ties and rope, Sir.'

'Anything else?'

'Cash. Bundles of twenties. A grand each, Sir.'

'How many are there?'

'Three.'

'His retainer,' said Dixon, turning back towards the hut. 'Serial numbers, please, Louise. Quick as you can.'

'Yes, Sir.'

Dixon slumped down on to the sofa in front of the fire next to Jane. Monty was curled up on the rug next to her.

'Is it over?' asked Jane.

'Nearly,' replied Dixon, closing his eyes.

Dixon spent the next two days interviewing Tamsin Kandes, when he wasn't asleep. Now he was on Berrow Beach with Jane, leaning into the wind and rain as they walked towards Brean Down.

'Look who it is,' said Dixon.

'Who?'

'Nimrod.' Dixon reached into his pocket for a dog biscuit as the Jack Russell came bounding along the beach towards him.

Monty was more interested in the seaweed washed up on the tide that morning, mercifully.

'I decided to keep him,' shouted the elderly lady running after him. 'He's such a lovely little chap.'

'Good.'

'And this'll be Monty?'

'It is.'

'He's looking well.'

'Thank you.'

'Do let me know if you have any other strays you need looking after.'

'I will.'

Dixon turned into the wind and put his arm round Jane.

'How much further d'you want to go?' she asked, squinting at Brean Down in the distance.

'All the way,' he replied, grinning.

'Stop mucking about,' she said, digging him in the ribs. 'So, how did you get on with Tamsin this morning?'

'A full confession.'

'Really?'

'Pretty much, although she blames her brother and says he forced her into it.'

'She'll probably get away with that now he's not here to say otherwise.'

'They came to the UK after their mother died, looking for Fletcher. That's when they met Hagley. He suggested Tamsin engineer a meeting with Brett Greenwood, fellow Canadian and all that, and Greenwood got her a job at Lings.'

'So they could find Fletcher?'

'That's right,' replied Dixon. 'Only Fiona Hull caught her rummaging through the file. Most people would have sacked her at that point, but Fiona was in too deep for that. She'd lost the firm a lot of money and was on her last warning. She'd have lost everything: her partnership, big house on Clifton Downs, kids in private school, the lot. And she'd taken the case on without insurance against paying the defence costs if they lost.'

'Why would she do that?'

'She couldn't get it. No insurer would take it on.'

'But surely the claimants would be liable for the defence costs if they lost.'

'Technically, but she never warned them, so they'd be able to sue Lings. And the court can also award costs against the solicitors themselves in some situations.'

'How much would that be?'

'Including an appeal?' Dixon grimaced. 'Well over a hundred thousand. A lot more if it went all the way to the European Court.'

'Bloody hell.'

'It wasn't just about that though. It was a test case don't forget, and if she could force the government to settle this one, then they'd have to settle the other cases waiting in the wings. Sixty of them, all military personnel suffering from mesothelioma and being denied compensation. She took their case when no one else would,' said Dixon, shaking his head. 'I admire her for that.'

'I suppose so.'

'So, she catches Tamsin rummaging through the file looking for Fletcher's address and demands to know why. Tamsin tells her the whole story, none of it in the witness statements of course, and the seed is sown. The no-win, no-fee agreement was Joel's idea, but he didn't need much persuading to help the marines apparently. And he wanted the money of course.'

'A killer on a no-win, no-fee,' muttered Jane, shaking her head.

'Ten percent of the damages, if he'd pulled it off,' replied Dixon. 'Anyway, Fiona moves Tamsin to work for Brett Greenwood and carries on as if nothing has happened, with a small retainer paid to Joel to cover expenses. The serial numbers match cash withdrawals from her bank. She must've been pretty bloody desperate by this point.'

'And Tamsin tipped off Joel when the barrister was going to be down the cave.'

'Alison Crowther-Smith, yes. She'd been advising the Crown to fight the case all the way to the European Court.'

'And Fryer?'

'He was adamant the Crown would fight it as well. Fiona tried to settle, but Fryer refused. There are telephone notes on the file. So Tamsin put Joel on to Fryer too. He was replaced by a more sympathetic lawyer at the Government Legal Department, but the Crown still wouldn't pay up. That's when she gave him Fripp's whereabouts.'

'What about Fletcher?'

'He was the odd one out. Fletcher got in touch with Hagley to ask if there was anything he could do to help them. That was the guilt I expect. Anyway, Kandes took the opportunity to kill him, and that was when the whole thing started to unravel.'

'Thanks to you.'

'You're too kind,' said Dixon. 'The original plan was to leave Fletcher until after the case was over.'

'After they'd won, you mean?'

'It was more about forcing the government to settle it.'

'Did the marines know about it then?'

'Only Hagley, but the money would've been paid by Fiona.'

'What a bloody mess,' said Jane, shaking her head.

'It was going well too if you think about it,' continued Dixon. 'Until Joel kills Fletcher. If he hadn't done that when he did, we'd never have made the connection and they'd probably have got away with it.'

'Will they win if the case goes to Europe?'

'We'll never know now.'

'Why not?'

'The court proceedings have been stayed – suspended indefinitely.'

'Why?'

'Because they did win in a way. There's a no-fault compensation scheme for mesothelioma victims funded by the government, and they've announced it's being extended to cover all service personnel.'

'So the marines will get their compensation?'

'They will. Lings will be out of pocket though. They won't get their costs paid, and they've still got the Border Agency fines to worry about as well.'

'After all that?'

'After all that,' said Dixon, looking at his watch. 'I spoke to Lewis this morning. He's persuaded the chief constable to recommend you for a medal.'

'What for?'

'Saving my skin.'

'I didn't do it for them.'

'I know that,' said Dixon, wrapping his arms around Jane's waist. 'And you know that. But they don't need to know that.'

He kissed her, neither of them noticing the rain running down their faces.

'C'mon, we need to get going. You're meeting your mother at six.'

'You are coming with me?'

'You have to ask?'

Acknowledgements

Thank you for reading *Death Sentence*, and I very much hope you enjoyed it.

There are several people without whom this book would not have been written, and I would like to record my thanks to them while I have the chance.

Firstly, to Alison Crowther-Smith, Florence Crowther-Smith and Will Reed, all members of the Wessex Cave Club, who very kindly (and patiently) escorted me down Swildon's Hole and then brought me back to the surface again in one piece.

I went as far as (but not through) Sump One, and it was a great day out. I cannot thank them enough for both the truly magical experience and the research, and if you have never been caving, I can heartily recommend it!

Secondly, to my father, Michael. I don't think I am giving away any state secrets when I say that he was based at the Royal Signals and Radar Establishment in Malvern in 1982, really did examine the Argentinian radar cabins when they were shipped back from the Falklands and really did find a turd in one of the drawers!

I should also like to thank Emilie Marneur, Katie Green and the team at Thomas & Mercer for their patience, as always.

And finally I should like to record my thanks to the UK government for extending the Diffuse Mesothelioma Payment Scheme to service personnel whose exposure to asbestos predates the 1987 repeal of the Crown Proceedings Act.

Thanks again for reading.

Damien Boyd
Devon, UK
April 2016

About the Author

Damien Boyd is a solicitor by training and draws on his extensive experience of criminal law, along with a spell in the Crown Prosecution Service, to write fast-paced crime thrillers featuring Detective Inspector Nick Dixon.